<u>OUT OF TIME</u>

<u>Paul Davis</u>

For Leah and Barbara.
One pushed me to finish.
The other didn't push me down the stairs.

Dedicated to the memories of Sean O'Gorman and Mark Byrne.

1. Sunny Afternoon

Molly Delaney was the archetypal, Dublin market dealer. Large of breast and hip, she had an overall rounded appearance and her perpetually rosy cheeks leant to her indeterminable age. She'd been selling flowers at Balgriffin Cemetery on Dublin's Northside for as long as anyone could remember, and some put her age between sixty and eighty, give or take, but nobody really knew for sure. The cemetery opened in 1954 but Molly didn't start selling there till ten years later, having made the journey out from a resident spot in Moore Street Market in Dublin's City Centre, and knew everyone who walked through those gates on a first name basis and always had just what they needed when they arrived.

She was standing outside her shop having a yap with the head grave digger who, in great Irish, humorous tradition of stating the obvious, was nicknamed Digger. They were both having a quick smoke, interspersed with him singing "Sunny Afternoon," and Molly telling him he was in fine voice. Digger smiled at this. He was renowned for his acapulco version of The Kinks classic - as in, "I don't need music, I'll sing it acapulco," – and broke into another verse.

Molly looked out towards the road and noticed a 1962, E-Type,

racing green Jaguar coming towards the car park and she got
the flowers ready.

"Here's Matthew in his lovely green car."

"Unusual to see him here on a Friday," Digger answered,
pulling stray tobacco from his roll up out of his mouth.

"It's Elaine's birthday today," she said, with an air of authority.

"Never misses her birthday or anniversary."

"What's it now, Moll?"

"Thirty years in June," she said, a note of sadness in her voice.
She knew all the regular mourners and got on with almost all of
them. She liked Matt and, if truth be told, had a bit of a girly
crush on him, despite her age.

"It's awful sad, Digger," she continued. "He was mad about
that girl and never got over her death. He's been miserable with
it for all these years. Won't even look at another woman."

"Aye," was all Digger had to say on the subject. A confirmed
bachelor, the only walk down the aisle he'd ever been interested
in was the one from the bookie's door to the counter.

They looked over to where Matt had pulled into a parking
space. He sat there and let the engine idle for a bit, listening to
the sound. For a person who was as much into music as he
was, people were always surprised to find that he never listened
to it in the car. There was just something about the sound of
the Jag he loved. He always preferred to hear the engine, in all

its glory. It wasn't every day you saw - or heard - a finely tuned vintage car like this, so he took advantage of it. Owning a garage helped. Keeping a car like that running was an expensive business, one which he himself charged others an arm and a leg to do. Vintage cars, motorcycles and scooters were his stock in trade, though he hadn't sat on a scooter in almost three decades, and never would again.

He checked his reflection in the rear-view mirror. His customary dark glasses always on, despite it being overcast and he thought of that night, almost thirty years ago, outside Bubbles.

They'd been at a housewarming in his brother's new flat in Rathmines that neither of them wanted to go to but had relented to his brother's continued pleas. It had rained that evening and the roads were slick, so he had to slow the scooter down considerably. What would have normally been a fifteen minute journey, took much longer. He remembered thinking, as they'd pulled out of the garden in Rathmines, that if they had to stop in a hurry, they were fucked. The journey through town proved to be uneventful, but just as they turned off Fleet Street and approached Adair Lane to turn towards the venue door, a stolen car came screeching around from Aston Quay. Matt turned the Vespa's handlebars sharply to the left, to get out of the way, but wasn't quick enough. The car hit them side on, snapping one of the mirrors off the front of the scooter, the glass flying up and into his open face helmet, slicing through his right eye. The only things he remembered from that instant, before the pain flooded through him and he lost consciousness, were the two boys driving the car, who couldn't have been more than fourteen, both wearing tracksuit tops, collars turned up, and a loud and cracking thud.

When he woke up in hospital the next evening, he realised when Lainey wasn't there, that the last sound he'd heard was her, hitting the laneway wall, as she'd been flung from the seat behind him. He'd picked up his watch from the bedside locker, the glass smashed and the hands still, resting on three minutes past two. The moment Lainey had died, and his world had ended. The rest was filled in for him by the Garda who was waiting to take his statement. He just sat in the bed, holding the watch, staring at it through the tears streaming from his one good eye. She'd told him that Elaine had died on impact. "She never suffered," she'd said, but how did she know? What went through Lainey's mind as the car sped towards them and Matt swerved to try and get out of the way but couldn't? What did she think – if she had time to think – as she saw the wall coming towards her face? The darkest, most beautiful brown eyes you'd ever seen, closing forever. Her auburn hair, a dirty black with congealed blood by the time the ambulance arrived.

7

And the car thieves? They'd reversed, drove around the wreckage, and sped down Adair Lane and cut back out onto the quays. The car was found burned out on the banks of the Liffey, up by the Garda Rowing Club the next day, probably in a final act of "Fuck You," to the Guards. They were never caught. All of this he tried to process, while being told that he'd lost his right eye in the crash. He didn't care. He'd lost the love of his life and that's all that mattered to him.

He turned the key and stepped out, buttoning his Crombie as he walked towards the gates, his cherry Oxfords making crunching noises on the gravel as he walked.

"Howaya, Matthew," Molly said, while Digger just nodded in his direction. "Here's some nice lilies for Elaine."

"Hi, Molly, thanks, she'd like them," he said and handed her a tenner. "Keep the change."

He took the regular and well-worn path up to Lainey's grave. The early January evening was beginning to close in, and the wind whipped around the gravestones making an eerie, whistling sound. He looked at the sky as heavy, black rainclouds began to rush in. Another hour and it would be dark.

He brushed debris from the gravestone and emptied the dead flowers from their vase, poured the water out onto the grass and arranged the lilies, before filling it up again with a bottle from his coat pocket.

"Happy birthday, Lainey, another one without you and I miss you, every day. We're celebrating your birthday at Sean's club tonight, as usual. Should be a good turnout, even with this weather."

He looked up again, as rain began to fall, making small rivers run down the gravestone and through her picture attached there. He ran his hand over it, tears mixed through the rain falling on his face.

2. Looking Back

Jools stood at the edge of the platform waiting to board a very late DART in a drab and dreary Tara Street station. A crowd had built up behind her to a point where she was now being pushed towards the wet and grimy doors of the train. Her Italian vintage coat would be ruined, she thought, if the soaking wet bodies behind managed to pin her against those doors, blackened by the pan Dublin crossing that the green of the train was barely visible. The mob pushed harder, in an effort to get on as quickly as possible and grab a seat. She stood her ground and hoped to God that what was sticking into her arse was just the umbrella of the ridiculously bearded, drunken hipster who had been giving her the eye. A hand in the crowd reached out to push the door button and the mob instinctively pushed forward. Mister Hipster was now so close to her she could almost taste his aftershave, and it wasn't pleasant. An odour somewhere between drain cleaner and stale beer assailed her nostrils and made her gag.

The doors opened with a whoosh and she stepped through quickly, spying a window seat across the carriage and practically leapt into it. Thank God for that, she thought as the crowd shuffled in and the carriage quickly became standing room only. Despite it being late January, it was unseasonably warm but, as usual, the Irish weather system threw whatever it could at you, all at once and the rain today had been torrential. Sitting in the relative safety of the window seat, she avoided the dripping umbrella appendages of the other commuters. The air in the train was stifling, so she removed her coat and suit jacket and absentmindedly brushed off an invisible speck of lint from the perfect crease of her pin striped trousers. A couple of her shirt buttons came undone in the process of removing her jacket, revealing a tantalising glimpse of cleavage for Mister Hipster, who had stationed himself at the edge of the row of seats opposite hers and she could see his eyes were directed towards her, but not at her face. She considered doing them up again for a second but thought, no, why should she? Let him leer. He looked late twenties at the most and here she was, forty-seven, looking mid-thirties and feeling and acting like she was still in her teens. She looked directly at his face and waited. Eventually he took his eyes off her cleavage and looked at her face and with some surprise, noticed that she'd been watching him and knew exactly what he'd been looking at. She waited a second to see the colour rise in his face which came up over his beard, colouring his face a nice light pink and laughed as he quickly looked away.

She reached into the inside pocket of her, again vintage and again Italian, leather bag and pulled out her iPod. This was her one concession to Twenty-First Century music playing technology and, although she hadn't joined the ranks of the anti-social, music listening commuters exactly kicking and screaming, she hadn't been the most enthusiastic participant. A Mod since she was thirteen and proud to still embrace the lifestyle, she felt there was just something wrong with how digitized music felt and sounded. Vinyl had a warmth and a feel to it that you didn't get with downloads or even CDs for that matter. At least with a CD (she had some, admittedly), you still got a booklet and.... something to hold. It was still tangible. But downloads? Just the track on your iPod and the first - and last - time she downloaded something, she felt cheated. There was no feeling of having something you could hold, cherish, and add to the already heaving shelves of records. It was nothing more than ether with a sound. She did admit though, when her daughter Jessica bought it for her two Christmases ago, after a while of using it that it was handy and with the digital record player her son Liam - Jessica's twin brother - bought her, she could transfer all her records to the laptop and upload them to her iPod. She embraced this new project with vigour and was currently up to four hundred L.P.s recorded and uploaded. No more downloads for her. When she was young, downloading a song meant taking a record down off the shelf and uploading meant putting it back when you'd listened to it. Back then, the only way she could get to hear the music she wanted was to record Beep's Got Soul on the radio, buy tapes from Noel, the DJ in Bubbles, or be in very early when Freebird Records got the latest Kent LP in as they sold out in a flash. The kids these days didn't know how lucky they were. Instant music at their fingertips. No waiting for a record dealer's list and sending off a postal order and waiting weeks sometimes for that elusive disc to arrive. Downloads, iTunes, Youtube, PayPal, eBay, all made getting what you wanted so easy, there was really no appreciation for music anymore. It's all about the latest thing, she thought and imagined Simon Cowell, herding lines of people into a virtual record shop saying, "Buy this, it's the latest thing."

The latest thing is dead, long live the latest thing.

She put the buds in her ears and pressed play. The setting was shuffle, but she knew whatever came on would be good, she didn't buy or play any crap. Looking around the carriage, she smiled as "Toe Rag" by The Rifles filled her head and she thought how appropriate it was, describing the monotony of the working week; "Same faces for the last ten years of my life.... see them more than my friends, couldn't tell you their names...." and there were many faces she did see and recognised. Life imitating art, or just a clever observation from

Messrs Crowther, Marsh, Pyne and Stoker? A download won't tell you the writers names or any other useful info either, she thought.

As the train pulled out of the station, the darkness of the January evening in Dublin turned the window into a black mirror, reflecting the inside of the carriage. The Liffey below her, a darker shade against the night which was punctuated by street and building lights, flowed its unending way to the sea as the train passed overhead and with the heat in the DART, even in the reflection of the black glass, she could see steam rising off coats and jackets towards the ceiling of the warm carriage, looking like a release valve on the working week as Friday evening was upon them and the train pulled out, bringing everyone closer to their two day hiatus. The weekend, as Cathy would have said, started here and it was going to be a good one. She began to think about the past few years and how it had exploded back into life again. It had certainly changed hers for the better. Meeting old friends again and going out on her own without Jimmy made her realise that she didn't have to put up with staying in, while he ran around God knows where, coming home stinking of booze and perfume and it gave her the confidence to finally kick him out.

Around 2008, as a lot of her friends approached the magical milestone of forty, almost every birthday party she went to, more and more people seemed to be wearing the style of their youth, the Mod style which, ironically, predated most of their births, and the Mod look came back onto the scene with a passion. Not that she had ever really abandoned it but most people through the Nineties got married, had kids and didn't go in much for vintage Mod clothes but now with the kids old enough to look after themselves, it felt right again, so Mod nights started popping up all around town and the one hundred percent original vinyl only Northern Soul nights didn't really seem that important anymore. The soul scene began to waver and was quickly replaced with a melting pot of sounds from Small Faces, The Jam, Secret Affair, The Chords, Makin' Time, Prince Buster, The Skatalites, The Specials, The Beat, and of course, still Northern Soul. The list was endless. There was now some kind of Mod, Soul, or Ska type night on every weekend, and more often than not, the nights that were on covered all the bases but that Friday night was her favourite, D-Town, named after the Sixties, Detroit record label, though the younger Mods assumed the D stood for Dublin.

Just as "Toe Rag" was fading out, she felt her bag vibrate and quickly pressed pause. She took the ear buds out and looked around the packed carriage quickly, to see if there was even a raised eyebrow of recognition as "Town Called Malice" played from her phone. Mr Hipster chanced a quick look, but it was more for her cleavage than recognising the song. She sighed, there was always the hope that some Mod from the old days, closeted away in domestic suburbia, unaware that there were still Mods and Mod nights out there, might pop his or her head up at the tune. She despaired. Not today.

She looked at her phone and smiled at the contact picture. It was Cyn, her best friend and general leader of those who wished to be led astray, even if they didn't know it yet.

"Hello there, my pretty little Modling, and how is the easy life of the stay at home Mum?" Jools asked her with a smile.

"Oh, you know," Cyn said, "sit around on my arse all day, eating chocolates, watching Jeremy Kyle and playing records. What's not to like?"

They both laughed and Cyn said, "Still on for tonight?"

"Of course," Jools replied, "you know it's the one club I wouldn't miss."

"What time do you want to meet?" Cyn asked.

"I'm still on the DART, it was late again, and I've got to go home and make myself beautiful."

"So I won't see you till Sunday then?" Cyn said, a cheeky giggle in her voice.

"Feck off you, you little tart," Jools said, giggling too. "Say.... ten…. under Cleary's clock?"

"Oooh, am I gonna get lucky?"

"I'm so out of your league, love, but you can have my cast offs." Jools said, the pair of them now laughing.

"Alright," Cyn said, "that's grand." Hesitantly she asked Jools, "Do you think Matt will be there?"

"Yes, Cyn, he'll be there. He goes to everything and especially as today is Lainey's birthday, he'll definitely go and so will we. She would want us to and she would definitely want him to go."

"I know, Jools, but she'd also want him to have moved on. It's nearly thirty years and he won't even look at another woman."

"I know," Jools said, "but they were engaged, and he said that he lost his soul mate that night. We miss her too, but she was just our friend. Imagine what he goes through, every January when it's her birthday and every June when it's her anniversary. Every time he looks in the mirror he'll remember that night and he blames himself, he always has. So, we'll go, and we'll be there for him."

"And what about Sean?" Cyn asked, a flirtatious note in her voice.

"Well, Cynthia darling, I presume he'll be there as it's his fecking club!"

"You know that's not what I mean."

"I know exactly what you mean, but do you think that wagon will let him out of her sight?"

17

"I don't know why she goes," Cyn replied. "She hates the music, hates the club, hates the people and fucking detests you!"

"That's exactly why she goes. If she even sees us talking she'll be in his ear all night and throwing me daggers."

"And you love to piss her off!"

"Oh yes! And he says the flak he gets is worth it just to see the look on her face!"

"I don't know how he lives like that," Cyn said. "If I was in his shoes she'd have got the push a long time ago."

"It's a lot more complicated than you know, more than anyone knows, including me and I know a lot more than anyone else. Maybe some day, but not today."

Jools thought about how close her and Sean were. They'd known each other since school and were as close as friends could be without being intimate, and never were. Oh, the attraction was definitely there, but the timing had just never been right.

"Ah well," she said to herself.

"What?"

"Oh, nothing. I'll see you later."

3. The Cock Of The Walk

Sean stood in front of the mirror, straightening his tie. He attached his dad's gold tie clip in place and put on his suit jacket, just to get the full effect. The jacket would be hung up in the car, he couldn't be having creases in it from sitting in the driver's seat, no, that wouldn't do, but just needed to see the full ensemble first. It was a nice suit alright. Hand tailored, from Cock Of The Walk Bespoke, a tailor's shop in Hull, England that catered to a lot of the Mod crowd.

Burgundy mohair, three buttons – all covered - single breasted suit with one ticket pocket on the right-hand side. He'd seen blokes wearing ones with three and four pockets on each side and thought they looked ridiculous and one bloke he saw had two side vents *and* a centre one. He looked like someone had slashed his jacket. Just the classic look for Sean. Slanted trouser pockets, because he didn't like frog mouth, and standard cuffs, no steps or butterflies. Individualism was all well and good, but not at the risk of looking shite.

A bloke came to the club one night wearing a black and white, full checkerboard square, check suit. Big squares the size of beer mats. He became a regular, but the suit was never seen again, after everyone called him "Chef."

Sean adjusted the pocket square and was happy with the overall effect.

"When the fuck will you ever grow up and start dressing like a normal bloke?"

His wife, Maria, walked into the room and threw her usual barbs at him.

"What? You mean dress like your brother? Or should I say dress like your brother's wife dresses him? That fucker has no mind of his own. At least I look stylish, he looks like he just walked out of the bargain bin at Tesco."

"Don't you talk about my brother like that!" She shouted, almost spitting the words at him. "And don't think you're slipping out of here without me tonight and meeting up with that lanky slut at your club!"

"And which lanky slut would that be?" Sean asked, knowing full well who she was talking about. "I have so many!" He smiled at this, which infuriated her more.

"Julia Fucking Sutton, that's who! That bitch hangs around you like a fly on shite. I'll kill her one of these days!"

"And why would you care?" He asked. "You don't give a shit who I see or what I do, as long as the money keeps rolling in. I could be riding every brazzer in Dublin and you wouldn't care, but if I even talk to her, you go mental. Now why's that?"

"She wants what I have!" Maria screamed, actually spitting now.

"You're mental. She's got a great job in the financial centre and doesn't need my money or anyone else's. You just don't like seeing me happy. I really don't know why I bother."

"Bother? Like, with me?" She asked, her sly smile appearing.

"Oh, go away," he replied, knowing she just wanted to goad him into a row and ruin his night.

"You bother, because, my darling husband, as I've told you before, if you even think about doing the dirt on me I'll use it against you and if you even dream of divorcing me, I'll take you for every cent you've got and the first thing I'll do is level that poxy little D-Town club you love so much."

Sean just shook his head and said, "Well you better get your arse in gear then, I've to be there before eight," and walked out of the bedroom, slamming the door behind him. Her laugh was still ringing out when he reached the bottom of the stairs.

4. Look At Sweet Julia

Despite her best intentions to have a quick bite and a shower and be back out the door by nine, Jools only stepped out of the shower at twenty-five to, so the likelihood of being showered, dressed, made up and in Dublin City Centre by ten was less than slim. Jessica had picked her up from Howth Junction, so there really was plenty of time for the turnaround, but, as usual, she spent so long debating what to wear while listening to records that the time just slipped by.

"Mam, your dinner," Jessica called up the stairs.

Jools ran down in her slightly too short for her long legs, red silk housecoat, her dark hair wet and tousled, and Jessica's boyfriend Sam raised his eyebrows.

"Hi, Sam, how's things?"

"Much better now, Missus Robinson," he said, with a smirk.

Wallop!

"Jesus," he cried. "What did I do?"

"Don't you be flirting with my Ma, you dirty shite," Jessica said, having clattered him with a pizza box.

"What's for dinner?" Jools asked.

"Pizza and curly fries."

"Seriously? I worked my arse off to put you through catering college and you give me pizza and curly fries for my dinner?"

"Ah, Mam, I've been working in a sweaty kitchen all day, last thing I want to do is cook when I get home."

"Did you even make the pizza yourself?"

"Well," Jessica said, with a smile, "I took it out of the freezer."

Jools turned to Sam and said, "You're lucky she took it out of the box before she hit you with it."

Thirty minutes later, she walked down the stairs and this time Sam actually gawped.

"Em…. Jools…. you look….. em…."

"Stunning, I think is the word he's looking for," Jessica said, kissing her Mam on the cheek and turning to Sam said, "Gobshite."

"Will I drop you to the DART, Mam?"

"It's grand," Sam said. "I'll drop her."

"Eh, no you won't," Jessica replied. "You look like you've just seen Stifler's Mom. I'll drop her down. You go and have a cold shower, I think you need it."

After a short wait on an empty platform, the DART pulled into Howth Junction and as she got on, her phone rang and again, it was Cyn's too young for her age face that filled the screen.

"Hiya, hon," Jools said.

"Where the fuck are you?" Came a barked reply from Cyn.

"What time do you call this?"

"Who are you, me Ma?"

"No, but if I was I'd make sure you were on time and leaving the house when you said you were."

"The DART was late," Jools said, grinning.

"Late, me arse! When I texted you earlier, you said you were walking out the door. Lucky you said you'd meet me at the Molly Malone instead, or I'd be under Cleary's clock like a stood up gobshite."

"I was leaving when I said I was, Cyn, honest. The DART was late."

"How come then when I texted Jessica straight after texting you and asked where her Ma was that I couldn't get hold of you, she said you were in the shower? Well? Ha!"

"Okay you got me, Cyn, but you know it takes time at our age to look this good."

"Speak for yourself!"

"You're breaking up, Cyn, we're going through a tunn." And she clicked the end button, laughing.

Cyn stepped off the bus in the City Centre, looked at the phone in her hand and said to herself, "There aren't any tunnels out that way."

Jools sat on the train and once again listening to her favourite music, settled in for the journey and one of her favourite pastimes of people watching.

She noticed a change in her fellow passengers. There were even a couple of the usual faces from her daily commute and she thought they looked different. The post-Christmas blues had been shaken off as it was the end of the month and most people had been paid. Temple bar would be hopping tonight with everyone falling from over-priced bar to over-priced club being force fed the latest thing, their iPods pulsing as Dr Dre sent nonsensical beats through their brains as they listened to "what's hot!"

She was happy. Happier now than she had ever been. Two beautiful children who had grown to be two beautiful and confident adults and that shitbag of a husband gone. Thank Christ I came to my senses, she thought. Great job, great mates, great scene she was involved in and so what if people judged her by the way she dressed or carried on? Those who knew her, really knew her, they knew Jools. To everyone else, she was Julia.

Her Mam and work colleagues insisted on calling her Julia, with their knowing nods and sad eyes and she'd heard all the comments, even if they thought she hadn't. "Why doesn't she grow up and get herself a fella?" "Why does she dress that way?" "She'll never get a man looking like that." And then there was her Mam, who always thought the sun shone out of Jimmy's arse. From the moment he walked into their house, on that fateful morning in 1985, comforting a very shaken Jools,

her Mam practically fell in love with "the son I never had."
Her mam had been devastated when they'd split up,
inconsolable when they'd divorced, but she never knew the full
extent of Jimmy's vices. It wasn't just the drink and the women.
Jools had lost count of the amount of times they'd almost lost
the house because he'd gambled away the mortgage repayment,
knowing her backup plan was selling her precious records
which, after he'd gone, she'd worked hard to get back. Even if
she did know, her Mam would have thought Jools was
overreacting, or had driven him to it, with her "strange ways."
She knew they thought she was pathetic because she wasn't
"with it," but then, she never really was.

Who's pathetic really? She thought. The girls in the office
practically inhaled the pages of Heat, Hello and other shite like
that to see what the celebs were wearing, so burdened by their
imagined freedom to express themselves.

"Have you seen what Cheryl is wearing? She's just soooo cool,
I have to get that look."

The latest thing is dead, long live the latest thing.

Jools knew. There was an air of superiority that came with it. It
was part and parcel of being a Mod. Knowing you were better
dressed than your boss even though she had six suits - all from
fucking Dunnes, mind - and she couldn't even be arsed getting

them tailored.

Off the pegs with the rest of the dregs.

Passing the Ugg boot brigade on her way to work each morning, in their outside pyjamas, dropping their kids to school. Yummy Mummies, now there's a laugh.

"Nice top."

"Thanks, Penneys."

And still they looked and sneered. She'd spend more on one outfit than they would on clothes in a month and quietly laughed to herself when she passed them hearing, "The state of that."

And even after all those years and with the whole retro thing that was in vogue, people still stared at her and she remembered the old days - well, remembered isn't exactly what she'd call it - when she'd come home from Bubbles, speeding on the last bus. She laughed at that memory and attracted a few glances from those who weren't plugged into the latest thing.

Look at Sweet Julia
Speeding on the late-night train
They're laughing at the way she dresses
Too smart and clean
But she don't care
because she knows she's right

Secret Affair were right with those lyrics from "Time For Action" that she could always identify with. She was right then, and she was still right now. Oh, not about the speed and God forbid Jessica and Liam ever found out, but it was a necessity to her back then and part of the scene. Always was, always will be she thought once, but not anymore. Too many friends gone bad with it. Paranoid people with wide eyes and shaking so hard now they needed two hands to hold their drink.

Dance all night and talk shite but it didn't matter, everyone else was out of the game and it was really all about the music. Had to stay awake for the night. Couldn't miss…. a…. single…. beat!

These days, "On the wrong side of forty," as her Mam put it, her youthful exuberance was just a memory, its edges dulled by amphetamines, but the passion was still there. Some thought it was a cliché but not her, it really was a way of life. And how did she look for being on the wrong side of forty? She stepped off the train at Tara Street Station to appreciative glances from men who knew a classy woman when they saw one and dirty looks from women who knew they could never look that good. She was forty-seven, looked thirty-seven and felt seventeen. Jools walked up around College Green to the bottom of Grafton Street and spied a small Mod girl with blonde hair in a five point bob wearing a Prince of Wales dress with black Peter Pan collars and black, vintage trench coat, casually thrown over her arm, standing beside Molly Malone, patent leather shoes glinting in the lamplight.

"Which one's the tart?" Jools called to her as she approached.

"Very funny, Jools," she laughed. "You got the gear, or do I have to chat up Robbo again?" Their old greeting from the Eighties never failed to get an outing and on a number of occasions, Cyn did have to chat up Robbo, the "go to guy" for gear in the Mod Clubs when they needed it, though there wasn't much chatting, either up or down with him. They were mates so he gave it to her anyway. She too, partook of the marching powder but shelved it when she met Eddie, and he whisked her off to the scooter scene after Bubbles closed. Lots of drinking, camping, riding scooters the length and breadth of Ireland and the UK, three kids and a fortieth birthday, plus a few years tagged on, all under her still size 10 belt later, she never left the scene but went back to the Mod look, as she thought a middle-aged woman running around in Doc boots and a Mohawk didn't look too cool.

"Of course I've got the gear, Cyn," Jools said, as she opened her coat and did a twirl, showing off her new navy dogtooth dress, with 2 front pleats and a button-down belt, all set off by matching navy sling backs and a bag you couldn't fit more than

29

a mobile, her purse, some lippy and her all-important music into.

"I.... have.... always.... got the gear! And you'll catch your death, put your coat on!"

"That's lovely," Cyn said, ignoring her motherly advice. "Where did you get it?"

"Carnaby Streak. That Angela Williams is an absolute genius when it comes to Mod designs."

"Tasty. How much?"

"Ah, now, that would be telling."

5. Leaving Here

Jools and Cyn linked arms and walked up Grafton Street as if they owned the place, stopping for a look in the window of Brown Thomas and talked about what they could do with the stuff in that window and a good dress maker, and by the time they'd negotiated their way through a line of scooters outside the door of a club off Baggot Street, what they'd seen in the boutique windows on Grafton Street had already gone out of fashion.

"Alright, Al, how's things?" Jools asked, as she kissed the cheek of a small, well dressed Mod standing at the door, his gold tonic suit catching the light perfectly. "Many in?"

"Yeah, it's jammed. I just stepped out for a bit of air, it's stifling down there"

"As usual, Al," she said. "I hope Terry kept us a seat."

"He's cordoned off two, up near the DJ box, scowling at anyone who tries to grab them."

"Ah, he's a Gent," Cyn said. "Nice whistle, Al."

"Ah, thanks, Cyn, I do me best. You don't look too shabby yourself, for an aul wan."

"Feck off, you cheeky git," she said, laughing. "See ya in there." They stepped through the door, the bouncer giving them a big smile. "Evening ladies, or what's left of it."

"Fashionably late, Shay," Jools said, "but I bet some of "The Faces" aren't even here yet!"

"No, you're wrong there, Jools," he said. "In my humble opinion, the two we've been waiting for have just arrived." Shay smiled, bowed at the waist and ushered them both through the door with a wave of his hand.

"Why, thank you, kind Sir," Jools said, smiling and they walked through the front door to a sparsely populated bar area, stopping to talk to two Skinhead girls sitting at a table near the entrance, both impeccably dressed and secretly enjoying the R&B and avoiding the stares they were getting from a middle aged Skin across the room.

"Hiya, Bree, hiya, June. How's things?" Jools said.

She looked over to the Skinhead standing near the bar and didn't recognise him. He was staring at the girls, a look of animosity plastered across his face.

"Story with him?" She asked.

"Hi, Jools, hi, Cyn. New Boy." Bree replied, with distaste.

Jools looked again. The bloke was easily in his fifties. Bleached jeans cut way too short over 18 hole Doc Martens - with yellow laces, of course - tank top and button-down check shirt, hair shaved to the bone. When he saw the four girls looking over, he took out his phone and posed for a selfie, middle finger extended, like he'd just read an "Everything You Need To

Know To Be A Skinhead" manual, written by someone who didn't.

Page 1. Buy Docs. Bleach jeans. Get bonehead haircut. Buy any check button down shirt (cover with tank top, so nobody will know it's from Penneys). If no tank top available, wear red braces to cover lack of logo on shirt.

Page 2. Extend middle finger and adopt tough pose. Practice until a photo opportunity becomes available.

"I've never seen him before in my life," Cyn said. "Who is he?"

"Mid-life crisis wanker. Probably saw a documentary on BBC4 and thought he'd have some of that," Bree replied, her distaste evident.

"I was at the bar earlier and heard him tell one of the young lads he'd been a Skin since the Seventies. Said he was on the Two Tone tour in Seventy-Nine as a roadie for, get this, The Babysnatchers! Said he copped off with the whole band."

The four of them looked over and laughed hysterically as the Skin looked on, face reddening.

Then Bree said, "The fact that he'd only have been about twelve in Seventy-Nine doesn't seem to have occurred to him."

"Well," Cyn said, "you know those Two Tone girls, he could well have been their roadie and got off with them. Dirty fucking baby snatchers."

They all looked over at him and again roared laughing. He was now pink from his collar to the top of his shaved head.

"Aldi Skin," June said, shaking her head.

"He's been giving us the sly finger. Maybe he's still twelve."

Jools and Cyn laughed, looking over once again as the Skin turned his back to the girls and nursed his pint.

"Catch you both later," Jools said. "Are you coming downstairs?"

"Yeah," Bree answered. "We're just waiting for my fella and we'll be down then. Sooner we get away from that gobshite the better."

"Alright," Jools said, "see ya later then."

They walked through the bar, walls painted dark red, with framed prints of Sixties and Mod Revival icons covering every inch. It was very reminiscent of London's 100 Club, but without the jazz greats photos. Instead, Jean Shrimpton, in a multitude of prints, looked down from the walls, as she sat on, and beside various Lambrettas, while a leopard skin fur coated Ursula Andress sat side saddle on a blue, Vespa SS90.

Twiggy, Peggy Moffitt, Mary Quant and David Bailey's iconic chair photo of Christine Keeler were all given pride of place too.

Secret Affair's Smash Hits cover was poster sized and framed and a black and white photo of Paul Weller, seemingly floating in mid-air while clutching a Rickenbacker guitar with his legs tucked behind him as he stared directly at the camera adorned the wall beside it. Framed album covers by The Specials, The Beat and Madness accompanied framed photos of The Who, Small Faces, Little Walter, Memphis Slim, Laurel Aitken, Prince Buster and various Motown singers and groups. Towards the back wall, beside the entrance to the basement club, was a DJ box, where two young Mods were behind the decks. One looked about sixteen and the other in his early twenties. The latter of the two was currently entertaining those who weren't downstairs dancing, with the Roger & The Gypsies record, "Pass The Hatchet."

"Hi, Ciaran, how's things?" Jools said. "Nice tune, I didn't know you had that."

"Alright, Jools, howaya, Cyn. I only got it tonight. Maryalice picked one up in Boston for me. Just walked in and said, 'Here, this is for you'. I was gobsmacked."

"Ah brilliant, I didn't know she was here. Nice present. When did she get in?"

"Just this morning, I think. Heading up to Belfast with the girls tomorrow for Back Track."

"Great," Jools said. "Me and Cyn are planning to head up too. Eddie said he'd drive."

"Eddie was told he's driving," Cyn said, matter of fact.

"Brilliant," Ciaran said, "there's a few of us heading up, should be good craic."

"Who's the young lad?" Jools asked.

Ciaran turned to the other DJ and said, "Ladies, let me introduce Ger, one of the scene's up and coming stars. Ger, meet Jools and Cyn."

"How's it going?" Ger said, smiling.

"Grand, thanks," Jools replied.

"Well, ladies" Ciaran said, "you'll have to excuse us, as we have very important work to be doing. These records won't play themselves and our audience demands quality."

Jools looked at the deck where Richard Berry's "Have Love Will Travel" was lined up. She looked around the bar and said, "Ciaran, you're playing R&B for two punks in that corner, two Goths in that corner and three Skins, one of which looks like he was put together by the work experience girl on Blue Peter! Everyone else is downstairs."

"I'll put on a bit of Ska for the Skins in a minute," Ger said, "I'm not allowed downstairs, but get this. The Buster Bloodvessel wannnabe over by the bar there came up to me earlier and said - wait till you hear this - he comes up and says 'Here, son, will you play some of that Base Reggae?' I said to him, 'It's Boss. Don't call me son.' So, then he says, Jaysus, he says to me, 'Okay, Boss, will you play some Base Reggae?'

Ciaran was drinking his pint and started laughing so much there was Guinness coming out of his nose!"

The four of them roared with laughter, and Buster, obviously feeling the vibes, sank deeper into his seat.

"Right, we better go on in," Jools said, finally getting control of herself. "See ya later, hon," they both cooed and blew him kisses.

They walked around the DJ box, through the door and down a wide set of stairs, into a large, square room, decorated in a very Sixties supper club style, all blue velvet and low round tables, surrounding a large, wooden dancefloor. A stage was set into a cavern in the wall at one end of the room with a separate DJ box to the left and they made their way towards it, coats draped over their arms, so everyone could see what they were wearing, stopping every few seconds for hellos, kisses, and hugs. They were in the home of Mod music in Dublin; D-Town, and it was packed to the rafters with Mods, old and young, all dressed to impress. Jools checked her watch, an old, gold Omega her grandmother had given her.

Ten to eleven. The place had been bouncing since half nine but Jools and Cyn couldn't be sitting in a club that early doors. No, an impression had to be made so a late arrival was paramount, and heads turned as they walked past.

She looked up and waved to the DJs as she walked towards the table by the DJ box. The two men waved back. Both with number one haircuts and who were often mistaken for brothers, they were playing, "Biff, Bang, Pow," by The Creation and had the floor flowing like a tide.

The song faded out and one of them picked up the microphone and spoke a very garbled link, the only audible words being, "Timebox," and, "Beggin,'" filled the room.

"He still doesn't realise nobody can understand him," Cyn shouted to Jools over the music.

"Have you ever heard any DJ on the mic at a club that you could understand?"

"True," Cyn said, as Jools turned to watch the dancers.

Side vents fluttered, tie pins glinted and shoes shined as they caught the occasional light in the dimly lit basement. The floor was filled mostly with male Mods, all dressed in their Peacock Suit best and amongst them, right in the middle, standing out in a knee length cream dress with matching long sleeved gloves, looking ever so elegant, while dancing like the only world that existed was in that very time and space, within the three feet of dancefloor she owned, was Maryalice, *The* West Coast Mod and we're not talking Galway. Growing up in Los Angeles, she was a big part of the Eighties Mod scene there, hanging out at The Roxy with The Untouchables. She found the Irish Mod scene by chance while doing a Facebook search and now, all her hard-earned money was spent on frequent trips to Dublin, to see her "new-found family," as she put it. Jools waved but, as always, the music took over every fibre of Maryalice's being and she was oblivious to everything but the beat. They spotted Terry at the table and headed towards him, only now noticing the four dark suited lads on the stage, getting ready to play. She hadn't seen them before and Jools raised an eyebrow.

"What's the story with these lads?" She asked Terry, kissing him on the cheek. "Nice suit by the way."

"Thanks!" He said, as he pushed his chest out and tried to look modest at the same time, which was a feat for Terry, as he didn't have a large chest and would always tell you he's gorgeous anyway.

"I got it in London a couple of weeks ago. The missus saw yer man Schofield wearin a nice suit on that strictly on ice thing, so I googled his tailor. Chris Kerr's his name, so I flew over and got measured. She said she'd buy it for me fiftieth present, though I don't think she realised how much it would cost, but hey, I'm worth every penny!"

He stood back so she could take it all in. Midnight blue mohair, three buttons of course with thin lapels and a high opening. Eight inch side vents, ticket pocket on the right hand side and all the buttons covered.

"How much?" She asked.

"Grand and a half…. Sterling," he answered. "And that's not

including flying over to be measured."

"Jesus, she must love you, Terry," Cyn said.

"Don't yis all hon, don't yis all!"

"So, what's the story with the kids?" Jools asked, nodding towards the stage.

"First gig in Dublin," he said. "Sean told them if they do well, he might give them a residency, but I don't know if that'll work, the oldest of them is fifteen, and they've been warned to stay away from the bar!"

The band were ready and didn't wait for an introduction as one of the DJs gave them a nod and faded the record out.

The opening bars of their cover of The Who's, "I Can't Explain," flooded from the speakers as they launched into their set. They looked like a younger Beatles with the edge of The Rolling Stones, all dressed in tailor made suits. These lads, despite their young age, got it.

The crowd started getting into the band's music and the enthusiasm from both the band and the crowd bounced back and forth creating an electric atmosphere.

The last note resonated as rapturous applause filled the air and the front man grinned and thanked the crowd, the spotlight reflecting in his Ray Bans.

"This is one by Slim Harpo," he said, and they effortlessly launched into the old Mod favourite, "I Got Love If You Want

It," and Jools and Cyn took to the floor.

"I love this," Jools said, as she floated across the floor in that way that only a Mod girl can, and others followed suit. Soon the floor was pulsating to the sounds of Rhythm And Blues and the floating movement of two hundred bodies as the band segued into another one from The Who, in their High Numbers guise, "I'm The Face," and the applause were thunderous.

The band played for another hour, packing the floor with, amongst many others, Eddie Holland, via The Byrds and, "Leaving Here," Bo Diddley's, "You Can't Judge A Book By Its Cover," and The Beatles song, "You Can't Do That," and finished to rapturous applause.

After an encore of the Johnny Watson classic, "Looking Back," a young female DJ took to the decks and announced another link, the only audible words that could be heard through the still cacophonous sound of whistles and applause were, "Dee Dee Sharp," as the floor quickly emptied for much needed drinks and the air filled with tinkling piano, drums and those unmistakable Philly strings, and, "What kind Of Lady," kicked in and the floor filled once again.

Jools headed over to the bar where the two previous DJs were deep in conversation with Phil and Kim, a couple from the UK who fell in love with Dublin when Phil came over to DJ at one of the nights and now came as often as they could. All four were standing with pints of Guinness in their hands, Kim always saying she couldn't be doing with any of that half pint shite she'd seen some of the women drinking. They all said hello and hugged Jools and then went back to their conversation, righting the wrongs of the strange world of Northern Soul, as they always seemed to do. All four had been on the scene a very long time and lived and breathed it.

She ordered drinks for her and Cyn, but the barman told her Sean had already got a round in and it was over at her table. She looked over and there he was, tall and handsome as ever, if you didn't count the botoxed leech that was clinging to him. Maria. His one mistake in an otherwise perfect life. They say love is blind, but marriage is an eye opener, well, it certainly was for him.

Jools and Sean had lost touch in the late Eighties for various reasons, just life, she guessed, and she always regretted that she never got the chance to stop him. Even if they were never destined to be together, she could have saved him years of misery by saying, "Don't do it!" But hindsight is great, she thought, and we'd all change things about our lives if we could and she knew from talking to him that Maria hadn't always been that way. As his first club became successful and the second and third ones took off too and the money started rolling in, he noticed a change in her. She became more snobbish and spent money as fast as he made it. He suspected affairs but couldn't prove anything and to be honest, he never really tried to. He needed to spend time at the clubs, but she never seemed to be home when he was. They had no kids - she never wanted them - so he put all his energy into buying an old building off Baggot Street and converting it to a pub and club. The result was D-Town. This was where he would see all his mates from the old days and it really was only a place for people from the old days. Hipsters weren't given a warm welcome and a sign above the door read, "We're not retro, we were there!"

Over the years, the marriage turned sour and in the days before most people had even heard the word, "Prenuptial," they were married, and now he just couldn't get out of it without her taking him to the cleaners. So he stayed.

Jools looked around the room and back to the table. So many faces from the old days and so many new ones too. There was Terry, looking cool as always, talking to Sean. Maria, of course, standing close by with a face like a bulldog, licking piss off a nettle. Cyn was chatting to Susan, Queen of cool, style and, oh, what a dancer, wearing her favourite, dark blue, with black polka dot, Orla Kiely shift dress, while Maryalice was chatting with Matt, who must have arrived when the band were on, the stripes from his boating blazer standing out in the neon lights above the table. Tash and Dee stood by the DJ box, looking like they hadn't aged a day since they were THE Mod girls in the Eighties and still dressed to perfection; Tash in brown, pin striped hipsters, with a white shirt and tan waistcoat, orange scarf tied at her neck and Dee, looking sleek in a long sleeved, navy and pink paisley dress, with a mandarin collar and both without a hair out of place. Jools took it all in. Everyone done up to the nines and oozing class and style.

She looked at the dancers. People from their twenties up to their fifties, all loving the music and the lifestyle and she thought, this is what it's really all about.

She walked back over to the table and joined the others. She was just about to kiss Sean on the cheek, but an almost imperceptible shake of his head stopped her. One look at Maria's scorpy face told her the rest.

Sean handed the drinks out and said, "Happy birthday Lainey, wherever you are."

"And wherever she is," Cyn said, "she's dancing."

They all clinked their glasses and drank, even Maria, though if she was swallowing poison, she couldn't have looked much worse.

"Hi, Matt," Jools said, giving him a hug. "I didn't see you come in. How's things? You DJing tonight?"

"Ah, grand, Jools, you know me, no complaints. Yeah, I'm on after Honey," he said, nodding toward the DJ, who looked like she'd just stepped out of a Sixties fashion shoot, her blonde hair, a perfect Nancy Sinatra look, tumbling down over the shoulders of her white, vintage, sleeveless, high neck top. She had the dancers in the palm of her hand with The Shangi-Las', "Bulldog," and the room was bouncing.

"She's playing some nice tunes," Matt said. "Sean heard her on some Australian radio show and brought her over."

"Yeah," Jools replied. "She's good. That one she's playing is a new one for me, but I like it."

"Me too and another one added to the wants list," he said. "Spending too bloody much on them, the prices have gone ridiculous. If I'd only known back then what I know now, I'd have picked up tons of stuff." Sean, standing close by and hearing the conversation, added, "That's something I say to myself all the time. If I'd known back in the Eighties, all the stuff that's going for mega money these days, Christ, I'd be loaded!"

"You are loaded, Sean," Jools said. "Anyway, you can't change the past."

She said this with a sad smile, looking at Matt, "But I'd do a bit of tweaking here and there if I could."

"You know what I'd do, Jools," he said, his mouth turning

down. "I wish I could have done something different that night. I still wake up some nights, screaming and trying to turn the scooter in my dreams. And when I look at the clock, it's always the same time, three minutes past two. The exact time it happened, Jools, that scares the life out of me. Five minutes either way, that's all it would have taken. Five minutes earlier and we'd have been inside, five minutes later and the car would have been long gone."

"We all wish we could have done something different, Matt," she said, hugging him.

Still holding the hug, he said, "If I had three wishes, Jools, I'd only need the one."

After another half hour where Honey gave a very appreciative audience a set of Girlie Soul and Sixties girl pop, signing off with her customary, "Thanks and remember, be kind, but be fierce," Matt slid in behind the decks and the next two hours went by in a blink, as he kept the crowd mesmerized with, "Cool Jerk," "Wade In The Water," John Mayall and Eric Clapton's version of "Hideaway," and it was Mod, Soul and Rhythm And Blues all the way till he finished with the whole of the room shuffling and singing along to The Action's version of "I'll Keep Holding On," and by then, even the walls looked like they were sweating.

Jools reluctantly walked off the floor as the last note faded and caught up with Cyn.

"What an amazing night! Was it ever this good back then?"

"Jaysus, I can't remember, I was off me tits most of the time!"

"Come on," Jools said, "let's get a taxi before this gang take them all."

They grabbed their coats, said their goodbyes and headed back up onto Baggot street.

Jools hailed a taxi and he pulled in on the opposite side of the street. She started to walk across and stopped, looking back to see where Cyn was. She'd stopped to talk to Tomo and Linda at the corner. Two stalwarts of the scene who supported everything and went everywhere, Linda being the only female DJ to play at Bubbles, at a time when the Mod and Northern Soul DJing scene was very much a man's world.

"Come on, Cyn," she called from the middle of the street.

She didn't notice a car as it turned the corner.

The car approached her and she just had time to see that the driver was looking down and there was a small glow lighting up his face. *He's on his fucking mobile!* she screamed in her head. He looked up too late, slammed on the brakes, but the road was too wet, and the car just kept going. She flew up onto the bonnet and her head smashed against the windscreen. She travelled another ten feet on the bonnet of his car before he stopped, and she rolled off and onto the ground. The taste of blood in her mouth felt metallic.

"Jools!" She heard Cyn Scream, and everything went black.

6. What's Going On

"Jools! Jools, honey, are you alright?"

Cyn's voice came from far away, sounding strange.

"Jools! You fell. What the fuck is wrong with you? You just fell over in the fuckin street!"

"I didn't fall. That fuckin eejit hit me with his car while he was on his mobile."

"What? What car? You're not making any sense….. and what's a fuckin mobile?"

Jools opened her eyes. It was a bright, warm summer afternoon.

"How long have I been out?"

"You haven't. You literally tripped, fell and smacked your head off that bin there," Cyn said, pointing. "Maybe a second or two but nothing more."

"Cyn, I was hit by a car when I was crossing the road to get into the taxi after we left the club. I didn't trip, I didn't hit my head off a bin and…. what's happened to you? When did you get changed? You weren't wearing those clothes tonight and, you look so…. young! What's going on?"

"What? You're not making any sense. We weren't at any club. It's the middle of the afternoon and we just got off the bus in town. We were about to cross O'Connell Street and all of a sudden, you looked like you just walked into a glass wall or something, stopped, and just fell. You hit your head off the bin. And what do you mean I look so young? Ah Jaysus, don't say that. We're meeting the lads in The Anvil tonight and if the barman thinks I'm too young, I'll never get served!"

Jools stood up and looked around. Things were strange. Everything looked strange. For a start, this wasn't Baggot Street and Cyn, well, Cyn had always looked young - the bitch – but she looked *young*, like she did when they were teenagers. A bus passed her. It was orange. There haven't been orange buses in Dublin in years, she thought.

She looked down towards the Savoy Cinema which proclaimed, "A Room With A View," was currently showing. Her head was swimming. This dream was so vivid, it almost felt real. She thought she must have got some serious smack when she hit that windscreen.

"Cyn…. I need to sit down."

"Okay, we'll go into Burger King and I'll get you some tea."

As they passed the large windows of Burger King, heading for the entrance, she caught their reflections. It wasn't just Cyn who looked young, they both did, and Jools was also wearing a white top and black pencil skirt, definitely not the clothes she was wearing tonight, last night, whatever! She just couldn't think properly.

She sat down at a table and put her head in her hands. A couple of minutes later, Cyn came back with two teas.

"There you go, hon," she said, "that'll make you feel better."

"What day is today?"

"It's Wednesday. Bubbles tonight. You must have hit your head harder than you thought."

Jools hesitated for a few seconds and with trepidation, asked the question she feared she already knew the answer to.

"What year is it?"

"Eh, what?"

"Tell me what year it is!" She shouted, panic creeping into her voice and a few people looked in their direction.

"You're scaring me now," Cyn said, with equal tones of panic, "and keep your voice down, people are staring, they'll think you're mental."

Jools whispered "What fucking year is it, Cynthia? Tell me!"

"For fuck sake, Jools, it's 1985! What else would it be?"

7. She Came Out Of Nowhere

It started to rain again. Cyn sat on the wet ground, cradling her best friend. Both were covered in blood and their dresses were soaked. People had run from the club when they heard the screech of brakes and now there was a circle around them. Someone must have called an ambulance, as Cyn could hear sirens approaching. Sean was being restrained by Shay, as he was trying to get at the driver, who just sat on the dented, blood covered bonnet of his car, in complete shock, muttering repeatedly, "She came out of nowhere," his mobile still in his hand.

The ambulance arrived at the same time as the Guards. Paramedics quickly prised Jools from Cyn's arms and began checking her vitals. She was still breathing. Thank God for that, Cyn thought. The paramedics put Jools in a neck brace, moved her onto a back board and loaded her into the ambulance. Cyn got in the back and Sean shouted, "Where are they taking her? I'll follow you there."

Cyn spoke to the paramedic and shouted back, "The Mater," and the doors closed.

A large Guard, with a thick country accent told Sean to back up, they were taking the driver to Store Street. Handcuffed and in the back of the car, he stared straight ahead, still in a daze, a small bruise on his face where he'd hit the airbag.

The rain came down harder. Sean, in a daze, felt someone touch his arm and turned, it was Maria. Tears streamed down his face as he looked at her and she said, "I'll get a taxi home if you're going to the hospital."

She didn't wait for an answer, just walked to the other side of the street and jumped in the back of a taxi, smiling.

Sean stood there, watching blood flow into the gutter and down the drain.

8. Dried Blood & Broken Bones

Jessica, Liam and Sam ran into A&E. They didn't have to look hard for Cyn. She was surrounded by their Mam's friends and her Prince Of Wales dress was brown with dried blood, which also stuck parts of her now, not so perfect blonde bob to her forehead, her hair in disarray. Everyone looked worried.

"Is she okay?" Jessica cried. "Where is she? Can I see her?"

Cyn stood up and gave Jessica a hug.

"No, hon, you can't. She's been rushed into the OR. She had a massive blow to her head, and she lost a lot of blood. Her right leg is broken too. They said they won't know the full extent of her injuries until she's out of surgery."

Sam put his arms around Jessica, and she sobbed into his chest.

"We'll just have to wait, love" Cyn said.

Four hours later, Jessica and Liam were called in by a nurse. Cyn stood up to go in but the nurse held her hand up, "Sorry, family only." She sat back down in the waiting room and cried as Sean and Terry tried to comfort her.

Jessica and Liam were led into a dimly lit, very cold room by the nurse, where Jools was in a bed, attached to monitors. A doctor was writing something on her chart. Jessica began to collapse but Liam caught her.

"How's she doing, Doctor?" Liam asked.

"She had a very serious head injury, Mister Sutton."

"Dowling," Liam said. "Me Ma never changed her name when she married." He laughed. "She said it was easier to change a husband than a passport."

The doctor just smiled an awkward smile. "Is her husband here?"

"Ex," Jessica said, "and he won't be either, not if I can help it. Now how is she, and why is it so cold in here?"

"Well, as I said, she's had a very serious head injury and when the brain is injured it tends to swell. But, unlike most parts of your body, it doesn't have anywhere to go. The inflammation can cause the brain to push up against the skull and increase pressure. Too much pressure and critical functions such as blood supply can be cut off. Your mother is in very bad shape, so we have had to induce a coma and we're keeping her at cold temperatures, which allows the brain to rest and not exert itself more than is absolutely necessary. We'll do a CAT Scan in the morning and we'll have more news then, but she's in good hands here."

"When do you think she'll come out of it?" Liam asked.

"I honestly don't have an answer for that," the doctor said.

9. I Wish I Could

Jools sat and stared at Cyn, trying to take it all in. Jesus, she looked so young. Her thoughts were reeling. This is a *very* vivid dream, she thought again.

"Sure, I don't even have a headache from hitting the windscreen," she said to herself.

"That's good."

"What?"

"You said you don't even have a headache."

"Em, no, I'm grand."

She looked at her tea. Cyn had left two small cartons of milk beside it but hadn't put them in for her. She had an idea. She lifted the lid and spilled some black tea on her hand.

"Jesus! That hurts!"

"Fuck sake, Jools. You're a clumsy bitch today."

That was real, she thought. This, whatever the fuck this is, is real. I'm here, in 1985.

She looked out the window. Summer sun was beaming down on O'Connell Street and Dubliners were walking about in shorts and T-Shirts. Summer, she thought. It's summer. Something nagged at her. She was in D-Town, she got a smack of a car and now, she's in 1985. But she's not her 1985 self, she's her 2015 self, in her 1985 body. Why was she back here?

Then it struck her.

"What date is today?"

Cyn thought for a second. "Well, the nighter is on June first, that's Saturday, so, that makes today, what? May Twenty-ninth?"

June first. The allnighter. Lainey's death. Then she remembered what Matt had said to her in the club. "*I'd give anything to change it, I wish I could have done something different that night.*" And then he'd said, "*If I had three wishes, Jools, I'd only need the one.*"

"He wished," she said to herself. "We both did." Then, louder, "I know why I'm here."

"Cos you tripped and fell, you clumsy shite!" Cyn said, with a laugh.

"I need to go to the toilet."

Jools got up and negotiated her way through the tables towards the toilets, without even thinking of the way. Some things just stay in your brain and she'd been there many times before, or was it many times to come? She didn't know, and it hurt her brain to think about it.

She pushed the door of the toilets open and walked in. The young girl in the large mirror, running the length of the wall above the sinks looked straight at her and she caught her breath. She walked towards the girl, someone she barely recognised and hadn't seen in many, many years. She looked around the bathroom and quickly checked the cubicles. She was alone. She walked back to the mirror and looked at Julia Sutton, 1985 Mod girl. Turned seventeen on January fifth. Eight stone nine pounds. Five Feet eight inches. Black hair in a short, box bob. White, short sleeved, knitted polo and black pencil skirt. Black Penny Loafers. She twirled. She was so much slimmer. She still had a great figure in 2015, but had forgotten how slim she was back then, back now, she corrected herself. Smaller boobs, smaller arse, smaller everything. She leaned close up to the mirror. No wrinkles. Not one! Her skin, which, luckily had never been blemished by acne, was clear and bright. And then she realised she'd no makeup on, apart from eyeliner.

I can't believe this, she thought. Wishes don't come true. People don't go back in time on a…. a wish. It's impossible. But I'm here.

Jesus, she thought, I can't tell Cyn, she'll think I'm mental. Cyn's a worrier, if I tell her I came back in time to try and stop Lainey being killed, she'll have me locked up.

"Right," she said aloud. "Bubbles tonight, Lainey and Matt will be there. Simple. I'll just talk them out of going to that party on Saturday night, so they'll be in the club when the car comes through the lane, spend a few days in 1985 and I'll wake up on Sunday in my own time after the accident didn't happen. That must be what'll happen. That has to be what'll happen."

She was still talking to herself and hadn't noticed the door open. An elderly lady looked around and seeing nobody else was there, asked her if she was alright.

"Yes, fine, thanks. Sorry, I was just singing while I washed my hands."

"Sounded like you were talking to yourself, dear," the old lady said.

"Yeah," she said, "I'm crap, everyone says I shouldn't sing."

When Jools sat back down, Cyn said, "You're in there ages, I was starting to get worried."

Jools silently laughed at this. Despite Cyn's outward bravado and don't give a fuck attitude, she was always a worrier. Nothing changes.

"Yeah, I'm grand. That bang made me a bit dizzy, I felt sick."

"Okay now?"

"Yeah, I'll be fine. Right, where do you want to go?"

"I thought we were going up to Jenny Vandar?"

"Oh yeah, right, sorry. What's the time? Can't be too late getting home and back out for tonight. You know how the DART is always late," Jools said this, laughing at their regular joke.

"DART? We don't get the DART. Why would we get the DART? It doesn't go to Coolock. You're still acting strange. Maybe we'll forget Jenny's and just go home."

"No, I'll be fine. Honest, Cyn. I was just a bit mixed up."

They finished their teas and linked arms as they exited Burger King, walking down to North Earl Street, to cross at the traffic lights.

"Go further down," Cyn said. "That Mary one freaks me out."

Jools looked across and smiled at what was, in 2015, a much missed, true Dublin character. Mary Dunne had stationed herself on the traffic island between North Earl Street and Henry Street for over thirty years and was once described as, "The most interesting thing on O'Connell Street since Nelson's Column." She carried a Gaelic bible and a crucifix and preached the word of God to anyone who would listen – which weren't too many – all while dancing about and singing. Jools remembered seeing an online article in 2014 about her recent death.

"Ah, she's fine," Jools said, "just a bit misunderstood. All the Dublin characters like her and The Diceman, you'll miss them when they're gone."

"Just keep walking," Cyn said, "and if you think she freaks me out, that Diceman scares the shite out of me. If we see him on Grafton Street, I'm running the other way!"

They walked down O'Connell Street and Jools smiled as they passed the corner of Abbey Street where, in 2015, Mod nights were regularly held in the basement of the pub there, but in

1985, was still a bank. They crossed O'Connell Bridge and instead of going straight up Westmoreland Street, Jools said, "Let's go this way," and turned Cyn in the direction of Aston Quay, hanging a left, to walk down the lane and past the entrance to Bubbles.

"Why are we coming this way?" Cyn asked.

"Well, it's on the way to Jenny's, and Rumours is on the way to that. If Tash's there, she might give us a discount."

That, of course, wasn't the reason she wanted to walk past Bubbles. The club had closed in 1987 and by 2015, the sign was long gone, but she just wanted to see it. She couldn't wait the extra few hours to go that night. Now that she was actually there again, she needed to stand outside. For Jools, it was always her place. Somewhere she met all her friends and kept in touch. This was *the* Mod club in the Eighties. She loved D-Town and had once asked Sean which he preferred and with no hesitancy, he said Bubbles. The club just had that kind of effect on you.

She stood at the shutters, looking up at the sign. The girl with the afro looked out, uncaring, unblinking, and Jools just took it all in.

"I've missed you," she said, under her breath.

She turned and Cyn was standing, hands on hips with her head cocked to the side, staring at her, a puzzled look on her face.

"What?"

"I don't know, it's odd. You look like you do when you haven't seen someone in years. You're acting really weird today."

"Must be just the bump," Jools said, smiling. "Come on, let's walk up to Rumours."

They walked and talked, about music, clothes, school finishing this Friday for the summer and starting again in September (their final year! Yay!) Talk turned to The Blades playing in the TV Club that Friday and the allnighter on Saturday. 8pm to 8am, twelve hours of Mod, Soul and Ska and, if she could see the night through without incident, Lainey still alive.

She was bursting to tell Cyn but knew she couldn't. Cyn would only think she was messing with her anyway. After all, how could she prove it? Tell her about things that were going to happen and see her amazed face when they came true? What could she tell her that was going to happen between now and Sunday anyway? Nothing. The only thing she remembered from the week preceding that awful night, was The Blades gig. Seeing the same gig twice, now that would be a déjà vu moment to mess with your head.

They walked across Temple Bar Square and saw Tash standing in the doorway of Rumours.

Jools smiled that not having seen someone in ages smile again, but Cyn didn't notice.

10. Gearing Up

Eight months after Sean's first night at Bubbles, the lads were gearing up for the allnighter – no pun intended - though there was a bit of that. It was Jayo's first, but Sean and Robbo had been to a few allnighters before, and were trying to play it cool, but Jayo could tell they were both as excited as he was. They'd all got new suits the weekend before and none of them looked the same, three button, single breasted withstanding. Robbo had a dark brown one, eight-inch side vents, steps at the back of his trousers that came down just above the heel of his shoes, with the front hanging just so. Frog mouth pockets at the front, pointed pocket flaps at the back, all the buttons covered and an extra ticket pocket on the left-hand side. Sean and Jay took the piss out of him when he showed it off for the first time, beaming with pride at his first tailor made suit.

"What the fuck is that?" Sean asked, fake incredulity in his voice.

"It's a suit, you dick, what do you think it is?" Robbo demanded, not picking up on the tone.

"What the fuck colour is it?" Jayo this time, wading in behind Sean, as usual.

"Brown! Are you blind?"

"It's not brown," Sean said, "it's not dark brown or even

chocolate brown, it's fuckin shit brown! It's awful!"

He told them to fuck off but knew they were just messing. It was a nice suit and it cost him a good few quid, but, although not exactly loaded, he wasn't short of a bob or two. Robbo was the go-to bloke for gear and when he walked into a club, the other kids started singing, "Here Come The Nice."

Jayo's one was black, with the side seams of the trousers opened in a little triangle at the bottom and a button sewn on each side of the opening. Sean's mam did that for him but apart from that he hadn't had any more alterations. He said it was minimalist, but really, what can you do with a black suit? It was off the rack Cavern brand too, as he didn't have a lot of money and only got it because his granny was about to drop off the perch, so when he begged his Mam for the money for a suit, she thought, why not? She told him to get a black one though, so they could kill two birds with the one stone, so to speak. The treatment he got when he showed it to the lads was similar to Robbo's but they didn't get as much mileage out of him.

"What d'yis think of me new suit?"

"Aww, did your granny die?"

"Fuck off."

Sean's was charcoal grey, mohair with seven-inch side vents, covered buttons and the jacket cuffs turned back in butterfly wings. He had the outside trouser seams opened at the bottom too but didn't go in for all the buttons on the bottom malarkey though. All three suits were carefully hung up in their respective wardrobes and wouldn't even get an outing at Bubbles that night, they were under wraps for the allnighter on Saturday.

Midsummer was just up the road and the sun was blazing. Sitting in the garden listening to tunes on their half day Wednesday from school was the order of the day and they would do that, all day and every day come Friday, when school kicked out for the summer. Seventeen was a great time. You're old enough for a part-time job to subsidise the endless flow of clothes and records, but young enough not to be stuck with a full time one. The upside of still being in school, Sean thought. He pitied the lads that had to sit in factories and work their arses off all day, with only Saturday and Sunday off and there they'd be, in two days-time, lording it. Plenty of time for proper jobs but there and then, they got the best of school days and three months off.

Sean had been a lounge waiter in the local for about a year at that stage and between tips and what the gaffer was paying him - under the table of course - he was coming out each week with more than his old man. He'd also been doing a bit of DJing at "normal" nights too, playing the pop stuff. Not much chance for Mod or Northern Soul at those nights, though he'd still squeeze in a bit of Jam or Style Council when he could and, of course, "Baby Love," and "The Locomotion," always got the aul wans going. "Special Brew," too, was always a banker with the lads who were still Rude Boys in their hearts, so he did alright and kept them dancing.

His brother's mate ran a mobile disco, which was code for when some bloke with a medallion and a lot of fake chest hair rocked up to your party with his twin decks and speakers the size of small bungalows to play the tunes.

The brother's mate was in the army and spent half his time peace keeping in Lebanon, which really meant just sitting around, scratching your arse, getting a tan and making sure that nobody started shooting rockets at each other. Sean asked him once what would he do if they did start shooting and, "fucked if I know," was all he said.

Mr Medallion had this big DJ rig and it was just sitting in his garage so told Sean he could do his gigs and just to put a percentage away for him. The brother got a score for driving him to and from the gigs and helping him set up, so it was easy money for everyone.

The Aces who ran the regular Mod nights frowned upon this kind of behaviour. Imagine playing chart stuff for normal people? They'd shit their suits! Most of the Mod nights were run in dingy, shitty little basements, where you'd have to wade through two inches of someone else's piss to go to the jacks. Oh, but that was way cooler than what Sean was doing; playing The Nolan Sisters and Gloria Gaynor to a bunch of pissed up fucks in a hotel function room, filling the floor and getting paid a hundred quid for it. What was not to like?

He threw twenty quid to his mam each week and she thought he was brilliant. She'd no idea what he was coming out with and he didn't tell her either, and although she must have wondered where all the clothes and records were coming from, "just tips Ma," seemed to placate her, for a while at least. Eyebrows were raised though when he bought the PX 125 and she actually asked him then how much he was earning to afford that.

"Ah, not much more than I give you," he told her.

"How did you afford the moped then?" She asked, oblivious to him cringing at the "M" word.

"You know those records I bought off yer man there a couple of months ago?" She nodded and said yes but he knew she didn't have a clue.

"Well, it turns out one of them was worth three hundred quid. The DJ in Bubbles offered to buy it off me but I wouldn't sell it, so he said he had a scooter that just needed a bit of work and he'd swap it with me for the record."

"You honestly expect me to believe that he swapped his moped with you for one record? I didn't come down in the last shower!"

"Honestly, Ma," he said. "You can ask Matt when he comes round, he's going to do a bit of work on it."

She gave him the, "I know you're lying," look, but couldn't prove it.

For the past couple of weeks they'd been listening to tunes in the garden after school and messing about with the Vespa. Matt came down after work a few evenings to do some bits and pieces on it – Sean didn't have a clue, none of them did - but were watching intently, just in case. They were going into town on the bus one night and saw a Mod at the side of the road, his scooter broken down. He was tying the exhaust back on with his scarf and was covered in oil. They weren't going to be that sad case, so watched Matt as he explained what he was doing. Jayo was even taking notes. Sean and Robbo took the piss out of him for that too, but he said he wanted to open his own business restoring old scooters and in 20 years' time, he'd be worth a fortune.

That Wednesday, after the lads had gone home for their tea, arrangements made to meet at Sean's house later to head into Bubbles, he was just chilling out in the garden, listening to tunes and "working on the scooter."

He sat on the step, polishing a chrome side panel and tapping along to "Suspicion," by the Detroit Prophets when he heard the gate open. Looking up, he saw two girls walking up the path, all dayglo pinks and yellows, hair sprayed up in impossible towers, with brightly coloured hairbands which served absolutely no purpose whatsoever, as that hair wasn't going anywhere. The look was completed with ironic, oversized, "Frankie Says Relax" and "Choose Life" T-Shirts, as both had gone out of fashion over a year before. One was blonde and the other, a tall redhead, which made him sit up and take notice. He was a sucker for a redhead.

As they got closer to the door, he recognised the blonde, she was one of the Cosgrove girls from around the corner.

"Howaya, Sean. Church collection."

"Alright, Jennifer, me Ma's in the kitchen, go on in."

The redhead leaned against the wall as her friend disappeared inside and said, "What's that on your stereo? Sounds very Motowny."

"It's not Motown," he answered, with a grin. "It's Northern Soul. But I'm impressed that you've heard of Motown."

"Jaysus," she said. "Everyone knows Motown."

"You'd be surprised," he answered. "Have you heard much of it?"

"I've a load of LPs and some singles. Heard my uncle playing it when I was about ten and just started picking stuff up whenever I could."

Christ, he thought, she's probably got more records than I do!

"Have you heard of Northern Soul?"

"Nope, but if it sounds like that, I reckon I'd like it," she said, as "Suspicion" gave way to The Four Tops doing, "I Just Can't Get You Out Of My Mind."

"Now that's Motown!" She said.

"Nah," he replied. "It's still Northern Soul."

"Well that's definitely The Four Tops," she said. "I'd know Levi Stubbs's voice anywhere."

"Yeah, it is," he said, "but I think they'd left Motown when they recorded that."

"That's a belter. Yeah, I like that."

"A what?"

"A belter! You know, it's really good."

"Oh, right," he said, "that's a new one on me."

She laughed and turned to go as Jennifer came out with the church collection envelope.

"See ya, Sean," Jennifer called over her shoulder as she linked her friend and they headed down the path.

"Yeah, em, right," he answered, distractedly. "Here, eh, Jennifer's mate, eh, do you want me to make you a tape or something?"

"Yeah, that would be good," she called back. "But stick more of that Modern stuff on it, I've plenty of Sixties."

"Modern?" He asked, a bit confused.

"Well, if it's not Sixties Soul, it's got to be Modern Soul, doesn't it?" She called back to him.

"Modern, yeah," he said to himself.

"I'll leave it here with me Ma for the next time you come for the collection," he said, "in case I'm not here. What's your name?"

"Kerry," she called back to him. "And I might do you a tape and all!"

"Yeah, I'd like that," he said. "Listen, I'm going to a club in town tonight called Bubbles, and the DJ plays loads of Soul and Motown, why don't you come along?"

"Ah, I'd love to, Sean," she said, "but I'm only fourteen, me Ma would kill me! See ya."

The pair of them walked off to the next house, doing their bit for the Catholic coffers and a dumbstruck Sean just stood there, side panel in one hand, polishing rag in the other and a gormless look on his face and said, "Fourteen! Bollocks!"

11. She Had A Way Of Looking At You

Wednesday in the garage of Clayton & Son was a day off for the staff, as they worked every Saturday, but Matt was there, working on an old Escort his uncle had dropped in for minor repairs. He was the only one in and had the stereo blasting out music. His dad had more or less retired by then and only came in a couple of days a week, leaving the running of the business to his son and the blasting out of music, particularly his kind, was the norm. The maintenance and repair of vintage cars and especially scooters, was a tricky business, so they hired mechanics who really knew their stuff and, of course, all drove scooters themselves and were involved in the scene. This explained the mountain of Mod, Soul and Ska tapes stacked beside the stereo, as they had all contributed to the collection. What he was listening to that day was a copy of a tape that Jools had gotten from her cousin Samantha in London, and that was a copy of a copy of a copy itself, and the stuff on it was mind blowing. Some he'd heard from various Mod rallies he'd been to in the UK, but most were new to him. The inlay card had been photocopied so many times it was barely legible, but one that he could read clearly and stood out, musically, above all the rest, was by Lawrence And The Arabians, "I'll Try Harder."

The first time he'd played the tape, when it came on, he wasn't too sure what was happening and looked at the stereo in disbelief. What was this nursery rhyme shit someone had put on in the middle of the tape? An acoustic guitar picked out a very childish melody and he walked towards the stereo to eject the tape, as if taking it out and looking at it would explain things better, but then it kicked in with drums, brass, vocals and a very uptempo beat. This was proper Northern! He was instantly hooked, and he couldn't help but dance away to himself as it played. A couple of phone calls to a record dealer resulted in a £100 postal order sent, and two weeks later, that lovely orange Hem record was sitting in his box. Bonus that he got an amazing version of Barrett Strong's "Money," on the flip too. Delighted, didn't quite cover it!

With an empty garage to himself, he was dancing to his heart's content. Completely lost in the world of Northern Soul, he didn't notice someone standing in the doorway until he looked up as the song faded out.

It was Lainey. The sun was behind her and her auburn hair caught the light, making it shine a beautiful, autumn red. She just stood there, watching him while he danced. He stopped and smiled as he looked at her. His heart jumped every single time he saw her, and he thought about how she had a way of looking at you. The tilt of her head, the curve of her mouth. It captured you. She could see everything with that look. Your heart. Your soul. Your joy. Your fear. And it didn't matter. You wanted her to see. And your biggest fear, when you saw that look, was never getting to see it again.

She had looked at him exactly that way the first time he saw her. They were at a Makin' Time gig in the CIE Hall in Dublin, and he saw her walk in and was mesmerized. Hair in an asymmetric bob, navy shift dress, cut straight, but not too tight and just above the knee, with matching jacket, slingbacks in the exact same colour as her dress and a navy granny bag over her arm.

He watched her dance, oblivious to her knowing that he was watching her. And then she stopped, turned and gave him the look. And he was instantly captured. She was sixteen, he was seventeen and by the time that sunny May afternoon had rolled around, they'd been together for three years. He'd proposed on her birthday in January and, of course, she'd said yes.

"I was looking for a flash Mod I heard works here," she said, smiling. "But all I see is some grease monkey in filthy overalls."

"There's nobody here like that, love," he said, approaching her, with his arms outstretched. "Just us dirty mechanics."

"Don't you come near me till you wash up," she said, running from his arms and laughing. "I'm not having oils stains all over my clothes."

"Ah come on," he said, chasing her. "Just one kiss for a lonely mechanic."

"I'm engaged to the boss, he won't like this. You could get sacked." She laughed.

He hopped around the garage, trying to remove his overalls, both of them laughing now. Finally, he managed to get them off and folded her in his arms. She looked up at him. Those brown eyes he always thought he could swim in, shining. They kissed and he said, "Sean asked me to head over after work and have a look at the scooter. Wanna come?"

"Yeah," she said, "why not? I might drop into Jools while you're doing…. whatever it is you boys do with your mopeds." That look was on her face again now. She was messing – and he knew it - but he faked exasperation, shook his head and said, "Fair enough. I'll meet you at Sean's then. An Ace Face like yourself wouldn't be caught dead on the back of a moped." He was grinning.

"Ah, sure I'll make an exception for a lonely grease monkey like you. Might give you a bit of class." She started giggling and he kissed her again.

"Right then, I'd better lock up."

12. Lace And Chiffon

Jools and Cyn walked over to Rumours, the small, second-hand clothes shop in Temple Bar, just as Tash was closing the door. "Are you closing?" Cyn asked. "Aw, we were looking for something nice for tonight. Kinda like that," she said, nodding at what Tash was wearing.

"Yeah, sorry," Tash replied. "I have to get home, I've a few things to do before tonight. Thanks, Cyn, I made it myself." Jools and Cyn admired Tash's clothes. A short red skirt, a navy boating blazer style jacket, with thick white stripes, all set off by a white shirt and red tie, an exact match to the colour of the skirt. Navy block heeled shoes, the same colour as the jacket, with a wide strap and gold buckle completed the outfit. Here was a girl all the others tried to emulate and as soon as someone did, she'd change again. When everyone wore their hair long, Tash wore hers short and when they started to cut theirs short, she'd let her hair grow out. Cyn would never find anything like the clothes Tash wore in Rumours or anywhere else, nobody would. Similar, yes, but never the same. Nobody really liked throwing the Ace Face title around, other than those who regarded themselves as such, but really weren't, and here was one in the flesh. Her short blonde hair shone in the afternoon sun, and not one was out of place.

"There is a jacket like it in there, Cyn, probably a little too long for you though, but would really suit Jools. I'll put it away when I get back in tomorrow, I've just really gotta run."

She said goodbye and started towards Merchant's Arch but stopped. She turned and called back, "By the way, I was up in Jenny's this morning. If you're heading up that way, there's some new stuff in."

"Yeah, we were on our way," Cyn called back. "Thanks, Tash, see you later."

"See you later," she replied and Jools thought, she looks exactly the same in 2015.

Jenny Vandar's was only a short walk from Rumours. Jools and Cyn strolled up Crown Alley and were about to walk towards the square of the Central Bank, to turn towards George's Street at the corner of The Foggy Dew, when they heard the music. To Cyn, it sounded like speeded up Heavy Metal, but Jools knew what it was. Someone was blasting out "White Power," by Skrewdriver and, although it was over thirty years since she'd heard it, there was no mistaking that sound.

"Let's go this way," she said to Cyn, looking towards the square and steered her to the right, back towards Temple Bar, so they could cut up Crow Street, at the back of the Foggy.

"Why?" Cyn asked, "This way is quicker."

"Boneheads," Jools said. "Hear that music? That shite that

they're playing, it's White Power, Nazi crap, I'd know it anywhere, and I've no intention of getting battered by Bonehead fucks who don't care if it's a bloke or a girl, once they're kicking the shit out of a Mod. There used to be, I mean there's a Bonehead wanker on my cousin's road. Asked me out once. The prick even had the cheek to say I'd look better if I shaved my head, and when I said no, he always gave me hassle when I went there after, and he was always playing that shite in the garden."

"I just thought it was heavy metal," Cyn said.

"They'll tell you it's Oi, which is kinda like punk for Skinheads, but that Screwdriver stuff is just filth."

"I've heard of Oi," Cyn said, "but that's the first time I've heard anything like that. Jesus, it's shite."

"Not all Oi is, but I'd steer clear of anyone listening to Skrewdriver, and whoever's listening to it is probably pissed, or off their heads on glue, so we're not going that way."

They got to the corner and just before turning, she took a look back and saw four shaved to the bone skinheads in eighteen hole Docs, bleached jeans and Swastika T-Shirts, arms covered in tattoos and one she recognised as the bloke from her cousin's road, but he didn't see her, he was too busy putting his head into a bag, and she could guess what was in it.

They got to Georges Street Arcade five minutes later and

walked down past the rows of stalls. The record shop in the middle was playing Stevie Wonder's "Part Time Lover," and Jools turned to Cyn, "Jesus, I hate that song. All the great stuff he did and wrote, and that's all he'll be remembered for."

"I like it," Cyn said, "I even bought it."

"Yeah, I know. And all those gobshites there," Jools said, nodding to the people sitting at the café, tapping along to the music, "wouldn't know Motown if it bit them in the arse. They probably think Jagger and Bowie's Dancing In The Street was the original too. I remember you buying that one as well, Cyn, what were you thinking?"

"What? I didn't buy anything by Jagger and Bowie. Did they do Dancing In The Street? Are you sure?"

Jools faltered. "Eh…. must have seen something on the telly," she said. "Maybe they were talking about doing it?"

She did remember Cyn buying the record. She was with her in Abbey Discs in Northside Shopping Centre when she had, but she couldn't remember when. Shit, she thought, it was 1985, I'd put my house on it, maybe it hasn't been released yet. Gotta be careful. Then she laughed a quiet laugh to herself as she thought, it's 1985, I don't even own a feckin house!

They walked into the shop all the discerning Mod girls went to. It was a small place, but gave the impression of vintage luxury, decorated with lots of lace and chiffon. The shoes were kept inside the door on the left, on small racks. Gorgeous, dainty shoes of various eras and again, Jools stopped and took a breath. It's like going back in time, she thought, and then laughed at the absurdity of that as Cyn gave her another puzzled look. Word must have got out that there was new stuff in, as the shop was packed, which wasn't difficult. Six people in and it was packed.

Jools, still not having fully recovered from the Panesque Tash she'd just met, was struck by the coincidence as Dee, who she'd only seen a couple of hours – and three decades in the future – ago, with Tash at D-Town, was standing at the counter.

Jools was suddenly struck by the resemblance to Audrey Hepburn as she looked at her. She was wearing a black and white, horizontal striped sweater, with black hipsters and shoes that were almost, but not quite, ballet flats, her black hair pulled back in a ponytail. Jools was reminded of a photo she'd seen on some café or bar wall somewhere of Audrey, sitting in an armchair, talking on the phone, legs dangling over the side, looking just like that. For some people, she thought, style comes effortlessly.

Dee paid for her purchase and whatever she'd bought, had disappeared into a bag before Jools and Cyn could get a look. She turned and saw the girls.

"Hi! How's things?"

"Grand, Dee. How are you? Love that top," Jools said. "Where did you get it?"

"Ivy market last Saturday," Dee said. "My Nana wanted to go up, so I tagged along. 50p! Can you believe that?"

"That's a bargain," Jools said, "It's lovely. Isn't it, Cyn?"

"Yeah," Cyn said, cooing, "but I couldn't be doing with that Ivy Market place, the smell of fish makes me gag."

The girls had a browse along the shelves but, for once, couldn't find anything they wanted and Cyn announced, "Jesus! Look at the time! We'd better be heading home, or we won't be going anywhere tonight!"

13. Going Home

The 42C pulled into a stop on the Darndale Road, next to Fairfield, one of Dublin's predominantly working-class suburbs. Jools and Cyn hopped off the bus, thanking the driver, who returned their thanks with a grunt and they walked towards Bonnybrook and home.

Home, Jools thought and for the first time realised that she was actually going home and her Dad, who'd died in 1992 would be there. Her heart began to pound, and a smile beamed on her face as she got that far away look again. This time Cyn did notice and said, "There it is again. You're acting really weird today, you look like you keep going off on some dream or something. What's up? Tell me."

Jools shook it off, thought for a second and said, "Cyn, I'm not Jools, well I am, but I'm not the Jools you know. I came here from the year 2015, to set something right, but I can't tell you what, in case it...."

"Affects the space time continuum?" Cyn said, cutting her off.

"What?" Jools was stunned.

"And I suppose you came here in a fuckin DeLorean too?"

"What?"

"Jools, you daft cow, we saw the trailer for Back To The Future when we went to see Ladyhawke. You were swooning over

Michael J Fox and said you couldn't wait till it came out next month and I said he doesn't look old enough to drive the fuckin car."

"Em…."

"Fuck it," Cyn said, "I suppose you'll tell me what's going on in that head of yours when you're ready, you always do. Probably just some bloke you've got your eye on."

Jools thought, even if I did tell her, she'd never believe me. She resigned herself to just getting the job done and getting - she laughed to herself - back to the future!

They walked towards Macroom Avenue and stopped at the corner as Cyn gave her a hug and said, "See you at half six, the lads said they'd be in The Anvil about seven."

Jools stood at the gate. She looked up the long driveway to the red bricked porch, her breath catching in her throat, her stomach tightening. Twenty-three years since she'd seen him. Her heart was beating so rapidly in her chest, she could almost hear it.

She opened the gate and instinctively closed it behind her. "Pull that aul gate," she heard him say in her mind. His thick, Offaly accent still as strong after twenty years living in Dublin.

She walked to the door and turned the handle.

"Is that you, Julia?" Her Mam called from the kitchen.

"Only me," she replied, sounding very far away to herself.

She walked down the hall and into the kitchen. There was her Mam. Young. Slim. Her hair an almost raven black.

I can't believe she was ever that young, she thought.

Her Mam turned, "There you are, love, dinner will be ready soon."

"Thanks, Mam," she said and looked towards the back door, seeing her Dad's broad frame almost fill the doorway, pipe smoke floating off into the air, the light shining off his brylcreamed hair.

She walked up and put her arms around his chest, putting her head on his back and took a deep breath. Her nose filled with the scent of tobacco and Old Spice.

"Hiya, Daddy," she said, a tear welling in her eye.

"Howaya, Jools," he said, "how was your day? Did you buy any new records?"

"Her name is Julia, not Jools!" The disapproving tone in her Mam's voice was noticeable.

Her dad turned around, "Sorry, May," he said, winking at Jools.

"You do that on purpose," Jools told him, looking up into his hazel eyes and grinning.

He smiled. "I have no idea what you mean," he said, giving her another wink. "Go on and get up to your room and sort out your clothes for tonight. Play All Or Nothing for me and play it loud, she'll be banging the sweeping brush on the ceiling when you do." He matched her grin and her heart nearly broke.

"That stuff will kill you," she said. "Give it up."

"I'm as strong as an ox," he replied, "I'll be grand."

She smiled again and kissed his cheek, thinking he'd be dead in seven years. Even if he did stop now – which he never did - the damage was probably already done, he'd been smoking since he was ten.

She went upstairs and opened the door of her bedroom. Sun streamed through lace curtains and reflected off the mirror set into the double wardrobe. She remembered how she'd loved that room and how bright it was on summer mornings, with the sun lighting up the cream, almost white coloured walls so when she woke, she could see the brightness beneath her eyelids.

The sun lighting up three of the walls, she corrected herself. One wall was given over to posters and clippings from various music magazines and fanzines, which, of course, the light did not reflect upon. All the usual suspects were there. The Jam, The Blades, The Who, The Kinks and her Dad's favourite, Small Faces.

Cyn gave her a photo of the Northern Ireland band, Them, once, which she refused to add to her collection, saying "Van's got a great voice and the songs are brilliant, but the Jaysus head on him! I'm not putting that on my wall, give me bleedin nightmares. And he's wearing a jumper under his jacket! My arse!"

"That's a no then?" Cyn had said at the time.

"Em…. yeah, maybe I overstated that a little."

"Ya think?"

She went to her record shelves and looked through the singles, till she got to D, for Decca. She was a bit nerdy when it came to her records. Singles sorted alphabetically by label and albums sorted alphabetically by artist. Cyn, who had very few records, couldn't understand this and was continually reprimanded for taking a record out and just sticking it back in where she liked on the shelf. Records were precious and if Jools wanted to hear something specific, she liked to know where it was and that she could put her hands on it immediately. She got frustrated after Cyn visited and she went looking for a record and it wasn't there. The next hour would be spent going through shelves looking for the misfiled record and restoring it to its proper home.

She looked through the Decca singles, till she got to Small Faces and instantly had "All Or Nothing" in her hands. Carefully placing it on the turntable, she switched on the stereo and whacked up the sound. A drum roll, a crash of cymbals, followed by bass and guitar and ten seconds in, Steve Marriott's voice singing, "I thought you'd listen….," and the bang of a brush handle on the ceiling, "Turn that down, you're not deaf!" She smiled, as she knew her Dad was smiling too downstairs and lowered it slightly as she sat down on her bed and, once again, tried to take stock of everything that had happened in the space of a few hours.

She really couldn't believe it was all real, that she was actually there. She'd gone past the point of thinking it was a dream, because if it was, it was the most vivid one she had ever had. Sights, sounds, smells even. Her bedroom window was open, and the smell of the steak pie her Mam was baking came wafting up from the kitchen.

"All Or Nothing" began to fade out and she went over and took it off, carefully putting it into the sleeve and back in the exact spot she took it from. She closed her eyes and ran her fingers along the singles and stopped, pulling one out at random. The Style Council, "My Ever Changing Moods." She took it from the picture sleeve, a blue cover with Paul Weller sitting, a cigarette in his hand, the smoke captured in the air from a light below, and put it on the turntable.

Nice dancer, she thought, but the slower version is better and made a mental note to put "Café Bleu" on while she decided what to wear that night as she lay on her bed and let the music wash over her.

Four minutes later she exchanged "My Ever Changing Moods" for "Café Bleu," and got down to the business of choosing an outfit while Mick Talbot played out a jazzy, piano instrumental, kicking off one of her favourite albums.

She opened both doors of her wardrobe. Clothes on two rails – one above and one below – filled it from wall to wall and stood back, astonished by the amount of clothes in there. She'd forgotten just how much she had.

She flicked through them, pulling out dresses and suits that she'd kill to have in 2015, but that sadly, would no longer fit her and she stopped. There it was. Her favourite.

A black, short sleeved dress, with a rounded collar and contrasting red skirt with buttoned patch pockets. Four red buttons down the front, covered in the same material as the skirt. No tights, she thought, and found a pair of black, pointed shoes, with two inch heels.

There were clothes to the left and clothes to the right and clothes on the rail below, brushing a plethora of shoes in the bottom of the wardrobe, but she didn't need to look any further. By the time Mick played the first chords of "My Ever Changing Moods," she'd sorted her clothes and laughed, Cyn would still be deciding what shoes to wear and then realised she'd done in twenty minutes what it had taken her two hours to do…. last night? She still had trouble getting her head around the whole time thing and hoped she wouldn't have to get used to it.

The doorbell rang.

"Julia," her Mam called, "Elaine's here."

14. Smiles And Dark Thoughts

Jools stood at the record player, rigid with shock, excitement, apprehension and an overwhelming desire to run downstairs and throw her arms around Lainey, screaming, "She's alive!" like a demented Henry Frankenstein, having brought life to Elsa Lanchester. She took a couple of seconds to calm herself, wiping away the tears that had suddenly sprung up, momentarily blurring her vision and walked over to the door. She stood at the top of the stairs and called down, "Come on up."

Lainey poked her head around the bannisters and smiled and Jools's heart skipped. That beautiful smile, she thought. And then a dark thought - you'll be dead in three days if I can't stop it.

Lainey walked up the stairs, a puzzled look on her face.

"Jools, what's wrong,?"

"What? Nothing. Why?"

"I dunno," Lainey said. "You smiled and then a really odd look came over your face, like you just got really sad all of a sudden."

"No," Jools said, forcing a smile. "I'm just a bit out of sorts today. I was in town with Cyn earlier and tripped on O'Connell Street and smacked my head off a bin."

"Jesus," Lainey said, a worried look on her face now. "Are you okay?"

"Yeah, yeah, I'm grand. You know me, I'm, "A clumsy bitch!"" they both said at the same time, and laughed.

Jools's smile broadened now, it was so good to hear Lainey laugh again.

They walked into her bedroom, where The Style Council were dropping their bombs on the White House and Lainey said, "You can turn that shite off, for a start."

"What is it with you and Tash?" Jools asked. "She thinks they're shite too. And The Jam."

"It's not Mod music, my dear, even if they do try to be jazzy" Lainey said. "They certainly weren't dancing to, or dressing like Paul Bloody Weller at The Scene or The Goldhawk, now, were they?"

She smiled, knowing how it wound Jools up.

"No, Miss Ace Face, but we do at Bubbles and unless you know how to go back in time…." And with this, she burst out laughing.

"If I could, I would," Lainey said, laughing at what she thought was the same joke.

Trying to keep some levity in her voice and not give away her concern, or the fact that she knew about the house warming, Jools said, "So, you all set for the allnighter on Saturday?"

"Yes and no," Lainey said. "Matt's brother is having some housewarming thing in his new flat in Rathmines and wants us to go. We plan to leave about twelvish and get to the nighter, but you know how these things go on."

"Can you not get out of it?"

"I wish we could, but Peter is giving Matt the whole, 'I'm your brother, you should be there instead of going to some poxy Mod do,' shite. Matt's tried to get out of it but Peter keeps nagging him. It wouldn't be so bad if Peter didn't work in the garage too, at least then Matt could avoid him. And the crap he puts on the stereo, Jesus. If that's what'll be played at his party, I really don't want to go. One of the lads threatened to throw his tapes into the waste oil barrel."

"That bad?"

"His latest kick is Marillion."

"Oh Jesus."

"Exactly!"

Jools frowned. "Try and get in as early as possible." And then she had a thought. "I heard they said it might be no admittance after midnight!"

"I never heard that," Lainey said. "Sure they couldn't do that, half the crowd will only be staggering out of the pubs at half eleven and by the time they get there…." She trailed off. Jools was about to try and press the argument when they heard a shout from the hall. "Julia, your dinner. Ask Elaine if she'd like to stay."

"Your Mam's steak pie," Lainey said. "Absolutely!"

15. A Bit Of Business

Robbo stood at the side entrance to Cleary's, watching the girls
in their summer dresses going in and out of Madigan's bar
across the street. Summer evenings in Dublin were great,
everyone in their light summer clothes, soaking up the
sunshine. It brought a smile to people's faces. Jaysus, he
thought, if the temperature in Ireland went into double digits,
everyone started peeling off, but it was warm that evening - not
even end of May warm but felt more beginning of August
warm - so he hadn't bothered with a jacket. It would still be
warm when he was leaving Bubbles, so decided on Navy Sta-
Prest and a white cycling shirt, with red and blue striped collar,
controversial at a time when the Irish Mod targets were all
green, white and orange and you could get your head kicked in
for wearing a red, white and blue one, but nobody touched
Robbo, everyone thought he was too well connected. As soon
as he finished his business here, he thought, he'd go across to
Madigan's for a quick pint to calm his nerves. He caught the
eye of a girl going into the pub, the spitting image of Samantha
Fox, ripped jeans, big tits and sprayed to fuck blonde hair, and
smiled. She looked across at him and his mind momentarily
relaxed. Might be worth checking out when he was finished.
She shouted over to him, "State o' yer shirt! Where did ya leave

yer push bike, ya Mod wanker! Bet ya'd love ta gimme a crossbar!" Her and her friends laughed hysterically, before disappearing inside.

"Bollocks," he muttered, his mood dropping again.

He was forty-five minutes early for this meeting, if you could call it that, but better to be early than late when it came to Freddie Collins and he couldn't sit still at home because he was so nervous, so he rang Sean to tell him he'd see him in Bubbles, and got the bus in early. He was smoking like a chimney, lighting up each smoke from the butt of the previous one, careful not to get ash on the suede of his Chelsea boots, as there was a pile of butts gathering at his feet. Freddie and his lads scared the shite out of him. He wasn't alone, Freddie scared the shite out of everyone he came into contact with, and it was always best to play it very cool with him, always be on time, always have his money and never disrespect him. When it came to gear on the scene, Robbo was definitely the go to guy, but it wasn't by choice. Okay, Freddie supplied him with the best stuff, and Robbo sold it to anyone who wanted it, and made a fair few quid, but he hadn't exactly sat in primary school, looking out the window, dreaming of being a drug dealer.

His Dad had died a couple of years earlier from pancreatic cancer. Now, no cancer is nice, but that one's a fucker. He was in hospital for a long time and they finally said there was nothing more they could do for him but make him comfortable. His Dad was a proud man, a big old docker who had wasted away to nothing, and decided he wasn't dying in any hospital, he wanted to go in his own bed at home and signed himself out, against strenuous objections from the medical team.

Unfortunately for his Dad, the cancer decided it would linger on a little bit, just to twist the knife, and he was in immense pain. Robbo had to do something, so approached one of the many dealers in Coolock who passed him up the line to Freddie, who was sympathetic, kind, even fatherly, as he supplied Robbo with enough morphine to keep his Dad comfortable for whatever remained of his life, with a, "don't worry about it Robbo, we'll sort something out later."

Robbo's Dad died six weeks later, off his tits on morphine, not knowing who he or anyone else was, but not in pain. At least that was something.

After the funeral, the family had the wake in the upstairs function room in Campions Pub, beside Balgriffen Cemetery. His Dad was popular, so the room was jammed, mostly with neighbours and friends he liked but there were also cousins he couldn't stand and others he didn't know, all turning up to get a free feed, so he had to get out of the room and went downstairs to the bar. He sat in the corner with his pint, enjoying the quiet. Apart from him, there was the bar man, reading a newspaper and two old men down the far end, both wearing flat caps and sitting back from a domino laden table, to accommodate their huge bellies, half their pints gone in one gulp. The only sounds in the bar were the occasional clink of a domino, a clock ticking and the sound of the newspaper turning. The walls were covered in old black and white photos of Coolock, Malahide and Belcamp, all in long lost days, when the area surrounding the pub was farmland. Men with horses attached to ploughs, holding pitchforks, looked on in their summer vests as haystacks littered the landscape behind them. Old women stood at half gates looking out from long demolished kitchens, while children played in the dirt of the yards.

The silence was broken by the creak of the bar door and all four looked up as three men walked in. The bar man folded his paper and walked into the back room and the old lads knocked back their pints, then one took off his cap and swept the dominoes into it, stood up and they both walked out the door. Robbo was alone in the bar as Freddie, all five feet two of him, dressed in a black three piece suit, shadowed by two, well over six foot thugs, walked up to him.

"Alright, Robbo," he said, sitting down on the stool opposite.

"So sorry about your Da, he was a lovely man."

You never even met him you midget fuck, Robbo thought.

"Ah, thanks, Freddie," he said. "Thanks for coming. I didn't see you at the funeral."

"Nah, sorry, I'd a bit of business to take care of. Some cunt thought he could get away without payin me for some gear I gave him." He laughed a humourless laugh. "Lucky I'm wearin black. The fucker's blood splashed me when I nailed his hands to the tree."

The thugs gave an obligatory laugh at this. Robbo didn't.

"So, now that your Da is gone and all that unpleasant business with the cancer, which is a bitch, by the way, is done and dusted, there's a small matter of a shit load of morphine I gave ya on tick. Now, how are we gonna work that one out?"

"Eh, you said it was okay, Freddie."

"Did I?" He said, looking up at the thugs. He turned back to Robbo and said, "Jaysus, I don't remember sayin that."

Freddie's voice was almost a whisper now, but there was no disguising the menace in it.

"I'm a businessman," he said. "How do ya think it'd look if I started giving every little fucker in the street with a hard luck story free gear? I'd be laughed at. Now, you wouldn't want anyone laughin at me, would ya, Robbo? Would ya?"

"No, Jaysus no, course I wouldn't."

"Well then, when's the insurance comin?"

"Fuck sake, Freddie, we only buried him an hour ago, I don't know. I'm not even sure he had any."

"Ah, Jaysus," Freddie said, a mock, sorrowful look on his face. "Well that's just very fuckin tough for ya, isn't it? Here, have a look out that window there." Robbo looked out.

Freddie leaned back, put all his weight into it and swung a left hook, catching Robbo on the right side of his face, just below the cheek bone and sending him off the couch to land on the floor on his knees.

"Jaysus, Freddie, what the fuck did you do that for?" He asked as he struggled back onto the couch, his hand on his jaw, which was already reddening. "That fuckin hurt!"

"Do what?"

"What?" Robbo said, shaking his head. "You gave me a fuckin dig for nothin!"

"No I didn't."

"Yes, you fuckin did!"

Freddie stood up and leaned across the table. Their faces were so close, Robbo could smell his breath. Minty. Not what he was expecting.

"Are you callin me a liar?"

"But…. you….. No. No, I'm not. It's just….."

"Just what? Ya said I gave ya a dig and I fuckin didn't. That sounds to me like you're callin me a liar. And nobody calls me a liar."

"I didn't mean….." Robbo said, shakily.

Freddie leaned back, put his hand in his jacket pocket and pulled out a flick knife. His eyes were still locked onto Robbo's and Robbo heard, more than saw the knife. Freddie put the tip of the blade inside Robbo's left nostril. He didn't move an inch, afraid the blade would cut through his nose if he did.

"Have ya ever seen Chinatown?" Freddie asked.

Robbo gulped. He had. And even if he hadn't, everyone knew that scene.

"Yeah," he managed to mutter.

Freddie just stared into Robbo's eyes, the tip of the knife bit into the inside of his nostril causing a tiny bead of blood to come out. It slowly trickled down the blade. Freddie smiled and pulled the knife away and it was folded and back in his pocket as quickly as it had come out. He sat back down and this time he looked out the window. Robbo followed his gaze, being sure to keep Freddie's fists in his peripheral vision.

"Tell ya what," Freddie said, "I'll even let ya pick the tree I'll nail your fuckin hands to, how about that? So, take a good fuckin look out that window and pick one. I'm just too kind to ya, son."

"Look, Freddie, I'll get your money as soon as I can, just don't nail me to any fuckin tree, please." He took a gulp of his pint, half gone in one go and thought he might piss himself and that he was lucky he was wearing black if he did.

"It's a lot. Ya never even asked me how much the Morphine cost. Ya just kept takin it and pumpin it into your aulfella, like there was no tomorrow." He laughed, as did the thugs. "And then, there was no fuckin tomorrow. The cunt was dead, and ya owe me seven hundred quid."

"What?" Robbo barked. "Where the fuck am I gonna get seven hundred quid?

"That's not really my problem, is it?" Freddie said. "And to think, that poor cunt that I crucified on a tree out there, probably thinkin he's Jaysus bleedin Christ himself, he only owed me five! You're fucked, Robbo. I reckon it'll be your kneecaps and all."

"Look, I didn't know what it cost. I'll get it to you, I promise."

"I'm not a monster, and it's yer Da's funeral, so I'll give ya a break. Have four hundred for me by Saturday and we'll work somethin out. Maybe ya can get some of your moddy friends to buy some gear. I heard them cunts like the speed. Maybe, if ya start sellin the gear for me in your mod clubs, ya can work off the debt. See? Business, Robbo, it's all just business."

He patted Robbo on the shoulder and said, "There's a good boy. Aren't ya glad we had this little chat?" He stood up and walked out the way he'd come in, not waiting for a reply.

When Robbo went back upstairs, he was white as a sheet.

"You alright?" Sean asked.

"I fucked up, bud," Robbo said. "Seriously, fucked up."

"What's the matter?" Sean asked, sitting down at a table with Robbo. He leaned in, so they could talk more privately.

"Freddie Collins. Me Da needed morphine and I had to go to him. I'm into him for seven hundred."

"Christ! Are you fuckin mental?" Sean said, shocked. "He's nasty. I heard he nails people to trees."

"Yeah, he told me to look out the window and pick which one I wanted. He was giving me the morphine and said not to worry about it. I thought he was just being nice."

"Seriously, Robbo? He's a gangster, I didn't think you were that stupid."

"I just wanted to look after me Da."

Robbo started welling up. The fright and the delayed grief got to him and he said, "What am I gonna do, Sean? Even if I sell my records, that won't get me more than a couple of hundred."

"When does he want the money by?"

"He wants four hundred by Saturday and said I can work off the rest by selling speed in the clubs. I don't even have the four hundred."

"I'll give it to you," Sean said.

"What?"

"I'll give it to you. Not the whole seven, I don't have that, but I'll give you the four."

"You mean lend me the four?"

"No, I mean give you. And no strings like with that bollocks either. Pay me pack when or if you have it. If you don't, it's no bother either. You're my mate and that's what mates do. But looking at it, Robbo, he set you up. He needed someone to sell gear in the clubs and didn't have an in. He came up to me once at some twenty first I was doing and asked if I wanted to make a bit on the side. I said I couldn't, it's not my DJ rig and if Johnny knew I was selling gear when I was doing his DJ jobs while he was in the Leb, there'd be a squad of soldiers kicking the shit out of me. He never came near me again after that. Freddie might be nasty, but he's not stupid. Them soldiers would murder him and he knows it."

"How come you never said anything?"

"Just never seemed important. You're gonna have to sell the gear though, there's no way out of it."

And that was that. Robbo was well and truly set up and well and truly fucked, but not in the way he'd first imagined and looking back, thought he'd have been better off being nailed to the tree.

If there was one thing that really pissed him off about Freddie

– and there were lots of things – it was his reluctance to take the money off Robbo on a regular basis, and just kept sending more gear over, so by the time Freddie did eventually arrange to meet him, Robbo could often be carrying a couple of grand around and there was three grand in his wallet that night, hence the nervousness.

He looked up North Earl Street and saw Jools and Cyn walking towards him.

16. Blame This Pair

"There's Robbo," Cyn said, turning from the window of Simon Hart's, where the latest Mod shoes were displayed, along with some hideous side laced ones the trendy lads were wearing.

"I thought he'd already be in The Anvil," Jools replied. "Let's walk up with him."

They walked up to Cleary's, noticing the pile of butts on the ground in front of him.

"Jaysus, Robbo," Jools said, "that's some habit."

"Howaya, girls. Ah, I'm a bit nervous. Meeting…. you know…. and he scares the shite outa me."

Jools had to think quickly and then remembered who Robbo was talking about.

"Ah, alright," she said, "he does that to people. What time are you meeting him?

"Half seven."

"No point standing here till then," Cyn said, "you'll smoke yourself to death. Come on to The Anvil and have a pint."

Robbo looked at his watch and at the mountain of cigarette butts at his feet.

"Alright then, yeah, a quick one."

He made loops of his arms and the two girls linked him on either side and they walked towards O'Connell Street, turning right to go to The Anvil, which was around the next corner, opposite the side of the Cathedral. There were two doors. One in the centre of the pub's red façade that led to the downstairs bar and one on the right, which led to the room upstairs. They walked in the door on the right and even from the bottom of the stairs, could hear the bustle of what sounded to be a fairly large crowd and "Sugar Beat," by Nine Below Zero playing on the jukebox.

The door to the function room upstairs was wedged open with a handful of folded beermats and the place was wall to wall Mods, a few moving on the small dance floor at the back of the room, near the toilets, but most sitting around in booths, drinking and chatting.

Most of the crowd in The Anvil were underage, but it was known as a place you could get served and with a barman who obviously didn't care, nobody was ever refused.

"What are yis havin?" Robbo asked them as they looked over towards a booth in the centre of the opposite wall from the bar, where Sean and Jayo were sitting. Sean looked up at Robbo and shouted over the music "What's the story, I thought you weren't coming in?"

Robbo yelled back, "Blame this pair," and turned back to the girls.

They both said they'd have Rum and Coke, as it was The Mod

Drink of the 60s, though in truth, Cyn didn't really like it. Robbo went to the bar and ordered two, and a pint of Harp for himself, taking his wallet from the back pocket of his trousers. Standing by the door, leaning on the cigarette machine, a small, skinny teen was watching him. A Mod in a light blue mohair suit went up to the machine and the teen had to move out of the way.

"Got any odds, Kev?" The skinny lad asked.

"Fuck off, Dosser, you little wanker."

"Ah, come on, man," Dosser said, in a high pitched, nasal voice. "I got me concession for Bubbles, I just need the money to get in."

"It a fuckin quid in," Kev said, turning his nose up. "You're probably fuckin loaded anyway. Frank just said you were over there trying to scrounge money outa him too."

"Ah, ya know, bud," Dosser said, shrugging.

"I'm not your fuckin bud," Kev said. "And again, fuck off!"

Dosser was one of those people who, no matter how hard he tried, always looked like he'd just rolled out of bed. When it came to the Mod look, Dosser was the antithesis of sharp. Nobody's actual friend, he just hung on the periphery of various groups, hoping to get in with some clique or other, but there was just something about him that people didn't take to. He had an air of untrustworthiness about him and carried stories to and from, just about everyone on the scene. It didn't matter whether those stories were true or not, and quite a lot of them he made up himself, but he'd tell you what he thought you wanted to hear and by the time you realised what was happening, he'd thrashed you to anyone who would listen, which, by then, were few and far between.

He hated Robbo. Especially with all the kids singing that Small Faces song they wrote about their drug dealer, "Here Come The Nice," when Robbo appeared. It made him sick. Who the fuck did he think he was anyway? Everyone thought Robbo was "The Man," and Dosser desperately wanted that to be that. What he didn't realise was that Robbo would have happily exchanged his current occupation with him, but Freddie knew Dosser only too well and didn't trust him either. Freddie believed himself to be a fair man and as long as Dosser stayed out of his business, then Freddie was happy enough to allow Dosser to keep breathing.

He watched Robbo with interest, a small sliver of saliva trickling down from the right corner of his mouth when he saw the bulging wallet.

Robbo, miles away as he watched one of the Mod girls dancing, put his wallet back in his pocket, not realising that the wallet wasn't actually in the pocket, but slotted, half in with the other half hanging over the side, picked up the drinks and started to walk through the crowd, towards the booth where Sean and Jayo were already on their second pints.

Dosser moved quickly, walking towards Robbo, slipping smoothly through the crowd and as Robbo turned sideways to slip between two people, Dosser's hand came down effortlessly, lifted Robbo's wallet without missing a stride and he went straight to the toilets.

He opened one of the cubicle doors, put the seat down, locked the door and sat down. He opened the wallet and stopped breathing.

His heart started beating faster and he began to sweat. It was stuffed. His eyes bulged as he counted out twenty after twenty, till he finally arrived at "three thousand and forty five quid," he whispered to himself.

He sat there for a good five minutes. Whatever Dosser was, he wasn't completely stupid. He knew this wasn't Robbo's money. He knew exactly whose money it was, and he thought about it for a minute.

He could give it back to him, saying he saw him drop it on the floor when he was at the bar and maybe get in with him and the other lads. Oh, and Cyn. He so wanted her. This could be the chance. But….

Robbo might only say thanks and buy him a pint and that would be the end of it. Back to being the snivelling little bollix that nobody wanted around, and he'd be no better off than he was before.

Three grand, he thought. That could get a lot of suits and a scooter. He could get yer man Des, that tailor the Dublin Mod Society lads used, to make some nice ones and then Cyn would be gaggin for him.

He whispered to himself, "Howya, Cyn, want a lift home on me Vespa?" His head filled with erotic images and the front of his jeans got noticeably tighter. He looked down at his crotch and his rising erection, stuffed inside his brother's hand me down Wranglers, which also grated on his pride, as his brother was a year younger than him. "They're not even fuckin Levi's," he said to himself. "Buy a lot of Levi's with three grand, Dosser." And then the clincher. "If Robbo can't pay Freddie," he quietly said to himself, "he'll end up without any kneecaps, or bits of him in a small hole in the Dublin Mountains. Then there'll be an openin for a new dealer and this time, I'll be The Fuckin Nice!"

He smiled. "Fuck you, Robbo," he whispered to himself and stuffed the money into his jeans pocket. He lifted the lid of the cistern and dropped the empty wallet in. "Let's see the cunt find it in there," he said and stifled a laugh.

Dosser took a deep breath and walked casually out of the toilet, pushed his way through the crowd and went back to his spot at the cigarette machine, feeling like every eye in the room was on him.

None were. Nobody ever noticed Dosser.

17. Here, Moddy Boy

Robbo looked at his watch. "Shit!" He jumped up, knocking the table slightly.

"What's the matter?" Cyn asked, wiping some spilled drink off the edge with her beer mat.

"I've gotta meet.... yer man."

"Ah, Jaysus," Cyn said. "Be careful, he's a nasty bollix."

"Tell me about it!" Robbo replied. "Sooner I can get away from him, the better."

Jools gave him a hug and echoed Cyn. "Be careful, Robbo, we'll see you in Bubbles later."

"That's the plan," he said, "but the last time I gave him a load of money, he insisted I go drinking with him in that pub he owns in Smithfield and you can't say no to Freddie."

"Well, hopefully he won't suggest it," Jools said, "and we'll see you later. Be careful!"

"I will," he replied and walked out the door as they were finishing their drinks.

Dosser looked at him from the corner of his eye.

Robbo ran down the stairs and out onto O'Connell Street, looking down towards the Parnell Street end for Freddie's car. He checked his watch again, he'd be here any minute.

He walked back down to his station at the side entrance of

Cleary's and noticed that one of Dublin Corporations finest must have been through with his cart and brushes and swept up the mountain of butts.

He leaned against the wall, not seeming to notice the bulge that had been between the wall and his arse earlier wasn't there, put his hand in his front pocket and pulled out his smokes, but a niggling thought crept into his brain that something was wrong, something was missing, and just before it had time to form, the Samantha Fox lookalike and her mates came out of Madigans and she noticed him. She said something to her mates and they all laughed. She turned back around and called over to him.

"Still there? I'm not surprised ya got stood up! Fuckin state of ya! Do ya not know that Cleary's clock is round the front?" Her mates all laughed at this as Robbo shook his head and looked down.

"Here, Moddy Boy!" She called. Robbo looked over as she lifted her top up, showing a bright pink, lace bra that looked like a hammock for a baby hippo. "That's as close as you're gonna get to diddies tonight!"

They all roared with laughter at this and he heard one of her mates say "Deirdre, you're a mad cow, showin him your diddies!"

Deirdre laughed and said, "Ah, Jaysus, would ya look at the state of the poor bollix, I pitied him so gave him a thrill. He'll never get a ride lookin like that, unless he's got a big fuckin wallet!"

She did a twirl, blew him a kiss and sashayed towards the corner.

Robbo watched them turn onto O'Connell Street and thought, love, if only you knew how big my fuckin wallet really is and he smiled.

The smile froze on his face and turned to a grimace, as the interrupted thought that had been forming, hit his brain, front and centre.

"No, no, no, no," he said, his hands shaking. He turned out his pockets, twisting around to look behind him and saw the empty pocket sticking out.

"No…. fuck, no…. Jaysus, he'll fuckin kill me."

He ran back to The Anvil and took the stairs two at a time, bumping into people who were leaving, making their way across town to Bubbles. Dosser came down, between two tall Mods, obscured by the parkas they were wearing, despite the heat and Robbo never even noticed him.

He got to the table where Sean, Jayo and the girls had been sitting. They were gone. He got down on his hands and knees and checked under the table and chairs.

The barman looked over.

"Are you alright there?"

115

"Me wallet!"

"What?" The barman asked.

"Me wallet!" Robbo said. "Have you seen me wallet?" He was sweating now.

"I had it coming in, I think I did."

"Did you buy any drinks?"

"Yeah," Robbo said, "A pint of Harp and two rum and Cokes."

"Jaysus," the barman said, "I don't remember. Half the fuckers in here ordered that. Maybe you dropped it down by the bar?"

Robbo ran to the bar, pulled out the high stools and scanned the floor. Nothing.

He turned and looked around the floor of the emptying room. "Bollocks.... bollocks.... bollocks."

He was sweating profusely now, the white of his cycling shirt turned cream at the back where it stuck to his skin.

"He's gonna fuckin kill me."

Tears welled up in his eyes and his vision blurred. He caught a glimpse of something small and brown beneath one of the tables and ran towards it, bumping a Mod girl as she ran from the toilets towards her friends waiting by the door.

"Here, watch it," she said, but he paid her no attention as he ran towards the wallet.

He knelt on the floor and through his tears, picked up a discarded chip bag that someone had sneaked in. "Not....

me…. fuckin wallet." The dam broke and he sat on the floor crying. By now, the room was empty, so at least his reputation was still intact.

18. Like He Owns The Place

Freddie's driver pulled up at the corner and one of the thugs go out.

"Is he there?" Freddie asked.

The thug looked down towards the side entrance of Cleary's and answered, "I don't see him, Boss, maybe he went round the corner for a slash."

Freddie looked at his watch, it was ten past eight. He laughed. "I'm only forty minutes late. I bet the little cunt's been pissing himself with the fright."

The thug laughed at this and said, "I'll have a look round the corner," and went off to see.

Freddie rolled up the window and shook his head.

"Little bollix. I don't like bein kept waitin."

"No, Boss, you don't," the driver said.

"Cunt's probably saunterin up North Earl Street, like he owns the fuckin place."

There was a tap on the front passenger window and the driver rolled it down.

"You know you're not allowed to park here?" The Guard said.

Freddie rolled down his window.

"What's that, officer?"

"Oh, eh, sorry there, Mister Collins, I didn't realise it was you,

118

Sir. It's just that, you know, there's a bit of traffic behind you."

"We're just waiting for someone, officer, we'll be out of your way in a minute. We wouldn't like to be causing you any undue distress in your work, now, would we?"

"Ah, th-anks, Mr Collins. W-ell, you just have yourself a fine evening, Sir."

"And you too, officer," Freddie said, as he rolled up the window. "Fuckin filth."

Just then the thug came running back. Freddie rolled down the window. The thug held his arms out to his sides and shook his head.

Freddie got out of the car and looked up and down O'Connell Street. The blood began to rise in his face, and he turned and kicked a bin over, screaming, "I'll fuckin kill him!"

Robbo watched this happen while sticking his head around the corner at the other end of the block, and felt vomit rising into his throat. He turned back towards The Anvil and puked.

"I'd better disappear," he said.

19. Do Me A Favour

Dosser stood outside the Three Lamps pub on Aston Quay, not knowing exactly what to do or where to go. He still couldn't believe his luck and thought he'd go in for a pint and calm his nerves a bit before going into Bubbles. He was standing there, wondering what to do, if he should even go to the club, in case he'd lose the money. It could just, like, drop out of his jeans pocket or something and someone might see it happen and questions would be asked and as soon as they all found out that Robbo lost his wallet, well, they'd put two and two together and it didn't bear thinking about. Nah, he thought, I'll just get the bus home and wait till Saturday.

He was just turning to go for his bus when a car beeped, and he heard someone call his name. His blood froze in his veins and a little bit of wee came out. There was no mistaking that voice.

"Dosser, ya little cunt, c'mere."

He turned slowly and looked into the flushed face of Freddie Collins, peering out through the window of his Merc. Thoughts barrelled through Dosser's head.

Freddie knows. Freddie's gonna have me kneecaps. He's probably got a nice little hole dug in the Dublin mountains, just my size. Run, he thought. Run Dosser and don't look back.

"Are ya deaf, ya little bollix? I said c'mere!"

Dosser's feet felt like lead. He struggled to move one in front of the other and slowly made his way towards the car.

"Ye-es…. Freddie?"

Freddie's eyes widened and he pulled his head back, as if slapped.

"Did we go to school together, Dosser?"

"Eh, no, I think you're a good bit older than…."

Freddie cut him off.

"Do I, perhaps owe ya some money then, for, say, a wager we might have had while playin a round of golf?"

Dosser was extremely confused.

"I've, eh, never played golf in me life. Why are ya askin if we played golf?"

"Because, Dosser, ya little toe rag, you're not me mate! So, if you're not me mate, who the fuck are *you* to be callin *me* Freddie?"

"S-sorry, Mister Collins…. I didn't mean…."

Freddie laughed a big belly laugh that frightened him even more.

"I'm only yankin your chain, Dosser, ya thick fuck. C'mere, do me a favour."

Dosser was totally confused now and stared at Freddie, like a sheep, looking into a spaceship. He had not got the faintest idea what was going on.

"Get in," Freddie said, and threw the door open.

Dosser's thoughts started reeling and every survival instinct he had, told him to run, but just like a sheep, he climbed into the back seat of the car, with no control over his movements whatsoever.

The car pulled out into traffic. Dosser sat next to Freddie, sweating profusely, and it had nothing to do with the summer heat.

"Ya know Robbo, don't ya?"

Dosser gulped. "Yes, Mister Collins, I do."

"Well," Freddie said. "That fucker was supposed to meet me tonight to do," he tapped the side of his nose, "a bit of business. But he never showed up."

Dosser gulped again, thinking he was going to swallow his tongue, his mouth was as dry as sand.

"Have ya seen him tonight, Dosser?"

He thought for a second about telling him no, but then thought better of it. Freddie might have seen them go into and come out of The Anvil and Freddie did love to play games.

"Eh, yeah," Dosser said. "He was in The Anvil earlier with his mates…. and two birds."

"What time was that?"

"Dunno, maybe, maybe bout half seven."

"Hear that, lads?" Freddie said. "That cunt was sinkin pints with two slappers in The Anvil when he shoulda been meetin me! Now that's just disrespectful."

He turned back to Dosser.

"Did ya talk to him?"

"Em, no, he doesn't, doesn't talk to me. None of them do. They barely even notice me. Especially the birds."

"Aw, Jaysus, Dosser," Freddie said, "that's an awful fuckin shame, you're breakin me heart. Is it because you're such a snivellin little cunt?"

Dosser didn't know how to answer this. Freddie was taking the piss out of him and he wanted nothing more than to burst the horrible, midget fucker who, in truth, wasn't much smaller than Dosser, but still.

"Em, yeah, probably," Dosser said, looking at the floor.

"Ah come on, son, don't be all sad. Here, ya can do me a favour and I'll give ya a score for your troubles. How's that?"

Dosser looked up and smiled. Freddie Collins was sitting there beside him and offering him twenty quid when Dosser had three grand of his money in his pocket. You're an awful thick cunt, Freddie, he thought.

"Sure, Mister Collins, that would be great. Anything I can do, I'd be delighted to."

"Good man," Freddie said and rolled down the window.

They'd driven down to Heuston Station, crossed the Liffey and drove back up the other quay and he hadn't even noticed. They were now back outside the Three Lamps.

Freddie pointed out the window. "I want ya to go into that moddy club of yours and see if that tardy cunt is there and if he is, come out and tell me."

Dosser just looked at him with that blank sheep look on his face again.

"Jesus, Dosser! Tardy! Late! Robbo left me sittin there for forty fuckin minutes waitin for him. I thought he was just late, but the pox never showed up!"

The thug in the front passenger seat looked at his watch, tapped the glass and put it up to his ear. He turned to the driver and mouthed, "Weren't we late?"

The driver just shrugged and looked straight ahead again.

"Oh, right, tarry, yeah, I get it," Dosser said.

"Well go on then," Freddie said, handing him a twenty pound note. "I don't have all fuckin day!"

"Em…."

"What?" Freddie snapped.

"Can I have a quid to get in?"

Freddie gawped at him. "I just gave ya a score, ya little bollix."

"Yeah, I know, but if I hand in a score, they'll think I robbed someone."

Freddie fished a pound note out of his pocket and handed it to

Dosser. "Get the fuck out and find him."

Dosser got out of the car and walked towards the corner, turning down Price's Lane. Once he was out of sight, he leaned against the wall and let out a big, deep breath. Then he laughed so hard, his ribs hurt.

20. Red Walls, Black Pillars

Jools and Cyn walked up to the door of Bubbles with Sean and Jayo. A queue had already formed, with people waiting for the club to open. There were a few Mods hanging about outside, away from the queue, sitting on scooters and others hanging around, posing in suits, making sure everyone could see them. The shutters went up. Jools looked at her watch, it was 8:15pm on the button. People moved in, regular faces, all well known. "Not tonight," one of the stocky bouncers said, the neon of the Bubbles sign reflecting off his sandy, red hair. A young Mod, who, despite his height, still looked about twelve, raised himself up to his fullest and stood inches away from him, his flat, boxers nose told tales of previous scraps and he smiled a humourless smile at the lad, but didn't budge.

There were giggles behind the boy, as the regulars gathered in the alley knew that he hadn't a chance. He deflated, turned and walked away, ignoring the laughter behind him.

Jools walked towards the door and looked at the rectangle of darkness behind the bouncer. Her breath caught, she couldn't believe it. Twenty-eight years after she left, after it had closed and her heart broke, she was going back in. Would it be as good as she remembered it? Was it really that special, or had speed and years rose tinted her memory?

She went to move past the bouncer, who said, "Well, Miss Sutton, I hope you don't start any trouble like you did last week."

"What? I didn't…."

"Fuck sake, Jools," Cyn said, "he's messing with you. You're acting so mental today."

She grabbed Jools's hand and dragged her in, Sean and Jayo behind them.

She walked down the stairs, turned right at the small landing and waited for her turn to pay at the ticket office.

Concession and pound note handed in, she walked towards the arch that led to the dancefloor and saw Noel, the DJ, behind the caged wall of the DJ box. He picked up the mic and with a nod towards her, said, "Back in time with Butch Baker, and here's The Just Brothers, "Sliced Tomatoes!"

"He remembers me," she said under her breath and then laughed.

Of course, he remembers you Jools, she thought, he only saw you last week!

She turned around and walked towards the cloakroom, saying hello to a bored looking attendant who wouldn't be doing much work this evening with the heat that was out there. She turned the corner and walked to the edge of the dancefloor and stopped, looking around and just taking it all in.

It was exactly as she remembered it.

The décor was very Sixties underground club style with red walls and seating all around the edges, also red. There was a tunnel leading away from the dancefloor area down to the toilets and further along, the soft drinks bar, which is where most of the crowd who weren't dancing or sitting would congregate. The floor itself was sunken and had steps down onto it, which were very rarely used. It had two massive, black pillars stuck on either side of it and the back wall by the DJ box was mirrored, from about halfway up the wall, to the black, painted ceiling, which was covered in spotlights, most of which pointed at a solitary mirror ball, hanging in the centre, the rest aimed at various parts of the dancefloor. On the left side of the room, near where the cloak room was, there was what looked like a large, rectangular white screen, which, if it was for projecting anything onto, Jools had never seen being used. Between this screen and the pillar, a purple fluorescent light hung, which would often see people scurrying from beneath it as it showed up any lint or fluff on your clothes in Persil White detail, but nobody else, unless they were very close to you, could see this. When the slow set would come on, you'd never see couples dancing in that area.

Cyn was already in their regular seat, halfway down the right-hand wall, which, even if Cyn hadn't been sitting there, Jools would have instinctively gravitated to. Everyone in Bubbles had their own spots, places they sat, week in, week out. She turned and bumped into a tall, dark haired Mod in a dark brown suit which, in this light, had a black look to it. She hadn't seen him in decades, as he'd dropped off the scene in the Nineties.

"Hi, Stevey!" She said. "How are you doing? I haven't seen you in ages!"

"You saw me in school yesterday, Jools," he said, his eyebrows raising.

"I did? Yes, I mean I did," she replied. "I mean, I haven't seen you here in ages."

"You saw me here last week," he said. "Have you been taking some dodgy gear? You should really stay away from that stuff."

"No, I'm grand, I fell in town today and banged my head off a bin, I've been a bit mixed up since."

"Yeah," he said, "just a bit."

The conversation halted a couple of beats as they both looked towards the floor where "Sliced Tomatoes" was giving way to "Lost Summer Love," and Stevey's mate, Lar, a Soul Boy in Adidas T-Shirt, combats and number one haircut walked off the floor, ignoring Jools as he looked at Stevey and they both said, "Girly shite."

She looked around for the third member of their trio.

"Is Chris not here?"

129

"Yeah," Stevey said, "he's dancing over in the far corner, hoping Mary Boyd will notice him."

"He shouldn't hold his breath," she said.

"You never know," Stevey replied, "though he's probably got more chance of getting off with Mary than he has of running a night like Bubbles."

"What's that?" Jools asked.

"He's been buying loads of records lately and said he'd love to be a DJ like Noel and that bloke Ady Croasdell, you know, yer man that's Harboro Horace off the Kent LPs?"

"Yeah, I know him."

"Says that's his dream, that he wants to be a DJ and run a club like this someday."

"Maybe," Jools said, "someday he might just do that."

"Yeah, right," Stevey said. "The way people are starting to drift off, I'd give the Mod scene two years tops."

You're not wrong there, she thought and said, "Ah, you never know, if he's that determined, he might just keep going and do it someday."

"I suppose," he replied. "You never know. One thing I will say about him is, whenever he puts his mind to something, he usually does it. Except Mary, he's no fuckin chance there."

Jools smiled. He would do it, she thought and looked over at the small Mod in the navy suit on the other side of the floor, desperately trying to get the attention of a cute, blonde bobbed Mod girl. He would end up running various clubs, years later, but never did get off with Mary.

21. Northern And Modern Rooms

Jools left Stevey and walked over to where Cyn was sitting, sat down and looked around.

The club was filling up now, with everyone going to their regular spots. Her heart was beating much faster than the music, as she spotted people, some of whom she'd seen only last night, but thirty years in the future and she was still amazed by that. Faces that were thirty years younger than they were the night before! She half expected to still wake up and find that it was all a dream.

And the music. This was the place she first heard "Biff Bang Pow" and "For Your Love." The first place she ever danced to "The Night." It all just washed over her and filled her up. She couldn't believe she was back and started to well up.

"I need to go to the jacks," she said to Cyn and quickly got up before she noticed her eyes. Cyn was already starting to think there was something up and if she just suddenly burst into tears, well, try and explain that.

She ran towards the ladies and pushed opened the door. Smoke and hairspray filled her nostrils and she gagged.

The toilet was packed but a cubicle was empty, and she went inside, shut the door and sat down on the toilet lid. She just sat there for a couple of minutes, drying her eyes and listening to the chatter of the teenage girls whose main topics of conversation were clothes, makeup and various boys outside. She smiled. Some things never change.

After she judged enough time had passed that any redness in her eyes had cleared up, she left the cubicle and went to the mirror to reapply her eye liner.

She left the toilets and walked to the mineral bar where Sean was in conversation with Joe Leonard, a small pudgy Mod known as Lenny. She ordered a Coke.

"Well," she heard Sean say, "If it's not Sixties, then it must be Modern."

Jools saw Lenny's face as he frowned at this and could tell the term was unfamiliar to him. He was well known on the scene and even in 2015, was still known as a perpetual pain in the arse. Calling him an anorak would give anoraks a bad name, he was just one of those know it all people who couldn't stand it when someone knew something he didn't and constantly pulled people up when they got a fact wrong.

In 1985, Lenny had a sizeable record collection, but it 2015 it was a monster one and he was, admittedly, quite knowledgeable, but it was widely believed that what he didn't know, he made up and some of the records he said he had, he didn't. Jools couldn't stand him.

"Oh, yeah, Modern," Lenny said, when he noticed her, "of

course."

Jools thought she'd have a bit of fun here. Nobody could argue that Lenny's knowledge was second to none – in 2015 – but in 1985, she had thirty years on him. She smiled.

"What's this?" She asked Sean.

"Modern Soul," Sean said, while Lenny nodded, knowingly.

"What about it?"

"Well," Sean said, "Like, if it's a Sixties record, it's Northern, and if it's a Seventies record, it's Modern, cos, like, well, it's not Sixties."

"Not necessarily," she said.

"Look, love," Lenny said, "this is man's talk. We don't interrupt you when you're talking about makeup and shoes and periods and that shite, so keep whatever you think you know about records," and he paused and winked at Sean at this point, "to yourself."

"Ah, now, Lenny," Sean said, "there's no need for that."

"It's okay, Sean," Jools replied, "I can hold my own with this misogynist."

Lenny looked aghast, though Jools could tell this was also a term he was unfamiliar with.

"Lenny," she said, "I've forgotten more about records, than you'll ever know, sunshine."

"I highly doubt that," he said.

Sean interjected quickly. "Anyway, what did you mean when you said not necessarily?"

"Just because it's Seventies, doesn't mean it's Modern and not all Northern was done in the Sixties."

"Like what?" Sean said, followed by a berating "Yeah," from Lenny.

"Frankie Valli," she said, off the top of her head, "The Night."

"Northern!" They both said.

"Ah, but it was recorded in 1972, so, shouldn't it be Modern?"

"Eh, well," Sean said, and Lenny said nothing.

"Keep On Keeping On?"

"NF Porter!" Lenny exclaimed. "Have it, total Northern, recorded in 1969."

"1973, love," Jools said, "but it's also Northern."

She thought for a second.

"Four Tops, I Just Can't Get You Out Of My Mind?"

"Motown!" Lenny blurted this out with a big grin on his face, "That's Motown! The Four Tops are Motown! Not Northern and not Modern."

"Oh, Lenny, you're an awful thick fuck," Jools said. "They recorded that when they moved to ABC, after they left Motown. But that could be considered both. Gets played in the Northern and Modern rooms."

Lenny was fuming. He'd not only never heard the term

"Modern" before tonight, he also had no idea there were rooms dedicated to it, whatever the fuck it was.

The colour in his face rose. Jools saw this and smiled inwardly. Then she remembered something. Lenny was forever saying that Bubbles had been shite and that he rarely went there because it wasn't progressive enough. Yet, she'd seen many photos of him in Bubbles, obviously having a good time.

"Sure, why are you here anyway, Lenny? I remember you saying on a few occasions that you didn't like Bubbles, that the music wasn't progressive enough for you, but here you are. What's that all about?"

Lenny became flustered. "Well, it's not! Same old shite, week in, week out. It's like DJing by fuckin numbers! He never introduces anything new!"

"People like familiarity, Lenny," she said. "They want to come here, week in and week out and hear stuff they know and like and maybe hear the odd new tune, but not so much that they're sitting in their seats all night, not knowing what to dance to. That's the difference between someone who's a good DJ and a self-indulgent prick. Noel is a good DJ."

"Well if I was DJing, I'd be different!"

"What would you play, dear?" She was enjoying this, and a few bodies had moved closer to the bar, for an earwig, as Lenny's voice got louder.

"I'd play the rare stuff!" He spat this out, like a petulant child and, although Jools was seventeen again - on the outside - she was still a forty-seven year old woman on the inside and had her fill of childish tantrums when her kids were in their terrible twos and that was multiplied by two, so she knew how to handle him.

"For instance?"

"Well," Lenny said, gaining some confidence, as he was on a subject he knew something about, "earlier on he played Sliced Tomatoes, by The Just Brothers. Every fuckin week he drags that shite out when he could be playing Carlena!"

"Maybe he doesn't have Carlena," Jools said, "and maybe the crowd don't know it."

"A lot of them do," Lenny said. "Tommo brought that tape back from Morcambe and made loads of copies. He even gave one to Noel! Jaysus, he could play it off the tape! Well, when I got that tape, I got the single shortly after, so that's one I'd play." He raised himself up to his full height and tried to look down on this mere, girl, but it didn't work, he was a good head shorter than her.

"I have that too." Jools said.

"Yeah, right! What label?" He asked, scorn and disbelief in his voice.

She laughed, "Garrison, of course."

"Ah," Lenny said, "the cheapie. I have the mega rare one on Wand!"

Jools laughed out loud at this and noticed the puzzled looks from the few kids who were looking on. "You don't have it on Wand!"

"Yes I fuckin do!" Lenny snapped.

"You can't," she said, "it never came out on Wand. It doesn't exist!"

"The tape that Tommo gave us has the artists, titles and labels written on the playlist," he said, "and it said Wand, so I got my cousin in America to get me one. He's from New York, where Wand was, and I have nearly all the Wand stuff anyway, so don't fuckin tell me what I have and haven't got!"

"I'm telling you now, Lenny, you can't have it. *My* cousin in London met Frank Bryant once and he told her that the song was sent to Wand to be pressed and was even given a catalogue number, but it never happened. Garrison was owned by Scepter, who owned Wand, so it was moved to Garrison and pressed on that!"

"Who the fuck is Frank Bryant?"

"What?" Jools asked, astonished.

"Who... the.... fuck... is.... Frank... Bryant? Are you fuckin deaf, love? What, is he your cousin's fuckin window cleaner?" He looked around at the assembled kids and laughed in an

"I've got her now" manner.

Jools shook her head. "Frank Bryant, from The Just Brothers, you moron!"

"Look, love, they're called The Just Brothers, not the fuckin Bryant Brothers." He laughed.

"You think their last name was Just?" She said, crossing her arms, sticking out her hip and raising her eyebrow in a "don't fuck with me" pose.

"That's what it says on the label, love," he said, shrugging his shoulders and opening his hands wide to the crowd around them.

She stood there and stared at him for a second.

"And," she said, "I suppose the Righteous Brothers are brothers and their last name is Righteous?"

"Eh…. yeah…." he said this, questioningly. How unsure he was could be heard in the tremble in his voice.

"Bill Medly. Bobby Hatfield. The Righteous Brothers, you fucking dipstick! Frank Bryant. Jimmy Bryant AND Willie Kendrick. The Just Brothers! Oh, and by the way, if you do have it on Wand, it's a boot and don't trust that tape that Tommo gave you, the playlist is riddled with mistakes."

"What's a boot?" Asked a kid who looked like he'd just made his Confirmation.

"Bootleg!" They both said, at the same time, neither looking at the kid.

"I don't fuckin have bootlegs! You'll see when it's my turn to DJ, you'll all fuckin see!"

He stormed off in a red mist, jumped on the floor and started dancing, only halfway through, he realised he was dancing to the theme from "Hawaii-5-0."

"Bollocks!" He said to himself and walked off towards the toilets.

Jools laughed and thought, you never did, son, you never got to DJ at Bubbles and it fucking killed you.

"And that," Jools said to Sean, who was standing at the bar with a massive grin on his face, "is how you put a prick like him back in his box!"

"I have never been so impressed in my life, Jools, you were fuckin amazing!"

"Aw, thanks, Sean," she said, gave him a hug and walked back to Cyn.

22. Special Missions

Dosser, who, at the best of times, nobody noticed, was now about as inconspicuous as a target painted on an elephant's arse. His "Special Mission" for Freddie had put him in full on Ninja mode and he slinked around the floor of Bubbles, to numerous stares and countless mouthings of "What the fuck?" The problem with spotting Robbo, a tall slim Mod, dressed in Navy Sta-Prest and a white cycling shirt, was that he was in a room filled with tall slim Mods, dressed in Navy Sta-Prest and white cycling shirts. And it was dark.

He did his awkward shuffle around the dancefloor, peering up into the faces of those around him, but if Robbo was there, he wasn't dancing, and no surprise, if Dosser had lost three grand of Freddie's money, he wouldn't be dancing either. He'd conveniently forgotten that Robbo hadn't actually lost the money.

He walked off the floor and headed down towards the bar, looking left and right, like a demented Green Cross Code Man, but anywhere he looked, he still couldn't see him. He wasn't really surprised. As he thought earlier, there was no way Robbo was going to Bubbles when he was three grand shy of Freddie's money. Nah, he'd be rolled up in a ball underneath his bed, crying his eyes out and making plans to hop on the boat to

England. Even then, would that be far enough for Freddie not to get to him? He checked the jacks, looking in all the cubicles. He even threw his eye into the girls' jacks, cos you never knew with Robbo, to a chorus of "Get the fuck out, Dosser, you little pervert!"

He was just about to head back outside and reluctantly give Freddie the bad news, when he spotted him. He was down the back, near the steps that went up to Fleet Street. He'd been down on his hunkers, talking to someone who was sitting there, and Dosser only saw him when he stood up.

He just had to see his face. He bet that Robbo's eyes would be all red and puffy from crying and he couldn't leave without seeing that because he knew, as soon as Freddie got his hands on him, that was the last time anyone would ever see the prick's face. Freddie wouldn't stop at nailing him to a tree, or even his kneecaps, no, Robbo was a dead man. Freddie had been rumoured to have kidnapped a rival dealer who'd been trying to move into one of his patches and brought him out into Dublin Bay on his boat. And just for the craic, Freddie had told his thugs to take the breeze blocks out of the rival's garden that were holding up his car and tied them to him. Over the side and there was no more rival.

The body was never found, and it could be all bollocks, but why would he whip the breeze blocks out from under the car to

142

stick him in a hole in the Dublin Mountains? Dosser laughed and started singing, "Here Come The Nice" to himself as he walked towards the back steps.

He tapped him on the shoulder, "Here, Robbo, ya got any odds, man?"

Dosser's face dropped when Terry turned around.

"What?" Terry said. "I'm not Robbo, you dick. He hasn't been here all night. Must have gone somewhere else after The Anvil."

"Sorry, bud," Dosser said, "I thought you were him."

"Jaysus, man, would people stop saying that to me. Though, I wish I had his money."

Terry laughed at this and Dosser made a bit of a giggle, just to be polite. He really thought he had him, and his impending promotion disappeared. For a while, at least.

"Alright, thanks," he said and headed back out towards the entrance.

23. Plan A & Plan B

Jools sat with Cyn, enjoying the night, but still on tenterhooks waiting for Lainey to arrive and another attempt at trying to persuade her not to go to the party on Saturday. The Jam were just winding up their rendition of "Move On Up", when she heard a quick drum roll and heavy piano come over the speakers, and Huey Piano Smith And The Clowns sounded out the first bars of "Don't You Just Know It," and she jumped to her feet. "I haven't heard this in years!"

Cyn gave her that look again.

"You need to get that bump seen to," she said, "he plays that every week!"

Jools ignored her and ran to the dancefloor, where she was quickly joined by two of the Donaghmede Mods, who, every time the line, "Don't You Just Know It" was sung, leaned in towards each other and wagged their fingers.

Jools burst out laughing, but stifled it quickly, though not before Gaz and Mick gave her funny looks.

The Dublin Mod Society lads had brought the record in for Noel to play and it went down a storm and the following week, he was playing his own copy. All the Mod Society lads danced to it of course and, for the laugh, had made up a dance to go with the song, all wavy hands and wagging fingers and then sat back and watched as the dance took off as the song gained popularity.

It had a very short sell by date, though some of the newbies still did it and Gaz and Mick got up and had a laugh, while the kid who looked like he'd just made his confirmation was in full flow, looking like he'd somehow managed to track down a tutorial on a yet to be invented Youtube.

As the song faded out and "Our Love Will Grow," by The Showmen took its place, Gaz sat down on the edge of the floor and Jools went over.

"How are ya doing, Gaz, you're looking well. I didn't know you wore glasses. When did you get them?"

Gaz, who was just about to sign up to the army, though he didn't know it yet, would drop off the scene for decades but, like many, he got back into it after Facebook exploded and people realised there still was a scene going in Ireland, but, as much as Jools had seen him in recent years, she had never seen him wearing specs.

"Yeah, I only got them today, though," he said, putting his fingers in through the holes in the frame where the lenses should be, "I'm not seeing any improvement."

She looked at him for a second and then they both burst out laughing and she smiled. For just a couple of seconds she was actually seventeen again and just enjoying Bubbles and all the

145

great music and great people that made it what it was. No thoughts of why she was actually back, just there, in the moment with that loveable headcase.

She looked at the dancefloor and saw Matt, who hadn't changed much between 1985 and 2015. Still tall and slim, dressed impeccably, but what she did notice was he wasn't wearing dark glasses. She looked around and saw Cyn engaged in conversation with one of the Belfast Mods, but no Lainey. She must have missed them coming in while she was dancing.

"I'll catch you later, Gaz."

"Yeah, see ya later, Jools."

She sat down next to Cyn and, as the song finished, Matt walked towards them.

"Hi, Jools," he said as she stood up and hugged him.

"Where's Lainey?"

"She couldn't come," he said. "Her Dad had to do a late shift and her Mam was going up to the Granny's, so she had to stay in with the younger kids."

"Ah, she must be gutted," Jools said, thinking, Shite! Shite! Shite!

"Sure there's always next week," Matt said, "and the nighter on Saturday, whatever time we get here at."

"You're not going to The Blades?"

"No, I'm up to my tonsils in work and Lainey's just not that pushed."

"And the party? You still can't get out of that? Lainey said you'd probably be there till twelve? That's not so bad, I suppose." She thought, if they go by twelve, they'll be fine.

"No, not a chance. Not only has he a new flat he wants to show off, there's some girl going that he's trying to impress and thinks the more people he gets to go, the more she'll be impressed because he's popular. He said she's the one, the real deal. Not like the last five or six weren't the one and the real deal too. And I doubt we'll be leaving by twelve. You know house parties, they never really get going till close to then and if we leave before it does, he won't be impressed."

"What time will you be here, do you think?"

"I don't know, we'll get out as early as possible, so, however long it takes us to drive over, but I can't see us getting here before half one, at least."

Half one, she thought. That's still fine, they'll be in and they'll be safe. But, just in case....

"Would you not leave the scooter at home and get a taxi? You know, like, so you can have a drink?"

Matt looked puzzled. "You know I don't drink."

"Ah, don't mind her, Matt," Cyn said. "She smacked her head off a bin today when she tripped. She's been mad muddled since. I think she's got concussion or something."

"I don't have fecking concussion! I just forgot Matt doesn't drink."

"Yeah, whatever," Cyn replied.

Okay, Jools thought, Plan B, like I ever had a Plan A.

24. There It Was Again

Dosser was outside the Three Lamps again, but Freddie's car was nowhere to be seen.

"Shite, Freddie, ya bollix," he said to himself, "makin me work and then not even bein here when I come out."

He was debating walking down to get his bus, when the Merc rolled up and the window rolled down.

"Here, Bollix!" Freddie shouted. A few people looked around. Dosser groaned and walked towards the car.

"Well?" The impatience in Freddie's voice was palpable.

"Where were you?" Dosser demanded, forgetting himself for a second. "I was waitin out here for ages, like."

Freddie's eyes widened.

"Dosser, it's been a long day and I'm tired and pissed off and three grand short and very fuckin impatient, but you're a gobshite and know no better, so, this time, I'll let ya away with that, but if ya ever, and I mean fuckin ever, speak to me like that again, I'll tie ya to the back of me Merc and drag your skinny little arse all over town, till there isn't a skinny little arse left on ya. Do ya understand me?"

"Eh, yes, Fred.... I mean Mister Collins. Sorry Mister Collins. I didn't mean it Mister Collins. It's just, like, ya scare the shite outa me and I got a bit mixed up. Sorry, Mister Coll...."

"SHUT THE FUCK UP, DOSSER!"

Dosser did as he was told. Immediately.

"Now, where the fuck is Robbo?"

"Em, he's not in there."

"Are ya sure?"

"Yes, Mister Collins, definitely not. I did think I spotted him, but it wasn't him, it was Terry, cos, like him and Terry look like each other and Terry said don't keep sayin that and that he'd love to have…."

"STOP FUCKIN TALKIN!"

Once again, Dosser did as he was told. Immediately.

"What I want ya to do, Dosser," Freddie said, in the most menacing tone he had ever heard him use, "is call me on this number," he flicked a card out the window, plain, white, no name, just a number, "if and when ya see that cunt and I'm tellin ya now, if I find out you've seen him and not told me, well, let's just say that ya really don't wanna know what I'll do to ya."

"But…. but…. Mister Collins…. I'm not gonna see him. He lives in fuckin Coolock. That's like a hundred miles from my gaff!"

Freddie snapped his fingers and one of the thugs in the front handed something back to him. He handed it out through the window. Dosser took it in his very shaky hands. It was a flyer for the allnighter on Saturday.

"I keep me ear to the ground, Dosser. Now, make damn sure you're at this thing on Saturday night and as soon as ya see him, run to that phone box there and call me and then it'll be bye bye Robbo."

Dosser just stared at the flyer, the reality of what was happening finally sinking in.

"Did ya get all that?"

He kept staring at the flyer and thought, this is real now. As much as he hated Robbo, Freddie was going to kill him.

"Earth to Dosser…. come in, Dosser." Freddie snapped his fingers again, but this time right in front of Dosser's face. He blinked, looked up from the flyer and said "Ye…. yes, Mister Collins."

"Okay then," Freddie said. "Now, fuck off."

He rolled up the window and the car took off into traffic without indicating, and Dosser, who was now looking back down at the flyer, heard the sound of horns and brakes screeching as motorists tried to avoid hitting the Merc.

He stood there for a couple of minutes, the proverbial good and bad angels sitting on each shoulder as he wrestled with what little conscience he had. Freddie would catch up with Robbo eventually and when he did, there was no way he could pay him back that money he lost (there it was again) and he wouldn't come out of this alive.

"Fuck him!"

25. Tonight Was Different

Jools was completely lost in the exuberance of youth. Bubbles had always been her happy place and she was absolutely devastated when it closed, so, being here once again, was beyond joy. The whole evening was going by in a blur. Song after song that had become classics in the years between 1985 and 2015 sounded so fresh and new and some were new, to most of the crowd there, but not her. Once she discovered that Lainey wasn't coming, there was really nothing else for her to do but just enjoy the night, and she danced like she'd never danced before.

In the Eighties – the first time round – she'd always danced to the Sixties Ska and Skinhead Reggae, always in the middle of the floor, doing the original Sixties Ska dance, but didn't generally do much to the Two Tone stuff.

Tonight, was different. From the moment Roland Alphonso called out the words, "Phoenix City," all through "Return Of Django," "Israelites," "Bonanza Ska," and right through "Too Much Too Young," "Night Boat To Cairo," "Mirror In The Bathroom," and "Too Much Pressure," she danced, with a massive smile on her face, completely oblivious to anything and everything but the music, and entirely unaware of a tall handsome Mod in a grey tonic suit, his dark brown hair in a classic, Mod French cut, leaning against the wall of the tunnel, watching her.

"As Too Much Pressure" faded out, Noel announced that it was "Back to the Sixties and slowing it down," and those unmistakable strings started, bringing in Lulu singing, "To Sir With Love."

The floor emptied before Lulu got as far as telling everyone that those days of biting her nails were gone and hesitantly, a few lads managed to persuade a few girls to have a bit of a twirl.

Jimmy watched Jools talking to Cyn. He'd seen her a good while before, but never had the bottle to approach her, but he was well and truly smitten.

She watched the dancing couples and looked around the room. She saw him, and her heart skipped. The first time she'd met Jimmy was at the allnighter, in three days' time. She'd never seen or met him any time before that. She remembered him telling her that he'd only been going for a few months before the allnighter, that none of his mates were Mods, so he wasn't too keen on going in on his own but had gotten to know a few of the lads there, so it wasn't as bad as when he'd first started and knew no one. He'd said he'd seen her weeks before the allnighter but just never got up the courage to talk to her till then and she admitted to him that she'd never seen him. But there he was. He'd asked her to dance at the allnighter but not tonight. She looked away, as if she hadn't noticed him but looked from the corner of her eye.

God, he really was good looking. She'd forgotten just how much. But what an arsehole he'd turned out to be.

She thought, what if he came over now and asked her to dance? Knowing what he did and how he turned out and what a shit life she had, or would have with him, what would happen if she said no? What might happen if she never went with him?

Then she thought about Liam and Jessica. They wouldn't be. If she fixed everything Saturday night but didn't get up to dance with Jimmy when he asked her, she'd go back, hopefully, to Lainey still alive, but her children not there. Would that happen? Her head hurt thinking about it. Still watching from the corner of her eye, while Lulu had stepped aside for Gene Pitney's "Backstage," she caught movement. He'd started walking towards her. She jumped up and ran towards the cloakroom, turned right, headed for the stairs to the entrance and hung a quick right again, to slip through the arch beside the DJ box and walked quickly across the dancefloor and straight into the toilets.

Once again, she went into a cubicle, shut the door, closed the lid and sat down, but this time she wasn't crying, she was shaking.

It wasn't until that moment that the magnitude of what was happening really hit her. She'd seen enough movies to know about the whole space time continuum thing and how messing with the past could drastically change the future, but until she ended up actually doing it, she thought - as anyone would – that time travel was complete bollocks.

Yet, here she was, a forty-seven year old woman in her seventeen year old body, trying to stop an event that happened thirty years ago and now having to worry about the kids she might never have.

Tears started streaming down her face. This was real, yet it just could not be happening. She couldn't do this alone and yet she couldn't ask anyone to help her. Imagine what Cyn would say. The way she'd been acting today, she'd be in a straitjacket before she could even say space time continuum!

"Right, Jools," she whispered to herself, "get your act together or you'll never get out of here. You'll be left like that bloke from Quantum Leap, bouncing around in the wrong time forever when your own body is…. where?" She thought about it for a second. Where the hell is the real me? Okay, the car hit me, I remember that much and then, what? I just end up on O'Connell Street, thirty years earlier. This is mental.

Bang!

She looked up, startled at the slam on the cubicle door.

156

"Will you hurry the fuck up in there, I'm bleedin burstin!"

"Okay, I'll be out in a minute."

She dried her eyes and stood up, lifting the lid and dropping the eye-liner stained tissue into the toilet.

26. Making An Effort

"Have you seen Robbo?"

Sean was standing at the bar, looking around for his mate. He'd caught Linda – the girl who'd be DJing at the allnighter on Saturday - by the arm, as she walked back towards the dancefloor with her friend, Lucy.

"No, Sean, I haven't," she said. "Have you seen him, Lucy?"

"No, I don't think so," Lucy replied. "We can give you a lookalike, if that's any good to you. Terry's down there." She laughed. "Doesn't Robbo usually come in with you?"

"He does, but not tonight. He had to see someone."

Linda rolled her eyes. By now, everyone knew what and who Robbo was into, even if you didn't partake - which she didn't - his reputation preceded him.

"I'm sure he'll turn up," she said. "He always does."

"Yeah, I suppose," he said, thinking Freddie must have persuaded him to go for a drink. But he was still worried. He always worried about Robbo. There was only a month between them, but they'd been mates since low infants and Sean always looked out for him.

He started to walk back towards the dancefloor, when he bumped into Jools coming out of the ladies.

"Oh, Jesus, sorry," she said, then, "ah, it's only you, Sean."

"Only me? Thanks very much."

"You know I didn't mean it like that."

"Yeah, I know, I'm only messing. Here Jools, are you okay? You look like you've been crying."

She froze for a second.

"Um, eh, yeah, I'm grand," she said. "It was a bit smoky in the jacks and it just made my eyes water. You know yourself."

She tried her best to construct another lie and sound convincing, which, to her own ears, was sounding less so as the day progressed, but Sean never noticed.

"Yeah, it's like a chimney in there," he said.

She smiled, the tension easing. "And you'd know it's smoky in the girls' jacks, how?"

He smiled, shrugged and said, "Ah, the lads pushed me in there one night, for the craic, like," and winked at her. Quickly changing the subject, he said, "Doesn't look like Robbo's gonna show. He must have gone for a pint with Freddie. I suppose it's not exactly like he can stand up to him, not with them thugs and Freddie's temper. I'm sure he'll give us the run down in school tomorrow."

"School! I forgot about school!" Jools said.

"We'll be doing sod all anyway. No classes, and Gerry said we could use his music room to play tapes. It'll be a doddle. Anyway, talking about music, the slow set'll be finished in a minute, so let's get back out there."

He took her hand and led her back out to the main area, where Cyn was shrugging off the advances of an Effort Mod – what, in the Sixties would have been called a Ticket, as in, he's making an effort, but just not hitting the mark - in black sta-prest and a white T-Shirt with badly painted arrows on it. The white stripes on his badger shoes a dull, beige colour.

"Look, just fuck off! I'm not dancing with you!"

He looked as if he was about to burst into tears as he walked away.

"Ah, Cyn," Jools said, "you're too harsh on the poor yunfella."

"Fuckin Effort. Why do these gobshites think I'm fair game? That prick Dosser is forever staring at me. Gives me the creeps. Always stands over there by the tunnel, just staring. I'm sure I saw him get a horn one night and then he ran into the jacks." She mimed sticking her fingers down her throat.

Sean looked over at Dosser's usual spot, which was empty.

"You must have scared him off, Cyn, he's not here tonight."

"I saw him earlier, slinkin round the dancefloor like a fuckin snake." She shuddered. "He's bad news. I just don't like him."

The Style Council were wrapping up the slow set with "You're The Best Thing," and Noel's voice came over the speakers.

"The Style Council finishing up the slow set there, back to the Sixties now and The Supremes!"

An electric guitar, with what Jools always thought of as a newsflash type sound played and before the drums even kicked in, she grabbed Cyn's hand and dragged her towards the floor to dance to a song that in 2015, had fallen out of favour with most of the scene's DJs and she hadn't danced to it in years. In 1985, it was regularly played.

"Come on, I love this!"

They both jumped down on to the floor and floated around, toe to heel, moving effortlessly, as only Mod girls can dance. Sean watched them, not knowing that in thirty years' time, he'd still be mesmerized by how they both moved.

About halfway through, the song broke and Cyn and Jools stopped, turned to each other, hands on hips and sang, "And there ain't nothing I can do about it," in unison with Diana. They laughed and started dancing again.

The remainder of the night went much like that. Jools, wrapped up in the sheer joy of being a seventeen year old girl again, put her worries about Saturday aside and decided to live in the moment.

Every song, from Brenda Lee's "Let's Jump The Broomstick," to Bobby Vee's "The Night Has A Thousand Eyes," Little Anthony And The Imperials with "Better Use Your Head," The Moments with "Nine Times" and Benny Troy pouring his heart out to his lover with "I Wanna Give You Tomorrow," and so many more lifted her up, spun her around and kept her moving until Noel wrapped the night up with the theme to "Match Of The Day," and she finally walked off the floor, giggling at a couple of young lads – obviously first-timers - who were dancing to what was Noel's signature, "It's all over for another week," tune that wasn't actually meant to be danced to, but always caught one or two of the newcomers off guard as, having heard "Hawaii 5-0" earlier, they thought, "This must be Northern Soul too!"

She walked over to where Cyn was standing, holding her bag and noticed that although she'd been dancing solidly to God knows how many songs, she wasn't remotely out of breath. She thought about how she'd be thirty years in the future and smiled. Although still fit and in great shape for her age, she wasn't seventeen.

"There it is again," Cyn said.

"There's what?"

"That faraway look and smile. You're just weird, Jools."

"I'd prefer to be weird than normal. It's more interesting."

"If you say so, love." Cyn screwed up her face and stuck out her tongue. "Weirdo!"

"Whatever," Jools said, laughing.

27. Maximum R&B

They walked upstairs to Adair Lane with Sean and Jayo and crossed town to Talbot Street, hopping on the 42C with minutes to spare, taking their usual seats upstairs, at the front. Sean looked around downstairs and then checked the back seats upstairs, but still no Robbo. Jools copped the worried look on his face and said, "He'll be grand."

"I thought he'd be on the last bus," Sean said.

"He's plenty of money for a taxi if he misses it."

"I know," he said. "I just hope he's alright. That Freddie is an awful prick. Dangerous and unpredictable. Can't hold his drink either. I heard he glassed some bloke in his pub one night for not holding the door for him when he went to the jacks, then carved his initials in his cheeks with the broken glass. If Robbo even looks at him wrong…."

"Robbo can take care of himself," Cyn said. "And besides, he's been knocking around Freddie long enough now to know what to do and what not to do. Like Jools said, he'll be grand. We'll be in school tomorrow and he'll be in a heap with a hangover. You'll see."

"I hope so," Sean said.

The rest of the journey home was taken up by talk of the night at Bubbles, the upcoming Blades gig on Friday and the allnighter on Saturday. Jools tried to put on a brave face and not give anything away but was having a hard time of it.

By the time they got to Coolock and she was saying goodnight to the others, she was in a heap trying to think of how to stop Lainey and Matt going to the party, or if she couldn't, get to them before they could drive down the lane. Everything she thought of just seemed like it would never work.

She fished her key out of her handbag and opened the front door.

"Is that you, Julia?"

"No, Mam, the house is getting robbed." She giggled and then her dad shouted down, "Well will you ask them to at least leave us the telly, I want to watch the snooker tomorrow night. There's money in the tea caddy."

She heard her Mam's voice then. "Don't you be encouraging her, Tom! And keep your voice down. I don't want all the neighbours knowing where I keep my money. Tom? TOM?!"

Then she heard the sound of snoring, knowing he was pretending to be asleep and she giggled again. Her smile faded quickly, knowing she only had a couple of more days with him before she - hopefully, she thought - finished all of this and went back to being a middle aged woman.

She went upstairs and undressed, once again marvelling at her figure in the full length mirror. She pulled open the top drawer of her dresser, knowing instinctively that that's where she'd find T-Shirts and pulled out one that was much too large for her that had Pete Townshend standing against a black background, windmilling his Rickenbacker and whispered to herself, "Maximum R and B."

She slipped it over her naked frame, the hem dropping to just above her knees and slid into bed. She was asleep as her head hit the pillow.

28. I Like This Dream

"Jools."

She heard a voice in the distance. It sounded so familiar. A voice she hadn't heard in a long, long time, pulling her up out of a very strange dream where she was seventeen again, but she was also in hospital and couldn't remember why. She struggled to remember, then it came back to her. It was the car on Baggot Street that hit her. That was it.

She flicked her eyelids open and shut them again quickly, the harsh bright light of the hospital room blinding her momentarily.

"It's not Jools, I've told you before, it's Julia. If you keep calling her Jools, it'll stick." A woman's voice. Was that her Mam?

"It's already stuck," the man said. "All her friends call her Jools."

"That doesn't mean you have to," the woman said.

She heard the man sigh. "Julia, it's time to get up."

No, she thought, I can't. I'm in hospital. I don't want to get up. I like this dream. I saw Lainey again.... and Dad, and I was so young. Do I have to?

She opened her eyes and as they adjusted to the bright sunlight coming through her bedroom window, she noticed the walls and the one above her bed coated with posters.

Not the hospital.

Then she saw her Dad's head around her bedroom door and her heart leapt into her throat. She smiled and tears welled up in her eyes, which she quickly brushed away.

"Dad."

"Come on, I've got your breakfast on," he said.

"Okay, I'm up," she said, smiling at him, which he returned, and her heart leapt again.

29. I Don't Like The Sound Of This

Sean and Jayo knocked on Robbo's front door. After a few seconds, his Mam answered.

"Howaya, Missus Mckenna, is Robbo there, I mean Robert?"

"Howaya, Sean, no, he went off last night to do a job for that Freddie fella, you know, the one that runs the pub?"

Sean and Jayo exchanged looks. If she knew what Freddie really ran, she was doing a great job of hiding it and if she didn't know, she must have had her head in the sand for the past God knows how many years. Freddie was notorious and very well known around the area.

"Yeah, I know him. Did he say what he was doing?"

"He just said that Freddie had bought some pub down the country and needed it to be tidied up a bit before they could open. Robert said it would only take a day or two, but Freddie wanted him to start on it as soon as possible. I thought it was a bit strange for him to be heading off at that time of night, but Freddie pays Robert well for the odd jobs he does for him, you can't really argue with the boss, now, can you?" She laughed a little at this.

Sean and Jayo again exchanged looks.

"No, no, Missus McKenna, you can't," Sean said. "He is the boss after all. Okay, I'm sure he'll give us a shout when he's back."

"When he rings, I'll tell him you were looking for him, Sean."

"Thanks, Missus McKenna."

The lads turned to walk down the path and Robbo's Mam called him back.

"Sean, hold on, I just remembered, he left an envelope for you."

Sean looked at Jayo with raised eyebrows.

"Man, I don't like the sound of this," Jayo said.

"Me neither."

Sean ran back up the path and Mrs McKenna handed him a pink, recycled birthday card envelope, with *Sean* written on it.

"Thanks, Missus McKenna."

"You're welcome, Sean, see you later." She shut the door and he walked slowly down to where Jayo was standing at the gate.

"What is it?"

"I dunno, yet, hang on."

Sean tore open the envelope.

"Read it out loud."

Sean

I'm seriously fucked. I had 3 grand for Freddie tonight, but when I left the pub, my wallet was gone. I don't know where it went. I think I had it going into The Anvil, but I can't remember. I checked everywhere after you all left but couldn't find it anywhere. I even looked on the street outside, but it's gone. Some lucky fucker must have picked it up and thought it was Christmas.

Anyway, I saw Freddie's car pull up at the top of North Earl Street and when he saw I wasn't there, he went mental. I'm heading down to Wexford to see my uncle Paddy. He said he can give me some of the money, but I don't know what I'll do about the rest. I might just have to get the boat and disappear. I dunno.

I'll lay low in Wexford for a while and see what happens. When he can't find me, Freddie will probably come and ask you where I am. Say nothing. I'm just gone, and you don't know where.

I'll give you a ring in a few days and let you know what the score is. If I can get hold of at least some of the money, I might be back sooner. Freddie might take some of it. Right now, I don't know.

Robbo.

Sean looked at Jayo, both were as white as the paper the letter was written on.

"Jaysus," Jayo said, "he's fucked."

"This time even I can't get him out of it," Sean said. "I just don't have that kind of cash.

30. A Cunning Plan

Dosser wasn't the sharpest tool in the shed. He could barely do addition, so any possibility of multiplication was way beyond him. He was also as lazy as fuck. There were dormant volcanoes that were more active than he was and he usually didn't crawl out of bed till the sun was high but was up early on Thursday morning. So much to do, so much to buy and a cunning – even for him – plan to explain how he'd just come by a load of money.

He jumped out of bed at just past eight o'clock and scurried over to the old - busted of course - Dansette record player in the corner of his bedroom. He removed the turntable and pulled out the money. He kneeled on the floor, holding the notes in his hands. He was naked, except for a pair of once white, but now yellowed Y-fronts and the excitement raised the hairs all over his thin, pale white body. If he'd caught a view of himself in the mirror at that moment, he'd have been struck by his resemblance to Gollum, kneeling on the ground, salivating over his precious, but the only thing Dosser would have done with a copy Lord Of The Rings, was used it as a door stop. His level of reading was just above street signs, and even some of those were a struggle.

He'd left school at fifteen - after a failed Group Cert – to be an apprentice fitter in his uncle Greg's engineering company, a job Greg had reluctantly given him after much begging from Dosser's Mam, but unlocked lockers, personal belongings, trusting workmates and his light fingers didn't mix, and it all became too much of a temptation for him.

Before his first month was out, wages and jewellery had gone missing and, although nobody could prove it, the finger of blame was pointed at Dosser, and Greg had to let him go. His reputation had preceded him into the job, and he hadn't failed to deliver.

Greg knew about Dosser's brushes with the law and the security guards all over town and both he and Dosser's Mam had hoped that knuckling down to a steady job and income would set him on the straight and narrow, but some people just can't be helped.

"It just isn't working out," Greg had told him, no mention of the missing money or jewellery, which Greg had compensated out of his own pocket. Dosser may be untrustworthy, but he was still family, so he wouldn't drop him in it. Still, he had to go. Walking by the lockers one morning, Greg heard one of the fitters say, "It's gotta be Dosser. I'm gonna burst that thieving little shit."

No accusations made, nobody brought to bear, just Dosser handed his marching orders and out the door by lunchtime

Friday, "With two weeks wages in me skyrocket," he'd told one of the winos round the back of the off licence that afternoon. "Here, have a sup of me Buckfast!"

That was three years ago, and he never got another job. What he shoplifted and sold kept him going till he was old enough to sign on, but even the thieving was drying up now, as every security guard and cop from Talbot Street to Mary Street and Capel Street to Wexford Street knew his face and kept him out. Now, after that prick Robbo had so carelessly dropped his wallet on the floor of The Anvil, he'd more than two weeks wages in his pocket. He'd three grand burning a massive hole there. He might not be very bright, but he wasn't stupid and knew he needed a way to explain away his new-found affluence, (not a word he would have had in his vocabulary), so he thought of his mate in the bookies.

He had absolutely no intention of gambling away any of it away, but thought a hot tip on a long shot might be just the ticket to explain the new suits and the scooter he was planning on getting.

That Thursday morning, he went into a bookies on Abbey Street where his mate worked and told him he was playing a trick on his Ma. He said he wanted to get a betting slip that showed about a grand and a half winnings – he also wasn't stupid enough to put the same amount that Robbo lost on the slip - and stuff it in his Da's trouser pocket, so his Ma would find it when she was doing the washing and go bananas that his Da had won loads of money and kept it for himself. He said he thought that would be just hilarious.

"Just one of them practicin jokes, Eamo, you know the ones?" Eamo, who did know the ones and was fond of them himself, nodded, but didn't correct him.

"How do you wanna do this then, Doss?"

"Fucked if I know, Eamo, I know nothin about the nags."

"Right then," Eamo said, grabbing a pen and some paper, as they both leaned over it and he began to write.

"I reckon we should do it this way. A one quid Yankee, that's eleven bets. It costs eleven quid. Each horse is doubled with the others, plus trebled, plus one four horse accumulator, and that should get you what you want. I'll go over some winners and throw in a good long shot too and you're sorted. What date do you want on the slip?"

Dosser just stood gawping at Eamo, with glazed eyes. In everything that he had just said, the only part that Dosser understood was when Eamo had asked him what date he wanted on the slip.

"Em, today, Thursday, whatever date today is."

"Grand. Drop in after lunch and I'll have it for you. I'd say she'll fuckin murder him!"

175

By now, Dosser was so mixed up with the intricate explanation Eamo had just given him, he'd lost his train of thought.

"Who'll murder who?"

"Your Da! Your Ma's gonna murder your Da when she finds the slip in his pocket. Jaysus, Dosser, are you on the glue again?"

"Oh, yeah, right. Yeah, sorry, I just got a bit lost there."

He laughed to show it was all a big joke and Eamo joined him, oblivious to Dosser's real intentions.

After a ten minute walk down through Dublin City streets, Dosser found himself looking in the window of Button Down, a small boutique type shop on Parnell Street that specialised in Mod wear. They carried most of the casual stuff; Sta-Prest trousers, T-Shirts, Polo and Cycling Shirts, but also some of the more formal wear like button down collared shirts (hence the name) and also a large line in suits, though none of the top Mods on the scene would buy one from here.

It was one of the very few shops in the city that he'd never lifted from. Being about fifteen feet square, the owner was always within view and it was just too difficult, even for a seasoned professional like Dosser.

His mouth watered as he looked at the clothes in the window. Brilliant white cycling shirts shone brightly in the sun, their green and orange striped collars standing out in contrast.

Sta-Prest of more colours than he'd ever seen, sat on a display in front of a mannequin that wore a pair of cream ones, and a black Fred Perry, with the twin tipped yellow collar and yellow wreath. The classic. His eyes bulged. He looked at everything in the window, taking it all in. Levi's 501s called out to him. Pre-shrunk too! None of that sitting in the bath malarkey, though he imagined himself to be a modern day Jimmy Cooper, doing just that. Then he saw it and he almost fainted. A bottle green, three button tonic suit. That's the one, he thought to himself. He pushed open the door, the bell rang over his head and walked into the dull light of the shop, his eyes adjusted and took it all in.

His senses exploded. The smell of fresh cotton and new clothes that hung on racks all around the shop walls filled his nostrils. Sun shining through the front window reflected off tall, slim glass displays in the centre of the room that stored tie pins and cuff links and pocket squares, though he just thought they were hankies. Ties, of every imaginable colour and design hung from racks and he just stood there, in complete awe. He'd only been in Button Down a couple of times. It was too difficult to steal from and when he had been there, the most he could afford was a couple of Mod T-Shirts, that the Faces wouldn't be caught dead in.

A tall, overweight, grey haired man, dressed in cream slacks and an immaculate, navy double breasted blazer, gold buttons polished to a shine that Dosser could actually see reflections in, approached him, an undisguised look of distaste on his face at what he thought of as an undesirable specimen of human detritus standing in his premises.

"Can I help you…. Sir?"

"Eh, yeah, em, I'm lookin to buy some gear."

The proprietor almost gagged.

"What would Sir be interested in?" He looked Dosser up and down and walked towards the T-Shirt section, pulling out a white one with a green, white and orange target on it. "This might suit Sir's pocket?"

Dosser, as has been noted, wasn't the sharpest tool in the shed, but he knew when someone considered him beneath them, which, to be fair, was almost everyone he came into contact with. He put his hand in his jeans pocket and pulled out the cash, now rolled up and almost the size of his fist. "Oh, I think my pocket is a bit bigger than the price of a fuckin T-Shirt, Mister."

The shop owner's face lit up and, completely ignoring Dosser's vulgarity, smiled his most charming smile and said, "Coffee?"

Dosser smiled in return.

"I don't mind if I do."

31. Frustration

The music room in the local secondary school in Coolock was a hive of activity. Only a day and a half left of the school year, all year end exams done and with the third years preparing for the Group and Inter Cert exams, and sixth years prepping for the Leaving Cert – all of which would commence the first week of June - meant that most classes were over for the term and a lot of students were left with multiple free periods that would be spent quietly reading in classrooms or, if obliging teachers allowed, hanging out in their classrooms, listening to music.

Jools and Cyn walked in and spotted Sean and Jayo sitting near a group of younger Mods over by the upright piano in the corner. At that time, in 1985, the school had no uniform policy, so the music room was filled with different groups. Mods in one corner, Goths in another, New Romantics or, by then, known simply as Trendies, though some still held onto their frills and eyeliner, and that was just the boys, in another. One or two from the different groups mixed with the others, but in general, stayed with their own.

Today, the Mods had control of the stereo – second years at the helm, and the current song coming from the speakers was "Frustration," by Purple Hearts.

Sean was sitting to the side of the group, foot tapping unconsciously along to the music, a worried look on his face.

Jayo sat on a desk beside him, looking out the window, biting his nails.

Jools and Cyn exchanged worried glances. They rushed over. Jayo turned, nodded to them and turned back to the window.

"What's going on, Sean?"

So lost in thought, he hadn't seen them come in and blinked.

"It's bad, Jools, it's really bad."

He put his hand into his jacket and pulled the envelope from the inside pocket. He handed it to her without a word.

She took it, almost afraid to and pulled out the letter, dropping it to Cyn's eye level so they could both read it.

"Oh, Jesus," she said.

"We're never gonna see Robbo again," Cyn said. "If he doesn't go to England, Freddie will murder him. What do you reckon the uncle can do? Does he have the money?"

"I dunno," Sean said. "Even if his uncle gave him a grand, the most I have is about five hundred. "Jayo?"

Jayo looked down and shook his head, "I've fuck all."

Jools and Cyn both shook their heads.

"Is there any way we can get in touch with him?" Jools asked.

"No," Sean said. "I don't have his uncle's number and I don't wanna ask his Ma in case she gets spooked. She doesn't know about what he does for Freddie and if I start asking to try and get hold of him, she might think something's up and I don't want her getting worried. Chances are she's not gonna see her son again, either way, and I'd rather she didn't work that one out right now."

"Well we can't just sit around doing nothing," Jayo said.

"What else are we gonna do? Freddie's gonna be out for our blood too if we even give him a hint that we know where Robbo is. No, if Freddie asks any of us, and I think he will – he's probably sitting outside the school right now waiting for Robbo or any of us to come out - Robbo said that he was going off to pick something up for Freddie and he'd be back soon. We know nothing! Right?"

They all agreed that they'd stick to that if asked and wait for Robbo to contact Sean.

"In the meantime," Sean said, "just act natural. No moping about, no worried looks or shite like that. Jayo, you'll have no fingernails left if you don't quit that shit!"

"Sorry, Sean."

"Come round to my gaff tonight, I'll tell me Ma that we're watching Top Of The Pops cos The Style Council are on it and we'll see if he rings. Blades tomorrow night and the allnighter on Saturday. He might be back for one of them if his uncle comes up with the dosh. We'll have to wait and see."

He took a tape out of his pocket and handed it to Cyn.

"Will you go over and change the tape please, Cyn? That little second year Mod fancies you and he won't kick up a fuss when you do. I can't think with all that Revival stuff, stick on some Soul."

32. Call Me

Just as Sean predicted, there was a big black Merc sitting outside the school gates, with Freddie leaning against the front passenger door. His thugs stood on either side of him, muscles bulging beneath their too tight T-Shirts. He had a hammer in his right hand, tapping the head on his left palm.

"Oh shit," Cyn said, "you were right, Sean."

"Just be cool, Cyn, he's not enough of a psycho to do anything in front of the school with so many people around."

"What if he tells us to get into the car?"

"He won't, don't worry," Jools said. "Let's just see what he wants."

"I think we all know what he wants," Jayo said.

As they approached the street, Freddie's maniacal grin broadened, giving Sean a momentary image of Cesar Romero, when he played The Joker in the old Batman TV show he'd watched as a kid. The image didn't make him any easier.

"Where's your buddy, Seany boy?"

"Which one would that be, Freddie?"

"Don't get smart with me, ya little bollix!" Freddie spat the words out, literally, there was spittle at the corner of his mouth. "That Robbo cunt, and if ya get smart with me again, I'll nail ya to the nearest fuckin tree!"

Sean was absolutely rattling inside, but his features didn't show it. He kept as calm as he could and, in the steadiest voice he could muster, said, "Freddie, we called for Robbo this morning for school and his Ma said that you'd sent him off somewhere to do something for you, so how the fuck should I know where he is if you don't?"

"I'm warning ya, Sean, don't fuck with me and don't speak to me like that or these lads'll rip your head off as quick as I can click me fingers. And it's Mister Fuckin Collins, ya little prick." The thugs took a step forward to show that they were just waiting for Freddie to say the word.

Sean ignored the instruction and said, "Freddie, like I said, all we know is that he went off to do something for you, and you or your lads aren't gonna touch me, because you know who I work for. Remember the mobile disco? Johnny and his mates have bigger guns than you have, so don't threaten me."

"Well then, maybe I'll just nail these pretty little brazzers to a tree instead?"

Jools looked at Cyn, the colour had drained from her face.

"Freddie, we don't know where he is, I swear. He went to meet you last night and never turned up at Bubbles, so we thought he'd gone drinking with you. And then this morning, like I said, we only know what his Ma told us. If he's doing some work for you, why don't you know where he is?"

Freddie thought for a second and, not wanting to look foolish in front of the kids, though he could feel the heat rising in his face, took a deep breath and said, "Yeah, that's right, he came for a drink with me last night and went to pick somethin up for me this mornin. He said it wouldn't take long and he'd meet me after school. But here we are and he's a no show."

"Well he never came in," Sean said. "I suppose he'll drop round to me when he gets back."

Freddie handed the hammer to one of his lads, fished inside his jacket and pulled out the same type of card he gave to Dosser. He walked towards Sean, who, despite the fear that was coursing through him, stayed as steady as a rock, even when Freddie put his arm around his shoulders. With the height difference, Freddie had to reach up to do it and it looked so comical, Cyn began to laugh, which was quickly stopped with a swift kick to the ankle from Jools, none of which Freddie noticed, he was too intent on trying to frighten Sean.

"Ow!"

Freddie looked at Cyn, questioningly.

"Cramps," she said, quickly. "Time of the month."

"Ugh," Freddie said, shuddering. He turned back to Sean.

"Take me card. If Robbo turns up this evenin, make sure ya call me, I need to talk to him."

"Right, Freddie, defo. As soon as I see him, I'll give you a bell."

"You're a good boy, Seany. Now, you, your two brazzers and that gormless cunt behind ya can fuck off home."

Freddie and his lads got back into his car and he sat in the front passenger seat, so he could watch them.

The four kids walked down the street and he saw Sean flick something into the road. Knowing what he'd flicked away, but still wanting to check, Freddie said, "Go and pick that up, will ya, George?"

George got out of the driver's seat and walked quickly towards the object on the road. Freddie saw him pick it up and shake his head. He came running back to the car, got in and handed his boss's card back to him. Freddie, uncharacteristically, didn't raise his voice. He didn't scream, he didn't shout, he spoke, and to no one in particular, said, "I'm gonna kill the lot of them."

33. The Penny Drops

Top Of The Pops that evening was a lacklustre affair, with nothing of interest for the four Mods sitting in Sean's living room, waiting for the phone to ring. Neither The Style Council or The Untouchables were featured on the show, as "Walls Come Tumbling Down" and "Free Yourself" were moving to the bottom end of the Top 40. The only mention of them was in the chart rundown.

"I never liked that song anyway," Sean said.

"It's no Solid Bond In Your Heart or Shout To The Top, that's for sure," Jools said. Then, lost in thought and once again forgetting when she was, rather than where she was, said, "That was kinda the beginning of the end for them. Come to Milton Keynes, what were they thinking putting that out as a single? Jesus wept."

"What?" It was Sean.

She came back to herself and all three were staring at her, Cyn with her, "she's doing that mad shit again," look on her face. "Hmmm?"

"You just said something about Come To Milton Keynes being a single?"

"Hmmm? Did I?"

"Jools, that," Sean said, pointing at the television, "is the latest single. Or was, as it's on its way out."

"Umm, eh, I think I read in Smash Hits that he said that would be the next single."

"When?" Cyn asked. "I don't remember reading that."

"Eh, maybe it was on the radio, I can't remember! Anyway, we're not here to talk about The Style Council! What are we gonna do about Robbo?"

"I honestly don't know," Sean said, and Jools relaxed, now that the subject had changed. She knew she couldn't keep making mistakes like that.

"He hasn't rang yet, but we can decide when or if he does. Till then, we just have to wait."

"He might show up for The Blades tomorrow?"

"I don't know, Jayo, if he hasn't got the money, what's the point? Anyway, the way Freddie was going on today, I reckon even if he does turn up with the cash, Freddie might still kill him anyway. If I was Robbo, I'd be out of here sharpish."

Jools thought back to the allnighter. She clearly remembered Robbo being there that night and he was also at The Blades on the Friday, so he might have sorted out all the trouble in time. But they were all close back then and if he'd had that kind of trouble with Freddie, she'd have remembered. Then the penny dropped. "I did this," she said, under her breath, but Cyn still heard her.

"No, you didn't," Cyn said, "how could you?"

Jools thought, I changed time, but you wouldn't understand.

"The Anvil," she said, tears welling in her eyes. "We convinced him to come to The Anvil with us last night. If we hadn't, he'd have met Freddie and he wouldn't be in this trouble."

"Jools," Sean said, "we don't know where he lost his wallet. It could have fallen out of his pocket walking up Talbot Street. He could have dropped it getting onto the bus, or off of it. If he'd met Freddie when he was supposed to and hadn't got the wallet then, Freddie would have put him in the back of the car and nobody would have ever seen him again. You probably did him a favour by getting him to go to the pub when you did."

He took a tissue from a box on the coffee table and handed it to her. She wiped her eyes and thanked him, but she knew better. She knew it wasn't really her fault. Okay, she had gotten Robbo to go to The Anvil, but she hadn't asked for any of this, she was just trying to get through the few days she was there and get to Saturday and then, hopefully back to her kids.

"I know," she said. "I'm just worried about him. He doesn't deserve any of this. One day that short arsed little fucker will get it, and I pray to God it's sooner than later."

"I think we all agree there," Jayo said. "Right, who wants tea?"

"This isn't your gaff, Jayo," Cyn said.

"That bollix practically lives here," Sean said. "Me Ma loves

189

him."

"Yeah," Cyn said, "cos he's got one of them faces only a mother could love!"

"Watch it you!" Jayo said, throwing a cushion at her.

"Right, let's go out to the kitchen and listen to some tunes," Sean said, "there's not much else we can do till he rings."

34. You're A Face Now

Friday morning, and for the second one on the trot, Dosser was up early. Well, relatively early for him. Not the stupid o'clock that his brother, sister, Ma and Da were up at for school and work, but a reasonable 10:30am instead of the 12:30ish that he usually dragged his arse out of bed at. Busy day today, he thought, lots to do, and thank fuck his Ma was in work, or she'd be wondering what he was up to. She'd long since given up on any hope that he'd get a steady job and just turned a blind eye to his light fingers. Mother's love prevented her from turning him in, but she secretly prayed every night that he'd be caught and get locked up. Prison, she thought, was probably the only thing left now to shock him onto the straight and narrow.

He'd made a phone call on Thursday after he got home from town to a bloke from Newry that he did some business with now and then. Gabriel Minor was a mechanic and ex-Mod from across the border who dealt in hot scooters. Not a particularly hard bloke, but he'd still take your head off with the monkey wrench he carried in his coat pocket for calling him Gabriel, or worse, Gay. The only person who was allowed to call him by his given name was his Mother. To everyone else, he was Morris.

Dosser had never owned a scooter, but he'd nicked enough and passed them on to Morris to be able to drive one. Now, there was one coming the opposite way and he was beside himself with excitement.

He'd jumped out of bed and threw on his new Levi's and black Fred Perry with the yellow trim, without bothering to shower or even change the Y-Fronts he'd been wearing for the past three days. Crusty socks found at the end of his bed were pulled on after a brief sniff and brand new Desert Boots completed the outfit.

Down to the kitchen and a bowl of cornflakes was wolfed down, wiping the milk that dripped off his chin and down the front of his shirt away with his hand. Less than ten minutes in his new gear and he was already manky.

He stood in front of the mirror in the hall admiring himself, not noticing the stains on the front of his shirt or the big, milky wet patch on the suede of his right boot.

"Top Mod, Dosser, you're a Face now," he said to himself. "Wait till Cyn sees ya, she'll be gaggin for it!"

He went out to the front garden and sat on the step, nervously biting his nails in anticipation of getting his new scooter and stopped. He sat up straight and looked at his grimy, bitten fingernails and, given his overall slovenly appearance and sickening lack of hygiene, ironically reproached himself. "Now,

now, Dosser," he said, "Top Mods do not bite their fingernails. They must be clean and tidy at all times."

After an hour sitting in his front garden with no sign of his habit stopping, the front of his shirt littered with nail bits, a black Transit van with yellow plates turned the corner. He jumped up and ran out to the street.

The van slowed down and came to a stop in front of his garden and the window rolled down.

"What about ya, Dosser, ya wee shite."

"Howaya, Morris, thanks for bringing it down so quick."

"No bother, mate. Stand back there and let me out."

Dosser stood back and Morris got out and walked around to the back of the van. He turned the key in the lock and threw open the double doors and pulled out a ramp.

Dosser looked into the gloom of the van and saw the most beautiful sight he'd ever seen. It was a Vespa, PX125, with silver grey metallic paint and whitewall tyres. The front was covered in lights and mirrors, above which, a fly screen had the word "FACE," written in capital letters.

Morris climbed up into the van, undid the straps, lifted the scooter off the stand and wheeled it down the ramp, where mid-day sunlight shone off the chrome on the front. He wheeled it up onto the pavement and lifted it back onto the stand, stepped off and said, "Voilà!"

Dosser looked at him, clueless.

"What?"

"Voilà, Dosser, ya thick fuck, here it is!"

"Oh, right, yeah, thanks, I love it. Gorgeous. I love that leopard skin saddle too."

"That'll have to go," Morris said. "And most of the lights and mirrors and definitely that stupid fuckin fly screen, so it will."

"Why?" Dosser's voice caught in his throat.

"Because this thing is hotter than any scooter you've ever given me. You said when ya rang me that ya wanted one by Friday and you'd pay me five hundred for it, so here it is. This is the only one I could get my hands on at such short notice, but if any of the Mods from up North see it, they'll know whose it is immediately. Ya might even have to get it resprayed. I'd have done it myself, but I didn't have time."

"I can't fuckin respray that, it's gorgeous!"

"Then at least change the saddle, take off the flyscreen and get rid of them lights and mirrors. Oh, and for fuck sake, unbolt that Jaguar on the front mudguard. And whatever ya do, don't forget to rob a new licence plate for the back!"

Dosser was looking at what he now thought of as his pride and joy, imagining himself driving along the seafront in Bray, Cyn sitting behind him, summer sun gleaming off the chrome.

"Dosser, Dosser! Are ya still with us?" Morris said, waving his hands in front of Dosser's face.

He shook his head clear, frowning at the lost daydream.

"What, yeah, okay, I'll change it up a bit, don't worry."

"Oh, I'm not worried, it's not me that'll get the hiding if you're seen on it. This belonged to Will McNeil, Billy McNeil's lad and if you're caught, he'll fuckin murder ya."

"Look," Dosser said, pulling a wad of notes from his jeans pocket, still irritated at being dragged from his daydream, "I'll be grand, I'll make a few changes and nobody'll notice, not even Billy Fuckin Big Deal or whatever his name is."

Morris shook his head, regretting having done this little bit of business, but the five hundred in his pocket eased his mind somewhat.

"Fair enough, Dosser, but I'll tell ya this now. If any fucker comes knocking on my garage door saying your name, I'll definitely fuckin kill ya."

"Yeah, right, thanks," Dosser said, once again drifting off into his daydream, as Morris climbed back into the van.

"Oh, by the way," Morris said, disappearing from view for a second and coming back up with a white, open faced helmet with a red peak and RAF targets on both sides. He threw it at Dosser and said, "You might as well have this too. The dozy prick left it on the scooter."

Dosser caught it and turned it over in his hands as Morris

keyed the engine and drove off.

"I can't wait to see their faces when they all see me on this beauty," he said as he popped the helmet on which was slightly too big for him. He turned the key and kick started the Vespa into life, smiling at the sound of the engine and the cloud of smoke that filled the air.

He drove the scooter up the garden path and parked it in the alleyway.

"Right, let's get this suit sorted."

35. He'll Turn Up

The bell rang and the school hallways erupted as students filled them, excited to be finishing for three months. Jools, Cyn, Sean and Jayo walked through the teachers' lounge to the staff entrance and Sean looked out through the curtains.

"No sign of Freddie," he said to the others.

"Still no word from Robbo either," Jayo said. "If he came back and Freddie caught up with him, we'd never know. That little bollix'll bring him swimming in Dublin Bay with breeze blocks for arm bands."

"Don't say that, Jayo," Cyn said. "He's probably still with his uncle. What's the bets he'll turn up at the gig tonight?"

"I dunno, Cyn," Sean said. "If he doesn't have Freddie's money, he'd be stupid to.", "Hopefully we'll hear from him today, at least then we'll know," Jools said.

"Yeah, hopefully."

36. Can You See The Real Me

"What the fuck do you mean you won't have it ready for tonight?"

"Don't you speak to me like that, Graham, I'll tell your Mam!"

Dosser tried to compose himself. He'd heard someone say once that money doesn't bring happiness, and he was starting to believe it. He had his scooter, and it was amazing. Fuck Morris and all those changes he told him to do. You don't get a scooter like that and ruin it with a respray or take the lights and mirrors off. Oh, and that beautiful saddle. He'd even decided that he wouldn't change the flyscreen. It said FACE, and that's what he was now, a proper Face, but what was a Face without a suit?

"I'm sorry, Missus Malone, I just got a bit frustrated cos I need that suit for tonight. There's a big gig on in town and I need to look me best."

"Graham, I'm sorry but there's no way I can have it done before tomorrow afternoon. I'm finishing off a wedding dress and I just don't have time to turn up your trousers and do all those mad alterations to the hems and cuffs. I really just don't have the time."

"I'll pay you extra!"

"It's not about the money. Jacinta Gorman is getting married tomorrow and there are last minute alterations to her dress. If I don't get them done in time, she won't be walking up the aisle. Now, don't you think that's a bit more important than you going to a disco?"

Dosser felt like screaming, but for once, thought clearly and kept his cool. If he started shouting at her, she'd tell him to go away and he wouldn't even have his suit for the allnighter. He should have listened to the bloke in the shop who'd offered to get it altered – for a small fee – thieving cunt, he thought, after the money he'd handed over. Nah, he'd thought at the time, Missus Malone will do it cheaper.

In the end, he'd just gone for the bottle green tonic suit, two Fred Perrys, a couple of pairs of Levi's, a plain white shirt, a cycling shirt and a pair of desert boots. A quick trip around to Simon Hart's secured him a pair of black bowling shoes. He knew he'd got loads of money, but the greed had kicked in and he didn't want to hand over too much for stuff that he'd normally lift.

"Okay, okay, sorry, Missus Malone. Will you definitely have it for tomorrow?"

"Yes, Graham, I promise. If you come round at lunchtime, I'll have it all done for you."

"Okay, thanks, Missus Malone."

Dosser walked out, silently cursing the Gods of tailors and

dressmakers, but then drifted off into his daydream where he drove along Bray seafront, with Cyn's arms holding him tightly around the waist and "Can You See The Real Me," playing in the background.

He smiled.

37. Looking Over My Shoulder

Sean went into his house, threw his schoolbag under the stairs and walked into the kitchen, to be greeted by his Mam, and Robbo, sitting at the kitchen table, drinking tea and eating brown bread. They smiled at each other and Sean had to resist the urge to hug his friend.

"Didn't see you in school today," Sean said.

"Yeah," Robbo replied, "I thought I'd go down and see me uncle for a couple of days. No classes so I skipped out early."

"I'll leave you two to it," Sean's Mam said. "Don't eat too much of that bread, son, you'll ruin your dinner."

"I won't, Mam, promise."

When she'd left the kitchen, Sean said, "What the fuck, Robbo? I thought we'd never see you again!"

"Yeah," Robbo said, "I know. You nearly didn't. Me uncle managed to get up fifteen hundred and I've a few quid stashed away, I thought Freddie might just take what I've got."

"I dunno, he's like a fuckin lunatic. Turned up at the school and all yesterday looking for you. Gave me his card and told me to ring him if you showed up. I threw it away."

"What did you tell him?"

"Nothing. I just said that your Ma told us you'd gone off to do some work for him and nobody knew when you'd be back. He bought it. I asked him if you were off working for him, why didn't he know where you were? I thought he was gonna have a stroke. His face went bright red. He didn't want to look stupid, so said that you had."

"Good. If I turn up with his money, or most of it, I reckon I'll be alright."

"Honestly, if I was you, I'd get the fuck out of here. I'd say he'll just take the money and bring you out on that boat. You're better off just leaving. I've about five hundred I could give you, so two grand should be enough to get you started somewhere."

"What, and have that midget fucker breathing down my neck? I'd be looking over my shoulder forever."

"That midget would need a stepladder to breathe down anyone's neck," Sean said, and they both laughed.

He walked to the back door, pulled aside the lace curtain and looked out the window, sunlight illuminated his face. Robbo could see the worry etched there.

He turned back and looked at his best mate, unsmiling.

"Seriously, Robbo, he's going mental. Even threatened to nail Jools and Cyn to a tree. I thought Cyn was gonna pass out!"

"I'll just have to see what he'll take. Me uncle said he might be able to get another five, he'll let me know, but he's not sure he can. Freddie's a businessman. Surely, he'll see I'm worth more to him alive than dead?"

"He's a dangerous bastard," Sean said, "that's what he is. Nothing reasonable about that fucker." He looked down at the holdall on the floor by the kitchen table.

"Does your Ma know you're home yet?"

"No, I wasn't planning on going home till I get this sorted. If he gets fed up waiting, he'll come to the gaff and I don't want me Ma seeing any of that. Can I crash here?"

38. Double Standards

The doors of the TV Club on Harcourt Street opened at 8:00pm, and at five to, an already long queue was building up outside.

Mod boys and Mod girls dressed in their finest, crowded the pavement outside, waiting to see Dublin's own Mod band, The Blades.

Jools, Cyn, Sean and Jayo were near the top of the queue and the band's roadie stuck his head out to have a look at the crowd. He spotted them.

"Jools," he called, "come in, bring the others. Robbo not here?"

"No," she said, "he wasn't feeling the best."

He just nodded and spoke to one of the bouncers who put his arm out to part the crowd at the top of the queue and let them through.

"Thanks," she said, "that's really nice of you,".

"Ah, no problem, thought you might like to get a spot at the front. I've just put the crowd barriers out, so as close to the front as you're all allowed." He laughed.

"That's great," Cyn said. Thanks again." She squeezed past one of the bouncers.

"Catch yis later," he said and as they walked into the lobby, he disappeared down a corridor on the left that led to the dressing rooms.

It had been a very long time since Jools was in the TV Club, so long in fact, that she couldn't remember exactly when, but as she stood in the lobby, looking at the staircase running up either side to the balcony, and the smell of stale beer and cigarette smoke filled her senses, it felt like she'd only been there yesterday.

"Come on, Cyn, let's go upstairs."

"But he said he let us in so we could get up the front."

"You want to be squashed against the crowd barrier by three hundred Mods then, and go home with a nice black line across that lovely white dress of yours?"

Cyn looked at the door to the dance hall and then to the stairs leading to the balcony.

"We're going up the front," Sean said. "Wanna see the band."

"Or is it Paul Cleary you want to see?" Jools asked, puckering her lips.

"Well, he is a handsome bloke," Sean said, winking.

"I think he gorgeous," Cyn said, drifting off. "But my dress is more important. Balcony, Jools!"

"Right, we'll see you later," Sean said as he walked towards the dance hall with Jayo, and the girls took the stairs.

At the top of the balcony there was a bar and a seated area, but they didn't stop and walked through, to lean against the balcony railings. They could see Sean and Jayo already up at the crowd barrier, right at the centre of the stage where the lead singer would be standing.

"They'll have a heap of girls knocking them out of the way so they can get a better look at Paul," Cyn said, Jools noticed the disappointment in her voice.

"We'll get a better view from up here and when you think about it, Cyn, I reckon they put those barriers up after you tried to jump on stage at the Baggot Inn!"

"But he's gorgeous," she said again.

Jools just laughed. She might look like a teenager on the outside, but inside, she was a divorced, middle aged woman who was no longer interested in teenage crushes.

As they looked down, the crowd started to pour in, and below and behind them at the bar, the noise level rose.

More and more people started to appear on the balcony and Jools noticed even more faces that she hadn't seen in years. She smiled that reminiscing smile again, but Cyn was too busy darting at every movement on stage, hoping to get a first glimpse of Paul, but it was the roadie, checking leads and amps and tightening the straps on the PA, as the speakers had a tendency to sway when The Blades played there, with the crowd bouncing to the music.

"Yis alright, girls?"

They turned to see two tall, immaculately mohair suited Mods behind them, holding out flyers.

"We're puttin on Makin' Time in the CIE Hall the August Bank Holiday Sunday," the slimmer of the two said, as both were around the same height, the other being broader.

"Ah, howaya, Darren," Jools said and looked down at the flyer which proclaimed, "The Dublin Mod Society Presents Makin' Time."

Cyn, for once, took her eyes off the stage and looked at the broader of the two Mods.

"Hello, Jeffrey," she purred, running her eyes up and down the length of his body.

Jeff, not a timid bloke by any stretch of the imagination, actually blushed.

Cyn, without taking her eyes off of him, said, "Yep, we'll definitely be there, lads, I'll be all over that!"

Jools looked at Darren and rolled her eyes as the lads made excuses about having to hand out more flyers and walked to the right hand side of the balcony.

"Jaysus, Darren," Jeff said, laughing, "I thought she was gonna rip me clothes off there and then!"

Darren laughed. "That one, Jeff, doesn't need to rip them off, by the time she finished looking you up and down, you were practically bollock naked with your suit gone over the balcony!"

"Cyn," Jools said, "do you think of nothing else?"

"What did I do?" She asked, all mock innocence. "I only meant we'd be all over that gig."

"Yeah, right, that's what you meant."

"Jools, I enjoy the company of men. What's wrong with that? If I was a bloke, nobody would bat an eyelid, I'd even be called a stud, or some shite like that, but just cos you're a girl, you're supposed to be all prim and proper. Now, that's just double standards."

Jools thought about that for a second and said, "You know something, Cyn, you're dead right!"

Cyn nodded, feeling justified and vindicated and said, "Come on, let's move down the balcony so we can get closer to the stage."

39. Jump

Downstairs, at the front, Sean and Jayo were pressed hard against the barriers, the crowd now so big, there was barely an inch of floor space available, as bodies jammed in and up against each other. The speakers were already booming with a mix of classics pouring out. "Louie Louie," by The Kingsmen came on and up on the balcony, on the opposite side to where Jools and Cyn were standing, a young, slim lad in a suit - very like the one Jimmy Cooper wore in Quadrophenia, as he too once stood on a similar balcony in a Brighton ballroom moving to the same song - stood up on the rails, his mate Bernard on one side holding him steady, and his girlfriend Liz on the other side trying to get him down.

The crowd began to cheer as he gyrated to the music. Sean and Jayo looked up as the crowd started singing the chorus and some gathered around the upstairs doors to stop the bouncers getting onto the balcony.

"Would you look at Danny," Sean said to Jayo, "Jimmy Fuckin Cooper!"

"He'll break his neck if he falls. Look at Liz, she looks like she's gonna kill him!"

Danny balanced precariously on the balcony's railing, doing a great impression of Jimmy while the crowd below, who, by now, had stopped singing along with The Kingsmen, and started to shout, "Jump! Jump!"

"Danny!" Liz shouted. "Get your arse down here now. If we get kicked out, I'll kill you."

He was so totally consumed by his Quadrophenia moment, he couldn't see or hear anything. As far as he was concerned, he wasn't in a club in Dublin, he *was* Jimmy Cooper, dancing on the balcony of that dancehall in Brighton in 1964.

Three bouncers pushed their way through the crowd at the balcony door as another two forced their way through the crowd below.

Danny looked over his left shoulder and saw the bouncers rushing towards him. "Let go, Bernard, I'm gonna jump!"

"Don't you fuckin da...." was all Liz managed to get out before he was gone, swan diving to the crowd below, who caught him, and then promptly dropped him on the floor.

"Ow, me head," he said as he hit the floor and two bouncers grabbed him under each arm and carried him towards the exit. He looked up at Liz, laughing. She just shook her head and shouted down to him, "Feck off you gobshite, I'm staying!"

40. Real Emotion

"Oh, here he is!" Cyn screamed as she saw the band walk onto the stage and the crowd cheered.

"We'll have to start putting parachutes on the balcony!" Paul Cleary said, and the crowd cheered again. "This is Last Man In Europe." The crowd cheered once again as the band launched into the song.

Jools smiled, remembering the gig from the first time she was there and how surreal it all felt.

"They'll do Ghost Of A Chance next," Cyn said, "I love that one."

"Bet you they won't," Jools said, remembering that's what they finished with. "I reckon it'll be Sadlands," she said, with a smirk. She couldn't remember everything they played that night, but did remember the first two and the last two.

"Last Man In Europe" finished to cheers and applause from an ecstatic crowd and with barely a pause, the organist played the first notes of "Sadlands," and Cyn turned her head sharply to Jools, her mouth making an O. Jools laughed and they both started to dance.

For the second time since she arrived back in 1985, she completely lost all memory of why she was there and got lost in the moment. "Sadlands" gave way to "Real Emotion," "Pride,"

"Boy One" and when they played "Tears That Tell The Truth," forgetting herself, she said to Cyn, "Jesus, I forgot about this one, what a song. Always sounded so Sixties to me."

Cyn turned to her and said, "What do you mean, you forgot about this one? They played it the last time we saw them."

"Oh, right, yeah," Jools said, "I must be mixing it up with something else."

She decided to keep quiet and just dance and enjoy the gig. Cyn was looking over the balcony at the crowd and between "Revelations Of Heartbreak" and "My Girl," she turned to Jools.

"Who's that bloke down there with Chris and Stevey?"

"Where?"

"There, beside the speaker on the left hand side of the stage," Cyn said, pointing at a tall, reddish blonde bloke in a Crombie.

Jools remembered, having met him at Bubbles back then and, coincidentally, she thought, the last time was at The Blades reunion gig in the Olympia in 2013.

"That's Don, can't remember his last name. He's a barman in the Belcamp Inn. From Galway, I think."

"Oooh," Cyn said, "I like that!"

"Of course you do, Cynthia, he's got a pulse, hasn't he?"

"Now, Julia, darling," Cyn replied, "A pulse is not the only requirement, otherwise I'd have let that horrible Dosser shit at me years ago. No, the pulse must be attached to a good-looking face, with a decent body. Money and a car is a bonus." She smiled.

"Not a scooter?"

"No, darling, this," she said, running her hands down her body, "does not get wet."

"That's not what I heard," Jools said, laughing.

"Cheeky mare," Cyn replied as she turned her nose up and looked away. Then, a moment later, "What kinda car?"

"A Cortina, I believe. You do like your Cortinas."

Jools didn't have a clue what kind of car he had, she just remembered he had one, but was hoping Cyn would get the song reference. She did.

"Oh I do. Fur trimmed dashboard. Stains on the seat?"

"In the back, of course!"

They both burst out laughing.

"I'm getting my hands on that later," Cyn said, looking over the balcony at the unsuspecting barman.

The rest of the gig was as amazing the second time for Jools as it was the first. She remembered correctly and they finished with "Young, Gifted And Black," as Cyn practically hung off the balcony watching Don skanking and then, after the crowd cheered for more, wrapped things up nicely with "Ghost Of A Chance."

They were amazing in 2013, Jools thought, but getting a chance to see them in their 1985 prime again, that was something else. "Ghost Of A Chance" almost brought the house down, with the crowd on the floor and the balcony screaming for more, clapping their hands and stamping their feet so hard, Jools felt the balcony shaking. The house lights came up and Cyn leaned over the railings, and shouted, "Chris, who's your mate?"

All three of them looked up and she pointed at Don and then pointed at herself and nodded.

Stevey nudged him and said something in his ear. Don's grin looked like his face was going to split in two.

"Evening, ladies!"

The girls turned as Gaz bowed to them and as he stood up, he once again pushed his lensless glasses back up on his nose and said, "There's a little after show soiree at my humble abode in Donaghmede, if you'd both care to join us? There are scooters a plenty for your transportation needs, M'Ladies."

"Is it raining?" Cyn asked.

"No, M'Lady," Gaz answered, again bowing. "It is not. Why, would that be a problem?"

"Yes, my good man," Cyn replied, "This…. does not get wet." Gaz just managed to get the words, "That's not what…." out of his mouth before Cyn interrupted him, saying, "Don't you say another fuckin word, Gary Reilly, or I'll stick them glasses where the sun don't shine!"

Gaz, totally unfazed, replied, "Very good, M'Lady, not another word on that particular subject. Various two wheeled carriages await your delicate bottom, should you so choose. I shall away to prepare for your gracious visit." He backed away, bowing, while intermittently pushing the glasses back up on his nose.

"He's fuckin nuts," Cyn said, smiling.

"He's gas," Jools replied. "Love Gaz."

41. This Looks Familiar

The crowd poured out onto Harcourt Street, where a line of scooters were parked. Right at the front, sitting on his new scooter, in a remarkably clean, white cycling shirt and Levi's so dark navy, they almost looked black, was Dosser. Even the cream coloured soles of his bowling shoes were still actually cream coloured.

"Howaya, Cyn," he said, leering. A sliver of drool escaped the left side of his mouth and dripped on to his now, no longer immaculate white cycling shirt. He didn't notice, but she did. No amount of dressing up could make Dosser into anything other than the pig that he was. Cyn looked him up and down, not impressed by his new clothes and sitting on what was obviously someone else's scooter. She muttered a disgusted, "Ugh," and shuddered.

"Can I give ya a ride?" He asked, looking directly at her chest.

"Dosser, you creep! Eyes are up here," she said, pointing at her face and surprised herself with that. Normally, she'd have no more than two words for him, the last always being "Off."

"And I wouldn't ride you if you had fuckin pedals!"

"Ah, no, Cyn, I don't mean it like that!"

"Yes, you fuckin do!"

"No, I mean on me scooter."

"That's yours?"

"Yep, I got it today," he said, delighted with himself.

The Dublin Mod Society lads came out through the doors at that moment and saw him on the scooter. Sam Kelly, one of the main organisers of their gigs looked at the scooter and asked him, "Where did you get this? It looks very familiar."

Dosser gulped. He was about to make up some lie when a young Mod in a boating blazer and Sta-Prest walked up to the scooter and said, "Face? Are you fuckin kiddin? I'm only 14 and I'm more of a Face than you are!"

"You're only what, son?" One of the bouncers asked him. The kid panicked and disappeared into the crowd. The Mod Society lads moved off and got onto their scooters, kicking them into life and smoke filled the air.

Darren called over to Jools and Cyn, "Party at Gaz's, want a lift?"

Cyn turned around and saw Don, Chris and Stevey come through the doors. She caught Don's eye. "No, thanks, Darren, I think we have one."

Dosser sat there, in his new clothes, on his new scooter, feeling dejected. No matter what he did, nothing worked. His dream of driving along Bray seafront with Cyn on the seat behind him was disappearing into the night air, just like the smoke from the scooter exhausts, as everyone pulled out, heading for the party.

The party he wasn't invited to.

"It's the cyclin shirt," he muttered to himself, "I shoulda got the suit altered in the fuckin shop and she woulda been gaggin for me. Fuck it!"

He kicked started the scooter and as he pulled out, two Mods were standing in a nearby phone box, the door was missing but he wouldn't have heard them anyway as one spoke into the phone, "Hello, Mister McNeil? This is Charlie's boy. I think there's something you need to know."

42. Capri Son

"Howya, I'm Don."

"I know," Cyn said, smiling her Disney Princess smile that melted every bloke she met.

"Oh," he said, returning the smile.

Jools rolled her eyes and turned to Stevey.

"He's no idea what he's getting himself into, does he?"

"Not a fuckin clue," he replied, as he, Jools and Chris got into the back of the car, which was a Capri, not a Cortina, "but I really don't think he cares."

Jools sat in the middle, Stevey on her left, Chris on her right.

"Enjoy the gig, Chris?"

"Yep," he said, blushed and looked out the window.

She smiled. She knew him from school. He'd always been quiet and shy, but she'd forgotten just how much. In 2015, people still said to him, "I don't remember you from Bubbles," she thought now, this was why.

"We're all going to the party then?" She asked, looking at the two occupants of the back seat. Chris just nodded and Stevey said, "Well, I'm going out with Gaz's sister, so I should probably show my face."

"Nice car, Don," Cyn said and they pulled out into traffic.

43. We're All Mates Here

Thirty minutes after they left the gig, the taxi carrying Sean and Jayo pulled up outside Gaz's house. The street outside was already packed with scooters, and bodies could be seen, silhouetted through the front room window, moving to Edwin Starr's "Twenty-Five Miles."

"Keep the change," Sean said, handing a note to the driver.

"Thanks, bud," the driver said, "That looks like a lively one, I hope nobody calls the cops."

"I think they're well used to it," Jayo said. "Half of Donaghmede are Mods and most of them are here."

"It's the other half you want to be worrying about," the driver said. "Have a good night, lads."

They got out and walked up the driveway, through the open front door and a wall of sound and smoke hit them.

Sean popped his head into the front room and saw a room filled with people dancing to the Edwin Starr song.

"See ya in a bit," Jayo said as he noticed a plastic shopping bag on a chair beneath the window, with the top of a still capped large bottle of Smithwick's sticking out.

"That'll do nicely."

Sean walked on into the kitchen, and standing at the back door, was Robbo, one hand on the waist of a tall, slim blonde girl and the other holding a can of Harp.

"Alright, Robbo, did you go to the gig? I didn't see you there," Sean said, with as much normality as he could.

"Nah, didn't go, wasn't into it."

"You shouldn't be here," Sean said, lower, as he got closer to his mate and stopped abruptly, as Robbo shook his head quickly, nodding at the girl in his arms.

"Hang on a minute, love," he said to her. She looked like she was about to pass out. He handed her his can, saying, "Hold onto this for me. Actually, no, I'll take it with me. Back in a sec."

They went out to the back garden where a gang of soldiers were standing by the wall, still in their combat gear, supping from cans. Gaz's brother Luke was in the army and they both knew the mobile disco mate. Sean had met a few of the lads here at his gigs and nodded over to them. They nodded back.

"What the fuck are you thinking, Robbo? There's too many people here and I'm sure by now that word has got out that he's looking for you."

"I'll be grand," Robbo replied. "We're all mates here, nobody's gonna run to that little fucker and tell him where I am. Have a drink and stop worrying."

The door opened and a couple almost fell off the step, trying to get to the dark end of the back garden.

"Do you think they're picking mushrooms?" Sean asked.

"I can save them the time," Robbo said, laughing "I've a bag of them here somewhere."

"Well, whatever you have in your various pockets, leave them there. Don't be doing any of that shit in Gaz's gaff, no matter who wants it."

"Relax," Robbo said. "I know I'm desperate for money, but I don't have anything on me, I wouldn't do that on Gaz. Anyway, remember the last time? Cops came in about four in the morning and broke up the party? No way I'm getting caught with gear on me if that happens. If I got locked up, Freddie would definitely have me done inside."

"You really gotta get out of this," Sean said. "I don't know how, but you have to, it's not good for your health."

"I know. Come on, let's go back inside and see what's happening."

44. It's A Two Door Car

Don pulled up outside the house, turned off the engine and opened the door to get out.

"Don't get out, Don," Cyn said, "they can go into the party, maybe we can take a drive?"

"I have to get out, Cyn, it's a two door car."

Cyn looked in the back and blushed at the three faces smiling at her.

"We can stay here," Jools said, "We don't mind, do we, boys?"

"Not much room," Chris replied.

"Ah I'm sure we can all bunch up," Jools said, laughing.

"Feck off the lot of you! Don, let them out. Smart fucks."

He got out, pulled his seat forward and let the three of them out. Jools leaned in the window and said, "See you later, Cynthia, hon, don't do anything I wouldn't do."

"That doesn't leave much!" Cyn replied, with a smile.

"Make sure he gets back here in one piece!"

"Aren't you supposed to be saying that to me?" Don asked her.

"Oh, darling," Jools said, with a laugh, "you really have no idea."

She stood up, linked the two lads and walked into the party, hearing the Capri drive away.

45. Ripples

As soon as they walked in the door, Gaz's sister grabbed Stevey and they disappeared, Chris went into the front room and started looking through records and Jools headed for the kitchen. Sean and Robbo had just come back in and were talking to Gaz and Jayo.

"Robbo!" Jools said and threw her arms around him. "What are you doing here? You should be keeping a low profile."

"I'm grand," he said, "just went through all that with Sean. The chance of that Jimmy Kranky fuck knowing I'm here is slim to none and even if he did, he's hardly gonna do anything in front of all these people."

"I wouldn't be surprised," Jools said, "he's a nutcase. Threatened to nail me and Cyn to a tree. Liberty taking fuck! I want my own tree!"

Robbo burst out laughing.

"There you are, it's good to see you laugh. It'll all work out, I just know it."

Jools knew that Robbo was still around in 2015, but she'd seen enough movies and TV shows to know that shit like time travel didn't really exist and when people in the movies did it, there was always a new timeline created and it wasn't always for the better.

But, here she was, travelling through time and it wasn't a movie or a TV show or even a dream. And she'd no idea what she'd changed by being back. How many ripples had been created when she persuaded Robbo to go to The Anvil and he lost that money? She didn't entirely remember that she had or hadn't gone there that night originally, though it was their usual haunt, pre-Bubbles, so they more than likely did, but she did know that he definitely hadn't been in this kind of mess with Freddie, she would have remembered that. What if it didn't work out? What if coming back to save Lainey ended up killing Robbo? Could she live with trading one friend's life for another? She began to well up and Robbo hugged her.

"It'll be fine, Jools, I'll have enough money to give back to him and he'll be grand."

46. You Know The Score

There weren't many people who knew Freddie Collins well. In his fifty-five years, there had been many acquaintances, but no real friends. People didn't tend to stick around him too long, his unpredictable nature and violent outbursts tending to scare everyone away and most people gave him a wide berth. That was fine with him. He wasn't an unintelligent man by any stretch of the imagination and certainly didn't mistake fear for respect. He knew it was more of the former and not so much of the latter and as far as he was concerned, the less people in his circle, the less people that could turn against him. Freddie was firmly of the mind that just because you were paranoid – and he was – it didn't mean they weren't out to get you, so trusted only one person with everything, including his life; his minder of thirty years, George Kearns.

George had been with Freddie from the beginning, when he was fencing stolen goods for every little toe rag in Dublin, but had quickly moved up to bigger things, organising gangs for warehouse and bank robberies and then drugs, brothels and strip clubs, and that's where the real money came in.

To keep an air of respectability, and keep the taxman off his back, he ran a lucrative and legitimate Imports & Exports business that did actually import and export all manner of goods for all manner of companies, with warehouses dotted all over Dublin. This also provided him with the logistics to move what he really needed to import and all through this, was George, his right-hand man. Freddie trusted George implicitly because George knew all the skeletons in all of Freddie's closets and quite literally knew where all the bodies were buried, he'd put most of them there himself. George also knew of Freddie's predilection for blonde haired, blue eyed, teenage boys, which was the one thing that never sat right with him, and Freddie knew it, but, Freddie being Freddie and considering he paid George's wages, really didn't give a fuck what sat right with George and what didn't. Freddie basically did whatever he wanted, to whomever he wanted.

George was sitting in his boss's kitchen with the radio on high. The DJ on the late-night Sunshine Radio show played some nice oldies and he needed loud music so he couldn't hear the noises coming from the room at the other end of the bungalow.

He hoped what his boss was doing in the bedroom would calm him down a bit. He had never seen him this mad. George knew and liked Robbo and thought what Freddie would do to him when he caught up with him, well, it really didn't bear thinking about. And it wasn't just Robbo. Freddie was going on about killing, "Him and all his little cunty mates." But the girls, they'd get the worst of it. The things he said he was going to do to them even shook a hard man like George. He just thanked his lucky stars that Freddie was taking all of this so personally, that he wouldn't get him to do any of it. Freddie said he wanted the pleasure of seeing the life drain from their eyes.

George had no problem breaking or cutting off the various appendages of most of the people who crossed Freddie - they were genuinely bad people – but just like with the poor boy in the room down the hall, this didn't sit right with him. Robbo, he knew, had been tricked into all of this. Freddie played him from the start. He heard the door open.

"Fuck off ya little cunt."

George looked down the hall and a small, skinny lad, who he hoped was eighteen, but had probably only just turned sixteen, if that, stood outside the bedroom, naked, bruised and bleeding from a puffed up and cut lip. Even from this distance, he could see the tears running down the boy's face.

"And if ya tell a single person ya were here, I'll cut your fuckin balls off and feed them to ya!"

The kid looked at George but didn't move.

"Are ya fuckin deaf? I told ya to get the fuck out!"

It happened so quickly, neither George nor the kid saw it coming. George just saw the kid's head jerk back and he staggered against the wall opposite the bedroom door, his legs gave out and he slid to the floor. Freddie had thrown an alarm clock, hitting him on the bridge of his nose, probably breaking it.

Blood poured down the kid's face and down his chest. George got up, walked down the hall, closed the bedroom door and helped him up, leading him to the bathroom.

"Go in there and clean yourself up, son. I'll get one of the lads to drop you back into town when you're done."

"George! What the fuck are ya doin? I told that little cunt to get the fuck outa my house!"

George opened the bedroom door, popped his head around and trying to ignore the vision of the half-naked, middle aged man on the bed in front of him said, "Boss, he's gotta get cleaned up. If we fuck him out, bleeding and without a stitch on him, the Guards will be down here pronto." He looked back over at the kid standing in the bathroom doorway and silently thought to himself, and I really don't think this one *is* even old enough to drink. He closed his eyes for a second. Freddie screamed and threw a shoe at the door, narrowly missing George's head.

"Fuck him! Fuck the Guards! Fuck Robbo and all them fuckin mates of his! Oh, and them two little fuckin bitches, I saw the way they looked at me, like I was a piece of shit. I'm Freddie Fuckin Collins! Nobody looks at me like that!"

George closed the door, turned to the kid and said, "Go in and wash that blood off and get dressed." He took a fifty pound note from his wallet and handed it to him and said, "You were never here, don't forget that. If anyone asks, you got mugged in town. If you mention Freddie's name and he finds out, he'll kill you. You get all that?"

The kid just nodded.

"Okay, clean yourself up, lad."

George went back to the kitchen, picked up the phone and dialled a number.

After a couple of rings, he said, "Benny, I need you round to the boss's in ten. Pick up and drop off in town. You know the score."

He'd only just hung up the phone and it rang.

"For fuck sake, Benny! Can you not take a simple instruction?"

"Eh…. Mister Collins? Eh…. it's not B…. Benny," came a timid and very nervous voice on the other end of the line.

"Eh, sorry, this isn't Mister Collins. Who's this?"

"It's Graham Doherty, eh…. I mean Dosser. Can I talk to M…. Mister Collins?"

"No, son, he's busy. This is George. What do you want?"

"Well, eh, it's about Robbo. There's a party in Donaghmede tonight, and he might be there."

"Oh really?" George said. "How are you so sure? We were

talking to Sean yesterday and he didn't even know where
Robbo was. If I go to Freddie and tell him Dosser told me
Robbo was somewhere and it turns out he wasn't, well, I don't
have to tell you what he'll do to you, now do I?"

Dosser gulped and said, "Eh, well there's a party at Gaz's gaff
and they all went off on their scooters to it. Everybody who's
anybody will be there, so I'd say Robbo will be too."

"Are you going?" George asked.

"Eh, no," Dosser said, "I wasn't invited."

"And where does this Gaz fella live in Donaghmede? It's a big
place, Dosser."

"I don't know, Miste…. eh…. Geor…. eh…. I don't know his
address. It'll be the one with all the scooters outside and the
music blarin."

"Righto, Dosser, thanks for the info. If it all works out and
Mister Collins catches up with Robbo, he might just give you a
little reward."

Dosser perked up at this. "A reward! Like, if an'thin happened
to Robbo, Mister Collins might be lookin for someone to sell
his…."

"Not on the phone, you dopey prick!" George shouted.
Freddie heard the shout and came out of the bedroom,
barefoot, with his bathrobe on.

"Who's on the phone?"

231

"It's that Dosser kid, Boss. Says he thinks he might know where Robbo is."

Freddie grabbed the phone off George.

"Ya better not be fuckin shittin me, Dosser! If you're sendin me on a wild fuckin goose chase, I'll cut your little fuckin mickey off!"

"Honest, Mister Collins," Dosser said, trembling, "I told…. G…. Geor…. tha…. that there's a party in Donaghmede and he might be there. Everyone's gonna be there."

"But Robbo is fuckin missin, isn't he?"

"I don't know nothin bout that Fre…. I mean Mister Collins. All I know is he wasn't at Bubbles on Wednesday, but this party, well, everyone's goin. Even Cyn."

"Even what?"

"Nothin. Look, Mister Collins, it's a big party and it's where all the big heads off the scene are goin. There's no way he'd miss that."

Freddie thought for a moment and said, "Alright. Good lad. Thanks," and hung up before Dosser had a chance to answer.

47. This Is It

By one o'clock, the party was off the scale. After some complaints about the pauses in music between records being changed, Gaz brought a stereo down from upstairs, put it beside the living room one and with all four speakers connected together, it was just like having a proper DJ set up and the crowd were loving it.

Jools heard the unmistakeable brass intro to "I Love Her So Much It Hurts Me," by The Majestics, and ran to the living room.

Behind the cobbled together decks, was one of the scene's finest DJs and collectors of Northern Soul, Declan Sheridan, with Chris sitting beside the stereos watching him at work. Declan was pulling records out of his box, handing them to Chris and saying, "Do you know this? Wait till you hear it," to almost every record, while Chris just sat there with eyes like saucers, wishing he had a photographic memory, as labels, titles and artists went by like a whirlwind.

Declan had the room bouncing. Jools smiled when she saw him and thought, he always could.

She found a spare six inches of floor space in the middle of the room and held her ground while Mod boys and Mod girls jostled around her, all vying for position. The living room filled and emptied out for the next hour or so depending on the record, but Declan never played to an empty floor. Noticing Gaz's brother Luke in the doorway with a few of his Skinhead mates, he thought some Reggae and Ska would be good for the party and with a quick look through the pile of records in the corner, he slipped one onto one of the stereos and as the last notes of Ron Baxter's "This Is It" was fading out, Dave Barker's voice took up the beat, saying, "I…. am The Magnificent…." kicking off "Double Barrell," and Skinheads filled the room.

Jools took the opportunity for a breather and made her way to the front garden.

"Robbo! What the fuck? You shouldn't be seen out here. What if someone tells Freddie you're here?"

"Ah, Jools, who'd tell him I was here? Sure, all these lads are my mates."

"I don't care, Robbo, get back into that kitchen, you can't be too careful."

"Fuck me, Jools, you sound like my Ma!"

Jools thought about that. She was just about to say that they were around the same age, and caught herself, instead, saying, "And you're not too big for a clatter, son."

Robbo held his hands up and said, "Okay, okay, Ma, I'm going."

He turned around and walked back into the kitchen, where the Blonde Mod girl he'd been with was slumped in a chair in the corner, snoring her brains out.

"Ah, fuck," he said.

48. Just Keep Driving

Whenever Freddie went out, he always sat in the back seat, but this time, he sat in the front, on the passenger side. He told everyone that he didn't like to drive, which was partially the truth. He hated not being in control and was so short, he couldn't quite reach the pedals properly without having the seat pulled right up to the steering wheel, a position that made him look like a kid driving Daddy's car and Freddie didn't like to look stupid, so he let the lads drive him.

Sitting in the front seat gave him a better view anyway and he looked out, eyes darting left and right, fingers fidgeting with a sawn-off shotgun.

"Boss," George said, "can you put that on the floor please? If we hit a pothole or something, you could end up shooting you, me or both of us."

Freddie looked down at the gun and back up at George, confusion on his face.

"What? Oh, sorry, George, wouldn't want to do that. Only fucker gettin shot tonight is that Robbo cunt."

"Donaghmede's a big place, Boss, we could be driving round here for hours."

"Just keep drivin, George. If he's anywhere, he'll be here."

"What about his gaff?"

"No, George, he wouldn't be stupid enough to go there. Besides, I have that little McCarthy fella watchin it and he said he's nowhere to be seen. Let's just check this out and see what's what."

They drove around the estates of Donaghmede, up and down deserted streets and didn't see one scooter, let alone a row of them. Just about to throw in the towel, they saw a group of kids behind the shopping centre on BMX bikes and pulled over. Freddie rolled down the window and leaned out.

"Here, yunfella, c'mere."

The young lad looked at him and said, "Fuck off, queer, I'm not gettin in your car."

Freddie held out a twenty and said, "I don't want ya to get in me car, ya little prick, you're not me type."

"What?"

"Never mind. There's a score for ya if ya can tell me if there's a moddy party round here somewhere. Should be a load of scooters outside."

The young lad cautiously approached the car and took the proffered twenty.

"Yeah, Reilly's, down Carndonagh…. somethin. Drive down here, turn left and then right and it's down there…. somewhere."

"If you're lyin to me ya little pox, I'll come back here and blow your fuckin kneecaps off."

"With fuckin what?" The young lad had moved back to the relative safety of his mates and was showing a bit of bravado. Freddie leaned into the footwell, momentarily disappearing from sight and came back up, pointing the shotgun out the window.

"Will this do, ya little bollix?"

"Scatter," the young lad said, and they all tore off in different directions on their bikes. After about three seconds, it was like they'd never been there.

"Let's find this cunt," Freddie said. "Drive."

George took the directions the kid gave him, but it was a dead end. After another ten minutes of driving around deserted streets, he cocked his head out the open window and said, "Boss, do you hear that?"

Freddie did the same on the opposite side and, adopting an upper class accent, for no apparent reason, said, "That, George, my old chap, sounds rather like music."

George, who knew his music, replied, "Frederic, old boy, I rather think that sounds like Mister Desmond Dekker."

"Who the fuck is Desmond Becker?"

"Dekker."

"Becker?"

"No, Dekker!"

"Like Double Decker?"

"No, Single Dekker."

"Whatever! Is that them, George? Is that what them moddy fuckers like?"

"It sure is, Boss, it sure is."

49. And he Liked It

The car pulled up outside the house which was unmistakeably where the party was happening. If the row of scooters on the pavement wasn't a giveaway, the music blaring from the open windows and the front garden full of Mods and Skinheads was. Luke Reilly stood on the front step. At over six feet, with Levi's and a black Fred Perry almost painted onto solid muscle, he was an imposing figure. Flanked on either side by shorter, but no less intimidating looking Skins, they looked to Freddie and George – who, himself, was a seasoned scrapper – to be something that should be avoided.

As it happened, they weren't troublemakers, they were really nice blokes who just happened to be Skinheads, but Freddie and George didn't know that.

Freddie, the narcissist that he was, believed himself to be something of a Tony Montana figure and with his don't give a fuck attitude, reached for the door handle. George put his hand on his boss's arm. Freddie looked down at it and then up at him.

George knew that look, knew exactly what it meant, but, for once, didn't budge.

"Boss, look at them lads, and I'd say they've got a lot of friends in there too."

Freddie lifted up the sawn-off again and said, "Then they need to say hello to my little friend."

George rolled his eyes and barely caught his exasperated sigh in time, but Freddie was too engrossed in his Scarface moment to notice.

He was still looking at the gun, his voice had an iciness to it that George had never heard directed towards him, when he said, "Now, George, I appreciate that ya've known me a lot longer than anyone else on this planet and that does allow ya a little extra familiarity with me, but," and here, he looked back at George's hand, still on his arm and said, "if ya ever take the fuckin liberty of layin your hand on me again, well, you're the one I trust the most, but there's plenty of lads who have no loyalty to ya and would love to take your place and I'll happily see them take ya to the farm. Still breathin."

George's heart almost stopped. Freddie's reputation for bringing people who crossed him to Dublin Bay and throwing them in, strapped to breeze blocks was well known and in fact, Freddie liked it be known, because it kept people in fear of him. He had done it, but only once. There were other people who had been stupid enough to cross him that had simply vanished and not a trace of them would ever be seen again. The Garda divers could search every inch of Dublin Bay and if they were lucky, they might find that one body, but Freddie had a way of making sure nobody ever turned up.

In the early Eighties, he'd read one of those true crime magazines while sitting in a dentist's waiting room which he, of course, rolled up and stuck in his pocket to finish reading later, and discovered that some bloke in America had been kidnapping young women, having his jollies with them in the cellar on his farm and when he was fed up, he'd kill them. He would then feed the body, feet first, into the woodchipper. When he was eventually caught, he told the cops everything. He'd driven across four states and abducted twenty-three hitchhiking girls – the cops found polaroids of them in the cellar – and in the most matter of fact way, he described, quite graphically, what he'd done to them and how he'd killed his first victim and put her through the chipper but puked at the mess it made. It was easy enough to clean up, he'd told the cops, just a quick hose down and it was gone but he had to think of something that would clean the mess up for him. So he welded a pipe to the outlet of the woodchipper and ran it straight into his slurry tank. The whole process, he'd told them, took a while to iron out the kinks but he got there. The cops who interviewed him, seasoned veterans, each one, were visibly shaken.

His Modus Operandi was to hit them over the head with a hammer and put them into the chipper, but he hadn't hit his third victim hard enough and she regained consciousness while the blades were tearing her feet off. This was an added bonus as it heightened the thrill for him of never knowing if he was going to get that extra little surprise when they went in and then suddenly wake up, screaming in agony. He never checked for a pulse as not knowing whether they were dead or alive was almost as good as what he'd done to them in the cellar. "It was like puttin them inna liqueedizah," he'd said to his interviewers, smiling.

When he'd read this, a lightbulb went off in Freddie's head. By the end of the week, he owned a disused farm in Meath. A week later, he owned a woodchipper, which he'd had modified to connect a pipe to a tank and by the end of that week, a nineteen year old junkie from Dublin's inner city was reported missing and Freddie had his first experience of what a woodchipper could do. And he liked it.

George didn't know about the junkie, but he did know about a couple of low rent drug dealers who'd crossed Freddie and been there when they were put in the woodchipper. At least Freddie had the mercy to shoot them first before having the lads throw the bodies in.

And for Freddie, the best part was the Guards would have nothing bigger than a tooth or bone fragment to make an ID. The slurry was spread across fields that would grow no crops, as none were ever planted there to begin with, on a farm where no hooves or trotters ever walked and the only animal sounds that could be heard, were the occasional squeak of rats and the constant buzz of flies around the woodchipper.

"The Guards would have some job makin an ID from them bodies," he'd told George after the drug dealers were taken care of and then sprayed across the fields. "They might as well be doin a fuckin jigsaw puzzle, with no picture on the box and half the pieces missin."

George had no intention of going to the farm alive or dead, so he took his hand off of Freddie's arm.

"Now, George," Freddie said, with warmth and even a smile on his face, like nothing had even happened, "let's go kill this cunt," and he opened the passenger door.

50. He's Not Here

"Who's this little prick?" The Skin to Luke's left asked the question.

"Too small for a Guard," the one on the right said.

Luke said nothing.

Freddie walked up the driveway, George, behind him, raising himself up to his full six feet four height, his stature still imposing, but belly and muscle starting to give way to fat, made him a bit slower than he used to be.

Freddie stopped in front of the Skins.

"Sorry, lads, can I get past?"

The Skin to the right spoke. "Who the fuck are you?"

George stepped forward, but Freddie raised a hand and opening his jacket, showed the Skin the shotgun tucked inside his belt and said, "My name is not important, to you, that is, but," he said, nodding towards the gun, "this is Mister Browning and he'll take your baldy, little fuckin head off." The Skin looked at Luke, who hadn't yet looked at Freddie, he was keeping his eye on George. Eventually, he spoke, still looking at George, but directing his words at Freddie.

"He's not here."

"Who's not here?" Freddie asked.

"Whoever the fuck you're looking for. Whoever the fuck you

think is your mate. Whoever the fuck you think will give you a reason to come into my house. He's not here."

"Your house is it? You must be this Gaz I've been hearin about then. That's good to know. I'll have me lads write your name on the bottle when we petrol bomb the gaff, so."

Luke took his eyes off George for a moment, looked over his shoulder and called, "Lads!"

The three Skinheads stepped off the front step and the doorway filled with Skins, Mods and, Freddie's worst nightmare, soldiers. There was no mistaking that combat gear. Freddie was a scary bastard and not a lot of things frightened him, but soldiers did. They were the only people he wouldn't fuck with because they shot guns for a living and they stuck together. You fuck with one, you fuck with them all. Suddenly his little friend felt very little.

Freddie and George both took a step back.

"Let's all just take a moment here, Gaz, and calm down."

"I am calm," Luke said. "And I'm Luke, not Gaz. Make sure you have the right name on that bottle of yours if you're thinking of throwing it but right now, we're all calm, and things will stay that way the sooner you both back the fuck up and get out of my garden."

"We're only here to have a chat with Robbo," Freddie said, as amiably as he could.

"Never heard of him," Luke said. "Gaz, have you ever heard of anyone called Robbo? There's isn't a Robbo in our gaff, is there?"

Gaz called out from the hallway, "Nope, never heard of anyone called Robbo in my life. There's no Robbo here."

"Every cunt knows a Robbo," Freddie spat. "There's probably have a dozen blokes in there called Robbo!"

Luke took a step forward. And so did twenty other blokes behind him. He bent down, his nose inches from Freddie's face.

"Did you just call my brother a cunt? And a liar?"

From behind Freddie, "Boss...."

Freddie stepped back and held his hands up. "No harm done, lads, we musta got the wrong house. We'll just head off and leave yis all to your party. Have a good night."

He turned and walked down the driveway and got into the car. George hesitated a moment and in a desperate move, mumbled to Luke, "You don't know what you've done, son. Do you have any idea who that is?"

"I know exactly who that is, and I know who you are too, George and that little fuck coming round my gaff waving a shotgun, well, we'll see what happens about that. By tomorrow morning, everyone in the army will know about this. You fuck with one of us, George, you fuck with all of us."

"Robbo owes him a lot of money, son. Freddie just wants it back."

"Told you, George, none of us have ever heard of anyone called Robbo in our lives. No idea what you're on about."

George shook his head. "I tried to warn ya, son."

Luke looked up to the night sky, looked at the car where Freddie was sitting, looked over his shoulder at the lads standing behind him and finally at George. "And I've just returned the favour."

George turned and walked down the driveway, his height a little lower than when he walked up. He got into the driver's seat, turned to Freddie and said, "What now?"

"Tomorrow's another day, George," and reaching into his inside pocket, he pulled out another flyer for the allnighter, "and this time, I know exactly where he'll be. And then he's fuckin dead."

"What about yer man, the skinhead?"

"He won't be with his army mates all the time, he can wait. Take me home."

51. That Was A Close Call

Jools ran into the toilet and pulled back the shower curtain.
"You absolute gobshite, Robert McKenna! Do you think he wouldn't find you behind the shower curtain? I told you coming here was a mistake!"

"Ah, now, Jools, you only told me that after I came. I was already here when you said it. And if I'd left then, they might have seen me walking home and anyways, I can't go home, Freddie's got that little McCarthy bollix watching the gaff. He thinks nobody notices him, but he sticks out like a pimple would on that fine, porcelain arse of yours."

"Fuck off, Robbo, I'm seriously annoyed with you!"

"Ah, come on now, Jools, please, I'll sort this out."

"Robbo, he had a fuckin shotgun! Do you think he came here just for a chat?"

Robbo thought for a second and said, "Well, no, I know why he came here and I reckon even if I do get all the money together, he's still gonna kneecap me."

Jools put her head down, once again thinking this was all her fault and replied, "No. No, Robbo, he's not just gonna kneecap you. He's gonna kill you." She began to cry.

Still standing in the bath, he tried to put his arm around her shoulders to comfort her, slipped, grabbed the shower curtain and fell out of the bath on top of her, the curtain ripping off the rings and covering them both. They burst out laughing. Suddenly the door flew open. Gaz stood there. He now had a wig on to go with his frameless glasses and in his best Peter Sellers a la What's New Pussycat voice he said, "Svines! Get out of my office!"

They pulled off the curtain and when they saw him, both looked at each other and burst out laughing again.

Sean stood at the kitchen counter, nursing a can. When they came back in, he said, "That was a close call, bud. If Luke and his army mates hadn't been here, we'd be scraping bits of you off the walls."

Robbo looked over at the blonde, still snoring in the corner, shrugged and sighed.

"So," Sean said, "what are you gonna do?"

Robbo thought for a second and looked at Jools, Sean and then over at the sleeping blonde.

"England, I reckon. I don't think I've any other choice now. Freddie won't stop till he finds me. How the fuck did I lose that money?"

Sean looked at Robbo, his face screwed up in thought.

"What?" Robbo said. "What is it?"

"I dunno," Sean said. "Are you sure you lost it?"

"Well I don't have it. It's missing. I must have. Wallet and all gone. Fell out of my pocket somewhere. Why?"

"Dosser."

"Nah, he's a prick but I don't think even he's that bad. What makes you say that?"

"Well, he was outside the TV Club tonight on a new scooter, and all dressed up in new clothes. Dosser's a Penneys Mod. He was wearing good gear tonight. Proper stuff. That shit doesn't come cheap."

"He won on the horses."

"What?" Sean said, turning in the direction of a bloke standing by the fridge. "What did you say?"

Marty, a Mod from Belfast, who'd been living in Dublin for a few years said, "Dosser got the money from a win on the horses. Fifteen hundred or something. Niall was talking to him outside the TV Club tonight, asked Dosser what granny he did over to get those new clothes and Dosser said he won the money. Some yankee thing or something. Showed Niall the betting slip, he said it looked legit."

"There you go," Robbo said. "It wasn't Dosser."

"Maybe he didn't rob your wallet, Robbo, sorry, I couldn't help overhearing, and trust me, I won't say anything, but he did rob something. That scooter he was on looked a lot like Will McNeil's one and if it is, whatever trouble you're mixed up in with Freddie Collins will make what he does to you look like a playground punch up compared to what Dosser gets. Will McNeil is Billy McNeil's son."

All three looked at Marty with blank faces.

"Billy McNeil is a big shot in the UVF. I mean, really, really big. He makes Freddie Collins look like a schoolboy."

"Freddie Collins does look like a schoolboy," Jools said, laughing.

"I'm serious, Jools," Marty said. "I know a lot of people up north, not in that way," he added quickly, "I'm not into any of that shit, but people know people who know people, if you get my drift and some of the stuff I've heard about Billy…. Jesus." He shuddered. "Dosser needs to be more careful. If he did rob that scooter and Billy finds out, he's fucked."

"Do you think we should say something to him?" Jools asked.

"Say what?" Sean replied. "We can't come straight out and ask him if he robbed the scooter."

"Knowing Dosser," Robbo said, "he'll deny it anyway, say it's just a coincidence."

"If that is Will McNeil's scooter," Marty said, "the best place for Dosser is sitting on the boat next to you."

The blonde in the corner fluttered her eyelids, stretched and stood up. "Robbo," she said, "where did you go?"

"I didn't go anywhere," he replied, "you went to sleep."

She stumbled, smiled and put her arms around his shoulders

252

and said, "I'm awake now."

"And about time we got you home," he said. "Tracey, you're still drunk and you'll be in a heap in the morning. Tomorrow night, you'll be grand then, as long as you don't overdo it before the allnighter."

"What do you mean, tomorrow night?" Sean asked, not believing what he'd just heard. "Robbo, please don't tell me you're thinking of going?"

"Why wouldn't I go?"

"Because Freddie will assume you are, and he'll kill you!" Sean said, his voice rising.

"He's right," Jools said and, not thinking, added, "and I'll have enough to worry about with Lainey and Matt without adding you to the list."

"What about Lainey and Matt?" Robbo asked.

"Yeah," Sean said, "what's up with them?"

Jools looked at Tracey, who raised her hands, shrugged and said, "Wha da fug do I know?"

"Eh, Lainey just said that they were going to Matt's brother's housewarming and they'd be late arriving and was worried they wouldn't get in. That's all. I was just worried they might not."

"The bouncers know the both of them years," Sean said. "If the two of them turned up, buckled drunk and said they'd lost their tickets, they'd still get in."

"I suppose," was all Jools could think to say. "I'd better see if Cyn is back, we should get going."

She walked out of the kitchen, feeling like she was trying to juggle a bunch of plates. Robbo, Lainey, Matt, Jimmy, come to think of it, and worried about which or how many she might drop.

She went back into the front room. She looked at her watch, it was after three and the place had emptied out. Don and Cyn were back. She was sitting on his knee on the couch with her face superglued to his. There goes my lift home, she thought as she turned and walked back into the kitchen.

Robbo and Sean were standing in silence, drinking from their cans.

"Where's Tracey?" She asked and then heard loud retching noises coming through the open back door.

Robbo nodded in that direction, shrugging.

"So, Robbo," she said, "what's the plan?"

"What do you mean?"

"That psycho is gonna keep looking for you till he finds you and whatever's left of you, he'll nail to a tree, at the very least. Forget the allnighter, you need to be on a boat in the morning."

"No. Look, I have to go away, we all know that but if I do, I want one last night out with my mates before I have to disappear. Is that too much to ask?"

"It is if it gets you killed," Sean said.

"It won't. There's no way Freddie's gonna come to Bubbles waving around a shotgun. The bouncers know who he is, and they wouldn't let him in. He might frighten some people, but not them. I heard once he tried to recruit them and was told to fuck off. Not just no, actually told to fuck off."

"Do they know you work for him?" Jools asked.

"Are you mental? They don't tolerate drugs in the club. Fuck, if they found out I was dealing for Freddie, they'd break my legs themselves. Anyway, I never sell anything in the club itself, I wouldn't do that. What if a Guard was undercover or something and saw me and the place was shut down? I don't want a few hundred angry Mods coming after me. Fuck no! I'd prefer whatever Freddie had in store for me to that!"

Don and Cyn came into the kitchen. He had a smile on his face that wouldn't have looked out of place on a Cheshire Cat and lipstick all over his neck. She had lipstick smeared up the side of her left cheek.

"Eh, Cyn," Jools said, "you've a little bit of lipstick there."

"Where?" Cyn asked, touching her mouth.

"Just there," Jools said, moving Cyn's finger up and up and further up.

Cyn ran out to the mirror in the hall, "Ah, bollix, it's all over me!"

Don smiled that enormous grin again and said, "Where's Chris and Stevey?"

"Stevey went upstairs as soon as he got here and never came down," Sean said, "and Chris left about an hour ago to walk Susan home and he never came back."

"Right then," Don said, "do ye all want a lift home?"

Tracey came staggering back into the kitchen, grabbed a tea towel and wiped her mouth.

Robbo put his arm around her waist and Don said, "If she's coming, she'd better not puke in the car."

Robbo looked at Tracey and said, "I'd better ask Gaz if we can borrow a bucket."

52. Respect

Saturday morning at ten o'clock. George sat in a chair beside the door of Freddie's office, pretending to read the paper, but looking over the top of it at his boss, with some concern. He'd seen Freddie go off on one before but never like this. Competitors were always nipping at his heels and he'd put every one of them down like, as Freddie had said, the little pups that they were. He just couldn't understand what it was about the Robbo situation that was getting under his skin. Three grand sure was a lot of money, but he'd been with Freddie at Cheltenham when he'd lost ten times that and shrugged it off, so it couldn't be the money. He looked up from his paper. No surreptitious look this time. He closed the paper and looked directly at Freddie, who was sitting at his desk, looking at the flyer for the allnighter in front of him. He'd circled 8pm with a biro and was circling the time over and over.

"Boss?" George said, cautiously. Freddie didn't answer. George coughed and a little louder, said, "Boss, are you okay?" Freddie looked up from the flyer and over to George, like he was seeing him sitting there for the first time. He blinked and shook his head, as if clearing it.

"What? Yeah, George, I'll be fine as soon as I get this business sorted."

"Boss," George said again, anxiously, "what is it? I mean, yeah, it's three grand and that's a lot of money but I've seen you lose thirty at the track and not even blink, so it can't be the money. What is it about all this that's affecting you so badly?"

Freddie sat back in his chair and looked at George for what must have been the longest and most unsettling ten seconds of his life. He knew that with one phone call or a snap of his fingers, the other lads that he had working for him would happily take him out with not so much as a first thought, let alone a second. He felt sweat running down his back. Freddie finally spoke.

"Respect, George, respect."

"Respect?" George repeated, and noticed the shake in his voice.

"That's right," Freddie said, "or lack of, which is more to the point. That little prick, Robbo has welched with three grand of *my* money and is runnin around Dublin like he's Billy Big Bollocks, flauntin it, throwin it in me face. And as for Seany boy and his two little tarts, I bet they're all havin a good old laugh at Freddie. Lookin down on me. Well, Seany's been holdin that army mates thing like a fuckin shield against me for too long. Wouldn't sell me gear at his gigs? Who the fuck does he think he is? By the time I'm done with all of them, George, that whole bunch of laughin cunts will know what it's like when they're goin into a woodchipper and they won't be fuckin laughin when they watch their fuckin feet disappear. But them two bitches, I'll make sure the pair of them hurt more than the others. I'm gonna do everythin I can fuckin think of to them until they can't fuckin bleed anymore. I'll fuck them so hard they'll be beggin me to kill them." Freddie laughed a cold, chilling laugh and said, matter of fact, "And I don't even like girls, but I'm gonna enjoy this. They'll be beggin me for mercy. No cunt looks down on or laughs at Freddie Collins. No. Cunt."

George just stared at him. He wasn't going red, he was calmer than he'd ever seen him before and that's what frightened George the most. Fuck me, he thought, he's finally, completely lost it. I'm too old for this shite. When all this Robbo business is done, I'm gone. Nice little bar in the Canary Islands or someplace like that. Someplace where it's always warm.

"George." Freddie's voice raised him from his musings.

"Yes, Boss?"

"You got Dosser's number?"

"Yeah," George said, "it's in my book. I think it's in yours too."

"Right, right," Freddie said. "Get him on the blower for me, would ya? And after that, tell Conn to come in, I've a little job for his yunfella."

George flicked through his book and dialled the number,

handing the phone to Freddie. After a couple of rings, Dosser's Mam answered.

"Hello?"

"Hello, Missus.... eh...." Freddie looked up at George, but he just shrugged, mouthing, "Doherty, I think."

Freddie spoke into the phone again. "Hello, sorry, can I speak to Dosser please?"

"His name is not Dosser, it's Graham!"

"Sorry, Graham, yeah, can I speak to Graham please?"

"Who's calling?"

"Tell him it's Robbo," he said, covering the mouthpiece, giggling. George stared at him again, his stomach gave a quick lurch. Freddie was losing it.

"Okay," she said, "I'll get him now, he's still in bed."

Freddie heard the sound of the phone being put down, probably on a table or something, he thought and, again, covering the mouthpiece, said to George, "Go out and tell Conn to come in! Do I have to fuckin tell ya twice?"

"No problem. Sorry, Boss," he said, walking towards the door, glad to be getting out of the office for even a minute or two. He looked back as he opened the door, Freddie has his chair pulled right up to the desk, cradling the phone between his left ear and shoulder and was fidgeting with his desk drawer. He pulled out the shotgun and put it on the desk in front of him, pulling the hammers and letting them click on empty chambers. When they got to the office that morning, George had taken the shells out of the gun and the very fact that Freddie was letting the hammers close on empty chambers worried him more than anything else so far, because Freddie hadn't seen him take the shells out. He hoped to God that Freddie had checked the gun himself and knew it was empty, or he'd completely lost it.

Mrs Doherty went up to Dosser's bedroom , knocked and opened the door.

"Jesus, Graham, it stinks in here," she said and yanked open the curtains and opened the window, "let some air in, for God's sake!"

"Ah, Ma," Dosser complained, "it's the crack of bleedin dawn, what are you wakin me for?"

"You're wanted on the phone," she said, "and it's not the crack of bleedin dawn, as you say with your filthy mouth, it's after ten."

"Who wants me?" He asked her, rubbing sleep out of his eyes with one hand and scratching his balls with the other.

"Some fella called Robbo."

He sat straight up. Oh shit, he thought. He knows it was me. The bettin slip didn't work. Oh fuck. If he tells Freddie, I'm fuckin dead. I can't even fuckin swim!

"Graham!" Mrs Doherty said to him. "Don't leave the chap waiting."

He pulled back the blankets and threw his legs over the edge of the bed and stood up, in nothing but his yellowed, piss stained Y-fronts. His Mam looked at him with disgust.

"And for God's sake put your dressing gown on make sure you have a shower! And throw those God awful things in the bin!"

He just waved her away and pulled the dressing gown off the hook on the back of the door and trundled down the stairs to the hall. He picked up the phone.

"He.... hello?"

"Hello, Dosser."

"What? This isn't Robbo. Who's this?"

"Don't you recognise my voice.... Graham," Freddie said, a menacing little chuckle in his voice.

By now, George had returned to the office with Conn, who, hearing Freddie on the phone and seeing his fingers fidgeting with the gun, looked at George, puzzled and questioningly shrugged, mouthing, "What the fuck?" George shook his head and mouthed back to Conn, "Don't ask."

Dosser held the phone to his ear and struggled to think who, if not Robbo would be ringing him and saying they were him. And then it clicked. He recognised the voice and he sat, almost fell onto the bottom step and said, "S.... s.... sorry.... M....

Mister C…. Collins…. I…. d…. didn't recognise ya there for a second."

"Ah, you're grand," Freddie said, "I was just playin a little joke on ya."

"T…. thanks," was all Dosser could think of to say. And then something occurred to him.

"M…. Mister Collins…. how do ya know me phone number?"

"Now, Dosser," Freddie, said, laughing, "I'm Freddie Collins. I've got everyone's number. All the thievin little fuckers from Dublin One to Dublin Twenty Four, I have all yisser numbers in a lovely little black book. Ya know, just in case I need to have a chat with one of yis. Now, shut the fuck up and tell me somethin. Are ya goin to this moddy thing tonight?"

Dosser was confused. For about ten seconds he had images of himself being thrown into Dublin Bay strapped to a breeze block and Freddie standing on the deck saying to George, "No need for two, George, one will be enough for that skinny little cunt."

Freddie raised his voice and Dosser had to hold the phone away from his ear.

"Are ya still fuckin there, Dosser?"

"Eh, yes, sorry Fred, I mean Mister Collins. The allnighter? Do you mean the allnighter? In Bubbles, like?"

"The very one," Freddie said, almost jovially.

"Eh, yeah, I am, M…. Mister Collins. Why?"

"Do ya have a ticket? It says on the flyer that it's ticket only."

"Yeah, I have a ticket. Why do you wanna know if I have a ticket?"

"I'll buy it off ya," Freddie said. "How much do ya want for it? Says here they're five quid. How about I give ya twenty?"

Dosser didn't know what the hell was going on. A million things rushed through his head at once, none of them good.

"Sorry, Mister Collins, did ya say ya want to buy me allnighter ticket off me?"

"Are ya fuckin deaf?" Did I not just say that?"

"But, you're not a Mod," was all he could think to say, his brain scrambling to catch up with what was going on and failing miserably.

"Why would ya want to go to a Mod allnighter?"

"Who's asking the fuckin questions here, ya prick?"

"Eh, you are M…. Mister C…. Collins."

"That's right. Now, I'm gonna give ya an address where me office is, and I want ya to come here. When can ya be here by?"

"I dunno, I…. an hour maybe?"

"If you're not here in thirty minutes, I'll cut your bollocks off. Now, here's the address."

Freddie gave him the address and hung up.

Dosser held the receiver at arm's length and stared into the mouthpiece, like something was going to come out of it and bite him.

He knows, he thought. This is a trick. He's gonna kill me when I get there cos he knows I robbed the money.

The thought of escape, regardless of the amount of money he had stashed away in the Dansette upstairs and with that, an opportunity to get as far away from Freddie as possible, never occurred to him. He slowly dragged himself up the stairs. With each step, another thought about what was happening. By the time he got to the door of his bedroom, he'd come to the amazingly astute, for him, and unknowingly accurate conclusion that if Freddie knew he'd taken the money, his living room would be on fire and he'd already be in the back of a van.

What the fuck is goin on? He thought to himself.

53. Sitting In The Big Chair

Freddie hung up the phone.

"Dosser's coming *here*?" George said.

"Yep."

"You gave that little prick the address to our place? Are you…." and here, he caught himself just in time. He was about to finish the sentence with, "fucking mental?" But had the savvy to complete it with, "sure?"

"Our place?" Freddie looked at George with cold eyes.

"Our place, George? What the fuck do ya mean, 'Our place?' Is your name over the fuckin door?"

"Eh, no, Boss, sorry," George said. "Collins and Son, it says. Even though you don't, like have a son."

"Fuckin semantics!" Freddie screamed. Then he lowered his voice, almost to a whisper and said, "You're gettin a bit too familiar with me lately. Puttin your hand on me, questionin me decisions. Ya wouldn't be looking to sit in the big chair, now, would ya?"

The thought that flashed through George's mind was, I'd need a bigger fucking chair if I did.

"No, Boss, course not. I just meant that he's a thieving little cunt and if he knows where we, I mean, you work from, he could tell all his other thieving mates and then…." he trailed

266

off.

Freddie laughed, like he'd just heard the best joke ever and said, "Do ya honestly think that little prick would steal from me? He must know that would be the biggest mistake of his short fuckin life. Jaysus, George, we'd only need one breeze block for that skinny, little cunt."

He roared again with laughter at this. Conn made the obligatory chuckle, but George just smiled a humourless smile and thought again of The Canary Islands.

"Now, Conn," Freddie said, "your boy Archie, he's done the odd few jobs for me from time to time, hasn't he?"

"Eh, yeah, Boss, he has," Conn replied. "Why?"

"Can he do a job for me this evenin? Tonight, like?"

"Eh, he's kinda studying for his exams next week, Boss."

"Conn," Freddie said, letting out a deep, exasperated sigh, "I think ya misunderstand me. I asked ya can he do a job for *me* this evenin? For *me*, Conn. Ya know, *me*, the chap that pays your fuckin wages? *Me*, Conn. Can Archie do a job for *ME*? That's what ya call a rhetorical question. So, basically, sunshine, I don't give a flyin fuck if Archie is studying for his fuckin master's degree in biochemical nuclear fuckin science, he's doin a job for me tonight! Now do ya understand?"

"Sure, Boss," Conn said, shakily. "He'll be only happy to."

Freddie looked at Conn, steel eyes boring into him. "And *you*?

267

Will *you* be only happy for Archie to do a little job for me tonight?"

"Absolutely, Boss, of course. Anything at all."

"Right then. Happy that's all cleared up. Go home and get him.

54. Just The Ticket

Dosser was in two minds whether to take the scooter or not but weighing getting to Freddie's garage in thirty minutes over being asked questions about where he got the money to buy a new scooter, well, it was no contest. He could lie about the scooter but was far too attached to his bollocks to have them removed for being late.

He was outside the garage in twenty. He put the scooter on the stand around the side, out of sight and they could assume he got there some other way. He'd think of something if they saw it and asked.

The shutters were down. The shutters were always down. No cars were ever serviced in this garage. He knocked on the door and after a couple of seconds, noticed there was a bell. He pressed the button and waited. After about a minute of him standing there, while fumbling with the allnighter ticket in his jacket pocket, George opened the door.

"Howaya," Dosser said, as calmly as he could, but he still couldn't mask the nerves in his voice.

George stepped out and pulled the door over, not shutting it, but closed enough so he couldn't be heard inside.

"When you go in there, answer everything he asks you, don't be a smart arse and don't give him any fucking lip. Trust me, he's not in the humour."

"Am I in trouble?" Dosser was now shaking so much his teeth were chattering. There was no disguising his nerves.

"No, you're not," George said. "Why would you be?"

Dosser wasn't prepared for this.

"I…. don't know. It's just," he looked around, "I've never been asked to come here before."

"Look," George replied, "don't worry, you're not. He wants that ticket off you and just couldn't be arsed driving out to you to get it. That's all."

"Oh, okay, that's fine then," Dosser said, still a bit unsure.

George opened the door.

"Go on in and remember, no fucking lip."

They walked across the garage floor, through stacks of pallets. Dosser's eyes widened at the contents. There must have been thousands of two hundred quantity packets of cigarettes on the pallets and there were even more pallets with brown bricks wrapped in cellophane. Bricks of hash the size of house bricks, he realised.

George caught his look, that wide eyed gaze.

"All of this, you didn't see, there's nothing here. You don't tell any of your mates about it, you tell no one, do you hear?"

"Jaysus," Dosser replied, "do ya think I'm fuckin mental?"

"There's that lip that'll get you into trouble," George said, "and no, I don't think you're mental, but I do think you're a thieving little shit with very little sense. So shut the fuck up and get up them stairs to the office."

They climbed the stairs and George stopped outside the door to the office and said, "Wait here."

He opened the door and stuck his head in.

"Boss, Dosser's here."

"Show him in, George. Don't leave the poor chap standing out there like nobody's child."

George turned back to Dosser and said, "Remember what I told you, no fucking lip."

He nodded, and George held the door open for him.

He walked in and quickly took in his surroundings, in case he needed an escape route if this all went sideways. George followed him and closed the door, the click of it shutting sounded very loud in his ears.

On the left, against the wall, was a set of filing cabinets, which was where George perched himself, elbow on the top. Next to the door was a chair. One of those plastic things, with steel legs. On the right was a couch that took up most of that wall and right in front of him was an enormous desk that filled most of the back wall. To the right of the desk was a big, black safe, with a faded gold coloured dial. In front of the safe was one of those stand up coat and hat racks that he'd only ever seen on the telly. There was a black suit jacket hanging on the rack, Freddie's, he assumed, because he didn't have one on. It suddenly occurred to Dosser that this was the first time he'd ever seen him without his suit jacket. There was one way in and one way out of this room and he'd just walked through it. Freddie was sitting behind the desk. An IN / OUT tray was on one side and a phone and a photo frame on the other, but it faced him, so Dosser couldn't see who was in it. He wondered who Freddie, an absolute fuckin nutcase who loved nobody but himself, could love enough to put in a picture frame on his desk and assumed that it was probably just a picture of himself. Then he saw the gun in the middle, sitting on top of the Bubbles flyer. The gun was, thankfully, facing towards the couch and away from Dosser, but he was still petrified, nonetheless.

"Come on in, Graham," Freddie announced, "so happy to see you. Would you like a cup of tea? Sit yourself down, take the weight off." He gestured towards the couch. "George, will you go downstairs to the kitchen and make Graham a cup of tea, please?"

Jesus, Dosser thought, noticing the change in his voice. This didn't sound like the scary Freddie he spoke to on the phone earlier, he sounds like a fuckin game show host!

"Eh, no, thanks, Mister Collins, I'm not a big tea drinker and," he said, looking at the couch and the barrels pointing in its direction, "I think I'd prefer to stand."

"Sit the fuck down," Freddie said, menace returning to his voice. "I'm not gettin a creak in me neck lookin up at a prick like you in me own fuckin office."

Freddie's complete change of tone left Dosser in absolutely no doubt that the wisest thing to do in his current predicament, was to sit the fuck down.

He shuffled over to the couch, head down and went to sit at the end farthest from Freddie and closest to the door.

Freddie tutted and Dosser looked up and saw him shaking his head. He gestured to the other end, closest to the desk and Dosser moved in the indicated direction and sat, sinking right into it.

The couch was deceivingly low, his knees came almost up to his chest and put him in direct eyeline with both barrels of the gun.

He could see the photo in the frame now and it was Freddie, posing with some cup, with horses in the background. "Prick," Dosser muttered, too low for anyone to make out. He got the shock of his life when Freddie said, "What was that?"

"Eh, nothing, Mister Collins," he replied, quickly. "Sick, I said. I mean, I just said I feel sick."

Freddie smiled and Dosser wilted under his gaze. Nobody had

ever looked at him liked that.

"Why would you be feeling sick, now, Graham?" He asked him, the game show host returning.

Dosser hesitated a second. "I was out last night. I musta drank too much."

This whole Graham thing was scaring him something rotten.

"Never touch the stuff myself, Graham. Teetotal, me. I have absolutely no vices. Only good, clean living. Isn't that right, George?"

George nodded and just said, "Absolutely."

Dosser hadn't got a clue what the man was on about. He'd used a vice in woodwork in school, but why Freddie was telling him that he didn't have any, was completely beyond him. No matter what George had said to him outside, he knew he was up shit creek. Nobody was told to come to Freddie's office for a fuckin chat that was ever, just a fuckin chat. He knew he wasn't the smartest bloke around, but he wasn't that stupid.

Freddie just sat there, staring at him. He put his left hand on the gun barrel and his right hand on the hammers. Dosser stared into the two, black holes, both so dark and wondered would it be that dark at the bottom of Dublin Bay. He gulped. His mouth had gone completely dry and he got a cramp in his stomach. He closed his eyes for a second, praying he could just get out of there. He opened them again. Freddie was still staring at him, hands on the gun.

He pulled back the hammers, cocking both. Dosser stared at the gun, wide eyed and trembling.

Freddie moved his hand from the hammers to the triggers. Dosser followed the movement of his fingers.

He pulled the triggers. *Click. Click. Ring.*

As both hammers clicked on the empty chambers, the doorbell rang, and Dosser jumped. Surprisingly, he neither pissed nor shit himself and for that, alone, he closed his eyes and thanked God.

When he opened his eyes, Freddie was still staring at him, still smiling, but Dosser noticed there was no humour in that smile. For a fleeting moment, he regretted not handing Robbo back his wallet. If he'd done that, maybe he wouldn't be sitting here with the craziest fuck he'd ever met in his entire life.

Freddie looked up at George.

"George, that'll be Conn and his yunfella. Go down and let them in. Why the fuck he didn't use his keys, I'll never know."

George nodded, turned and went out of the office.

Freddie stood up, put his hands in his trouser pockets and walked over to stand in front of Dosser. He looked down at the now shaking kid looking up at him and thought, you're maybe just a tad too old, and I do like a bony little arse like yours, but if it was the last arse on the planet, I'd rather put me dick in a fuckin mincin machine before I'd let it touch you, ya filthy little cunt.

"Ticket," he said.

Dosser looked up, confused.

"What?"

"The ticket, ya moron! Why the fuck else would your pox ridden filthy fuckin arse be sittin in me office right now if I didn't need that ticket?"

The words settled into Dosser's brain. The ticket. All he wants is the fuckin ticket. Jesus fuckin Christ, he only wants the ticket.

"Come on, prick, I haven't got all day," Freddie said, clicking his fingers.

Dosser pulled the ticket out of his pocket and handed it over. Freddie looked down at the dog eared and grubby thing in his hand and said, "What the living fuck is this?"

"That's the ticket."

"Dosser," Freddie said and, with having reverted to his nickname, Dosser breathed a sigh of relief, "you are, I was about to say, 'possibly,' but no. You are *the* most disgusting cunt I have ever had the misfortune to clap eyes on. I've had some right grubby shit in me hands over the years, but this takes the fuckin biscuit. It's filthy. What the fuck did ya do to it?"

"Eh, n…. nothin…. Fr…. I mean, Mister Collins."

Freddy shuddered.

"I dread to think."

He pulled his wallet from the back pocket of his trousers, took a twenty out and threw it at Dosser.

"Now get the fuck out of me office and," he said, taking another twenty out and throwing that down too, "invest in some fuckin soap, ya dirty little pox bottle. Honestly, Dosser, if I ever need your help again and we have to meet, ya better be fuckin clean." Freddie looked over his shoulder and nodded towards the gun. "Or them chambers won't be fuckin empty and the only thing we'll have to worry about cleanin, is your tiny little brain off me office wall. Now get the fuck out! Oh, just one more thing. Where do them moddy boys get their clothes?"

"What? Oh, eh, Button Down, a shop on Parnell Street," Dosser said, as he struggled to rise out of the low couch. He fell back in, but eventually got to his feet, stumbling. Freddie kicked him in the arse, sending him sprawling towards the door that George had left open. He smacked his forehead off the edge, causing a small gash and sprawled on the floor just as George stepped in. He'd gotten about two thirds of the way down the stairs when he saw Conn open the garage door.

"He found his keys, Boss," he said to Freddie and noticed the prostrate kid at his feet. He grabbed him under the arms, saying, "You done with him?"

Freddie said nothing, just waved a hand indicating he was.

"Okay, Boss, I'll see him out then."

"Make sure you wash them hands after handling that filthy little bollix."

George pulled the dazed Dosser out the door and whispered, "Remember, son, you were never here, you know nothing, you saw nothing."

Dosser, tears in his eyes, spilling out onto his cheeks, just nodded.

They got to the bottom of the stairs and passed Conn and Archie, who were standing to one side. Conn looked at George, fear for his boy evident on his face. George returned the look, shaking his head.

He brought Dosser outside and said, "For some reason, Freddie has taken a real disliking to you, son, so, if you can, stay out of his way as much as possible."

"George," Dosser said, tears and snot now streaming down his face, "the gun. I thought it was loaded. I thought he was gonna kill me."

George, not thinking, said, "Not you, it wasn't meant for you, but Robbo's a dead man."

Realising what he'd just said, he grabbed Dosser by the shirt front, lifting him off the ground. Their noses were actually touching as George said, "You open your fucking mouth about that to anyone, and I'll kill you myself."

"I won't! I won't! I promise. That's what he wants the ticket for. He's not mad enough to walk into Bubbles with a shotgun and blow Robbo away in front of everyone. Is he?"

George put him down.

"No, he's not, but that's none of your concern. Just get the fuck out of here."

As frightened by everything that had just happened as Dosser was, and with what he knew was about to happen, his greedy little mind couldn't help but see an opportunity.

"If he kills Robbo, who's gonna sell his gear at the Mod nights?"

George looked at him, dumbfounded.

"You horrible little cunt! I swear to Jesus, if I ever see you again, I'll rip your fucking head off!" He went in the door of the garage, slamming it behind him.

Dosser stood for a few seconds, staring at the closed door and then walked around the side of the building to where he'd parked the scooter, bent over beside it and puked. He stood up, wiping his mouth on his sleeve and then felt an unmerciful urge to piss, so whipped it out, there and then and pissed on the side of the garage wall. An old woman pulling a shopping trolley walked by on the other side of the fence and, noticing him, called over, "You dirty little boy! If Mister Collins knows you're urinating on the side of his building, he'll be very annoyed."

Dosser didn't stop pissing and turned completely around, so she could see his dick and shouted at her while he waved it, piss flying everywhere, "Take a good look missus and then mind your own fuckin business, ya nosey aul cunt!"

Finished, he put it back in, zipped up, pulled the helmet on and drove out onto the main road.

55. Do You Know This Place?

Archie walked into the office and sat down on the arm of the couch. He'd been there before. Nobody ever sat on the couch if they could help it. The gun was gone from the desk.

Conn leaned against the filing cabinet, George sat in the chair beside the door and Freddie was back sitting behind the desk. He lifted up the flyer and waved it towards Archie.

"Do ya know this place?"

Archie walked over to the desk, took the flyer and looked at it.

"Yeah, it's around the corner from The Apartments. All the Mods go there."

"I want ya to go tonight."

Archie looked back down at the flyer and then up at Freddie.

"You want me, to go here, tonight?"

Freddie turned to Conn.

"Is everyone fuckin deaf today?"

Conn shrugged.

"Archie, son," Freddie said, "there'll be a bloke there tonight that I want to talk to. I want ya to go in there and get him to come out. Simple job."

"How am I gonna do that, Freddie? I'm not a Mod, I don't know anyone in there. Jaysus, I don't even have the clothes. I'll stick out like a sore thumb. Why's he just gonna walk out of the club with me? He's not a queer, is he? I don't have to try and get off with him, do I? I can't do anything like that, Freddie, I'm not into any of that queer shit."

Freddie's face began to redden and Conn, knowing about Freddie's preferences, and it now being obvious that Archie didn't, thought, no, Robbo's not queer and neither is Freddie. What he is, is a vile, disgusting piece of shit that preys on kids and if he ever even looked at you that way…..

Conn spoke, so Archie didn't see his boss's rage or embarrassment.

"No, son, he's not…. like that. You don't have to do anything like that. It's just a small job. Simple in and out." He looked at Freddie again while Archie was still looking at him.

Freddie's face had returned to normal.

"What's the plan, Boss?"

Freddie took a deep breath and turned back to Archie.

"There's this bloke called Robbo. Everyone knows him in there and he's always hangin round with a bloke called Sean. Them two are joined at the hip. Ya find one, ya find the other. Ya go in, ask anyone where Robbo is and when ya find him, start a fight with him. The bouncers come, ya both get fucked out and then we grab him, and I have that chat with him. Easy peasy, lemon squeezy. And for that little bit of work, I'll give ya a ton. What do ya say?"

Archie looked at his dad, who shrugged.

"Says here it's ticket only."

Freddie reached over to where the ticket was beside the phone and lifted it up, waving it.

The grubby card flopped over, it was that grimy. He handed the ticket to Archie, who reluctantly took it.

"I'd be amazed if I get in with this," he said. "It's so fuckin dirty, you can barely see the writing. Anyway, I can't wear these clothes." He pulled at his T-Shirt to emphasise his point.

Freddie looked him up and down, opened the same drawer where the shotgun was, reached in and pulled out a roll of cash. He threw it at Conn, who caught it, barely moving from his position.

"Take the lad down to that Button Down place and get him kitted out. He has to look the part."

56. The Smell Of Two Stroke

Dosser stopped the scooter outside Mrs Malone's house, pulled it up onto the stand and revved it hard, so the air filled with smoke and he breathed it in.

"Nothin like the smell of two stroke," he said to a passing kid who looked like a miniature Robert Smith. The Goth kid looked him up and down and responded with, "Fuck off, ya mod prick."

Dosser was delighted. Someone had actually recognised him as a Mod and that never happened.

He turned the key, turning the engine off and walked up the driveway, a spring in his step. He didn't care that he hadn't got a ticket for the allnighter, he'd drive up on his new scooter and pose in the laneway, outside the entrance. New suit, new scoot, new Dosser. He rang the bell. The curtain twitched and after a few seconds, she answered, the suit on a hanger, covered in a dry cleaner bag.

"You cleaned it?"

"God, no," she replied, "I've loads of these bags in there, but I did give it a little press for you." She lifted the bag and carefully pulled one of the trouser legs out, showing him. "You could cut yourself off that crease, Graham," she said, with pride. "It's a grand job, even if I do say so myself."

"Yeah, Missus Malone, it looks deadly," he said, smiling. "What's the damage?"

"Ah, a tenner will do, son," she said, "and I'll throw in the second leg for free!" She burst out laughing at the joke, her huge bosom and jowls bouncing. Dosser watched, wondering if they'd ever stop moving. He pulled a ten pound note from his pocket and handed it over.

"Thanks, Missus Malone, I can't wait to wear it out tonight."

"You'll look really handsome, Graham. If I was ten years younger," she said, with a sigh.

In a rare moment of quick wittedness, he replied, "Missus Malone, if you were ten years younger, I'd only be eight!" They both laughed at this and Dosser strode down the path to his scooter, suit hung over his shoulder, feeling like a million dollars.

57. Give The Lad A break

On the way from Freddie's to town, Archie had been thinking. The plan wasn't going to work. Freddie had said that if he asked anyone, they'd tell him who Robbo was and so if everyone knew who Robbo was and nobody knew who he was, if he started a fight, he stood a good chance of getting the shite kicked out of him by Robbo's mates and the bouncers would probably just throw him out and not Robbo. The only way to get him outside, he thought, was with a bird and he thought of just the right one.

Archie knew Karen Flynn from school, and they'd hung around a bit from time to time, so he knew she was sound. Karen's sister used to be a Mod and if she still had all her old clothes, he might be able to get Karen to wear them and go with him and lure Robbo out. She was a cracker, after all, no way this Robbo bloke could resist. Now, if he could just figure out how to get her in without a ticket.

Conn pulled the car up outside Button Down and they both got out, but Archie said no. He didn't want to go in with his Da and look like a kid shopping for his Confirmation suit. He'd see what he could find himself and sure the shop owner could help him out. Conn said that was fine and handed him over the money.

"How much can I spend?"

"As much as you need," Conn replied. "I'd be surprised if Freddie even knows how much he threw at me and I doubt he's looking for change."

"Grand. I won't be long."

"Take your time, son, it's not like I've anything else to be doing."

Conn got back into the car and Archie went inside. He started to look through the suits and everything else that hung on the racks that covered every wall and discovered that he was a lot more impressed with the clothes than he expected to be. There was a nice style to them, he thought. The owner had music playing through the speakers in the shop and while he was there, three teenage Mods had come in, two blokes and a girl and were nodding along to the music, which Archie thought was pretty good too.

He liked the look of the girl. What was it they were called? Modettes? Wasn't that it? She was dressed in a Black skirt and had a cream jacket on with brown stripes on the collars and cuffs. Her hair was a bob, he thought it was called. He looked over at the lads, one was wearing tight, straight trousers in a lovely dark blue but not navy colour and a sky blue cycling shirt. He knew it was a cycling shirt from watching the Tour De France, but on this bloke, it looked cool as fuck. Then he saw the shoes. Fuck sake, he thought, they're bowling shoes! But they were black, not them mad colours you saw in the bowling alleys. Maybe this Mod thing wasn't so bad after all.

The other lad was wearing Levi's, a red and white striped shirt with buttons on the collars and some cream coloured boots with laces. Archie had never seen them before, but they looked alright. The lad with the cycling shirt saw him looking at them.

"Y'alright there, mate?"

"Yeah, grand," Archie said, awkwardly. "Just looking at that cycling shirt you got there. Where did you get it?"

"Over in London," he replied. "Place called Sherry's on Carnaby Street. All the Mods go there. The ones they have here are nice, but you don't wanna be wearing something everyone else has, know what I mean?"

"Eh, yeah," Archie replied, "that's important, like?"

"You only getting into it then?" Cycling Shirt asked.

Archie thought for a second and said, "Yeah, I used to go to The Apartments but when I saw all the Mods and Modettes dressed up, I thought, that's what I want."

"We're not Modettes!"

"What?" Archie said, looking at the girl.

"We're not fucking Modettes," she said. "There are Boy Mods and there are Girl Mods, just Mods. But, seeing as you're only getting into it, I'll let you slide this time."

"Jaysus, Emma," Cycling Shirt said, "give the lad a break."

"I just did," she replied and turned back to look through the rack of clothes on the opposite wall.

"Anyway," Striped Shirt said, "we are so much better dressed than them trendy pricks. And their music, for fuck sake. Karma Fuckin Chameleon! Jaysus."

The two Mods laughed, and Archie laughed awkwardly with them. Emma seemed like she hadn't even noticed.

Archie actually liked Culture Club but the music that was playing now, this was something else. It had an edge to it that he'd never heard before. He nodded to the speakers while looking through the trousers, noticing a pair that looked exactly the same as the ones Cycling Shirt was wearing. The tag said Sta-Prest – Petrol Blue.

"That music," he said, "that's brilliant. Who's is it?"

Striped Shirt answered him. "That's one of mine. The owner asked me to make a few tapes to play when customers were in, so I made that for him."

"That's you?" Archie said. "That's you playing! Like your band? That's brilliant!"

The two Mods laughed, and Striped Shirt replied, "No, you dope, it's my tape. I made the tape for the shop. That band is The Small Faces. The song is called Tin Soldier."

"Oh, right," Archie said, "I like that."

Cycling Shirt said, "Are you going to the allnighter tonight?"

"Yeah," Archie said, "that's the plan. I got a ticket off a mate that can't go, he has to work. Only thing is though, I couldn't get one for me bird and she really wants to go. Do you know anywhere I can get one?"

"Allison can't go."

Cycling Shirt turned to Emma. "What?"

"Allison can't go," she said. "She's after coming down with something. She rang me earlier. Said she's in bed, dying. Thinks it might be the flu. Said there's snot and phlegm all over the gaff."

"Lovely," Striped Shirt said. Emma ignored him.

"Anyway," she said, opening her bag, and after a quick rummage, pulled out a card and held it out to Archie. "I have her ticket. If you want it, it's yours."

Archie couldn't believe his luck.

"How much?"

"It's only a fiver," she said.

He pulled out the roll of money and they all exchanged glances.

"Tax back," he said quickly, pulling off a tenner and handing it to her.

"I don't have any change," she said.

"It's grand, keep it."

"Great, thanks," she said as she took the money and handed

over the ticket. "That'll get me a couple of drinks in the Three Lamps tonight, before we go to the allnighter. That's where a lot of the crowd will go first."

Archie smiled, things were going to plan but, having met these Mods and getting on so well with them, he felt a pang of guilt with the deception and he'd no idea who this Robbo bloke was, but whatever he'd done that Freddie wanted to "talk to him" so badly, well, Archie certainly didn't want Freddie talking to *him* about anything, no way. He'd been around that psycho long enough to know that didn't end well. Just get the job done and that'll be that.

He went back to the racks of clothes and noticed a jacket the same as the one Emma was wearing. He turned to her and said, "I thought this was a men's clothes shop?"

"It is."

He pulled on the sleeve of the jacket and held it out. "This is the same jacket you're wearing."

"So?"

"Is that not a girl's jacket?"

"Jesus," she said, "you've a lot to learn. No, it's called a Monkey Jacket. Both boys and girls wear them. Same with Harringtons and flight jackets. Told you, there's no Mods and Modettes, just Mods."

"So does that mean I can wear a skirt?" Cycling Shirt asked, laughing.

"You do, and you won't be going out with me anymore."

Archie looked down at Cycling Shirt's shoes.

"Where did you get them? They're the business."

"Simon Hart's, up on North Earl Street. Loads of nice shoes in there, but stay away from them Badger and Jam shoes, they're fuckin atrocious. Only the Tickets wear them."

"I've a pair of Jam shoes," Striped Shirt said. "And a pair of Badger shoes!"

"See what I mean?" Cycling Shirt said. "Fuckin Tickets."

Archie was just about to ask what a ticket, jam and badger shoes were, before Emma spoke.

"Leave him alone," she said. "Are you buying anything or what? I've still to get my hair done."

"I'll just take these Sta-Prest," Cycling Shirt told her and turning to Archie said, "nice meeting you, bud, see you there tonight and if you're buying a suit in here," he indicated a silver grey mohair one, "that looks the most expensive. But with that roll of money you have, you should be going to a tailor. Oh, and when you go to Simon Hart's, get yourself a pair of Loake's if you plan on wearing a suit. The bowling shoes are more for casual wear."

They said their goodbyes and went to the counter to pay,

leaving Archie to pick whatever he fancied off the rails. He was beginning to like this Mod business.

58. There's Nothing To Tell

Jools stood in Cyn's bedroom, looking at the mountain of clothes on her bed.

"Are you sure you've enough there, love?"

"I need two outfits for tonight," Cyn replied. "One I've never worn out before because, well, we can't be having anyone see me in something they have already, you know that and another for a change during the night after getting hot and sweaty shaking my fine little arse to the superb music of Mod, Ska and Northern Soul!"

"Speaking of shaking that fine little arse," Jools said, "how did it go with Don last night? You were superglued to his face when you got back."

"He's a lovely chap. I might see him again."

"How was the back seat of the Capri?"

"Adequately spacious," Cyn replied and they both started laughing.

"Is he coming tonight?" Jools asked her.

"He may be lucky enough to," Cyn said, tossing Jools a wink.

"Jesus, Cyn," Jools said, laughing, "sometimes with you it feels like being in a Carry On movie."

Cyn replied, "Do you like some inuendo, Jools? I like some in my endo!"

They both laughed and fell onto the mountain of clothes on the bed.

"I suppose you, Miss Perfect, has her outfits already chosen for tonight?" Cyn said.

"Hon, my outfits were picked thirty years ago!"

"Oh yeah, of course, only original Sixties stuff for you."

Jools just smiled. Maths was never Cyn's strong point.

Cyn rolled over so she was looking directly at Jools, their faces almost touching.

"You've got that strange look again."

Jools shook her head. "It's nothing. I'm just tired. Late one last night. You should know, you were there."

Cyn wasn't buying it.

"Jools, I know there's something up. You're the most carefree person I know, well, maybe not as carefree as me, but…."

Jools cut in. "There's a difference, Cynthia, between being carefree and just not giving a shite. You, my dear, most definitely fall into the latter category!"

"I know, I know," Cyn held her hands up, "but something's different. You're my best friend and since we were in town on Wednesday, you seem, I don't know, older? More responsible? I can't put my finger on it."

"I told you, Cynthia," and, waving her hands in front of her face said, in as spooky a voice as she could manage, "I'm from the future."

"Oh fuck off you and your Michael J Fox shite. Future, me arse." She laughed and then said, soberly, "If there was something wrong, you'd tell me, wouldn't you?"

Jools thought and said, "There's nothing to tell. There's isn't anything wrong. Okay, I'm worried about Robbo and this shite he's mixed up in with Freddie and I think he's mental to go to Bubbles tonight, but call it a feeling, I just think something really bad is gonna happen. I don't know what, I just do."

Cyn sat up and said, "Well, let's hope it doesn't. Come on, help me find something. That gorgeous BOAC bag I got last weekend is not going to fill itself!"

59. Suited And Booted

Archie sat in the car on the way home from town, looking out of the window and thinking about later, again. The bags from Button Down and Simon Hart's were on the back seat. There was still a good chunk on the roll of money, but he'd spent a fair bit. Two pairs of Sta-Prest, one pair of which were the petrol blue ones he saw, a red cycling shirt with red and white striped collar, three Ben Sherman shirts, one white, with red vertical stripes, the other sky blue with extremely thin, white pin stripes running through it, and the third a plain white Oxford, two pairs of Levi's, the same Monkey jacket he'd seen Emma wear, a black Fred Perry with twin tipped, white stripes and, of course, the silver grey mohair suit that was recommended. The owner was so delighted with the sale he threw in a couple of pocket squares and a dark grey with silver polka dot tie to go with the suit.

"Why are you giving me hankies?" Archie asked him.

"Young man," the owner said, "they are not hankies, they are pocket squares. No discerning gentleman wears a suit without one."

He laid one out on the counter – silk, in a shade of grey, almost identical to the tie, but without polka dots – and showed Archie how to fold it. He placed it in the breast pocket and stood back, hands clasped together at his chest, admiring his handiwork. Archie did agree that it gave the suit an extra splash of colour. The Simon Hart's bags contained a pair of black bowling shoes and after a discussion with the assistant about "What are Loake's?" and "I was told to steer clear of Badger and Jam shoes, but don't know what they are," the pin holed, tassled loafers were purchased too.

When the assistant showed him the Badger and Jam shoes, he agreed, yes, they were hideous. Both were black but the Badgers had a white stripe down the middle, from tongue to toe and stripes at the side whereas the Jam Shoes had the whole front of the shoe white, again from the tongue to the toe. He did like the look of the suede Chelsea Boots though, so a pair of them were added to the bill and suddenly, as far as he was concerned, Archie was a Mod.

"Dad, can you drop me off at Karen's on the way home?"

"The Flynn young one?"

"Yeah, I think I might need some help tonight. I've been thinking about it and I don't think Freddie's plan is gonna work. He might think the only way to sort things out is with violence and go in all guns blazing, but I don't."

Archie then explained why he thought this way and what he thought was the best way to get Robbo out of the club and so, a woman's touch was required.

"That's a better plan than Freddie's, I have to say. Do you think she'll do it?" Conn asked him.

"I reckon if I throw her a score and buy her a few drinks in the Three Lamps beforehand she might. It's a night out and she doesn't really have to do much. Chat him up, get him outside and then leg it. She won't even have to get off with him."

"Okay, you might be onto something, I'll drop you off."

60. You're Out Of Your Mind

Sean, Robbo and Jayo, sat in Sean's kitchen, drinking tea and eating his Mam's porter cake.

"Where's the butter?" Jayo asked.

"You're a sick fuck," Robbo said. "You're gonna ruin this fine lady's porter cake by putting butter on it? Jaysus, where did we get you from?"

"Have you tasted it with butter?"

"No, and I haven't tasted shite either, but I instinctively know it's not gonna taste nice."

"You two gobshites quit it," Sean said, "Jayo, just eat the fuckin cake. It's free. What do you want? Jam on it?"

"I can have jam too!"

"Enough of this bollocks," Sean said, laughing.

He turned to Robbo, with a serious look on his face, all the laughter gone in a flash.

"Robbo, you're mental. I don't know how many times I have to say it. If you think you can just waltz into Bubbles tonight and not end up dead by the morning, you're out of your mind."

Robbo shrugged.

"Look, same as I said last night. If I have to leave, I want one last night with everyone."

"And Tracey, if you haven't already," Jayo said.

"No, Jason, I haven't. I'm a gentleman."

"Yeah, right. If she hadn't been so wasted last night…. you might be lucky tonight though."

"Nah," Robbo said. "I rang her before you came around. She said she's not going, something about a stomach bug. Says it's coming out both ends. Said she'd love to go and it's a waste of a ticket, but she's in a heap."

"Maybe Freddie will buy it off her," Jayo said. "I reckon there's plenty of three button Communion suits knocking about that he could wear."

"Don't even fuckin joke about that," Robbo said, "I wouldn't put it past him."

"He wouldn't get in anyway. The bouncers would break him in half as soon as look at him," Sean said. Then, "So, what's the plan? Anvil first?"

"No way," Robbo said, "bad juju in that place now. That's where I got into this mess. Well, that's where I think I lost the money. Anyway, that's the first place he'll look if he is looking for me. No. Three Lamps. That place is gonna be heaving, he'd never see me."

"One door in, one door out," Sean said. "All he's gotta do is sit outside and wait."

"The allnighter starts at eight and I plan to be there as soon as them shutters go up," Robbo said. "It's the beginning of June, it'll be broad daylight and the place will be jammed with people we know, going in and out of that pub. He might be stupid enough to turn up at a party in the middle of the night in Donaghmede, but he's not stupid enough to lift me off the street in the middle of town."

"Good point," Sean said.

"I'm going. That suit cost me an arm and a leg and I'm gonna wear it to Bubbles at least once. No way it's that staying on that hanger."

"Okay, okay, you win," Sean said, holding his hands up in defeat. "We'll just have to make sure we keep an eye out for him."

"I'm going to Northside to get me hair cut," Jayo said. "are yis coming?"

"Have you been listening to any of this, Jayo?" Sean said. "He can't go traipsing round Northside Shopping Centre like he doesn't have a care in the world. And certainly not because you fancy the bird in Peter Mark's!"

"They do a better cut in Peter Mark's than they do in the barber's," Jayo protested. "She, I mean they know how I like it."

"You fuckin wish, Jayo," Robbo said.

61. No Good Samaritans

Jools went home after finally helping Cyn select two outfits for the night. What she herself was wearing was firmly stamped in her memory from the first time around and it was just the first outfit she'd brought that night. She'd never had a chance to wear the second. After the crash, everything stopped. There was a dead girl outside that everyone knew and suddenly, dancing wasn't important anymore.

Strangely enough, the dress she'd picked quite resembled what she'd been wearing on the night she was hit by the car in 2015. That was a navy dog tooth dress, this one was white, with black checks. She thought about picking something entirely different to try and break the spell, as it were, but decided, no. Enough things had been changed for one or even two lifetimes and God only knew what even a small change like wearing a different dress might do. What she remembered from that night was going to The Anvil, as usual and then over to Bubbles, so that's what would happen again. She looked at her watch. It was just after 2pm. Another twelve hours to try and make things right, but there was so much now. It wasn't just Lainey, it was Robbo too.

She walked into the hall and dialled a number from memory, surprising herself that it came to mind so easily after thirty years. Maybe, she thought, there was still a bit of the seventeen year old Jools in there, occasionally piloting the ship. After a couple of rings, a voice she knew and could never forget, no matter how many decades had passed, said, "Hello?"

"Lainey, it's Jools!"

"Hi Jools," Lainey said in that always bright and bubbly voice of hers.

"You literally just caught me, I was walking out the door to the hairdressers. What's up?"

"Oh, nothing, just wondering if you were popping into The Anvil before the allnighter tonight?"

"Did I not tell you? I thought I had. We're going to this stupid housewarming. I'd been pushing Matt for us to get there early and leave about twelve but he said most house parties don't even get going till that time and Peter will throw a fit if we walk out and it's not even started properly. I gave in. By the sounds of it, I reckon we won't be there till close to two. My memory must be going, I was sure I'd mentioned it."

Jools's heart sank. "It's just me, Lainey, you probably did. I've just had so much on my mind with Robbo that I forgot."

"What's up with Robbo?"

"Oh, shit, you don't know. Course you don't, you weren't out on Wednesday. You know how Robbo does some…. stuff for…."

"Yes, I know what he does and who he does it for and how the poor sod got roped into it, but I still don't approve."

"Yeah, I know, but he's in big trouble. He had a heap of money to give him, around three grand and he lost it."

Lainey, who never, ever said anything stronger than gobshite, just said, "Fuck."

"That's putting it mildly."

"How in God's name did he have that much money to give him? It's not like Robbo's Michael Corleone! He doesn't sell enough gear to accumulate that amount of cash."

"According to him," Jools said, "Freddie wasn't making any arrangements to collect it. He just kept sending some young lad over to his house with more gear. He said he hadn't seen Freddie in about six months and, of course it built up."

"Does he have any idea where he might have lost it?"

"He thinks in or around The Anvil, but in that part of town, if someone found a wallet with three grand in it, they're hardly likely to hand it in like a Good Samaritan now, are they?"

"I would," Lainey said.

"I would too," Jools said, "but unfortunately, you, nor I found it."

"The poor sod. What's he gonna do?"

"I reckon he'll be on the first boat in the morning, straight from Bubbles."

"He's going to Bubbles!"

"Yep, that's what he said."

"Does he have a death wish?"

"Probably, or he's just too far gone now to care. Says if he has to skip to England, he wants one last night out with his mates."

"I think he's crazy," Lainey said.

"Yeah, me too," Jools replied. "But there's no talking to him. Anyway," she continued, "two o'clock? Are you serious? You'll miss six hours! Is there no way to just ditch the party and come to Bubbles?"

"I'd really love to," Lainey said, "but there's really no getting out if it and we'll still have six hours and by the time we arrive, it'll have cleared out of most of the eejits that can't hold their drink and can't stay awake. More room to dance."

Jools thought, there's no talking to you either, Lainey and I can't come right out and say it.

"Just, just do me a favour, please. Promise me you'll be careful tonight?"

"What's wrong? You're sounding really odd."

"It's just…. I heard on the news that it's gonna lash, so the scooter, you know, just be careful."

"Jools, you caught me going out the door, the sun is splitting the trees, there isn't a cloud in the sky. I seriously doubt it's going to lash. Anyway, how many storms and rain and hail and snow has Matt driven in and we've never even come off it once? If it does, we've got the rain gear, so we'll be grand. Now will you just stop worrying?"

"Okay," Jools conceded. "Just try and get there earlier than two. Will you promise me that?"

"I promise you we'll try," Lainey said. "Gotta run or I'll miss my appointment. See ya later. Muah!" And with that, she hung up the phone.

Jools stared into the phone and started to cry.

She hung up and was just walking up the stairs when the doorbell rang. Quickly, drying her eyes, she opened it. Sean was standing there, smiling when he saw her, but that quickly changed.

"What's wrong?"

She couldn't tell him, of course, so she lied.

"It's just this business with Robbo, it's really starting to get to me. I think he's mad going tonight, because I reckon that psycho and his thugs will be standing outside waiting for him to arrive and if he does make it through the night, he'll be gone by tomorrow, Monday at the latest. We won't see him again, either way. Come into the kitchen, I'll make some tea."

"It wasn't his fault that he got into this," Sean said, following her down the hall.

"All that stuff with his Da. Freddie just hooked him and reeled him in and there really wasn't any way out. I reckon he would have skipped to England eventually anyway. The way the experts are talking, they're predicting a bad recession and most people will finish school and hop on the boat."

"I remember," Jools said, thinking back to the late Eighties when so many Irish moved to England for work. Had to move. Sean didn't though. He got a job with his Dad and the DJing continued to be a sideline. In the early Nineties, he'd had enough of what he'd called "wasted factory years," and quit. He decided to try his hand at event management, not just Soul – by that stage, there was no call for Mod nights in Dublin - but booking large venues and putting on Techno and Rave nights, promoting bands and that kind of thing. All that led to opening a small pub with a basement bar and it just took off from there. But that Maria wagon dragged him down. Talk about getting the hooks in. As far as she could remember, he met her in Dublin around Eighty-Nine.

"What?"

"I mean I remember hearing it on the news or somewhere." She bustled around the kitchen, filling and putting the kettle on, taking two mugs down from a shelf.

"Oh, right."

"What will you do, Sean?" She asked, sitting down, knowing the answer already.

"Do the exams and then my Dad said he could get me in with the draughtsmen in his job. I've always been pretty decent at mechanical drawing."

"What about your DJing? Wouldn't you like to keep that up? Try your luck in London? Maybe start your own club some day?"

"Yeah," he said, "it is something I've been thinking about. Not the London bit, though. But, you know, the factory will give me a steady wage and all that. Plus, I love the scene here."

"It's not gonna last," she said. "I reckon, two years, tops and the Mod scene is gone. It'll be all scooter rallies and the odd Northern Soul nights."

"Do you really? Bubbles is jammed every week and so are the gigs The Dublin Mod Society lads put on. Tonight is gonna be off the scale."

"Yeah, I know," she said, "but there have already been different groups passing through Bubbles. Some of the early Revival Mods left when Noel started playing Sixties Soul like the Arthur Conley and Markays stuff and then more left when he started playing Northern Soul and there's a lot more Northern played now than in the early days. A lot of the Mods don't like that."

"The dancefloor always seems to be full," he said.

"Just saying what I see. I've friends in England and they've said that seems to be the way things are going over there too. The music is moving away from Mod and more towards Northern with each passing month. And Sean, you're more into Northern than you are into Mod and Ska."

"True," he said, as Jools stood up, popped a teabag into each mug and poured in the boiling water.

"Just milk, right?" She asked.

"Only a drop," they both said at the same time and laughed. She took the teabags out, dropped them in the bin and put only a drop of milk into both teas. She sat back down and said, "I love the scene here as much as you do, but it's too small for you. You've got great records and could do really well in London. Much better than you could here." She thought of something just then and said, "I think I have some record lists upstairs...."

"Yeah," he interjected, "but most of that stuff none of us know. What's the point in spending money on something that might turn out to be shite?"

She smiled. She remembered that she used to keep all of her record lists in a shoe box on the top shelf of her wardrobe and with no worry about spending ages to go through clothes to wear that night, she could use that time to go through the lists.

"I've a cousin in London, as you know," she said. Sean nodded. "Samantha, we write to each other all the time, and she's been telling me all the stuff that the big DJs are starting to play and some of them are like only five and ten quid at the moment on Soul Bowl and Domar's record lists. Maybe fifteen or twenty for some, but not mad expensive. I'll get some of the lists and put a line under the stuff she's been telling me about and give them to you. I'm telling you, Sean, you land in London with a box of records like that and you'll get gigs all over the place."

"It's definitely something to think about," he said. "I've never really given London much thought but that's always been where everything stemmed from."

"Apart from Northern Soul," she said. "It wasn't called Northern for nothing." She smiled. He loved that smile. They'd been friends for God knew how long but, nothing. It just never seemed to go beyond that.

"Anyway," she said, "it is definitely something to think about but what's happening this evening? Anvil?"

"God, no," Sean said. "Robbo told me he's not setting foot in that place again. His exact words were, 'Bad Juju!' Fuck, Jools, I thought I was gonna wet myself."

"He didn't say that?" She replied, laughing. "Shit, I know I shouldn't be laughing, Sean, but bad fucking juju! That's so funny." She paused, the laughter draining from her. "It's really getting to him, isn't it?"

"If I lost that amount of money, it'd get to me too," he said.

"No, we'll go to the Three Lamps. I heard the weather on the radio earlier and it's to rain tonight, so we don't want to be walking across town getting wet. Quick bolt around the corner and we're in."

"Alright," she said, "sounds good. What time?"

"Kicks off at eight and Robbo said he wants to be in there as soon as the shutters go up. That little McCarthy fella is still watching his gaff for Freddie. Sits in the long grass in Mitchell's garden across the road with sandwiches and a flask like he's on a fuckin stake out! I've seen one of his mates go by mine on his bike a few times, so we're gonna go out the back gate, through the lane and Jayo will meet us there. We'll get the 42C or a taxi on the Darndale Road and they'll be none the wiser."

"See?" Jools said, "You're always the one with the plan."

"I do me best," he said. "Right, gotta go and get ready. My gaff, six bells?"

"That's grand," she said. "I'll tell Cyn half five so she's ready." He laughed. "See ya later, Jools." And just as he was about to walk out the door, she grabbed him and gave him a massive hug. He stood back, not knowing what to say.

"I love you, Sean," she said, "you're my best mate."

"Isn't Cyn your best mate?" He was smiling.

"Well, you know what I mean. See you later."

62. Life Changing Moments

Jools shut the door, went upstairs and pulled the shoe box down off the shelf and sat at the dresser in her bedroom. She took a pen and a ruler out of a side drawer and started going through the record lists, highlighting stuff she recognised that was massive and massively expensive in 2015, but were no more than twenty pounds in 1985 and some even considerably cheaper. There were the odd one or two for fifty or one hundred, she noticed, but they were few and far between and were the ones that in the Twenty-first Century, were fetching thousands.

By the time she'd finished going through and underlining every record she knew in all of the lists, she'd calculated his spend and smiled. If he did buy everything she recommended – some of which he would have known already, but most he wouldn't have because they hadn't started to get spins till the late Eighties and early to Mid-Nineties – it would set him back about a thousand pounds, but for that, in 2015 prices, he was probably looking at about a hundred grand's worth of records. "That'll do nicely," she said to herself and carefully placed them all back inside the shoe box, wrapped an elastic band around it and put it on the floor, beside her shoes and bag, so she wouldn't forget it. If she was going out tonight and Jools Sutton, forty-seven year old mother of two, divorced (thank fuck), IT consultant in a multi-national investment bank was going home, she wanted to make sure Sean was set up.

But what about herself? She sat on her bed and looked at her reflection in the mirror on the dresser.

"What would you do?" She asked herself. "This is your moment, Jools. They say everyone has one, defining, life-changing moment. Is this yours?"

There were things she knew would happen, because she remembered, but there were others that she'd no clue about, because she didn't know what she'd set in motion.

She knew Noel would start the slow set – as he nearly always did – with "To Sir With Love," and she knew that Jimmy would wait till it was halfway through before he asked her to dance. She also knew that if she said yes, it would be three or four songs later that they kissed, ironically, thinking back, to The Jam's "The Bitterest Pill."

Had she looked the picture of contented new wealth on her wedding day, in her white lace and wedding bells? The photos definitely showed she was contented, but never wealthy.

Yes, she thought, I was. I am. Never in a monetary sense, but with Liam and Jessica, she was.

So, Jimmy would turn out to be a prick. Worse than that, a cheating, gambling, alcoholic prick. There weren't enough Anonymous groups for him to attend, he was addicted to every possibly vice you could think of, but he hadn't started that way and she really didn't know when he changed.

Was it the kids? Some people can't handle having one, let alone two and some would crack up with two at the same time. She remembered it always seemed like she had one hanging from each hip, and him not being around to help. It hadn't all been miserable. Cyn was a godsend who took her Godmotherly duties on with relish, apart, of course from their spiritual wellbeing, to which, in the church, she answered, "Yes," but in private said, "I will in me bollix!"

If it hadn't been for Cyn looking after them as they grew up when Jools had college to go to, she'd probably have lost everything, with Jimmy only interested in himself. What then? Move back in with her Mam? God forbid! She was interfering enough, but what Jools did in her own house, was nobody's business but hers.

So, would she dance? She knew exactly where they'd be when he'd ask her. She'd been at the bar and he'd spoken to her and they'd chatted at length. She knew what she did when he asked her to dance originally, but what she didn't know, is what she would do this time.

What would happen if she said no? Would she go outside at two o'clock and wait for Matt and Lainey to arrive and wave them down? Would they all go back into the allnighter and

315

enjoy the rest of the night and then she'd go home to her parent's house and wake up forty-seven again? But with what and where? If she didn't dance and kiss Jimmy that night would she ever? If she didn't get together with him, there would be no Liam and no Jessica.

Maybe she'd end up with some other bloke and go back to something in the future where there was a version of her kids, just slightly different? It hurt her head to think about it.

Liam and Jessica's faces filled her mind. It was like when people say you see your whole life flash before your eyes when you're dying, but she was watching her two beautiful children, from the first moment she held them both in her arms, right through their terrible twos times two, primary school, Communion - cost a fortune – Confirmation – cost an even bigger fortune, secondary school, college and numerous trips to the beach and laughing and messing around at home. The one constant in her life, no matter what else happened, were her children. They always made her happy. She smiled again, walked to the top of the stairs and shouted, "Mam, will you put the immersion on, I want to have a shower."

63. A Feminine Touch

Archie's Dad dropped him off at Karen's, around the corner from his house.

"See you in a bit, Dad."

He rang the doorbell and she answered in a couple of seconds.

"Archie! Haven't seen you in a while."

"Busy studying. Need to ask you something."

"That sounds serious," she said.

"No, not at all. Just wondering if you sister still has all her old Mod clothes?"

"Are you considering turning into a cross-dressing Mod?" She asked, with a laugh.

"No, no," Archie said, laughing himself. "I've to do a job for Freddie tonight and it kinda requires a feminine touch. So, I thought of you."

"A feminine Modette touch?"

"They're not Modettes. There's girl Mods and boy Mods. Just Mods."

"Get you!" She said. "Defending the rights of the ladies. You'll be going on feminist marches next!"

"Hey," he said, "it was news to me too. Only discovered it today. Anyway, it's a simple job, but we have to go to Bubbles and get some bloke Freddie wants to talk to out of the place.

So, I was thinking, if you kinda chatted him up a bit and then…."

"I'm not getting off with some bloke I've never met!" She snapped. "What's he look like anyway?"

"I've no idea. But apparently everyone knows him there, so shouldn't be too difficult to find him. Freddie suggested I start a row with him so we both get fucked out, but if everyone knows him, and that probably includes the bouncers, they'll just fuck me out and Freddie won't be happy."

"Oh, I dunno, Archie," Karen said. "Sounds like a lot of trouble."

"I'll give you twenty quid, buy you a few drinks beforehand and make sure you get a taxi home. No, we'll get a taxi home together once the job's done. Freddie can't seem to track this bloke down and he said he just needs to talk to him and he's pretty sure he'll be there tonight. That's all it is."

"Archie, we both know what it means when Freddie wants to talk to someone. He usually does the talking and the other person can't, cos they've had their teeth knocked out. I dunno, I really don't."

"You'd be doing me a real favour, Karen. You know what Freddie's like if someone says no to him and I really don't wanna be that someone. And I don't wanna go in there on my own and probably get my head kicked in."

"Especially looking like that. The Mods will spot someone who isn't, a mile off."

"Not tonight," he said. "You should see the gear I picked up today. Lovely stuff. Those Mod clothes are pretty decent."

"Well, I have to say, the stuff my sister used to wear always looked really sharp. Ah, feck it, it's a night out, few drinks. I'll give you a dig out. Come back around six, I should be ready then."

"Thanks, Karen, I owe you one."

64. Plausible Deniability

"Where's that little bollix, Conn? I'm gettin real impatient."

Conn's wife Gwen was standing at the kitchen counter and looked over at her husband. She took a deep breath, but he raised his hand slightly, indicating not to react.

Freddie was sitting at their kitchen table, like it was his kitchen table.

"He'll be along soon," Conn said. "We had a talk in the car about tonight and he thinks there might be a better way of doing things. Best let him explain when he gets here."

"He?" Freddie said, exasperation and disbelief in his voice.

"He thinks there's a better way than how I think?" He looked astonished.

The front door opened, and Archie called out "Just me." He walked into the kitchen.

"You took your fuckin time," Freddie said. "And what's this shite about ya knowin better than me? Ya wanna be runnin me business next? Well? Do ya?"

Gwen opened the drawer and put her hand on the hilt of the carving knife.

"Ya can close that drawer, Gwen, love," Freddie said, without looking around. "I won't be doin an'thin to your yunfella, ya have me word on that."

She closed the drawer, turned and leaned against the counter, but said nothing.

"Right, what's this plan then, Mastermind?" Freddie said to Archie, who looked at his dad. Conn nodded. Archie sat down and just before he started to explain, Gwen cleared her throat with a louder than needed, "Ahem!"

Archie only got as far as "Well…," and stopped, as everyone looked at her and she said, "I need to go to the shops." She went over to her son, kissed him on the top of the head, then kissed her husband on the cheek and left the kitchen, saying a silent prayer that her son would be safe and both him and her husband would get as far away from that prick as soon as possible. She also didn't want to hear the ins and outs of whatever the plan was, with two words rolling through her head that she'd heard said on TV in some film or other. Plausible Deniability.

Archie began saying what he thought of the whole plan and how, if this Robbo fella was so well known and Archie started on him that he, himself, would probably just be thrown out and Freddie would be nowhere closer to getting to talk to him. If he could get Karen to chat him up and maybe go outside under the pretence of getting off with him, George and Conn could be waiting in the lane, just out of sight of the bouncers and grab him. Into the back of the van and gone. Job done.

Freddie sat in silence for probably ten seconds that seemed like an eternity to Conn and Archie.

"And this Karen one, ya can trust her?"

"She's grand," Archie said. "I've known her since we were in primary school."

Freddie rubbed his chin and looked up at Conn.

"The kid might just have a plan here, Conn. This might work."

"That's what I thought, Boss. What do they say? You catch more flies with honey than vinegar?"

"That's what they say, Conn, that's what they say." He turned to Archie and said, "Right, use the girl, but don't just rush in and get her to drag him out. He needs to be in there a while, let his guard down. She could be Linda Fuckin Lusardi and he's not gonna leave that place with her if he thinks there's somethin up. If we leave it a while, he'll probably be so off his head on the gear he's supposed to be sellin for me that he won't even give a bollocks. She's definitely up for this, yeah?"

"Yeah. Defo. I promised her a few drinks and a taxi home, plus a score. As long as she doesn't have to get off with him, she's grand. She's no slapper, Freddie, but she could flirt for Ireland. And she's absolutely gorgeous, I doubt he'll take his eyes off her once she turns on the charm."

Freddie thought for a moment, whether she was gorgeous or not, or even Linda Fuckin Lusardi, that meant nothing to him.

She was a tool. Nothing more than a crowbar in a skirt. Something he needed to get the job done. He nodded, leaned to one side and reached around to his back trousers pocket and pulled out a wallet as thick as a paperback book, took out ten twenties and put them on the table. He put his mug on top of the cash.

"That'll do yis both. If she's doin this, she should be gettin more than a score. Give her fifty. But I'm tellin ya now, Archie, don't get pissed and make sure she doesn't get pissed either, cos if yis do and Robbo's not outside that club, ya really don't wanna know what'll happen to the pair of yis." He looked at Conn. "And you, you'll go down with them too."

Pointing at Archie, he said, "Make sure you look like one of them moddy pricks. And the bird too."

Archie looked at his Dad and back at Freddie and nodded.

"Right, let's agree on a time to get that lanky streak of piss outside then," Freddie said, rubbing his hands together and smiling.

65. Strange, How?

"I really don't want to go, Matt. All his mates are gobshites, they'll all be drinking Buckfast and the music they play will be awful. As much as I don't like The Jam and The Style Council, I'd rather be listening to that than fecking Marillion. Every time I was in your Mam's over the past few weeks, he was going around with his Walkman on, singing that Kayleigh shite at the top of his voice. Are you sure he's not adopted?"

Matt smiled. "Lainey, he's been in my ear all week about it. There's some girl he's trying to impress and wants to make sure he gets as many people there as he can. He wants to look like he's really popular."

"Who does he think he is? Hugh Hefner? It's a house party in a bedsit in Rathmines, not the Playboy Mansion. You probably couldn't swing a cat in it."

"Well, more than likely not," Matt said, "his lease stipulated no pets!"

Lainey just smiled, but it wasn't her normal smile, the one that lit up her whole face.

"What's wrong?"

"I dunno," she said. "Just something about Jools. She was on the phone to me earlier and sounded…. just a bit strange."

"Strange how?"

"I can't put my finger on it. She doesn't want us to go to the party. Like at all! I don't understand it, she sounded really weird. Just come to Bubbles, ditch the party, she was saying. I said we'd be there late, but we would be there."

"Ah, you know Jools," he said. "She loves the place and just wants to make sure nobody misses out on anything. Linda and Flavo are filling in for Noel with a couple of spots, so he doesn't have to do the whole twelve hours himself. We see Noel DJing week in, week out and as good as he is, it's not that often you get to see Linda and Flavo DJ in Bubbles. That's probably what it's all about."

"Maybe," was all she said, but she wasn't convinced.

He put his arms around her.

"It'll be fine," he said. "Are you gonna wear that lovely little brown suit I like with the short skirt?"

He kissed her.

Still slightly distracted thinking about Jools, she said," No, I'm wearing a trouser suit. Might put the brown one in the bag to change into during the night, but it's supposed to rain later, and I'm not hoisting rain gear over a skirt and look a mess when I get there. Bad enough having to put a helmet on a new hairdo."

Matt looked out the window. For a day that started like a perfect summer's morning, he could see dark clouds moving in from the horizon.

66. The Giggle Line

Archie put the mohair suit trousers on, cuffs stopping just above the Loake's, no crumple, crease like a knife edge. No alterations, they simply just fit. The crisp, white Oxford shirt his Mam had ironed for him went on next. With the grey and silver polka dot silk tie in a Windsor knot and the collars buttoned down – with the third button at the back done, the shop owner told him that was extremely important - he put the jacket on and for the first time ever, he felt this was what he had been missing. The pocket square in his breast pocket that almost matched the tie, looked the absolute business.

After discussing the music with the shop owner, he discovered that it was just background music to him, that he was more of a classical head and said he just played it to keep the customers happy, so threw a couple of tapes into the bag with the suit.

So there was Archie, at 10am that morning, no inclination of even wearing a pair of Levi's and now, early evening the same day, wearing what looked like a tailored mohair suit and listening to The Who singing "Daddy Rolling Stone." Who'd have thought?

He walked down the stairs to a wolf whistle from Conn. Gwen started to well up.

"You look so handsome, son," she said, "just like your Dad did when he was your age."

"Am I not still handsome, darling?" Conn said, twirling her around, laughing, as Gwen pulled away and hit him with the tea towel she was holding. "You're only gorgeous," she said and blew him a kiss. Archie looked at the pair of them with a what the fuck look on his face and said, "Right, so, I'm off. I'll see yis later, but this thing is an allnighter, so if I like it, I might stay."

"Just you be careful now," Gwen said.

"I'll be fine, Ma, nothing to it."

He looked at Conn, who nodded, a worried expression on his face.

Five minutes later, he was standing in front of Karen's hall door and just about to knock when it opened. Karen's older sister Jeanette stood there, an almost identical version of Karen, just a couple of years older and about a head taller. She still retained some of the Mod look but had stopped with most of it a couple of years previous. Didn't like "All that Northern Soul shite," as she put it. She raised an eyebrow.

"Is that Archie, or The Face from Quadrophenia?"

"The what?" Archie asked.

"Jesus, yunfella, you're brutal. Karen! Your date's here!"

From upstairs, Archie could hear her shout, "He's not my date, we're just going to a club. I'll be down in a minute. Do I have to wear these stockings? Can I not wear tights? This dress is a bit short for stockings."

Jeanette stifled a laugh and looked at Archie, raising the eyebrow again and said, "In any language, Archie, that's a date! Come in, will you and don't be standing there like a gormless shite."

Archie stepped into the hall, Jeanette shut the door behind him and they both heard feet on the top steps and looked up. Archie's heart nearly exploded. Yes, the skirt was short and yes, he could clearly see where the stocking tops ended, and the inner thigh began. Jeanette nudged him and pointed at the bare flesh he could see. Karen stopped on the stairs as she spoke.

"Archie, see that line at the very top of her stockings?"

Archie gulped and just nodded, as Karen turned bright red.

"That's called the giggle line."

Archie, also going redder by the second, managed to mumble out, "Why's it called the giggle line?"

"Because, Archie," she said, slapping him on the back, "If you get past that line, you're laughing!" She burst out laughing, herself and looking up at Karen said, "You dozy cow, I can't believe you put the stockings on, go back up and get them black tights on that are over the back of the chair."

"Jeanette Flynn, you horrible fucking bitch!" Karen shouted, turned about face and stormed back up the stairs. A bedroom door could be heard slamming and various curses being shouted.

"Wanna cuppa tea while you're waiting?" Jeanette asked. "She's gotta take the skirt off to get at the suspender belt before she can take the stockings off."

Archie's face started to go red again as Jeanette went into the kitchen, laughing.

Ten minutes later, Karen entered the kitchen, not in the skirt and top she had been wearing, but in a navy, sleeveless A-Line dress with a stand up collar and white stripe running down the front, from neck to seam. She'd no tights on, choosing bare legs instead and navy block heel shoes with pointed toes. Archie's jaw dropped.

"That one was always my favourite," Jeanette said, "you look amazing."

"Oh piss off, Jeanette! Fucking stockings!"

"I can't believe you swallowed it. Oh, Jesus, that was funny. And you," Jeanette said, prodding Archie in the chest, "that's the closest you'll be getting to her giggle line tonight! You hear me?"

Archie, wide eyed and red faced again just nodded at Jeanette and said to Karen, "You right then?"

Jeanette said, "Grab that navy mac at the back of the door there, Karen, that always went well with it too."

Karen did and as they walked out the door, Jeanette stood

watching them, like a proud Mam and said, "Have a good night, me two little Moddy babies."

Karen, without turning, gave her the finger.

67. Wide Eyed Girl On The Wall

It didn't take Jools long to get ready with, of course, Small Faces blasting from the stereo, her Mam banging the brush handle on the kitchen ceiling again, as she knew her Dad would be standing by the open kitchen door below her bedroom, smoking and tapping along to the music, a smile on his face. The album she was playing, "The Autumn Stone," was their record. Originally her Dad's, she fell in love with the band when he first played it and remembered distinctly where she'd been when she first heard her favourite one by them, "Wide Eyed Girl On The Wall." She was ten years old and her Mam was out, so her Dad was blasting the stereo while he did some DIY. He'd accidentally put Side Four of the album on instead of Side One and when "Wide Eyed Girl" played, she had actually been sitting outside her front door, on the garden wall. She couldn't believe what she was hearing. Her and her Dad had always had a strong bond, but this brought them even closer. When it came on, she smiled a sad smile, reminiscing about that day when she came running into the house, actually wide eyed and asked, "What's that? It's brilliant!" She remembered his smile then and her love of music grew from that moment.

Still smiling at the memory, she looked in the mirror and said to herself, "Well, this is it. For better or worse, whatever happens, happens."

She walked downstairs and put her bag and the shoe box on the table. Her dad was still standing at the open kitchen door, smoke rising up around his head.

"You'll go deaf," her Mam said to her.

"What?" Jools replied, smiling. She could see her Dad's shoulders rise and fall as he chuckled.

"You'll go deaf," her Mam repeated and then, realising she'd been caught out, said "Oh, feck off," and shook her head.

She went over to her Mam and hugged her.

"What's that for?"

"Just because," Jools said. Then she went over to her Dad, once again, standing behind him, putting her arms around him and resting her head on his broad back.

"You'll never know how much I love you," she whispered to him.

"I know," he said, "as much as I do you."

He turned and put his arms around her. She was almost, but not quite the same height as him, but he was twice the width. Whenever she thought of him, she remembered a line from The Quiet Man, their favourite film that they'd watched together, countless times, where one of the men in the pub says he remembers Sean Thornton's father having "shoulders on him like an ox!" That was her Dad. The biggest man she ever knew, with the biggest heart. She thought, no matter what happened tonight, this was probably the last time she would see him alive and began to well up. She took a deep breath, regained control of herself and, standing on tip toes, though she really didn't need to, she kissed him on the cheek and said, "I love you, Daddy."

"I love you too, Jools," he said, and kissed her on the forehead. "Now go and have a good time!"

"I will, Dad, thanks."

"Don't be too late," her Mam said.

"Mam, it's an allnighter."

"A what?"

"Jaysus, May," her Dad said, "an allnighter! They'll be there all night!"

Her Mam looked at her, not understanding what she meant.

"Eight tonight till Eight tomorrow morning, Mam."

"God, you'll be dead!"

"Nobody's dying tonight," Jools answered. "See yis tomorrow!"

Five minutes later, Jools rang Cyn's doorbell and she answered, for once, ready. Jools stood back and looked at her.

"Sorry, I think I have the wrong house. I was looking for a girl I know called Cynthia Keeling, who should still be in a dressing gown, fighting through a mountain of clothes on her bed and still not having a clue what she's going to wear. And then discovering that the hairdryer she's been looking for all evening is buried under that mountain of clothes and has been since three o'clock this afternoon. Who are you and what have you done with my incredibly disorganised best friend?"

"Oh, very fuckin funny, Little Miss Perfect! And you're late. It's ten to six. You said you'd be here at half five."

Jools just smiled and ignored Cyn's comment about being late. Instead, she said, "Little? You…. you are calling me little? Cyn, you're five feet one, I'm five feet eight and I also have two-inch heels on."

"Okay," Cyn said, "but you know what they say about the small ones." She winked at Jools.

"Lucky you ended up with Don last night then. You were looking to go after Jeff originally and although Don isn't small, he's a good bit shorter than Jeff."

"Height makes no difference to me," Cyn said. "A fallen tree is easy to climb!"

"Oh you dirty little shite!"

"I'm just a woman who takes what I want," Cyn said, "but I'm no slapper, I won't go off with just anyone. There must be that certain something."

"Yeah," Jools said, "like, he's still breathing."

"No, still warm will do." She laughed and then said, "Why do you have a shoe box?"

"Oh, it's for Sean, just some record lists I was throwing out. Thought he might like to look through them."

"You boys and your records." She reached into the hall and grabbed her bag.

"I'm off, Mam, see you in the morning."

"Have fun," came the reply from the kitchen.

68. Fifty-Fifty Chances

Dosser sat looking out the kitchen window. Thick, black clouds had rolled in from nowhere.

"Bollocks," he said to himself. "That looks like rain. If I drive that scooter in the lashing rain, me suit'll get soaked."

"Who are you talking to?"

"What?" He looked up at his brother, who was standing there staring at him.

"Were you just talking to yourself, you mental head?"

"Look, just fuck off back up to your room and leave me alone," Dosser said. "It's cunts like you that put me in a bad humour."

His brother looked out the window.

"You're gonna get soaked on your moped if you go out on it tonight. Maybe you can borrow one of Ma's pink plastic macs?" He laughed. "That'd really suit you, you little queer bollix."

"I'm not a fuckin queer! Now just fuck off!"

He looked at the clock. It was nearly six.

"I'm goin in to watch the news."

His brother opened the back door and called out to his Mam, who was frantically trying to get the washing off the line before it started to pour.

"Ma! I think Graham is sick! He said he wants to watch the

news!"

"Just the fuckin weather, ya knob," Dosser said. "Then I can turn it off."

His brother looked at him, smiling. "You're an awful dozy prick, do you not know anything?"

"What?"

"Nothing," his brother said and walked up the stairs laughing.

Dosser went into the living room and sat down in the opposite armchair to his Dad, who looked at him, as if seeing an apparition, or an alien landing. Perhaps a unicorn? No, definitely not a unicorn, they were always clean, but certainly not something he'd ever seen before.

"You alright, son?"

"Yeah, I'm grand. Why?"

"It's six o'clock and you're sitting down to watch the telly."

"Yeah."

"You know the news is on at six o'clock?"

"Yeah, course I know."

Dosser's Dad shook his head and settled down to watch the news.

After the longest thirty minutes of his life, Dosser stormed upstairs and threw open his bedroom door. His brother was lying on the bed, looking through any unstuck pages of a Mayfair he'd found under the bed.

"You get the weather then?" He asked.

"At the fuckin end!" Dosser shouted. "They put the fuckin weather on at the end of the fuckin news! Why the fuck would they do that? People have to go out! Do they think people have all fuckin day just to sit around watchin the fuckin news just so they can see if the fuckin weather is alright so they can go fuckin out?"

His brother got up, walked to the door and flung the magazine at Dosser's head and said, "Is it?"

"Is it what?"

"Is the weather okay for you to go out tonight on your moped, you fucking numbskull?"

"Eh, yeah. The bird on the telly said there was a fifty percent chance that it was to rain in the evenin but should clear up before midnight."

"So, you know what that means then? You know what fifty percent means?"

Dosser just looked at him blankly.

"Fifty percent is half, Graham. It means, really, it might, or it might not. She may as well have just stood on the telly and tossed a bleedin coin."

"So, it will, or it won't rain then?" Dosser asked, even more confused.

Dosser's brother shook his head, put his hand on the door

handle and before he left the room, said, "You know something, Graham? You're the thickest cunt I've ever met in my entire life. First off, the weather is always on at the end of the news. It always has been and, presumably, always fucking will be and second, you know that thing in the hall, the black yoke, with the roundy bit in the middle of it, with all the numbers, that makes the ding-a-ling sound?"

"The phone?"

"Yeah, you dozy cunt, the phone. Assuming you can actually read, there's a thing on the shelf under the phone called a phone book and in that book there's a number that, if you call it, you can get the weather any old time you like. You absolute fucking moron."

He walked out into the hall and just before he closed the door, he heard dosser say, "ah bollocks."

69. Record Loving Freaks

"There you go," Jools said to Sean, handing him the shoe box. "What's this?"

"Remember earlier I was talking to you about all the records my cousin was recommending to me?"

"Yeah."

"I've been underlining anything she's told me about. Bought a few myself, but I've no interest in DJing and I never will, but you, on the other hand, might get some use out of them." She remembered something then. "Pass them on to Matt when you're done."

Sean put the box on the kitchen table, they all crowded around it, except Cyn who had absolutely no interest in records and stood looking out the window and said, "We'd better get a move on, before it starts to piss down."

"Hang on a sec, Cyn," Sean said, "I just want to have a quick look."

He pulled the band off and opened the box, which was almost filled to the brim, picking one of the lists out at random and opened it to the first page.

By 2015, the knowledge of Northern Soul records Jools had was off the scale and she smiled, with great satisfaction as Sean's jaw dropped. On the first page alone, there were probably no more than ten items listed that she hadn't underlined. Sean read one of them aloud.

"The Magnetics – I Have A Girl. Thirty quid. Is it any good?"

Jools, who'd heard it played and only had a reissue herself in 2015, thought, yes, Sean, it's about seven and a half grand good.

"Yes, I'd certainly recommend that. Also, see that one, Cookie Jackson, Do You Still Love Me?"

"Another twenty quid one," Sean said.

"Yep, snap that one up. My cousin, who's well in with some of the dealers – record dealers – I should add – reckons the prices will start going through the roof. In ten to fifteen years, people will be paying thousands for them."

"Yeah, right," Cyn said. "Whoever would pay that much for a record has more money than sense."

"I can't disagree with you there, Cyn," Jools said.

Sean was still looking through the lists.

"Hamilton Movement," he said. "She's Gone. Heard anything about that? Says here that it's a nice Seventies dancer, could go big. That's a bit pricey, fifty quid."

"At this moment in time, Sean, could you afford to spend fifty quid on a record?" Jools asked him.

"Well, yeah, I could, but not much more."

"Do me a favour then. If you only buy one record from that list, buy that. If you only buy two, get The Magnetics as well."

"For fuck sake, you record loving freaks! Will you come the fuck on! I want to go!"

"Okay, Cyn," Sean said, "we're going."

He put the list back in the box, carefully placed the lid on and wrapped the band around it again. Just about to go, he thought for a second. If he left it there, his Mam might think it's just rubbish and throw it out.

"Back in a sec," he said, running up to his bedroom and putting the box on his bed.

Back downstairs in a flash, he opened the back door and ushered his friends out, to Cyn saying, "Bout fuckin time!"

70. Mister Hyde

"What do ya reckon, George?"

"What's that, Boss?" George said, looking up from his paper. Freddie was sitting at his desk, opening and closing his flick knife.

"Robbo. Think he'll be there tonight?"

George, who had been around Freddie long enough to know when he was baiting someone, thought for a second. He was a good foot taller than Freddie and had at least seven stone on him, but Freddie was an unpredictable fuck. George knew he could break him in half if he wanted to, literally. He could just pick him up and break his spine in one, quick movement, but Freddie could just as quickly be over the table and onto him before he had a chance to move and next thing he would know, he's missing an eye, at the very least. He concluded that Freddie was just mulling over everything and really speaking out loud, to himself, more than him, but still, so he chose his words carefully, thought again and finally spoke as noncommittally as he could.

"Well, if he isn't there, you've gone to an awful lot of trouble for nothing."

"Yeah," Freddie said, still musing. He looked directly at George.

"What do ya think happened? Why did Robbo welch on me?"

"Honestly, Boss, I don't think he did."

"What do ya mean, he didn't?" Freddie asked, his voice rising.
"Am I sittin here with three grand on me desk?"

"No, but…."

"But what? Robbo was supposed to meet me on Wednesday
and the cunt hasn't been seen anywhere since! Neither has me
fuckin money!"

"Robbo's a smart kid, Boss. He's worked for you for long
enough to know what happens when people cross you and
that's the reason I think what's happened here isn't
intentional."

"What do ya mean?"

"Let's just say that, eh, your reputation precedes you. There's
no way on God's green earth that Robbo would steal from you
and if he was to, it certainly wouldn't be that much."

"Go on." Freddie said, the knife now remaining open, the
pointed end on the desk, the hilt being twirled around between
his thumb and forefinger.

George took a deep breath, closed his paper and folded it over.
He put it on his lap and leaned forward on his chair and said,
"He lost it, or it was lifted off him, one or the other. He's too
smart to just walk off into the sunset with that much money
belonging to you."

"Unless he was plannin it."

"Why would he do that?"

"He never wanted to work for me in the first place. He bought that carin uncle type shite I gave him when his old man was in a jocker and then he was in me pocket. Maybe he was waitin for a big pay day just to get the fuck out and tonight is his one, last big hoo ha with his moddy mates before he fucks off to London or Manchester or who the fuck knows where with *my* money!"

George thought about it. Freddie might actually be on to something there. This could be a way out for Robbo. For years, George had been sticking money in a hollowed-out section of the wall in the old outside toilet in his back garden that he'd used as a tool shed. Last count, there was about fifty grand there and looking over at his boss now, the normally maniacal look in his eyes was even worse. He thought, it's not even like he's Doctor Jekyll and Mister Hyde anymore, it's like he's only Mister Hyde, just gone even more fucking mental.

George decided that no matter what happened tonight, he was getting a plane ticket to Gran Canaria on Monday morning and never looking back. Robbo, whatever happened and whatever caused him not to show up with Freddie's money, was a good kid. George had made his peace a long time ago with what Freddie did and he wasn't even very much a part of it, he was ingrained in it. He'd always known Freddie was a few houses short of a Monopoly set, but for some reason, Robbo had gotten under his skin and he knew what Freddie would do to the poor lad once he got hold of him. No amount of explaining would work and even if Robbo did come up with the cash, even if he walked into the office right that instant and dropped three grand on the desk, he knew that the knife Freddie was playing with would end up in Robbo's throat and Freddie would just walk out, not even blinking and tell him to "Clean that shit up."

This was a young man's game and he was getting way too old for it.

"Maybe you're right, Boss. If you get your hands on him tonight, we'll get to the bottom of it."

"Not just him, George," Freddie said. "And ya know what, it really doesn't matter about the money anymore. Him, his mates, them two brazzers and that big skinhead fucker, they're all on me list now and by the time we're finished, not one of them cunts will be left breathin. We'll take the van tonight, might be lucky and even get more than just Robbo and they'll be watchin the sunrise in lovely Meath and none of them will be laughin at me again."

71. Just Like Louise Brooks

The Three Lamps was heaving. Not the largest bar in Dublin, it has to be said, but it could adequately hold about a hundred people, with a bit of a squeeze.

Sean held the door for Jools and Cyn, who thanked him and walked in, Jayo and Robbo behind them and finally Sean, all dressed in their best and the heat hit them.

There was easily pushing a hundred in the room already, and they could barely squeeze through the crowd. The one thing that hit Jools more than anything else, after having been in the few different pubs and venues since Wednesday, was the smoke. In 2015, everyone had to go outside for one, but in 1985, a grey haze hung over the room. She noticed Dee and Tash standing by the end of the bar nearest the front window which, partially opened, afforded little, but not much ventilation.

"Sean," she called to him as he was moving through the crowd towards the bar, "we're just going to chat with the girls for a bit."

"Alright," he called back, "do yis want a drink?"

"No," she replied, "we'll sort ourselves out. Thanks."

"No worries," he called back over the noise of the crowd. "I'll see you later."

Robbo, after his lesson learned in The Anvil on Wednesday, had his new wallet tucked in the inside pocket of his suit jacket. Nothing was going to fall out and nobody was going to lift it, if that is what had happened. Sean caught the eye of the barman and there were three pints of Harp in front of them in an instant.

Jools and Cyn said hi to Dee and Tash, and Jools stood back, well, as far as she could, given how packed the place was and looked at them both, admiring what they wore and thinking, they never once lost it. Not in thirty years.

She looked at Tash's dress, shook her head and said, "Where did you get that? It's gorgeous!" She certainly wasn't expecting a "Thanks, hun, Penneys," reply.

"Jenny Vandar," Tash said, smiling at the compliment.

Jools was stylish and very rarely envied how anyone looked, but admitted to herself, she'd have killed for this dress.

Purple paisley with a boat neck and no sleeves. Fitted and knee length with a slight flair at the hem. Bordering on psychedelic but stuck neatly in 1966. Worn with almost flat T-bar pointed toe, brown original Sixties shoes.

"And Dee," she said, "you look incredible."

"Thanks, Jools. I know I've worn this to Bubbles a few times before, but it is my favourite."

Dee's look was something that others had tried to emulate, but just couldn't come close. Even Cyn, who always admired the way Dee dressed and herself was in a dark blue, but not quite navy, two-piece skirt suit with a white, round necked top beneath, thought she could never pull off what Dee wore. A crimplene two-piece. Sky blue and off white with a white turtleneck. Three covered buttons on the jacket. Hush Puppies with white knee socks. Some girls would have worn tights, but Dee always thought the knee socks just went better with it. Jools had a good memory, but she couldn't remember seeing Dee in this outfit before and smiled. Again, thinking, for some people, it's just effortless.

"Looking well, ladies, how's it going?"

Jools looked at the young lad that had just spoken, he was standing there with his mate, both dressed in suits, sharp as tacks and considerably younger than the last time she'd seen either of them but recognised them both in a flash.

"Mark! Gavin!" She leaned over and kissed them both on the cheek. Not something that was done very often between the Mod boys and Mod girls in Eighty-Five and they both seemed a little taken aback.

"Did you order, Cyn?"

"What? No, I thought you did. What do you want? The usual?"

Just about to say yes, Jools thought about the night ahead and what it potentially entailed.

"Just the Coke," she said, "I'm not in the humour of drinking tonight."

Cyn turned to Dee and said, "She's been acting weird all week, now she's off her drink."

"I'm just popping to the loo," Jools said to Cyn, "back in a minute."

She made her way through the crowd, stopping beside the lads.

"Any sign of him?" She asked Robbo.

"Well, we'd hardly see that short arsed little bollix in this crowd, but no. I was checking for the Merc along the quays before we even crossed O'Connell Bridge and nothing. Not a sign. And if George and Conn were hanging about, we'd spot them a mile off."

"Good," she said, "but keep your head down anyway and leave it till just after eight to go round. If you get into the middle of a group going out, if he is there, he might not see you. You can't be standing outside waiting for the shutters to go up and he walks around the corner."

"No, you're right, Jools. I'll be careful. I promise."

"Just popping to the loo, back in a bit," she said and started pushing her way through the crowd again.

Jayo looked over towards the corner, where Chris was standing with Susan, who was chatting to the most exquisite girl Jayo had ever laid eyes on. Chris was just standing there, an untouched pint in his hand, mouth half open, staring at her, looking like a rabbit caught in headlights. Jayo was Five-Ten and this girl looked about the same, a little shorter maybe, her loafers bringing her up to about equal height. Slightly tanned, slim, her black and white shift dress accentuated her figure, opaque tights completed the ensemble.

Her dark eyes were hypnotic, with black eye liner and big lashes and with jet black hair cut in a bob and skin so flawless, she could be a model.

Jayo had seen a silent movie on BBC2 a few weeks before with some actress called Louise Brooks in it, from the thirties or something, and this girl's hair was cut exactly the same. That Louise one was tasty, he'd thought at the time, but the girl he was looking at now, there wasn't another person in the place that came even remotely close to her. He reckoned ninety-nine percent of the lads in here would crawl across broken glass just to chat to her, which was a distinct possibility in the pub they were in. The other one percent probably just hadn't seen her yet.

She looked over, caught his eye, smiled and turned and said something to Susan, who looked over and waved to him, beckoning him to join them.

"Lads," Jayo said, "I'll see yis in there."

"What?" Robbo said and looked towards where Jayo was

looking.

"Sweet mother of Jesus!" He said. "I have never seen a bird like that in my entire life."

"Robbo," Sean said, looking over, "that's no bird and no girl, she's a woman! Jayo, she's so out of your league, you might as well be on different planets!"

Without taking his eyes off of her, Jayo said, "I'd rather go down in flames than stand here and forever wonder, 'What if?'"

He picked his pint up and moved through the crowd like a hot knife through butter. Not a drop was spilled, not a button thread was pulled.

"Howya, Susan. Howaya, Chris. How's it going?"

Chris looked up at Jayo, still with that wide-eyed look on his face and muttered a "Howya, Jayo. Grand."

Susan elbowed him in the ribs, which brought him back to life a bit and said, "Hi, Jayo, you're looking well. New Suit? It's a lovely shade of, eh, black."

"Yeah," he said, distractedly, looking at the dark-haired girl, "I got it last week."

Chris looked the suit up and down and said, "Who died?"

Susan gave him another elbow in the ribs for that.

She looked at her friend, a coy smile on her face, knowing that Jayo desperately wanted an introduction.

"Jayo, may I introduce you to my cousin, Nicki."

Jayo put out his hand and Nicki offered hers.

"I haven't seen you here before," he said, awkwardly.

"For fuck sake, Jayo," Susan said, "is that the best you can come up with? That's almost as bad as asking her does she come here often."

"I, eh, well," was all Jayo could manage.

Susan prodded Chris in the shoulder and looking at Jayo said, "See this gobshite? I introduced him to Nicki a half hour ago and he went bright red and has barely spoken since!"

"I, eh, well," was all Chris could manage.

"Men!" Susan said. "Or should I say, boys! See a beautiful woman and you go to pieces."

Nicki turned to Jayo and said, "Jayo? Short for Jason, I presume? What do you prefer?"

"Eh, Jayo is fine, thanks. Now, that's definitely not an accent from around here. Where are you from?"

"Sheffield," she said. "I came over this morning for the allnighter. Susan's been telling me all about Bubbles and I just had to see for myself."

"Well," Jayo said, "you've definitely picked the best night for it. The music is top notch and," he said, indicating the packed bar, "it's gonna be jammed."

"I'm looking forward to it," she said. "What do you think, Chris? Are you looking forward to it?"

"I, eh, well," was all Chris could manage and Susan grabbed him by the elbow, spilling some of his beer over a young Mod who couldn't have been more than fifteen and already passed out. She looked down at the stain the beer had left on his grey Sta-Prest, shook her head and said, "He's really gonna last the night, isn't he? And you, Chris, I think need some air! Nicki, Jason, we'll see you in a bit."

She dragged Chris towards the front door, leaving Jayo and Nicki already deep in conversation.

"I'm amazed," Sean said to Robbo. "I never thought he'd even get a look in, never mind a word in."

Robbo looked over. "Jaysus, she's laughing now. And it actually looks like she's laughing with him, not at him. She must be really nice."

"She is," Susan said, as she passed them. "And so is he, so stop taking the piss."

Sean and Robbo looked at each other and then at her, snapped to attention, saluted and said "Yes Miss!"

"Oh, fuck off, you pair of wankers," she said, laughing.

"Chris," Robbo said, "are you gonna let your bird talk to us like that?"

"You both know Susan, yeah?" He said. "You think I have any say in the matter?"

"That's the most words you've spoken since I introduced you

to Nicki," she said.

"I, eh, well," was all Chris could manage as she pulled him through the crowd and out the door.

72. Disguises

"Sorry, love," Archie said as he opened the door that Susan was just about to push, and she stumbled forward. Archie caught her.

"Oh, thanks," she said. "Christ it's warm in there. Need some air."

"No problem," he said. "It didn't look like your boyfriend was gonna be quick enough to catch you."

"You're a Gent. He's not my boyfriend." She smiled. "We're just good mates."

Chris shrugged an unsaid, "It is what it is," which Archie picked up on and smiled, himself.

"No problem," Archie said again, as he let them pass. He turned to Karen.

"My lady." He said, and she walked into the pub, through the door he held open and into a wall of bodies.

"Jesus! It's packed. Over there, by the window," she said. "It's a bit open, so there might be some air."

They pushed their way through the crowd to the bar.

"What are you having, Karen?"

"Bottle of Ritz please."

"You want a glass with that?"

She looked at him with disbelief. Wide eyed and jaw dropped.

"Are you seriously asking me if I'm going to stand in a pub, dressed up to the nines and drink from a fucking bottle? Of course I want a glass!" She turned her eyes up to heaven and, under her breath, muttered, "Gobshite."

"Okay," Archie said, "I was only asking." He turned back to the bar and ordered a Guinness and a Ritz, with a glass of ice. She could take the ice out if she wanted.

"They don't have a clue. Boys, they are, not men. All of them." Karen turned to the small, blond girl in the dark blue suit standing beside her and said, "Sorry, what?"

Cyn nodded her head in Archie's direction. "Your boyfriend. You come in here, in an absolutely gorgeous dress like that and he thinks you're gonna stand there and swig from a bottle. We're Mods, we'll leave that shite to the tramps in the Apartments."

At first Karen didn't know what to do, or to say. She wasn't a frequent patron of The Apartment Club, the other teenage disco around the corner from Bubbles, but had been there a few times and knew that you never spoke to someone you didn't know the way this girl had just spoken to her, because you were liable to get the bottle that she probably was swigging out of across the head and you never, ever spoke to a girl about her boyfriend. That was a no go, minefield, danger filled area. There'd be bits of you all over the dancefloor.

The "disguise" had obviously worked then. This, Modette, correction, she told herself, Mod, had thought that her and Archie were Mods too. Well, the dress was superb and so fitted, it showed her figure off really well. Granted, she didn't have a bob haircut, but she quickly looked around the room and noticed that a lot of the girls didn't either, so that was alright. She remembered the story they'd give if anyone thought, as Cyn had, that they were boyfriend and girlfriend. Archie had explained to her about how he'd got the ticket off the girl in the clothes shop for, he'd told her, his girlfriend, but if Karen was to chat up this Robbo bloke, even if she could find him, she couldn't be Archie's girlfriend.

"Him? He's not my boyfriend. He goes out with my mate who can't come cos she's sick, so he offered me the ticket. I've never been."

"Really? Oh, you don't know what you've been missing. Lucky you got a ticket then. It'll be a great night. I'm Cyn, by the way." She offered her hand.

"Karen, pleased to meet you," she said, smiling and took Cyn's hand.

Archie came back from the bar and handed the Ritz and the glass of ice to Karen, who introduced him to Cyn. Some of the cream from the top of his pint had rolled down the side of his glass, onto his hand, so he reached over and put the pint back on the bar, before going into his jacket pocket and pulling out a plain, white cotton handkerchief – another tip he got from the shop owner – he wiped his Guinness soiled hand with it before taking Cyn's.

She raised her eyebrows and looked at Karen.

"You have a proper gentleman here, Karen, even if he isn't your boyfriend."

"Ah, he'll do."

Jools came back from the toilets and after introducing her to Archie and Karen and then both of them to everyone else as the names Dee, Tash, Mark, Gavin and Jools went by Karen in a flurry, Cyn gestured for Jools to come down to her level, as she wanted to whisper something.

Jools bent down, turning her ear to Cyn's mouth.

"While you were in the jacks, both Mark and Gavin were chatting me up!"

Jools turned back and whispered, "What's wrong with that?"

"I thought they were a couple!"

Jools laughed loudly at this, as the others looked at her but returned quickly to their conversations.

"Not at all," she said, dispensing with the whispers. "Those lads have been around the block a fair few times."

"Well then," Cyn replied, with a wink.

Jools laughed again and said, "Aren't you forgetting something, or someone?"

"Who?"

"Don. The bloke you had your face glued to last night."

"Don and I have an understanding."

"Which is?"

"Well, I haven't actually told him yet what that understanding is, but, well, he's doing his bar apprenticeship in Dublin and he won't be here forever."

"Would you not like to be Missus Don someday, running a pub in Galway?"

Cyn laughed. "Jools, I wouldn't trust myself to run a bath, never mind run a pub. I'd be an alco in a week."

"Are we nearly ready?" Sean said, as he and Robbo moved in beside Jools and Cyn.

Jools looked at the clock above the bar, which proudly proclaimed that it was "Guinness Time," but she'd have to take Arthur at his word, as she'd never tasted it. Just didn't look very appealing to her. The bar clock said it was five minutes to eight. "Do you want to have another here and then head in about quarter past?

Robbo looked at his watch. He wanted to be there as soon as the shutters went up.

"Yeah, I suppose, but would one of you have a quick look outside for…."

He didn't have to finish the sentence.

"I'll go out now," Jools said. "Oh, you haven't met the two new additions to our gang. Cyn is doing her best to lead them astray already." Karen and Archie smiled politely.

"Cyn, you do the introductions, I'll just pop my head outside for a minute."

"No problem," Cyn replied. "Karen and Archie, meet Sean and Robbo."

They both looked at each other and the same thought quickly passed between them – what incredible luck!

"Nice to meet you," they both said, smiling.

73. Boys!

Jools went out onto the street, which was crowded with Mods who'd spilled out from the bar. The forecasted rain which was really ever a 50/50 chance, began to fall, though not in earnest. She felt a few light drops on her face as she walked down to the corner and around to Adair Lane. It was already jammed with people waiting for the shutters to go up, which would, at eight o'clock on the button.

There was no sign of Freddie or his lads. She ran back to the pub.

"Did you order those drinks yet?"

"No," Sean said, "I was just about to."

"Don't bother. It's already jammed around there and there's loads of new faces who won't know who sits where. If we don't get in straight away, we won't get a seat. Also, it's starting to rain."

"Right then," Robbo said, "let's head round." He knocked back what was left of his pint and put the empty glass on the bar, looked at the others and said, "What are yis all waiting for?"

Tash, whose glass was still half full – she never was and never would be a glass half empty girl – looked at him with complete distaste.

"You, want us, to knock back our drinks? Is that what you're asking?"

"Tash," Dee said, "I don't think he was asking. That sounded to me more like he was telling."

They both put the hand that wasn't holding their drink on the opposite hip, cocked their heads to one side and looked at him with piercing gazes.

"Well, Robert McKenna," Tash said, "is Dee right? Are you telling us to knock back our drinks? Is that an instruction? Perhaps, a…." she looked at Dee as she said this, who was desperately trying to keep a straight face, and then back at Robbo, "a command? That wouldn't be a command, now, Robert, would it? Will you be calling us Modettes next?"

Robbo stood looking at the two of them, all faces on him now. Sean put his arm around his shoulder and said, "You know, Robbo, when your Ma is talking to you and she uses your full name? You know what it means when she does that, don't you?"

"Yeah, it means you're fucked."

"No, Robert," Sean said, "it means you're totally, proper, up shit creek, absolutely fucked. Tash there, the lovely girl that she is, just called you by your full name."

Robbo gulped.

"Look, girls, I mean, ladies, I didn't mean any disrespect, I just…."

Dee couldn't hold it in any longer and burst out laughing. She looked at Tash, they both shrugged and knocked back their drinks.

"Robert McKenna," Jools said, "you have just been taken to the cleaners by these two very lovely young ladies."

Tash and Dee smiled and did big stage bows.

"Aw, very funny," Robbo said. "You had me going there, Tash."

All five girls looked at each other and said, simultaneously, "Boys!" Before erupting into laughter.

"So, ladies," Robbo said, "may we have the pleasure of your company as we walk around to the fine establishment around the corner? That is, if you'll allow us to be seen in your presence?"

"Oh, I suppose," Cyn said.

Just then, Jayo and Nicki appeared beside them and Mark almost choked on his pint. Turning to Gavin, he said, "Where did she come from?"

"I dunno, but it looks like Jayo might have things wrapped up already."

"Howaya, Jayo," Mark said, "are you not going to introduce us to your friend?" Then, looking him up and down, said, "Sorry about your granny."

"Ah Jaysus, not you too!"

74. The Way It Should Be

They all left the pub and Karen sidled up beside Robbo.

"Nice suit, Robbo," she said, flashing a dazzling smile and batting her eyelashes at him.

"Nice dress, Karen," Robbo said back, smiling. "Haven't seen you here before."

"First time. I've been into it a while but just never got round to going. Archie's girlfriend's a mate of mine and she couldn't go, so gave me the ticket."

"You're not with Archie?"

"Nope."

"I thought…."

"No," she said, quickly interrupting him and smiling that dazzling smile again, the one she knew made boys go weak. "Just mates."

She looked around at the throng of Mods standing outside Bubbles as they reached the doorway, just as the shutters went up.

"There seems to be a lot of that here," she said. "I don't think I've ever come across a group of people like it where all the lads and girls treat each other equally."

"It's the way it should be," he said. "That Modette word freaks me out as much as it does the girls. Somehow implies that they're less than us, know what I mean? We're all Mods here, simple as that."

Karen looked at Robbo and smiled. Then she thought about the reason she was really there and struggled to keep the smile on her face. Whatever he had done for Freddie to want to get hold of him didn't bear thinking about, and she felt really guilty already and she'd only known him ten minutes. But she was more afraid of Freddie to cross him, than she liked Robbo. Whatever happened, she'd make sure she'd have him outside later. Whatever Freddie did with him after that, really wasn't her problem.

75. I Can't Put My Finger On It

"She seems nice." Cyn said to Jools, with a quick look over her shoulder at Karen.

"Yeah," Jools said. "I love her dress. And the Archie fella. They both seem nice but…."

"But what?"

"I dunno. I've never seen either of them before in my life and they both show up tonight, out of nowhere and she just latches onto Robbo. They're certainly not regulars."

"Pretty well dressed and on the money for complete newbies." Cyn said.

"Oh, they definitely look like Mods. but I just can't put my finger on it. Might be my imagination, but I'm sure a look passed between them when they were introduced to Robbo."

"It's all in your head, Jools. And this is Robbo, Here Come The Nice. They probably heard from someone that if they needed some gear, he's the bloke to go to."

"Maybe you're right."

"Well," Cyn said, "they both seem fine to me."

76. Monsters In Shadows

The crowd poured down the stairs and handed their tickets in at the box office. There was already a queue forming at the cloak room and Jools and Cyn joined it. About ten minutes later, by the time they'd deposited their coats and walked around to their usual spot, she noticed that the lads had already held their seats. She looked around and checked the crowd. Archie was standing chatting with Sean, while Jayo was about two seats down where Susan and Chris sat, chatting to that Nicki girl he'd met in the pub and Robbo sat on the arm of one of the seats, deep in conversation with Karen, both their heads inches apart as the music was already quite loud. A few bodies were shuffling about to "A Touch Of Velvet, A Sting Of Brass," as Noel was getting into his stride. Karen's foot was tapping along with the music. Her sister would have hated this already.

Most of the regulars were there, all sitting or standing near their usual spots. She took a deep breath and tried her best not to worry about what lay ahead. She'd just have to try and put on the façade of enjoying herself while secretly worrying about what she had to do.

She was about to sit down and noticed something dark on the seat. She picked up Karen's mac.

"Is this yours?" She asked her.

"No," Karen replied, "well, yeah, kind of. It's my sister's. Thought it might rain tonight so brought it, just in case.

Jools held it up and looked at it. "You should put it in the cloak room."

"Why? Is it not alright where it is?"

"Well, it's up to you, but I wouldn't. It's nice. If you leave it here, someone might lift it if we're all up dancing."

Karen gulped. She'd never thought about dancing and looked at the girls on the floor who seemed to be floating from side to side and forward and back again. She thought she'd never be able to dance like that, even if the music was good, which she was surprised she liked.

"Oh, I probably won't be dancing much."

"Still," Jools replied. "It's fifty pence. Better than going home and telling your sister you lost her mac."

Karen relented.

"Where's the cloakroom then?"

"Just over there," Jools said, pointing.

"Back in a minute," Karen said to Robbo, standing up and taking the coat from Jools.

She walked off towards the cloakroom.

"What's the story with her?" Jools asked him.

"Dunno," he replied. "Only just met her. And him, tonight," he added, nodding towards Archie. "Why? What do you mean?"

"She comes in from nowhere, Robbo and latches onto you?"

"Have you seen me?" He said to her, smiling. "Especially in this suit. I'm amazed there aren't more birds latching onto me." He laughed.

She didn't.

"What's wrong?"

"Freddie Collins is out for your blood. Literally. And two people you've never seen before just show up and next thing you know, one of them is your new best friend. And you don't find that a little bit suspicious?"

"Well, no," he said. "They're clearly Mods. Look at his suit for starters, that's definitely tailor made and mohair, fits him like a glove and as for Karen, dressed like that, you might as well be looking at Jean Shrimpton. I've been around yer man and enough of his headcase friends long enough to spot a bad one and she's definitely not."

Jools thought. Maybe he was right. Maybe she was just being paranoid. Everything weighing down on her felt almost like an actual, physical weight and maybe it had all finally caught up with her. Maybe she was seeing monsters in shadows where there weren't even any shadows.

Maybe.

She looked at her watch.

Ten minutes past eight.

Cyn grabbed her hand as Noel announced, "Time for The Style Council, this is Speak Like A Child," and Cyn dragged her towards the floor, patting her blonde bob and laughing as Weller sang about hair hanging in golden steps.

"I hope you're right," she called back to him, as Karen sat back down.

Robbo looked at his watch. Twenty-five to nine, and thought, good long night ahead and if it's my last one here, I might as well make the most of it.

"Am I keeping you up?" Karen asked him, smiling.

"What? No, not at all." He laughed. "Just thinking we've still nearly a full twelve hours here, it's gonna be a cracker."

Before she could reply, a tall, slim Mod in a dark suit came up to him.

"Robbo, you got any…."

"Nope." Robbo replied, quickly. "I'm out."

"Bollocks. Gonna be hard to stay awake till eight."

"Get some coffee at the bar," Robbo said. "You'll be grand."

As he walked away, Karen asked, "What was that all about?"

"Ah, nothing," he replied.

That's when the penny dropped for her. She knew Archie long enough to know what his Dad's employer was into and that exchange brought her back a couple of years previously to

371

looking through her sister's handbag for some lipstick and finding a small square of silver foil, which, when she opened it had contained a white powder.

"What the fuck is this, Jen?" She'd asked her sister. "Are you doing coke? Don't fucking tell me it's heroin?"

"Course not, you daft cow," Jeanette had replied. "It's just a bit of speed. All the Mods do it. Keeps you going when you're knackered. Nobody does coke, it's too expensive anyway and heroin's a mugs game. Karen, Mods have been taking speed since the Sixties. It's harmless, just gives you a bit of a buzz, a bit of energy. But don't tell Mam, she'll have a fucking heart attack!"

She looked at Robbo. He was looking out at the dancefloor, tapping his foot and mouthing along with the lyrics. She'd only just met him but there was something genuinely nice about him, yet, if he was mixed up with drugs, how nice could he really be?

She knew what Freddie did and she knew – or suspected – some of what Archie's Dad did for Freddie, but, again, Conn was really nice. Good people have to do bad things sometimes, she thought.

Why had she agreed to do this? She knew now that if Robbo was selling gear, he was either selling it for Freddie and had fucked him over or was selling gear and shouldn't have been if he wasn't working for that gangster, but either way, if drugs were involved, Freddie most definitely didn't just want a chat with him.

Robbo was still looking out towards the dancefloor and she managed to catch Archie's eye. She nodded her head in the direction of the tunnel, which she assumed led to the bar and toilets – she was correct in both assumptions - and Archie nodded back, said something to Sean and walked off in that direction.

"I'm just going to the ladies," she said to Robbo, squeezing his hand. He looked down at their hands touching and smiled.

"Alright," he said, "see you in a bit."

77. You Can't Leave

"What the fuck, Archie? You never said it was anything to do with drugs!"

Archie had stopped just short of the bar as Karen grabbed his elbow and now stepped back, with the full force of her anger in his face. He held his hands up in defence.

"Honest, Karen," he said, "I didn't know! I was just told to get him outside so Freddie could get hold of him and I couldn't have done that myself. You saw how many people said hello to him as they passed. Everyone here knows him and looks like they like him too. If I'd started a row with him, I'd have got my head kicked in."

"Everyone fucking knows him, Archie, because he sells them drugs!"

"Not everyone's doing it, Karen, and anyway, it's probably nothing worse than a bit of speed. Relax."

"Don't you fucking tell me to relax, Archie Boylan. You're my mate and we go back a long way but if I had known this was about drugs, I'd have said no from the start."

"Well I didn't know, Karen. Honest! Freddie wants him outside, that's it, that's all."

Karen sighed. "He seems really nice. If I get him outside later and Freddie grabs him, you know what he'll do. I really don't want to be a part of that."

"You're not thinking of leaving, are you? You can't leave! If we don't get him outside later, Freddie's gonna kill the pair of us. Sorry, Karen, but he more or less told me that in the kitchen earlier."

"Us?" She said. "What do you mean, Us? That prick knows who I am?"

"Well, yeah, I had to tell him."

Karen punched him in the chest, drawing looks from a group of girls standing near the bar. "Couldn't you have just told him it was some girl you know?" She said. "You didn't have to give him my name! For fuck sake, Archie!" She was fuming.

"Sorry, but what was I supposed to do? Dad arrived home and said I had to go to the office, that Freddie wanted me to do a job. I said does he know I'm in the middle of studying for the leaving and he said Freddie told him he didn't give a fuck if I was studying for my master's degree in biochemical nuclear fuckin science, that I was doing the job tonight. End of. His actual words, Karen. It wasn't that I even had much of a choice, I didn't have any choice. You don't say no to Freddie!"

"I'm studying for the leaving too…." she said, trailing off, but knew her argument didn't hold any water.

"I know that," he said, "and I'm sorry but his plan, well, it was shit. Freddie thinks that he can get everything sorted with

375

violence and I knew that wouldn't work here and I was right. Look at you, Karen, you look gorgeous. I knew you'd catch his eye and get me out of this but if you leave now, there's no way I'm gonna get him outside and if Freddie doesn't get hold of him, I really don't know what he'll do to us. Yer man Robbo might be nice, but...."

"He is!"

"Okay, he is nice. But we don't know him from fucking Adam and I'm sorry I got you roped into this, I really am, but there wasn't any other way. Nobody says no to Freddie Collins and lives to tell about it."

Archie began to well up.

"Come here, you soft shite," she said and hugged him. "I'm really not happy about this but I said I'd help, and I will."

Archie reached into his pocket and took out his wallet. He took all of the money that Freddie had given him and handed it to her.

"What's this?"

"Freddie gave me two hundred quid to go out tonight. He said to give you fifty, but you're doing all the work, so here, take the lot."

"I don't want the money," she said, pushing his hand away.

"I'm enjoying talking to him, and it's not as bad here as I thought it would be, in fact, I think it's pretty decent, and I will make sure he's goes outside, but I don't want money for it. What would that make me? I feel guilty enough already. No, keep the money."

"I don't want it either."

"Well, I don't know, give it to the Vincent De Paul or something tomorrow, I don't want it. Now come on, let's get back, we've been gone long enough."

78. Bullseye

Dosser got out of the shower, wrapped a towel around his scrawny waist and with his shoulders back and head held high, wiped the steam off the mirror and had a look at himself. He felt good. He'd even shaved, and properly too. Normally when Dosser shaved, there were bits of hair left sticking out here and there, making him look like he'd tried to do it with a fork. But tonight, he'd made a special effort and his face was as smooth as a baby's bum. He still held onto the misguided illusion and unreasonable hope that he would, one day, eventually get together with Cyn. Oh, he fancied all of the other girls on the scene, but, for Dosser, there was just something special about her. He thought if he looked like a proper Mod tonight, in his new suit, on his new scooter, both him and it sparkling clean, maybe, just maybe, when she came out of the allnighter for some air, she'd see him differently and that virginal monkey that was on his back would fuck off away. He'd dreamt of it so many times and cracked a fair few out to fantasies of her too, all the while calling her name. He'd done it one time while listening to a Northern Soul tape he'd bought off Noel, on a Walkman he'd lifted from Peate's in Parnell Street and with eyes closed and hearing impaired, he didn't know his Mam had walked in on him with his washing, while he was mid-stroke, and saw him in full flow, hearing him moan the words "Sin, Sin."

His Mam, a devout Catholic if ever there was one, didn't know what to make of this and asked the priest the next time she was in confession if masturbation was still a sin if you knew it was and said the words, "Sin, Sin," while you did it? The priest, just out of the seminary and newly appointed to the parish, went bright red, got flustered, said it was and gave her ten Hail Mary's and told her that a woman of her age shouldn't be doing anything like that, before getting up and running from the confession box.

Dosser, of course, was blissfully unaware that he'd been caught and never thought to question why, all of a sudden, his clean washing began to appear outside his door, neatly folded, but on the floor of the landing.

Dosser's brother was waiting outside the bathroom, ready for another round of his favourite pastime of slagging his smaller, but older sibling.

"Ma! I really think Graham is sick," he called out as Dosser exited the bathroom and passed him in the hall, before making his way upstairs to his bedroom. "He's just had a shower and it's not even Christmas."

"Oh, shut the fuck up, Brian," Dosser said. "You're an awful smart prick, you know that?"

"Graham, of course I'm smart, but that's good coming from you. Everyone is smarter than you. That plant," he said, indicating a plastic fern in the hallway, "that fucking yoke is smarter than you and it's not even real."

"Just fuck off!" Dosser shouted at him.

"Language, Graham," came his Mam's voice from the kitchen.

"Jaysus, Ma," he called back, "it was him, starting his fuckin shite again. He's always takin the piss out of me!"

"I won't tell you again, Graham," she called back.

"See?" Brian said. "You don't even have the cop on to stop cursing when she tells you. It'd be gas if she said you weren't going out tonight, that you were grounded for talking to her like that."

"She can't do that," Dosser said, uncertainty creeping into his voice and thoughts of getting off with Cyn beginning to slip away. "I'm eighteen. I'm an adult. I'm even old enough to vote. She can't tell me what to do. Can she?"

"Her house, her rules," Brian said. Dosser just shook his head, his shoulders now dropped once again. He didn't say anything as he went up the stairs to his room.

"Bullseye!" Brian said to himself, smirking.

79. Old Habits Die Hard

Dosser sat on his bed, towel wrapped around his shoulders. He looked at his suit, which was hanging on the handle of the wardrobe door, still in the cellophane cover Mrs Malone had put it in. Beside it was the plain white shirt he'd also bought in Button Down – though the collars of the shirt weren't.

"Why the fuck didn't you buy a Ben Sherman?" And then something else occurred to him. He didn't even possess a tie. There were probably hundreds of ties hanging on racks in the shop, but he never even thought to buy one. He'd been so excited and even more delighted that the owner had treated him with a bit of respect when he'd seen all the money, that he'd forgotten to get the most important bits to go with his suit.

He went into his Mam and Dad's bedroom and had a look through his Dad's ties. Every was about five inches wide at the bottom, and most of them were brown. "What the fuck is it with him and this brown shite?" He said, shaking his head. "Bollocks. I'll just wear a Fred underneath it."

He went back into his bedroom and took the light blue Fred Perry he'd bought but hadn't worn yet out of the wardrobe. He held it up to the suit. Even someone as devoid of taste and fashion knowledge as he was knew that a light blue Fred Perry would look shite underneath a bottle green tonic suit, but he put it under the jacket to see anyway. It didn't go. He thought about wearing just the white shirt instead but knew that without a tie, the collars would just stick out and he'd look stupid. He once again admonished himself for not thinking to buy a button down shirt and a tie. He looked around the floor. The black Fred Perry with the milk stains down the front was in a ball beside the record player. He picked it up and after a quick look and a sniff, concluded that it would do, and under the suit, nobody would see the stains.

The piss stained Y-Fronts he'd been wearing for God knew how many days, that he'd left on the floor of his room before he went downstairs for his shower had mysteriously disappeared and now inhabited the deepest, darkest recesses of the bin out the back. Once his Mam had heard the shower going, she'd ran upstairs with the tongs from the fireplace and removed the offending article, almost gagging.

He never noticed. He opened the top drawer of his chest of drawers and took out a brand new, clean white pair that he'd lifted from the local Dunnes the day he was in Button Down. Even with a pocket stuffed with cash, old habits die hard. He put them on and pulled back the curtains. It was lashing.

"Fifty percent, me bollix," he muttered to himself.

80. Is She Here?

The drive from Lainey's house in Baldoyle to Matt's brother's flat in Rathmines was a long one. The rain that Jools had correctly predicted came and by the time they crossed from one side of Dublin to the other, their rain gear was soaked.

"This is going to be awful," Lainey said after they pulled into the garden and ran up the stairs to the flat. Matt rang the bell and a few seconds later, his brother, Peter, opened the door.

"You two look like drowned rats," he said.

"Lovely," Lainey replied, as they stepped into the hall. "Exactly what a girl wants to hear. Now, can you get us towels, please? We need to dry this gear off if we need it later."

Peter opened a cupboard in the hall and took out two bath towels.

"Will these do?"

"Perfect," she replied, and turning to Matt said, "Turn around, I'll do you and you do me."

Peter was just about to speak when she said, "Shut it, you dirty minded shite."

When their gear was dry, removed and hung up, Peter showed them into the living room, which quietly surprised Lainey. She'd had a small, dingy room in mind, with a bed and a kitchen beside it, bathroom tucked away in an alcove somewhere, but no, the living room, bedroom, kitchen and bathroom were all separate and the space surprised her. Also because there was barely anyone in it.

"Where's everyone?"

"Oh, there's still a gang of people in the pub, they'll be around soon," Peter replied.

"Matt," she whispered to him. "There are eight people here, including us and your gobshite brother."

"Give it a chance," he said, "It'll be grand."

"Is she here?" Lainey asked Peter.

"Who?"

"Her, the girl you're trying to get off with?"

Peter blushed.

"You told her?" He said to Matt.

"Course I told her, she wanted to go to Bubbles. She's here doing you a favour."

Peter rolled his eyes.

"No, she's not here yet. Do yis want a drink?"

"Just Coke for me," Matt said.

"Same, thanks," Lainey replied.

"Coming right up," Peter said, exiting towards the kitchen.

"How long do we have to stay?" Lainey asked Matt. "They're already staring at us. And the music is terrible."

The song that was currently playing was "Shout," by Tears For Fears and Matt said, "They were a Mod band once. The

Graduate."

"The operative word in that sentence, Matt, is 'Were.' That," she said, nodding towards the stereo, "is not a Mod band."

"Fair point," he said, as Peter returned with their drinks, just as the doorbell rang.

"Sit down," he said, ushering them towards the couch, "there's a few more coming in now."

81. That Strange Feeling Again

After The Style Council, Noel played The Jam, Purple Hearts, The Chords, Makin' Time and Nine Below Zero and then followed that with one of Jools's all-time favourites, The Action's "Shadows And Reflections," which kicked off the Sixties Mod set and Jools and Cyn kept dancing to "Baby Please Don't Go," "Yeh Yeh," "Sha La La La Lee," "Anyway, Anyhow, Anywhere," Mel Torme's version of "Comin' Home Baby" and The Creation, with the song that inspired one of her favourite Eighties Mod bands, "Makin' Time."

Noel came back on the microphone and announced that it was "Time for a bit of Ska" and the sound of a car screeching filled the air when "Al Capone," by Prince buster started to play.

Jools shook her head.

"I can't, Cyn," she said, "I need a breather."

They walked back to their seats and they sat down.

She hadn't danced as much in the last thirty years as she had done in the past few days, she thought. Or, the next thirty years, if you thought about it another way.

Sitting there, she started to think about that night. This night, she corrected herself. She could never remember much about it and kind of knew why. In 2015, they had a term for it, but in 1985, not many people had heard of post-traumatic stress disorder, which, although never actually diagnosed, is what she thought had blocked most of the memories out.

She remembered what she was wearing, which was exactly what she was wearing right now. She remembered meeting Jimmy at the bar, and they had chatted for what seemed like ages. She remembered him asking her to dance and remembered they kissed while "The Bitterest Pill" played, she never did lose sight of the irony there.

She only knew the exact time of the accident afterwards, but how long after that the ripple of an accident in the laneway above had started to spread through the club, what exact time that was, she couldn't remember. All she remembered after she heard, was making her way upstairs with the rest of the crowd to see what had happened.

Up to that point in her life, the only dead person she had ever seen was her Granny, her Grandad having died before she was born. And even then, when she saw her Granny in the coffin, the funeral directors had done such a job of tarting her up with all the wrong makeup, the kind of stuff she would never have worn when she was alive and would probably have said that she wouldn't be caught dead wearing, although now, she was, it didn't actually look like her Granny. But when she made her way through the crowd of shocked and silent faces and saw her friend on the ground, so very and completely dead, even with blood on her face and in her hair – she guessed someone had removed her helmet - her body twisted and broken, it was still Lainey. Undoubtedly, Lainey.

The following week had been a blur. She had absolutely no recollection of the funeral home viewing, and very little of the funeral itself.

But now, sitting here, on the same night, bits and pieces began to fall back into her mind. All the records that Noel played in the slow set before Jimmy and her kissed. Standing at the bar when Mick told Gaz how he came home from work that afternoon and his baby brother, who was only three at the time, was sitting in the front room playing pretend records on his little Fisher Price record player while he shushed everyone as he talked into a hairbrush and told them all he was on the radio. She didn't remember that till now, but she smiled, because that's exactly what he did end up doing when he grew up. Linda and Flavo both doing sets, but for the life of her, she couldn't remember what they played.

And Jimmy. She'd been at the bar and that's where he first spoke to her and she knew that's where he'd first speak to her tonight. She'd seen him on the previous Wednesday – this time around – but had avoided him. Would she avoid him now? She remembered how handsome he looked when they'd met and sometimes it really was love at first sight and she thought that's what it was for her. But Prince Charming wouldn't always be either a prince or charming and she remembered the years of misery, but she also remembered the good times, there were some, she had to admit. And what if, when he spoke to her at the bar, what if she just said no, not interested? What would her life be like? How different would it turn out? Extremely different, she thought. No Jimmy, no struggling, but also no determination to not ever have to be dependent upon anyone. But the biggest no, was no Jessica and Liam. She thought again, as she had earlier, if she wasn't with Jimmy and ended up with someone else, there might be another *version* of her kids, but they wouldn't be them. Like it or not, there was a part of Jimmy in both of them and with someone else, they'd be very different. She'd go to the bar and when he spoke to her, she knew what she'd have to do. They'll chat, he'll ask her to dance and they'll kiss. And that's when the deal will be sealed.

She also remembered what Cyn had in her BOAC bag and it was automatic, unthinking. She was hot after dancing so much and badly needed to cool down.

"Can I have one of those fans you have in your bag please, Cyn?"

Cyn looked at her, surprised.

"How do you know I brought fans?"

"I dunno. You must have told me during the week that you

were bringing them or earlier tonight, I don't remember."

Cyn was completely mystified. Up till that afternoon, *she* didn't even know she was bringing fans. Up till that afternoon, she'd forgotten they even existed.

The previous August, her aunt had been in Benidorm and brought two fans home for her sister, Cyn's Mam. They were dark, ugly things with badly painted flamenco dancers on them, a man on one and a woman on the other. Her aunt had told her Mam that they'd look great spread open on the living room wall, and, of course, her Mam smiled, said they really would and thanked her. As soon as the sister went, they were thrown in the drawer of the china cabinet and forgotten about, which was also where the sewing kit was kept. Cyn had gone rummaging in the drawer that afternoon for the kit to sew a loose button on a pair of hipsters she'd brought to change into later and found the fans. She threw them in the bag thinking they might come in handy if it got really hot and had actually forgotten about them.

"Jools," she said, "I didn't even know I was bringing the fans till today. Up till this afternoon, I had no clue we even had fans in the house. I'd forgotten I'd even put them in the bag. So, if I didn't know, how did you know I had them?"

Jools sighed, "Maybe I'm psychic, or maybe I just saw them in the bag when you went looking for something earlier."

Cyn thought about that. She couldn't remember opening the bag before now, but she also couldn't remember *not* opening the bag. That strange feeling she'd gotten about Jools being somehow different swept over her again. She shuddered. She opened the bag and, although she thought she had thrown the fans in first, and they should be right at the bottom, they were both there, right at the top, sitting on her towel. Maybe Jools had seen them. She had to have, Cyn thought. There's no other explanation. She took them both out and handed one to Jools who took it, flicked it open and revealed it to be the one with the male dancer. Cyn flicked open the other one.

"Jesus," Jools said, looking at both of them, "these are fucking hideous! Where did you get them?"

"My aunt," was all Cyn said.

82. Confidence

Dosser dressed in most definitely the best clothes he'd ever worn since his Confirmation and hunkered down beside the Dansette. He carefully lifted off the turntable which had long ago stopped working and placed it on the floor. He took the wad of cash out from the hole beneath where the turntable was, counted off five twenties and replaced the still quite substantial remainder back into the hole and put the turntable back in place. He stood up and looked at it. Just a record player, that's all it was, nobody would think any different.

His Mam had noticed the new clothes and scooter, but she said nothing. She'd either been afraid to ask because she didn't want the truth, or didn't want the lie, or just when it came to caring, like the turntable, had long ago stopped. His Dad was either at work, or in the pub or when he was at home, was too engrossed in his paper or the TV to notice much of anything. Only Brian asked where he'd got the money and Dosser had simply told him to fuck off. Brian had just shrugged and walked away without a word. Dosser must have caught him on an off day.

He looked out the window. It was just after eleven and the rain had stopped. The bird on the telly had been right on the money.

Without a ticket and with no way to get in and dance, he'd no need to bring a bag with a change of clothes – not that he would have anyway – and ran down the stairs, full of confidence in his new-found look and wealth. For once, Brian was nowhere to be seen to ruin his mood.

"I'm off to Bubbles, Ma," he called into the living room. "See ya in the morning."

83. You Can't Hurry Love

"This is awful, Matt," Lainey said. "That girl over there keeps looking at us and sniggering. You know how much I dislike violence, but if she keeps that up, I'll go over there and burst her!"

"No you won't," he said. "That's not you, and we both know it. Come on, we'll go into the kitchen and see what Peter's up to." They got up off the couch and he took her by the elbow and led her in. She reluctantly let him. She'd have preferred if he'd led her towards the front door.

Peter was standing by the fridge, chatting with a girl who was, presumably, "The One," if his body language was anything to go by. They were standing very close together, him touching her arm and her playing with her hair. They hadn't seen her arrive, both of them stuck in the corner at one end of the couch while the flat had filled up with drunken revellers fresh from the pub, dancing to Now That's What I Call Music! Volumes One to Four, though not in consecutive order. She almost puked when Phil Collins came on singing, "You Can't Hurry Love," and she heard some gobshite say, "Oh I love Motown!"

Even The Style Council, who she didn't particularly like, but tolerated, because Matt and most of her mates liked them, was whipped off with an extremely loud scratch as they began to sing "You're The Best Thing." The same happened when "Shout To The Top" started. Another scratch and the needle was lifted and dropped onto another God awful pop song. The person in charge of the music proclaiming that The Style Council were "Absolute fucking shoite."

Where had Peter picked up these arseholes? She wondered to herself. They all seemed like Trinity or UCD heads. Privileged college kids. Why on earth would they be hanging around with a mechanic from Raheny? When she asked Matt what he thought, he looked around, saw the crowd knocking back the mountain of beer and spirits Peter had bought for the party and said, "That," waving his hand around the room. "Free booze and a free party in a free gaff. There's probably a couple of them going at it in his bed right this minute. There's been so many people in and out of that room since we got here, he should install a revolving door."

They walked into the kitchen and Peter was grinning from ear to ear.

"Erin, this is my brother Matt and his girlfriend…."

"Fiancée," Lainey said, correcting him and holding up her left hand, to show the ring.

"Sorry," Peter said. "My brother Matt's Fiancée, Lainey."

"Lainey?" Erin said. "That's unusual. Never heard that one

before. L-A-N-Y?"

Lainey smiled. Erin was not from these parts, as the saying goes. Her accent was so different from those in the other room. "No, L-A-I-N-E-Y. It's short for Elaine."

Erin looked up for a second and, smiling, said, "It's actually the same length."

Lainey laughed. "Yes, you're absolutely right. I never thought of that. So, how did you end up with that lot?" She asked, nodding in the direction of the other room. "You're definitely not a Southsider."

"College," Erin said. "And I am Southside, actually. Ballyfermot. But definitely not a Southsider in their sense of the word. All that Dublin Four, Daddy's Beemer and let's all cheer for the rugger, shite gets on my nerves. One of the girls I know from college and one of the few I actually like," she paused and pointed out a small, red haired girl dancing over by the stereo, "that one there, Winnie, she gets her car done in the garage Peter and Matt work in and I went with her last week. I got chatting to Peter, he seemed nice and a couple of days later, Winnie got a call inviting us to the party. Bring your friend, she told me he said, and then changed it to friends." She laughed. "So here we are. And here they are. Nice little flat. I'm still at home with Mam and Dad."

"He's a bit of a gobshite sometimes," Lainey said, "and his taste

396

in music is atrocious, but he's not the worst."

"No," Erin said, looking at Peter. She tugged on his shirt collar, smiled and said, "No, he's not."

"That's a relief," Peter said to Matt, smiling, as the girls fell into conversation, "I was hoping they'd get along."

84. Not Long Now

"I'm getting real anxty, George. Wonder what's happenin? Is the bird doin her job?"

"We'll find out soon enough, Boss," George replied. He looked up from the chair to where Conn had taken up position against the filing cabinet. Conn looked worried. Of course he's worried, George thought. That was his yunfella in there with her and if they didn't have Robbo outside when Freddie arrived, Conn would feel the brunt of it.

Conn looked at George and they both looked at Freddie, the same thought passing through their minds. We could kill him now, straight through the woodchipper and nobody would be any the wiser.

"He'd better be there," Freddie said. He looked at his watch. "Not long now."

85. Making An Impression

"Want a drink?" Jools asked Cyn.

"No, I'm grand, thanks," she replied. "There's Linda over by the DJ box with her records, I think she's going on now, I reckon I'll be dancing in a minute."

"Okay then, I'm going up to the bar, I'm parching."

She looked over to the DJ box and Linda had slid in behind the decks. By the time she reached the bar, Ronnie Dyson's "Lady In Red" was blasting out of the speakers and people were running to the dancefloor.

She ordered a Coke and heard Gaz laughing and saying, "That's priceless." He was talking to Mick and she knew what he'd just been told.

"Jools," Gaz said, "wait till you hear this."

Mick relayed the story she'd remembered earlier, and she smiled.

"Sounds like a determined young man," she said.

"Oh he is," Mick replied, beaming with pride.

"You never know, he might even DJ at Bubbles one day."

"That would be something to see," Mick said, still beaming.

Jools got her Coke and turned around, leaning against the bar, watching the throng of people going around the venue, to and from the dancefloor, in and out of the toilets and just generally hanging around in groups, chatting and laughing. And, of course the couples here and there snogging. Those teenage hormones running wild.

She looked to the end of the bar where Sean and Lenny were talking, that Archie chap standing with a Coke in his hand, wide eyed and taking it all in. Even dressed as sharp as he was, he may as well have had "Newbie" written across his forehead.

She walked down to them and said to him, "Don't listen to this pair, Archie, they don't have a clue about the bits they think they know about and make up everything else!"

Sean laughed, but Lenny didn't. She smiled as she saw the anger cross his face.

"Haven't seen you here before," she said to Archie.

"No," he replied, "First night."

"Really?" She said, trying not to let on. "You must be a Mod a while, you're certainly dressed the part."

She ran the tips of her fingers over his pocket square and, having noticed neither Lenny or Sean had one, and come to think of it, neither did most of the other lads, said, "This, boys, is that final touch that makes the difference."

Sean smiled, loving how Jools was baiting Lenny, as he saw that both him and Archie were going red, but for different reasons. Archie's frame extended upwards with the compliment, whereas Lenny's lowered, with embarrassment. She smiled. She wasn't normally a vindictive person, but she really, really didn't like Lenny who would, at any given opportunity put others down if he got the chance, using his superior knowledge of music as a weapon.

Just then, she saw a tall, slim red haired bloke approach who looked vaguely familiar, but she just couldn't place him. He clapped a hand on Sean's shoulder and said, "Alright, Sean, mate, ow you doin?"

Sean jumped and spilled his drink, put it down on the bar and turned to see who was accosting him.

"Del!" He said, shaking the other bloke's hand. "I didn't know you were coming. I haven't seen you since…."

"Brighton!" They both exclaimed.

That's when Jools recognised him. Del McGrath was one of the Brighton Mods that had DJd in Dublin a few times back in her own time. She remembered seeing him in the Grand Central one night and he played a stormer of a set and she'd been introduced to him afterwards. She was just about to give him a hug but caught herself at the last second. In 2015, they knew each other, but in 1985, they didn't and, despite bits and pieces of the night coming back to her, she didn't remember having met him.

Ripples, she thought. Some things would remain the same, but others would be different and as much as she was trying to do the things she remembered and be the places she should be, there was still a certain element of free will to it. Maybe she'd walked back to Cyn after having heard Mick tell his story the first time round but didn't this time. She remembered the story but couldn't remember what she'd done directly after hearing it, so, there always was the possibility that Del had talked to Sean at the bar and she just hadn't been there to see it.

"What are you doing here?" Sean asked him. "By the way, this is Jools, Lenny and Archie." Del said "Alright, nice to meet you all." Turning back to Sean, he said, "Robbo got me a ticket. I was gonna be in Westport this week wiv me Nan anyway, so I thought" - the word *Thought* coming out as *Fawt* – "I'd come up on the train and surprise you, mate. Lots goin on in Brighton right now, but you can't beat a night at Bubbles, and I've only been ere the once!"

"Brighton, yeah mate, I love a bit of Brighton." Lenny said.

"You been to Brighton, then?" Del asked.

"I don't remember you going to Brighton," Sean said. "You weren't there when we were."

"Nah, nah," Lenny said. "I went with my cousins. They're all top London Mods, proper geezers. Best mates with that Eddie Pillin bloke."

"Piller." They all said, except Archie, who hadn't got a clue. Lenny continued, unfazed.

"Yeah, we drove down on the scooters my cousin owns. All original. I drove a TV Two Hundred, just like Jimmy's one in Quadrophenia." He smiled, believing he'd impressed them all.

"Jimmy drove an LI One fifty, mate," Del said. "Series Three," which came out as *Free*.

"Yeah, yeah, that's what I meant. Great weekend, fightin trendies on the beach, stuffin they're faces in the sand."

"Ain't no sand on Brighton beach, mate." Del said.

"What?"

"Brighton," Del continued, taking a sip of his Coke from the straw. "Brighton ain't got no sand, it's pebbles. Stones. Brighton is not a sandy beach. You was never there if you think you was avin a go at some casuals on a sandy Brighton beach, mate."

Lenny, flustered, pulled the first thing he could from his head.

"Nah, sorry, I was a bit confused there. Musta been all the pills we had. I meant Clacton. Yeah we drove down to the coast and were fightin casuals on Clacton beach. We were gonna stop in Brighton for a kickin, but just drove straight past and went to Clacton."

"Clacton's the other way, mate."

"What?"

"Where was you stayin in London when you was there?" Del asked. "Like, where does your cousin live?"

Again, Lenny wracked his brains and pulled out the first thing he could think of.

"Wimbledon...." he said, unsurely.

"North East London," Del said. "So, you had to drive all the way through the city and down through Surrey, to get to Clacton, on the South coast?"

"Yeah," Lenny said, "We had some buzz drivin down."

"Lenny, is it?"

Lenny just nodded his head. At this stage, he was so caught up in the lie, that he wasn't even sure of his own name.

"Right, Lenny," Del said. "Wimbledon, ain't in North East London, it's in South West London, so you was never driving South through the city to get to Clacton on the South coast. Clacton is on the East coast. If you was in Wimbledon, you'd av to drive North East of London to get there. Av you actually been to Brighton or Clacton or even Wimbledon, or did you just think all of this up while you was watching the tennis on the telly?"

All faces were on Lenny now and any possibility of him keeping his one cool was gone, as the colour rose from his neck, through his cheeks and continued past his forehead. Jools thought he looked like a thermometer.

"I..." Lenny said, "I'm going to dance."

He turned completely around and without another word,

walked towards the dancefloor to the sound of Alfie Davison singing "Love Is A Serious Business," but didn't get far enough away that he couldn't hear Del say, "Muppet," which came out as "Mappet."

"What the hell was that all about?" Jools asked.

Sean just stood there, stunned.

"I knew Lenny could bullshit with the best of them but that, I really don't know what to say.

"I think he was trying to impress you, Del," she said.

"Well, Jools, I really do av to say, he made an impression alright."

Sean just stood there, shaking his head. Still bewildered.

"Hi. Jools isn't it?"

She turned and almost gasped.

"Yes, Ji…." She was about to say Jimmy, but quickly corrected herself, "Jools, yes."

"I'm Jimmy," he said.

God, he really is good looking, she thought and despite herself, she smiled.

86. Dance, Dance, Dance

Cyn had been dancing non-stop since Linda went on as she'd been pulling blinders out of her record box from the first disc, though, the highlight of her set for Cyn was when she played The Vel-Vets, "I Got To Find Me Somebody," as she loved that bit where everyone shouted "Wooo!" along with the track, but she danced to everything. "Picture Me Gone," "Love Love Love," "My Sugar Baby," "Dance Dance Dance," and "Rosemary What Happened," from Detroit's finest, Richard "Popcorn" Wiley was followed by one of her all-time favourite records and one that would still be played in 2015, though she didn't know it yet, The Detroit Prophets, "Suspicion," which nobody knew at the time was an unissued Motown song by The Originals as everyone who had it in 1985, had it on a bootleg. Cyn couldn't have told you if it was The Originals or The Detroit Prophets, she didn't care, that was more what Jools and Sean were into, she only cared about two things; if it was good or if it was bad and as far as she was concerned, everything Linda was playing was good. She so needed a breather, a pee, and a Coke, but every time a record ended, there was another gem to follow it.

"Two more for me and then you've got Flavo for the next hour," Linda spoke into the microphone and Cyn silently prayed that at least one of the last two would be a song she didn't like so she could go to the toilet, get that Coke and see what Jools was up to, before Flavo came on because, as Cyn had said, multiple times whenever she saw him DJ, "He's got some amazing records," but no, Linda had other ideas and, as "The Night" faded out, those unmistakable guitar licks of the intro to Billy Butler's "The Right Track" flooded from the speakers and Cyn said, "You've got to be fucking kidding me," and she kept dancing.

Two and a half minutes of trying to keep hold of that space she'd been dancing in on an increasingly packed floor later, as Billy was fading out, she saw Flavo move in behind the decks and thought she wouldn't last another hour if she didn't go now and no matter what was played, she had to go, or she really would *go*, there and then on the dancefloor and thankfully, finally, Linda finished with one that Cyn wasn't too hot on, Willie Tee's, "Walking Up A One Way Street," and she walked off the floor, in the direction of the toilets, at this stage, almost bursting, and clapped her hands for a fine set from Linda who, although with that one record, didn't cater to Cyn's taste, still had a full floor of appreciative Mods and Soulies swaying to the Northern Soul classic.

As she entered the toilets, she saw Jools standing at the bar, chatting to a bloke, but with his back to her, she couldn't see what he looked like. Jools was smiling though.

As Cyn finished up, so did Willie Tee and she walked out of the toilets to Flavo's voice saying "Thanks to Linda for the last hour, you've got me for the next one, let's stick with the classics and stay with Atlantic, this is Rex Garvin, Sock It To 'Em JB," and the drums kicked in, with a cheer from the crowd. Cyn looked at her watch, which told her it was twelve forty-five and marvelled at how quickly the night was going and that she still had so much to look forward to.

She walked down to the bar.

"Jimmy," Jools said, "this is my best friend Cynthia, or Cyn as everyone calls her."

"I know," Jimmy said. "Everyone here knows who you two are."

"Is that a bad thing?" Cyn asked.

"Not from what I can see," Jimmy said. "Isn't it better to be well known and popular than not at all?"

"Are we famous, or infamous?" Cyn asked, laughing as she tried to adopt what she thought was a Hollywood starlet pose.

"Oh, you're most definitely infamous," Jools said, with a smile. "Cyn by name, sin by nature! And, speaking of sin, here's Don," she said, looking at her watch. "He must have got off early."

Cyn turned to see the strawberry blonde, flat topped Rude Boy

408

behind her, a broad grin on his face. He opened his Crombie with a flourish, and a big, "Aha!" And there, sticking out of each inside pocket, they could see the red caps of two naggins of Smirnoff vodka.

"Who's for a couple of spruced up Cokes?" He asked.

Cyn smiled. "This is turning out to be a great night."

87. Let's Get The Show On The Road

Freddie sat at his desk, pulling the hammers back on the sawn-off shotgun and then pulling the triggers to click on the empty chambers. He looked at his watch.

"Time, gentlemen, please," he said, grinning. "Is the van ready, Conn?"

"Yep."

"Rope? Batons, in case we're lucky enough to catch a few of them?"

"Yep."

"Then let's get this show on the road."

He leaned down, opened the drawer in his desk and took out two shotgun shells, put them into the chambers and said, "Yous hang back at the entrance to the lane. I changed me mind. Soon as I see Robbo, he's a fuckin dead man, and when all his little fuckin moddy mates come runnin out, we scoop them up, into the back of the van and by tomorrow mornin, tiny little bits of them are gonna be sprayed across the lovely fields of County Meath."

He snapped the gun closed with a loud click.

88. Shooting From The Hip

Matt looked at his watch. The party that neither of them had wanted to go to had been shite, as they predicted, but only music wise with absolutely nothing they liked being played, but the good conversation made up for it and the time flew. Lainey and Erin were getting on like a house on fire and Peter was happy that it had turned out so well, though he'd probably have to change his sheets before he got into bed, whenever that would be.

When he told the Style Council hating bloke who had dubbed himself "The Master Of Ceremonies," and would not relinquish control of the stereo to anyone, to play "Kayleigh," the self-proclaimed MC put it on and shouted, "Now that is a fine choice, Pedro!"

Lainey shook her head and turned her eyes up to heaven and when Erin said, "God that's one of the worst songs I've ever heard! And yer man, what does he call himself, Fish, is that it? Jesus wept."

Lainey laughed and said, "Thank you, Erin. See, Peter, I told you, even your girlfriend thinks it's shite!"

Both Peter and Erin blushed.

"What? What did I say?"

"He hasn't actually asked her out yet, Lainey." Matt said,

smiling at his Fiancé's faux pas.

"She's here, isn't she?" Lainey replied.

"Yes and came with her mate, Winnie."

"Who she hasn't spoken a word to all evening. She's been standing in the kitchen talking to us, well mainly me but she kept looking at this gobshite." That remark was punctuated by her prodding Peter in the chest. "And if he doesn't properly ask her out, he's a bigger gobshite than I thought. She's clearly into him. You are into him, right?" She said, turning to Erin.

Matt interjected quickly to save either of them any further embarrassment and said, "Lady, and gentleman," nodding at each of them in turn, "the future Missus Elaine Clayton. She shoots from the hip."

That broke the ice as they laughed and she said, "You think I'm taking your name? Lainey Clayton is too much of a mouthful, I think I'll stick with my own, thanks. What time is it anyway? We'd better be going."

"It's twenty-five minutes past one, dearest," Matt said.

Lainey turned to the living room, put two fingers into her mouth and whistled like a builder. Everyone in the room stopped and looked into the kitchen.

"Oi, you, the gobshite at the record player with the awful taste in music, be a love and look out the window there and tell us if it's still raining."

He just stared at her, not knowing what to do. She waved her hand towards the window and nodded as he walked slowly in the indicated direction.

He pulled back the curtains and said, "No. But it's wet."

"Thanks, love." And turning back to Matt said, "We should still probably put the rain gear on."

89. Six Down, Six To Go

Flavo, just as Linda did before him, was playing a blinder. He kept the floor full, with classic after classic. Joe Tex followed Rex Garvin with "Show Me," and The Dells followed Joe with "Wear It On Our Face," which was followed by Sugar Pie DeSanto singing "Go Go Power." He moved from Chess but stayed in Chicago with Major Lance and "You Don't Want Me No More," which he expertly followed with Sandi Sheldon and "You're Gonna Make Me Love You," and just when he'd whipped the crowd into an absolute frenzy, he took it up another notch with Larry Williams and Johnny "Guitar" Watson doing "Too Late," and then confused everyone by playing an instrumental that they all knew as "Boogaloo Investigator," by the Matt Parsons Orchestra, by introducing it as Mike Vickers, "On The Brink." And they still danced.

As the instrumental began to fade out, he picked up the microphone and said, "I think I'll give you all a bit of a breather and slow it down," and when everyone was expecting a slow set to start and were about to walk off the floor, he played Doug Banks, "I Just Kept On Dancing," which was exactly what the crowd did.

Jools was still standing at the bar, chatting with Jimmy. She loved that record and had finally managed to track down a copy of it herself in 2010 and so wanted to dance but had forgotten how much she enjoyed talking to him and regardless of how she knew he'd eventually turn out, was enjoying this. Who, she thought, got to fall in love with the same person twice, and both times for the first time? And she finally admitted to herself, that's what was happening, but she could still enjoy it, for a while anyway. She checked her watch again, there was still plenty of time. She'd be standing up on Fleet Street waiting for Matt and Lainey to arrive and get them to stop. When the car came flying down the lane, past them, and they were safely pulled over to the side, they'd say they were lucky she'd been there. Still time and still time to enjoy Jimmy's company. She thought of her kids and thought, yes, they were safe.

Doug Banks faded out and without introduction, The Supremes kicked in with "Love Is Like An Itching In My Heart," which was followed by a handful of Motown classics and then, segueing nicely, was The Four Tops with "I Just Can't Get You Out Of My Mind" and more Seventies classics, before he announced "Last one from me, and then you've got Noel back. This is a new one and it's gonna be massive. Carlena Jones, Quack Quack."

A drum roll was followed by a heavy bassline and then a high pitched voice came in singing, "There's a brand new dance, yeah, that's sweeping the nation, yeah-eh-eh," and Jools, who was taking a sip of the "spruced up Coke" that Don had given her, spat it out when she realised she was hearing The Peanut Duck for the second first time, narrowly missing Jimmy's jacket.

"What the....? He said.

"I'd forgotten about that," she said. "The Peanut Duck!"

"The what?"

"Nothing, the song," she said. "Carlena Jones, Quack Quack. I'd forgotten Flavo was the first to play it."

Jimmy looked at her, eyebrows raised.

"If he's playing it tonight for the first time, how have you heard it?"

"Oh," she thought quickly," my cousin in London has it. Only getting big there, she put it on a tape for me."

"Oh, right," he said, none the wiser.

She looked down at the dancefloor and saw an incredible sight. For a record that everyone – except her, Flavo and a few of his close mates – were hearing for the first time, the floor was jammed. She could see Cyn and Don from where she stood and even he was moving around the floor to it and he was a dyed in the wool Rudie. She smiled, what an amazing night it was, and she'd make sure it still would be and they'd all be walking out that door at eight o'clock on Sunday morning.

The Peanut Duck faded out and Noel's voice came on, saying

"Put your hands together for Linda and Flavo, two great sets there. Now it's time to really slow it down," and once again, as it had the previous Wednesday, those trembling strings started and a nineteen year old girl from Scotland began to sing, "To Sir With Love."

Jimmy looked at her and smiled.

"When he played this on Wednesday, I finally got up the courage to ask you to dance, but just as I started to walk towards you, you jumped out of your seat like someone had set it on fire and tore off in the direction of the cloakroom. I'd seen girls running away from yer man Dosser that fast, so I looked around, thinking he must have had the same idea as me and you saw him coming."

She laughed and lied.

"No, I didn't see either you or Dosser coming. I just needed some air. Hadn't been feeling too well all day and it was just a bit hot. What better time to get out for some air than during the slow set? You won't miss anything good then. And anyway, Dosser's not into me, though I'd say he'd have a go given half the chance. He's into Cyn. She said she's sure she saw him getting a horn while he was watching her here one night and then he ran into the jacks. I don't even want to imagine how that ended. Ugh."

Jimmy laughed. "No way! To be honest, I reckon if Dosser was given half the chance, he'd give me one."

Jools laughed at that. "Speaking of, I haven't seen him here tonight, that is unusual."

"He's upstairs in the lane on his new scooter, in his new suit, posing," he said. "Though the word is that it's not actually his scooter."

"Yeah," she said, "I heard something like that myself."

With Lulu halfway through thanking the man who took her from crayons to perfume, they looked at each other and for the first time that night, lapsed into silence.

Hesitantly he said, "Do you…."

"Yes," she said, not giving him time to finish the sentence. He was about to take her hand and lead her to the dancefloor when she did just that.

They finished off dancing to Lulu, and as Tracey Thorn began to sing The Style Council's "The Paris Match," the gap between them began to close.

By the time that song had ended and Noel followed it with another Style Council song, "You're The Best Thing," their cheeks were brushing and her head was almost on his shoulder.

When Gene Pitney was halfway through "Backstage," you couldn't have gotten a razor blade between the two of them.

It had been an extremely long time since she'd danced with Jimmy, and an even longer time since they'd danced like this.

She looked over his shoulder and saw Cyn dancing with Don. She was so small compared to him that she couldn't get her head near his shoulder, it was resting on his chest. Her eyes were closed, and she was smiling.

Noel's voice came over the speakers again as Gene Pitney was belting out his final notes and said, "Back in time with Gene Pitney, this is the last of the slow set and then it's Two Tone time. Six hours gone and another six to go. This is The Jam with The Bitterest Pill."

This is it, she thought, this is the song they kissed to, the one that sealed the deal, and then something Noel had said just hit her. *Six hours gone and another six to go.*

She looked at her watch, but in the dark basement, couldn't see it. She pushed away from Jimmy and moved over to stand under one of the spotlights, holding her wrist up. Eventually, the light caught it and told her that the time was one twenty-five. *Six hours gone and another six to go....* that can't be right. She grabbed Jimmy's wrist, trying to hold it up to the light, but she couldn't see.

"What time is it?" She shouted at him, over the music.

He pressed a button on his watch and the face lit up. It was digital and it said 02:01.

"Fuck!" She screamed. "My fucking watch is slow!" She pushed him away and ran towards the DJ box and up the steps beside it that led to the stairs, leaving Jimmy standing in the middle of the dancefloor, totally confused.

When she got to the stairs, she considered for a split second trying to take them two at a time but immediately discounted that idea. She'd probably trip and break her leg and what then? She ran up the stairs as quickly as she could and ran through the door, almost bowling over the bouncers, hearing one of them say, "Whoa there, Jools, you'll do someone an injury." After being in the hot, dark basement, suddenly her senses exploded with light, sounds and smells.

The bright lights over the door of the club reflected off the chrome of the lights and mirrors on the scooter parked opposite, that Dosser was sitting on. No, posing on. The smell of cigarette smoke hung in the air. The material of Dosser's suit shone a dark green in the bright light. Dark patches of rainwater stood out on his desert boots. Puddles were on the cobbles of the laneway, one so large she could see the Adair Lane street sign reflected upside down in it, like someone had taken it off the wall and thrown it on the ground. She looked and saw Robbo and Karen kissing in a doorway of a building that backed onto Price's lane at the junction of the two laneways, her bare left leg wrapped around his right one, bright white in contrast to the colour of his trousers. A short, dark suited figure walked towards them, one arm longer than the other. The sound of a scooter approached from the right, from Fleet Street. She could hear the screech of brakes to the left, on Aston Quay. She ran into the laneway, towards the junction that suddenly intensified with light and sound. There were two silhouettes standing at the entrance of the lane on Aston Quay, they looked like two large men, but she couldn't make out who they were, the lights from the car blinding her. She then realised who the dark suited figure was as the lights from the scooter's headlight to her right and the car approaching from her left lit the whole scene. It was Freddie and he didn't have one arm longer than the other, he was holding a shotgun. And then she suddenly realised….

I'm not here to save Lainey, I'm here to save Robbo!

She screamed.

"Robbo!"

He stepped away from Karen and turned to see Jools, and Freddie, who was levelling the gun at his chest.

The driver of the car saw people who shouldn't be there, brightly lit in three headlights only a few feet from the front of the car and pulled the handbrake, turning the steering wheel sharply to the right.

Jools tried to move but couldn't. Her eyes locked onto Karen's, both of them paralyzed with fear, Jools with a car quickly approaching her and Karen with a shotgun pointed straight at her face.

Freddie's thumb cocked back both barrels and his finger moved to the trigger.

The rear wheels of the car skidded through the huge puddle and sent rainwater up into Jools's face, snapping her out of her daze. The back end of the car spun to the left, while the driver fought to control his turn to the right. She heard a thump, followed by two loud bangs, saw a bright flash and Matt's scooter dropped behind the car. Robbo went down. Then the car hit her.

90. I'll Look After You

Jools woke.

She flicked her eyelids open and shut them again quickly, the light in her bedroom was too bright. She had to do something about those walls.

"She's awake." Jools heard the voice close by and felt someone squeeze her hand. She knew that voice and smiled. She'd know that voice anywhere. The voice said, "she's smiling." It was her Dad.

"Thank God, Tom, I thought we'd lost her." That was her Mam.

She opened her eyes. She wasn't in her bedroom.

"Where am I?"

"You're in The Mater, love," her Dad said.

"What happened? Why am I here?"

"The accident, last night. Don't you remember?"

"Last night? What do you mean, last night? It's Wednesday afternoon."

"It's Sunday," her Mam said.

"Sunday?" Jools thought for a few seconds. "No, it can't be Sunday. It's…. it's Wednesday. I remember now. Me and Cyn…." she looked around the room, Cyn was sitting in the corner, looking at her with tear filled eyes, Sean was standing beside her, right hand on her left shoulder. They waved at Jools.

Jools continued, looking at Cyn. "We were in town, going to Jenny Vandar's and…. I was walking down O'Connell Street and…. I can't remember anything after that."

"You tripped and hit your head on a bin," Cyn said. "You started acting all weird then after that, talking about the future and shit. Ooops, sorry Missus Sutton."

Jools's Mam gave Cyn a disapproving look but said nothing.

"I don't remember," Jools said. Then, her eyes widened.

"It's Sunday!" She barked.

"Yep," Cyn said.

"So I missed the fucking allnighter? Ah Jaysus!"

"No, you were there," Cyn said, "and lucky you were. You honestly don't remember a thing about last night?

"Honest, Cyn, I don't remember a thing since we were in town on Wednesday."

"Well, I told you that you'd been acting all weird. It was mad, kinda like you knew something bad was gonna happen."

Jools looked at her best friend, confusion on her face. Cyn continued.

"Lainey and Matt were driving down the lane to Bubbles when a robbed car came round the corner from Aston Quay, just at the same time Freddie Collins walked up to Robbo with a shotgun to shoot him. You ran into the lane and the robbed car swerved. Matt had to swerve to avoid the back of the car and the scooter dropped to the ground and slid, clipping Robbo and knocking him out of the way. The car hit Freddie and the gun went off. Lainey and Matt came off, just a few bruises and Robbo's fine, the shot completely missed him, but the smack of the car spun Freddie around. Dosser was posing on his new scooter near the doorway and got hit with shotgun pellets, but the distance between Freddie and him was too big to kill him. Most hit his face, I heard he only had a few stitches, but one hit him in the eye, and he lost it. Freddie died on the spot, and good riddance to the cunt. Ooops, sorry Missus Sutton. The two yunfellas driving the robbed car definitely weren't expecting a laneway filled with people and scooters when they drove in and turned the car to avoid everyone. The side of the car clipped you as it swerved and you were flung against the laneway wall and that knocked you out, but the arse end of the car hit Freddie square in the back and threw him against the wall. Matt said he'll never forget the sound of Freddie's head hitting the bricks. Just a loud, cracking thud. His face hit the corner and it was nearly split in two. There was blood everywhere. The lads reversed and tried to drive down the lane, but Dosser's scooter was in the way and they crashed into that. It went under the wheels and the car wouldn't move then. They jumped out and tried to run but the bouncers grabbed them. I reckon the Guards gave them a medal for taking out Freddie. He was one of the scariest fuckers in Dublin. Oops, Sorry Missus Sutton."

"That's okay, Cynthia," Mrs Sutton said, "Freddie Collins was an unbelievable cunt."

"Mam!" Jools said, astonished.

"Well he was," Mrs Sutton said. "Sometimes no other word will do."

"Why was Freddie trying to shoot Robbo?" Jools asked Cyn.

"I'll tell you later, it's a long story."

"Ah, she's awake."

Jools looked up and saw a tall, handsome Mod in a blue suit, his dark brown hair in a classic, Mod French cut. He was quite good looking. She smiled.

"Who are you?"

"Jimmy," he said, "You don't remember? We met last night."

"I don't remember anything since Wednesday, apparently."

"He's been here all night, only just left your side a few minutes ago to ring his Mam," Mrs Sutton told her, smiling at Jimmy. "Lovely young man."

Jools looked at Jimmy and for a fleeting moment, had a vision of him in twenty years' time, still trying to hold on to the vestiges of youth in a cheap suit, sitting at a casino table, a blonde hanging out of him. She shook her head. "What the fuck was that?"

"What was what?" Jimmy asked.

"Nothing, I must be just tired."

Jimmy smiled, took her hand and Jools relaxed.

"Get some rest now, Jools," he said, "I'll look after you."

She smiled and drifted off into a peaceful sleep, where she danced on the floor of Bubbles in the arms of a tall handsome Mod.

91. Burned And Gone

Dosser stood in the hospital bathroom, looking at his reflection in the mirror. Never the most handsome of faces, the one that looked back at him was even less so today. His face was littered with stitches from where shotgun pellets had been removed, and around his head and covering his left eye was a clean white bandage.

He leaned closer to the mirror and gently lifted the bandage and the pad beneath, that covered the puffy, red, stitched up skin where his left eye used to be.

He stared at the blank space on his face and a tear rolled from his good right one.

The last thing he remembered from Saturday night was sitting outside Bubbles, posing in his new suit and sitting on his new scooter. He remembered Jools running out the door in some kind of panic and then the screech of brakes, the sound of what he thought at the time was a car backfiring and the worst pain he had ever felt, before he blacked out.

The only visitors he'd had since the accident were his Mam, Dad and his mate Eamo from the bookies, all of whom filled him in with bits and pieces they'd picked up from friends and relatives of Jools in the hospital corridors.

Freddie was dead, that was a good thing. Robbo was alive, that wasn't so good.

The robbed car had completely totalled his new scooter, that was a very bad thing and a shotgun pellet had taken out his left eye. That was a fuckin awful thing.

The beautiful tonic suit he'd been wearing was destroyed with blood (who knew an eye could bleed so much?) and the suit was thrown out, but that was okay, there was still a shit load of money in the old Dansette in his bedroom, so he could buy another scooter and lots of suits. This time, he'd go to a tailor. Despite the image that looked back at him, he smiled. He'd still have enough money to be a Top Mod and the scars were just battle wounds from the night he jumped in front of a robbed car outside Bubbles and saved Jools. That was a story that would get him some mileage. The fact that everyone would know it wasn't true escaped him.

He walked back to his bed where his Mam had arrived with a change of clothes, which he picked up and some wash up stuff, which he ignored.

"How are you feeling, Graham?" His Mam brushed her hand over his hair.

"I'm grand, Ma, thanks," he said, pulling his head away from her over motherly touch. "I'll be fine, just stop fussin over me."

"Your Dad is outside," she said. "He borrowed Mister Finnerty's car to bring you home."

"That's great, Ma. It'll be good to get home. I just wanna get back into me own bed."

"Well, we've a lovely surprise for you when you get home, Graham, you'll be delighted."

"Ah brilliant," he said, not really giving a shit about what his Mam had got him. "Thanks Ma, that's really nice of ya."

He sat in the back seat of the car, with his Mam talking non-stop to him on the journey, nodding in what he thought were the appropriate places, but not really taking any of what she said in. She was talking a lot about hospital stuff and what the doctors had said about his injury. He vaguely heard stuff like "Risk of infection," "Clean environment," and "Follow up appointments," but it all went in one ear and out the other. After about a half an hour of not really listening to his Mam's drivel, they pulled up outside their house and his Dad said he was dropping the car back to Mister Finnerty and would be back in a minute.

As they got out, Dosser saw his brother and sister standing at the hall door and affected an invalid limp, hoping for more sympathy than he was due.

As they got near the front door, Brian said, "Why are you limping, you dozy cunt, you didn't get shot in the leg!"

"Watch your language, Brian!" Dosser's Mam said. "Get back out to that fire in the garden and make sure it doesn't spark and burn the shed down!"

"Fire?" Dosser said. "What fire? Why is there a fire in the back garden?"

"Were you not listening to me, Graham," his Mam said in an exasperated tone.

"You never listen, though, in your current condition, I'm not surprised, you must have had quite a shock. If that car had been going any faster you might have been, well, it really doesn't bear think…."

"MA!" Dosser shouted. "Will you stop with your bleedin prattle and just tell me what's goin on?"

"The doctors said we had to make sure you were in a clean environment or there was a risk of infection."

"Ma, what the fuck did ya do?"

"Graham, don't you use that language with me! That's the thanks I get for doing up your bedroom!" She tutted and stormed off into the kitchen.

Dosser ran down the hall and threw the back door open. Right down the end of the garden, a fire burned, the stench of black smoke filled his nostrils.

"Brian," he called to his brother, "what's on that fire?"

"Your whole fucking bedroom. Da and me spent the past couple of days ripping everything out. Ma said everything had to be clean and new for Graham. She's going on talking about a

431

clean slate or some shite."

Dosser's face went as white as the bandage round his head. He ran to the stairs and took them two at a time.

When he got to the top, he put his hand on his bedroom door handle and took a deep breath before throwing the door open.

It was like walking into a furniture showroom. New bed, new duvet, new wardrobe, new chest of drawers. New shelves for his few records but no record player.

He ran down the stairs and caught his Dad as he came in the door.

"Da, Da! Where's me record player?"

"What?" His Dad replied. "The one from your bedroom?"

"Yeah, Da, that one, where is it?" He demanded, hoping beyond hope, but he already knew the answer.

"That thing was broken," his Dad said. "I plugged it in, and it wouldn't even turn on. I tried changing the fuse, but it still wouldn't work."

Dosser shouted at his Dad, "I know it didn't fuckin work! Where the fuck is it?"

"I threw it on the fire with the rest of the old stuff from your room. Your Mam said she wanted everything clean and new for when you got home."

Dosser felt faint. Everything started to spin but he managed to run to the back door and down the garden to the fire, where he dropped to his knees in front of the burning remains of his old bedroom furniture, carpet, curtains and a Dansette record player, all the wood and anything remotely flammable on it and in it, burned and gone, just the remnants of a long stopped working motor glowed red in the flames.

"What the fuck else is gonna happen on this God poxy day?" He muttered and his answer came immediately.

"Graham," his Mam called from the kitchen. "There's someone here to see you."

"What the fuck now?" He muttered to himself.

"Who is it?" He called out.

There was a pause and his Mam called back, "She says her name is Lisa! She met you at your disco on Saturday night?"

What? Who? He wracked his brain. He couldn't remember anyone called Lisa talking to him on Saturday night. He couldn't remember any girl talking to him at all. This was a turn up. No girl had ever called for him. Never.

He walked quickly up the garden through the kitchen and into the hall, where the front door was open. He stopped when he saw her, his heart skipped a beat and his breath caught in his throat. She was about the same size and shape as Cyn, and she was gorgeous. He looked her up and down quickly, hoping she wouldn't notice. Jesus, he thought, them checked ski pants she's wearing coulda been sprayed onto her. You can see every bit of it. And the tits, fuck me, look at them tits! And to top it all off, a perfect, blonde bob too!

"Eh, howaya, Lisa, how's it goin?"

"What about ya, Dosser," she said, "I hope you're feeling better after your wee accident on Saturday night."

"Em, yeah, I'm grand. Lost an eye though." He almost started to cry again.

"Oh, you poor wee lad, I'm so sorry. I thought I'd drop round to see how you were doing after meeting you on Saturday night."

Dosser thought hard, but he really couldn't remember.

"You don't remember me, do you?" She looked sad.

"Ah, no," he said, "course I do. You were out by the door with yer mates. Three or four of ya, I think."

"That's it," she said, brightening up. "We were admiring you're lovely scooter."

"It's not lovely anymore, Lisa, it was totalled in the crash."

"No it wasn't," she said, "there's barely a scratch on it."

"What? What do you mean? That car, it wrecked the scooter!"

"Not at all," Lisa replied. "You must have got a bigger bump on your head than you thought, you poor, wee thing." She put her hand out and stroked the side of his face, just below where his eye once was. He thought his heart was going to burst.

"Sure that's why I'm here. I saw it all happen and when the

ambulance took you away, well, I couldn't leave your scooter there, it might have been robbed. I rang my Daddy and he came down with his van and loaded it up. I've been keeping it for you till you got out of hospital."

Dosser couldn't believe his luck. At least one good thing was coming out of today, he'd got his scooter back. And the way this girl had stroked his face, maybe two good things.

"Where is it?"

"There," she said, indicating a Transit parked outside next door's garden. With this vision of loveliness before him, he'd never even noticed it.

"It's in the back of the van," she said. She took his hand, saying, "Come on, you're gonna get everything you deserve." She smiled and his heart leapt.

Dosser was beaming as she led him down the path and over to the back door of the van.

An extremely large man dressed all in black got out from the driver's side and opened the back doors. Dosser looked in, expecting to see the gleam of chrome from lights and mirrors, but saw nothing but gloom where the scooter and accompanying gleams should have been. Two men, also dressed in black were sitting down on upturned milk crates on each side of the van and in the middle, he could see someone towards the front of the van wearing a parka with a red, white and blue target on the back, bent over a tarpaulin. He couldn't see a scooter. He tried to peer into the gloom of the van, hoping his eye was playing tricks on him, maybe with only the one, his vision was a little bit dulled, but it wasn't. There was definitely no scooter in the van. He felt a hand tighten on his left arm and looked around to see a fourth man, also large and also dressed all in black. He heard a noise in the van and looked back in.

The tarpaulin moved.

The figure in the parka stood up, turned towards him and said, "What about ya, Dosser, ya wee, thievin shite."

Dosser was extremely confused and very, very scared.

"You don't know who I am, do you? I'm Will McNeil. That there, with a nice firm grip on your bony little arm, is me Da and I see you've already had the pleasure of the acquaintance of my girlfriend, Lisa."

Dosser looked all around him, finally meeting Lisa's eyes. She smiled, or rather, smirked and said, "Pleased to meet ya, Dosser," and then gave him a sarcastic little curtsey.

The tarpaulin moved again, and Dosser looked towards it.

"Oh," Will said, "excuse my manners. I forgot to introduce you to the final member of the party." He whipped the tarpaulin away with a flourish and tied at the wrists and ankles, with a gag in his mouth, was Morris. Bruised and bloodied, with both eyes

436

badly swollen and a left knee that was far too big for his jeans. Dosser's heart started beating so quickly, he thought it was going to come through his chest.

"But I hardly think I need to introduce you to your good friend and, I think, Business Partner is the correct term, is that right?" He kicked Morris, who groaned so loudly, it could be heard through the gag.

"I said is that right, you thievin cunt?" He kicked Morris again, who groaned and tried to say something, but the gag prevented Dosser from making it out.

Will walked to the back of the van and sat down on the edge. Lisa came over, jumped up beside him and kissed him on the cheek, then turned to smile at Dosser.

His heart broke and his face fell.

Will looked at Dosser and then at Lisa and then back to Dosser again. He laughed, its mocking tone stung Dosser's ears and broke his heart all over again.

"Seriously? Her? You honestly thought a fine lookin bird like Lisa would be caught dead with you? Jesus, Dosser, I heard you were a thick fuck, but come on. She'd rather touch shit on her shoe than put a finger near you!"

Dosser mumbled.

"What was that?" Will asked, cocking his head to the side.

Dosser mumbled again.

"Speak up, you wee prick, we all want to hear."

Dosser, finally accepting that he was in a whole heap of trouble, looked Will straight in the eye and said, "She touched me face, she held me hand. The only thing worse than her touchin shit is her touchin you. You're the cunt!"

Billy McNeil punched Dosser in the left kidney, and he dropped to the street. Billy picked him up and whispered in his left ear, "Nobody calls my boy a cunt!"

Will waited for Dosser to catch his breath and said, "The scooter, Dosser. My scooter. Morris nicked it for you and then you drove it around Dublin like you owned the fuckin place. Did you think I wouldn't find out? For fuck sake, man, you didn't change a fuckin thing on it! I was told by two wee Mods that you'd been seen on it and you dozy fuck, you hadn't even got the brains to change the number plate. Now, it's all over Belfast that Will McNeil can't keep a hold of his stuff, that any little Moddy prick can take what's mine. Sure, some cunt tried to chat up Lisa in front of me last night! Givin her the eye all night and smilin at her, so he was. The fuckin cheek!" Will started to laugh. "Well, I'll tell you somethin for nothin now, that cunt has two fine gashes on his cheeks and a permanent fuckin smile."

Dosser's bladder finally let go and his jeans turned dark blue. "Oh you dirty wee fuck," Lisa said, her face screwing up in disgust.

Will continued. "Now, what are we to do with you, Dosser?"

"Let me go," he mumbled.

Billy started laughing. "Son, he says we should let him go! Aw, why don't we do that?"

"Because, Daddy," Will said, "everyone knows what we do to thievin wee shites like him."

"Aye, son," Billy said. "Aye, they do."

Will turned to the man on Dosser's right side and said, "Throw him in, tie him up."

Dosser begged as Billy and the other man put their hands under his arms and lifted him into the back of the van. The two men on either side who were sitting on the milk crates stood up, grabbed him and threw him roughly to the floor of the van. His head hit Morris's swollen knee when he was flung down and Morris cried out again, his cry turned to a dull moan by the gag. They stuffed a gag in his mouth and tied his hands and feet. Lisa jumped off the back of the van and walked around and got in the front. Will stood up, walked to where Dosser and Morris lay, both now crying, and kicked the two of them. He nodded to his dad and he closed the doors of the van. Dosser watched the light disappear, until he was enveloped in darkness. Will's voice came from the dark and said, "You lads, you're fucked."

A zippo lighter was flicked on and held close to Dosser's face, so close, he thought it was going to burn him. Will's face appeared out of the darkness behind the flame and smiled.

"Proper. Fucked."

The zippo was flicked closed and once again, Dosser was enveloped in darkness. He said a silent prayer to a God he didn't believe in for a miracle.

None came.

The last sound he heard was the engine turning, before the hard heel of a loafer came down on his head, knocking him out.

Dosser's Mam walked out to the front door.

"Graham?"

She called upstairs too but heard no reply. She walked to the end of the garden and as she turned to look up the road, she saw a black Transit van turning the corner, but took no notice.

92. Her Daddy's Eyes

Jools woke.

She flicked her eyelids open and shut them again quickly. I've really got to repaint this bedroom, she thought.

"She's awake."

Jools heard the voice close by and felt someone squeeze her hand. She knew that voice and smiled. She'd know that voice anywhere. The voice said, "she's smiling."

It was Jessica. She was back.

"Ma." It was Liam.

"Don't call me Ma."

She opened her eyes and looked at her children. She smiled, tears welled in her eyes and she hugged them both. Then, a voice from the doorway.

"She's awake! Mam, Dad, she's awake!"

Jools looked up and saw Lainey running towards her, as young and slim and beautiful as she always was, her auburn hair shining in the sunlight coming through the window. She looked at her children and looked at Lainey. This was impossible. The teenage Lainey and her children couldn't possibly be here together! Oh no, she thought, not another dream! You're either still in the Eighties or in hospital or, fuck knows, you might even be dead!

She began to cry.

"Auntie Jools, it's okay."

Jools wiped her tears away with the back of her hand.

"What did you call me, Lainey?"

"I'm not Lainey. Auntie Jools, don't you remember me?"
The girl took her hand and leaned in closer, wiping away her
own tears.

Jools looked at her.

She looked like Lainey, talked like Lainey but, the clothes, the
hairstyle, it was all different. And her eyes. They weren't
Lainey's, they were Matt's.

She looked towards the door at the two people who had just
walked in. There was no mistaking them. Both older, but both
still impeccably dressed and unmistakably Lainey and Matt.
They smiled.

"The doctor said you might be a bit confused when you came
round," Matt said.

Jools looked from the girl to Lainey and back again, shaking her
head.

"I…. I don't understand."

"That's your God daughter, Jools," Lainey said, happily. Then,
"You had us worried. That would have been some present if
you'd died on my birthday." She smiled a sad smile.

"I'll do my best not to do it again. Come here."

Lainey rushed over to Jools, who hugged her tightly. Turning to Lainey's daughter, she said "I'm sorry, I had an awful bang, I don't remember much. What's your name?"

"Mam just told you, it's Jools!"

"Jools!" She hugged her Goddaughter and looking over young Jools's shoulder at Lainey and Matt, she mouthed, "Thank you."

She looked over towards the window and for the first time noticed Sean standing there. Beside him was a woman she didn't recognise, tall, slim, elegant. Her bright red lipstick stood out beautifully on her pale features, her face framed by fiery red hair.

"Sean," Jools said, smiling. Then, looking at the woman, said, "Where's Maria?"

"Who?"

"Maria. Your wife."

"That was some knock you got Jools. This is my wife, Kerry."

Jools looked at the woman, taking her in and recognition slowly dawned. "Kerry? From around the corner from your Mam's?"

Kerry smiled. "The very one, Jools. The doctor said you might have forgotten some things when you woke up, but they'd start to come back soon."

Jools, again confused and looking from one to the other said, "How? I can't remember. Sorry."

Sean explained.

"It's mad that you can't remember. I'd seen Kerry around for a bit but there were a few years between us, she was only fourteen when we first met, just a kid, so I wasn't going there."

He looked at Kerry who laughed and elbowed him.

"Ow!" Sean said. "Anyway, after I moved to London, which, I remember you were extremely insistent I did, I never saw her again, till one day, I'm on holidays with the lads in Tenerife and we walked past a bar and heard Northern Soul coming from inside. I went in to check it out and who's DJing?"

"Kerry," Jools said.

"And that, as they say, was that," Kerry said, looking at Sean as they both smiled.

"Thank God, Sean, that Maria was an awful geebag."

Sean, looking totally confused, said, "Who the fuck is Maria?"

But Jools interrupted him, frantically looking around the room.

"Robbo?" She said. "Where's Robbo? Please don't tell me Freddie killed him?"

Sean shook his head.

"Jools, that was like, thirty years ago."

"I don't care when it was," she said, "did Freddie shoot Robbo?"

"God knows what's been going through your head while you were out, Jools, no, Freddie didn't shoot Robbo. He tried to but that robbed car hit him, and you too. But Freddie was killed. Robbo's fine."

"Where is he? I want to see him."

"He said he'd be in to see you after his shift. He's been in the last couple of nights."

"Shift?" Jools said, "what shift? What are you talking about? What does Robbo do?"

"Jesus, Jools," Sean said, "when the doctors told us you could have some memory loss, they weren't kidding. Robbo's a Guard. Drug Squad."

Jools stared at him, wide eyed, a completely astonished look on her face and then suddenly burst out laughing.

"Robbo! A Guard! In the fucking Drug Squad! That's the funniest thing I've ever heard." She was laughing so much she got a stitch in her side.

"Well," Sean said, "who better to know what's what when it comes to drugs?"

Jools was still laughing hard when a nurse came in and said, "There's too many people in here, she's very weak and needs her rest. Come on, out you all go, you can come back later when she's feeling better."

The nurse looked at the still laughing Jools and thought, maybe she already is.

Jessica kissed her Mam on the cheek. "I'll be back later, get some rest."

Jools lay in the bed, watching them all leave and then put her head back and looked up at the ceiling, trying to make sense of everything.

She couldn't remember any of last night after she ran into the lane, there just seemed to be lights and noise all around.

Then…. nothing.

It all seemed to have worked out though. A few things changed but definitely for the better. The most important things though, both Lainey and Robbo were alive, and Jools still had her kids. All's well that ends well.

She thought of the kiss that never happened, almost thirty years in the past. Back when she was really seventeen, the first time round, Jimmy had kissed her on the dancefloor during the slow set at the allnighter, but it hadn't happened last night. Running out the way she did, he never got the chance, so something must have happened that they ended up together. She guessed some things are destined to be and, as he wasn't there when she woke up, she guessed that some things just weren't destined to be and no matter what you do to change it, they remain the same.

Just then Cyn came bursting into the room like a tiny, blonde whirlwind, Jayo and Terry trailing behind.

"Out!" Screamed the nurse. Cyn ignored her while the lads

stopped just inside the door.

"You're awake! I only went for a fuckin coffee and I miss all the drama."

"You're one to talk! You're late for everything, Cyn, you'll be late for your own funeral."

"I think that would be more you than me," Cyn said and then, quickly, "oh, I'm sorry, I didn't mean, we nearly lost you. I thought you were dead when that car hit you." She burst into tears.

"Stop bawling, you sad shite," Jools said. "Look at me, I'm fine. The picture of health. As fit and gorgeous as ever." She laughed.

Cyn looked at Jayo, who looked at Terry. They both looked at Cyn.

"No way, Jayo," she said, "I'm not telling her."

"Tell her what?" Jools barked, then grabbed Cyn by the arm. "What are you not telling me Cynthia?"

"Em," Cyn said, "Eh, they had to, em, do a bit of an operation on your head and, well, had to cut away a bit of your, em…."

"Get me a mirror, NOW!"

Cyn rummaged in her bag and pulled out a makeup mirror. Jools flicked it open, took a deep breath and looked at her reflection. Her head was bandaged but her hair, well, there was significantly less of it than there was before.

"My hair! Where's that bastard that hit me with the car? I'll fucking murder him!"

"The three of you, get out!" The nurse was now losing her temper. "And you," she said, turning to Jools, "you're lucky to be alive, your hair will grow back. Now get some rest."

Jools lay back and thought, yes, she was lucky. Friends like hers didn't grow on trees and, as it happened, didn't get nailed to any either and thanked whoever or whatever had sent her on that little adventure as now, there was one more person here who wouldn't be around if that car hadn't hit her on Baggot Street. Two if you counted young Jools.

She smiled at the thought of her Goddaughter and now, with the quiet in the room as everyone had left, she could faintly hear sound drifting in from a radio playing somewhere, the jingle for RTE Gold followed by a string laden intro that she knew well. Chris Farlowe began to sing "Out Of Time," and she smiled and said, "Not anymore, Chris," before drifting off into a peaceful sleep, where she danced on the floor of Bubbles, seventeen again.

93. The French Have A Word For It

Molly Delaney stood outside her shop at Balgriffen cemetery,
chatting with the head grave digger, interspersed with him
singing, "House Of The Rising Sun."

"Sing something different, Digger," she said. "I don't like that
one."

He cleared his throat and launched into, "Sunny Afternoon,"
by The Kinks.

"Yes," she said. "You do that one well."

Digger smiled.

Molly looked out towards the road and noticed a 1962, E-Type,
racing green Jaguar coming towards the graveyard. She screwed
up her face in thought. A memory of the sort that you just can't
grasp, a fragment of a memory, something you haven't seen in
a long time, crossed her mind.

"Do you recognise that car, Digger?"

"Doesn't look familiar to me," he replied.

"Strange," she said, "I just got one of them feelings. You know,
like when you've seen something before but just can't place it?
The French have a word for it."

"Sacra Blue?" Digger offered.

"No, that's not it," she said. "I don't know. Maybe I'm just
tired."

She watched the car as it passed the turn in to the cemetery car park and before it continued on down the road, she saw there was a couple in it. The sun shone through the windscreen lighting up the woman's auburn hair, making it shine a beautiful, autumn red. She was laughing.

"Pretty lady," Molly said, but Digger was too engrossed in his singing to notice.

Paul Davis 20/08/2020

Authors Note

In 1985, I walked into Bubbles for the first time. My mates had been going since they were fifteen, but, always being small for my age, I waited till I was sixteen, and had my birth cert with me in case I was refused. The last thing I wanted was to have to get the bus home on my own, disheartened that I hadn't got into the club that they constantly talked about, and I would have been alone, as I'd never have expected them to not go in, just because I couldn't. But I needn't have feared. I got in and it opened up a whole new world for me.

Many years later, I took part in a creative writing course and the lecturer told the class to write about something we loved. People wrote about their dogs or their kids, but as, at the time, I had neither, I wrote about a place I loved. Bubbles. That story, entitled "Wade In The Water," was about my first night there and was published in a book about Irish Mods called "To Be Someone," which was a collection of anecdotes shared by Irish Mods, from North and South of the border, compiled by Marty McAllister and Adam Cooper.
"Wade In The Water" formed the basis of "Out Of Time," and people who read it, said it brought back memories of the place we all loved to go and hear music that you couldn't hear

anywhere else. Well, apart from the odd night that the Emerald Mod Society were doing or the rallies various scooter clubs put on, but I didn't have a scooter and I was too young to get into the pub function rooms that those events took place in, so really, for me, the only place I could hear and dance to that music, was Bubbles.

It was that feeling, that youthful exuberance and camaraderie that you got in Bubbles that I wanted to write about and so the idea formed about a person on the present day scene reliving their youth and I hope you, Dear Reader, felt that passion when you revisited Bubbles, or even visited Bubbles for the first time in the pages of this book. If I had you imagining being there and smiling as you remembered when you had first walked down those stairs, that's the best I can hope for.

Special thanks need to go to a few people, without whom, Out Of Time would never have been written.

For their incredible knowledge of the clothes, hairstyles, shoes and various shops to get it all in, Fiona Mellon and Anne Doyle, I can't thank you enough.

I've lost count of the amount of times Fiona was texted, asked stupid questions (I know virtually nothing about 80s Mod girls, only that they looked fantastic) and was given exactly what I needed and some of her explanations are written verbatim. So, if I got anything wrong, that's on me. Writers say this all the time, but I really do mean it, without Fiona, this would have been an even bigger struggle than it was and believe me, there were times there was almost a laptop shaped hole in the window. Fiona, you, above all others kept this book true to the style of the 80s Mod girl and it could not have been done without you.

(She's blushing now.)

Thanks to Mill Butler for his knowledge of the layout of the TV Club, Anne from The Blades Facebook Fan Page and Brian Foley for their help with bringing the gig to life.

Noel Synnott for technical info on what went on behind the decks at Bubbles and for just being.

Noel is, for me and many others, Bubbles. Without Noel, it wouldn't still be going in the 21st century. As a DJ and promoter of Mod and Soul nights, it was Noel and Bubbles that inspired me to start on that course and remain on it thirty plus years later. The energy he created in that small basement club on Adair Lane in Dublin has always been my benchmark. If I could put on a night that even captured a percentage of that atmosphere, I was doing well and I hope that, over the years, I have.

Thanks to Linda Doran, Eamon Flavin and DJ Honey, all of whom, along with Noel, agreed to be DJs in my story, thank you for allowing me to cast you. It added that little touch of realism to it and you all played magnificent sets.

Jason Brummell, author of two incredible Mod books – All About My Girl and All Or Nothing - who gave me great advice at the beginning and again at the end, you helped immensely and I hope you enjoy my story as much as I enjoyed yours.

Barney Taylor, author of the incredible Viro books who gave me some great advice towards the end. That Barney Taylor who does D8 Soul Club? Yep, the very same. Get his books, they're well worth a read.

Joe Moran, the recognised, resident scribe of the Dublin Mod and Soul Scene, your input was right on the money and helped to shape it into the final draft that is being read now.

All three lads mentioned above, I can't thank you enough and am forever in your debt.

Sharon Tennyson, Carlow Mod and Teacher, who read it from the perspective of both and proofed it for me. She was even apologetic in her texts when pointing out my punctuation and spelling errors. I certainly didn't know there was an accent in Voilà! (She teaches French.) Thanks, Sharon.

Tomo Doran and, again, Linda. You were a constant source of encouragement and support and gave me exactly what I needed, when I needed it. Thank you.

Dave Cairns of Secret Affair who allowed me to use his Time

For Action lyrics, thanks, Dave and thanks to Tracey Wilmott for putting us in touch.

Ollie Slaney who allowed me to use the lyrics of Toe Rag by that superb band The Rifles.

John Dunne for help with the betting because I, much like Dosser, know nothing about the nags.

My wife Barbara for putting up with me rabbiting on about storylines she knew nothing of (she's not and never was a Mod) and my daughter Leah, who kept encouraging me to finish the book, though not without an agenda. She said she hopes it's such a success that it's made into a movie and she gets to star in it.

At least she's honest!

And last, but by no means least, you, Dear Reader. Thank you for taking the time to read my story. It was a long time coming but I got there in the end. I hope you enjoyed it.

CPSIA information can be obtained
at www.ICGtesting.com
Printed in the USA
LVHW091530090221
678829LV00032B/511

9 781838 263805